DARE SHE DATE THE DREAMY DOC?

BY
SARAH MORGAN

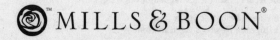

MILLS & BOON

To all the readers
who asked me to write another book set on Glenmore.

First published in Great Britain 2010
Harlequin Mills & Boon Limited,
Eton House, 18-24 Paradise Road, Richmond, Surrey TW9 1SR

© Sarah Morgan 2010

ISBN: 978 0 263 87902 5

Printed and bound in Spain
by Litografia Rosés, S.A., Barcelona

Dear Reader

Four years ago I wrote two books based on the ficti-
tious Scottish island of Glenmore. I enjoyed writing
them so much and had such enthusiastic feedback from
readers that I wrote a third—THE REBEL DOCTOR'S
BRIDE.

This summer I decided to return there again. Jenna
is a single mother who moves to Glenmore intent
on building a new life for herself and her teenage
daughter. Bruised and still in shock after discovering her
husband's infidelities, the last thing she is looking for is
love. Dr Ryan McKinley isn't looking for love either.
But the people who live in the tight-knit community of
Glenmore have other ideas, and Jenna discovers once
again that life doesn't always turn out according to plan.
Like all mothers she has to juggle numerous demands
on her time and her emotional energy. She is so used to
putting herself second that she has never really allowed
herself to consider her own needs. Until now.

Glenmore and its inhabitants are so familiar to me
that setting a story there is like returning to a beloved
holiday destination. Writing this book allowed me to
explore so many aspects of living and working in a
small island community. I loved giving Jenna her much
deserved happy ending, and I hope you enjoy reading
her story as much as I enjoyed writing it.

I love hearing from my readers. Your kind, generous
and enthusiastic feedback is what keeps my hands on
my keyboard! You can contact me via my website at
www.sarahmorgan.com, and find me on Facebook and
Twitter.

Warmest wishes

Sarah

xx

Sarah Morgan is a British writer who regularly tops the bestseller lists with her lively stories for both Mills & Boon® Medical™ and Modern™. As a child Sarah dreamed of being a writer, and although she took a few interesting detours on the way she is now living that dream. She firmly believes that reading romance is one of the most satisfying and fat-free escapist pleasures available. Her stories are unashamedly optimistic, and she is always pleased when she receives letters from readers saying that her books have helped them through hard times. *RT Book Reviews* has described her writing as 'action-packed and sexy'.

Sarah lives near London with her husband and two children, who innocently provide an endless supply of authentic dialogue. When she isn't writing or nagging about homework Sarah enjoys music, movies, and any activity that takes her outdoors.

Recent titles by the same author:

Medical™ Romance
THE GREEK BILLIONAIRE'S LOVE-CHILD
ITALIAN DOCTOR, SLEIGH-BELL BRIDE
THE REBEL DOCTOR'S BRIDE**
THE ITALIAN'S NEW-YEAR MARRIAGE WISH*

Brides of Penhally Bay
**Glenmore Island Doctors*

Sarah Morgan also writes for Modern™ Romance. Her sexy heroes and feisty heroines aren't to be missed!

Modern™ Romance
POWERFUL GREEK, UNWORLDLY WIFE
CAPELLI'S CAPTIVE VIRGIN
THE PRINCE'S WAITRESS WIFE

CHAPTER ONE

'I CAN'T believe you've dragged me to the middle of nowhere. You must really hate me.' The girl slumped against the rail of the ferry, sullen and defiant, every muscle in her slender teenage frame straining with injured martyrdom and simmering rebellion.

Jenna dragged her gaze from the misty beauty of the approaching island and focused on her daughter. 'I don't hate you, Lexi,' she said quietly. 'I love you. Very much.'

'If you loved me, we'd still be in London.'

Guilt mingled with stress and tension until the whole indigestible mix sat like a hard ball behind her ribs. 'I thought this was the best thing.'

'Best for you, maybe. Not me.'

'It's a fresh start. A new life.' As far away from her old life as possible. Far away from everything that reminded her of her marriage. Far away from the pitying glances of people she'd used to think were her friends.

'I liked my old life!'

So had she. Until she'd discovered that her life had been a lie. They always said you didn't know what was going on in someone else's marriage—she hadn't known what was going on in her own.

Jenna blinked rapidly, holding herself together through will-power alone, frightened by how bad she felt. Not for the first time, she wondered whether eventually she was going to crack. People said that time healed, but how much time? Five years? Ten years? Certainly not a year. She didn't feel any better now than she had when it had first happened. She was starting to wonder whether some things just didn't heal— whether she'd have to put on the 'everything is OK' act for the rest of her life.

She must have been doing a reasonably good job of convincing everyone she was all right because Lexi was glaring at her, apparently oblivious to her mother's own personal struggle. 'You had a perfectly good job in London. We could have stayed there.'

'London is expensive.'

'So? Make Dad pay maintenance or something. He's the one who walked out.'

The comment was like a slap in the face. 'I don't want to live off your father. I'd rather be independent.' Which was just as well, Jenna thought bleakly, given Clive's reluctance to part with any money for his daughter. 'Up here there are no travel costs, you can go to the local school, and they give me a cottage with the job.'

That was the best part. A cottage. Somewhere that was their own. She wasn't going to wake up one morning and find it had been taken away from them.

'How can you be so calm and civilised about all this?' Lexi looked at her in exasperation. 'You should be angry. I tell you now, if a man ever treats me the way Dad treated you I'll punch his teeth down his throat and then I'll take a knife to his—'

'Lexi!'

'Well, I would!'

Jenna took a slow deep breath. 'Of course I've felt angry. And upset. But what's happened has happened, and we have to get on with it.' Step by step. Day by day.

'So Dad's left living in luxury with his new woman and we're exiled to a remote island that doesn't even have electricity? Great.'

'Glenmore is a wonderful place. Keep an open mind. I loved it when I was your age and I came with my grandparents.'

'People *choose* to come here?' Lexi glared at the rocky shore, as if hoping to scare the island into vanishing. 'Is this seriously where you came on holiday? That's totally tragic. You should have sued them for cruelty.'

'I loved it. It was a proper holiday. The sort where we spent time together—' Memories swamped her and suddenly Jenna was a child again, excited at the prospect of a holiday with her grandparents. Here—and perhaps only here—she'd felt loved and accepted for who she was. 'We used to make sandcastles and hunt for shells on the beach—'

'Wow. I'm surprised you didn't die of excitement.'

Faced with the sting of teenage sarcasm, Jenna blinked. Suddenly she wished she were a child again, with no worries. No one depending on her. Oh, for crying out loud—she pushed her hair away from her eyes and reminded herself that she was thirty-three, not twelve. 'It *is* exciting here. Lexi, this island was occupied by Celts and Vikings—it's full of history. There's an archaeological dig going on this summer and they had a small number of places for interested teenagers. I've booked you on it.'

'You *what*?' Appalled, Lexi lost her look of martyred boredom and shot upright in full defensive mode. 'I am not an interested teenager so you can count me out!'

'Try it, Lexi,' Jenna urged, wondering with a lurch of horror what she was going to do if Lexi refused to co-operate. 'You used to love history when you were younger, and—'

'I'm not a kid any more, Mum! This is my summer holiday. I'm supposed to have a rest from school. I don't want to be taught history!'

Forcing herself to stay calm, Jenna took a slow, deep breath; one of the many she'd taken since her daughter had morphed from sweet child to scary teen. When you read the pregnancy books, why didn't it warn you that the pain of being a mother didn't end with labour?

Across the ferry she caught sight of a family, gathered together by the rail. Mother, father, two children—they were laughing and talking, and Jenna looked away quickly because she'd discovered that nothing was more painful than being around happy families when your own was in trouble.

Swallowing hard, she reminded herself that not every modern family had perfect symmetry. Single-parent families, stepfamilies—they came in different shapes. Yes, her family had been broken, but breakages could be mended. They might heal in a different shape, but they could still be sturdy.

'I thought maybe we could go fishing.' It was up to her to be the glue. It was up to her to knit her family together again in a new shape. 'There's nothing quite like eating a fish you've caught yourself.'

Lexi rolled her eyes and exhaled dramatically. 'Call me boring, but gutting a fish with my mother is *so* not my idea of fun. Stop trying so hard, Mum. Just admit that the situation is crap.'

'Don't swear, Alexandra.'

'Why not? Grandma isn't around to hear and it *is* crap. If you want my honest opinion, I hope Dad and his shiny new girlfriend drown in their stupid hot tub.'

Relieved that no one was standing near them, Jenna rubbed her fingers over her forehead, reminding herself that this was not the time to get into an argument. 'Let's talk about us for a moment, not Dad. There are six weeks of summer holiday left before term starts. I'm going to be working, and I'm not leaving you on your own all day. That's why I thought archaeology camp would be fun.'

'About as much fun as pulling my toenails out one by one. I don't need a babysitter. I'm fifteen.'

And you're still a child, Jenna thought wistfully. Underneath that moody, sullen exterior lurked a terrified girl. And she knew all about being terrified, because she was too. She felt like a plant that had been growing happily in one spot for years, only to be dug up and tossed on the compost heap. The only difference between her and Lexi was that she had to hide it. She was the grown-up. She had to look confident and in control.

Not terrified, insecure and needy.

Now that it was just the two of them, Lexi needed her to be strong. But the truth was she didn't feel strong. When she was lying in bed staring into the darkness she had moments of utter panic, wondering whether she could actually do this on her own. Had she been crazy to move so far away? Should she have gone and stayed with her parents? At least that would have eased the financial pressure, and her mother would have been able to watch out for Lexi while she worked. Imagining her mother's tight-lipped disapproval, Jenna shuddered. There were two sins her mother couldn't forgive and she'd committed both of them. No, they were better on their own.

Anger? Oh, yes, she felt anger. Not just for herself, but for Lexi. What had happened to the man who had cradled his daughter when she'd cried and spent weeks choosing exactly the right dolls' house? Jenna grabbed hold of the anger and held it tightly, knowing that it was much easier to live with than misery. Anger drove her forward. Misery left her inert.

She needed anger if she was going to make this work. And she *was* going to make it work.

She had to.

'We're going to be OK. I promise, Lexi.' Jenna stroked a hand over the teenager's rigid shoulder, relieved when her touch wasn't instantly rejected. 'We'll have some fun.'

'Fun is seeing my friends. Fun is my bedroom at home and my computer—'

Jenna didn't point out that they didn't have a home any more. Clive had sold it—the beautiful old Victorian house that she'd tended so lovingly for the past thirteen years. When they'd first married money had been tight, so she'd decorated every room herself…

The enormity of what she'd lost engulfed her again and Jenna drew in a jerky breath, utterly daunted at the prospect of creating a new life from scratch. By herself.

Lexi dug her hand in her pocket and pulled out her mobile phone. 'No signal. Mum, there's no signal!' Panic mingled with disgust as she waved her phone in different directions, trying to make it work. 'I swear, if there's no signal in this place I'm swimming home. It's bad enough not seeing my friends, but not talking to them either is going to be the end.'

Not by herself, Jenna thought. With her daughter. Somehow they needed to rediscover the bond they'd shared before the stability of their family had been blown apart.

'This is a great opportunity to try a few different things. Develop some new interests.'

Lexi gave her a pitying look. 'I already have interests, Mum. Boys, my friends, hanging out, and did I say boys? Chatting on my phone—boys. Normal stuff, you know? No, I'm sure you don't know—you're too old.' She huffed moodily. 'You met Dad when you were sixteen, don't forget.'

Jenna flinched. She had just managed to put Clive out of her mind and Lexi had stuffed him back in her face. And she wasn't allowed to say that she'd had no judgement at sixteen. She couldn't say that the whole thing had been a mistake, because then Lexi would think she was a mistake and that wasn't true.

'All I'm asking is that you keep an open mind while you're here, Lexi. You'll make new friends.'

'Anyone who chooses to spend their life in a place like this is seriously tragic and no friend of mine. Face it, Mum, basically I'm going to have a miserable, lonely summer and it's all your fault.' Lexi scowled furiously at the phone. 'There's still no signal. I hate this place.'

'It's probably something to do with the rocky coastline. It will be fine once we land on the island.'

'It is not going to be fine! Nothing about this place is fine.' Lexi stuffed the phone moodily back in her pocket. 'Why didn't you let me spend the summer with Dad? At least I could have seen my friends.'

Banking down the hurt, Jenna fished for a tactful answer. 'Dad is working,' she said, hoping her voice didn't sound too robotic. 'He was worried you'd be on your own too much.' Well, what was she supposed to say? Sorry, Lexi, your dad is selfish and wants to forget he has responsibilities so he can spend his summer having sex with his new girlfriend.

'I wouldn't have cared if Dad was working. I could have hung around the house. I get on all right with Suzie. As long as I block out the fact that my Dad is hooked up with someone barely older than me.'

Jenna kept her expression neutral. 'People have relationships, Lexi. It's part of life.' Not part of *her* life, but she wasn't going to think about that now. For now her priorities were remembering to breathe in and out, get up in the morning, go to work, earn a living. Settling into her job, giving her daughter roots and security—that was what mattered.

'When you're young, yes. But he's old enough to know better. They should be banned for everyone over twenty-one.' Lexi shuddered. 'Thank goodness you have more sense. It's a relief you're past all that.'

Jenna blinked. She was thirty-three. Was thirty-three really past it? Perhaps it was. By thirty-three you'd discovered that fairy tales were for children, that men didn't ride up with swords to rescue you; they were more likely to run you down while looking at the pretty girl standing behind you.

Resolutely she blocked that train of thought. She'd promised herself that she wasn't going to do that. She wasn't going to generalise and blame the entire male race for Clive's shortcomings. She wasn't going to grow old bitter and twisted, giving Lexi the impression that all men were selfish losers. It wasn't men who had hurt her; it was Clive. One man—not all men.

It was Clive who had chosen to have a rampant affair with a trainee lawyer barely out of college. It was Clive who had chosen to have sex on his desk without bothering to lock the door. There were moments when Jenna wondered if he'd done it on purpose, in the hope of being caught so he could prove how virile he was.

She frowned. Virile? If she'd been asked for a word to describe Clive, it certainly wouldn't have been virile. That would have been like describing herself as sexy, and she would never in a million years describe herself as sexy.

When had she ever had wild sex with a man while still wearing all her clothes? No one had ever been that desperate for her, had they? Not even Clive. Certainly not Clive.

When Clive had come home from the office they'd talked about household accounts, mending the leaking tap, whether or not they should have his mother for the weekend. Never had he walked through the door and grabbed her, over-whelmed by lust. And she wouldn't have wanted him to, Jenna admitted to herself. If he had grabbed her she would have been thinking about all the jobs she still had to do before she could go to bed.

Blissfully unaware that her mother was thinking about sex, Lexi scuffed her trainer on the ground. 'There would have been loads for me to do in London. Cool stuff, not digging up bits of pot from muddy ground. I could have done my own thing.'

'There will be lots of things to do here.'

'On my own. Great.'

'You'll make friends, Lex.'

'What if I don't? What if everyone hates me?'

Seeing the insecurity in her daughter's eyes, Jenna hugged her, not confessing that she felt exactly the same way. Still, at least the people here wouldn't be gossiping about her disastrous marriage. 'They won't hate you. You make friends easily, and everyone on this island is friendly.' Please let them be friendly. 'That's why we're here.'

Lexi leaned on the rail and stared at the island mournfully. 'Change is the pits.'

'Change often feels difficult, but it can turn out to be

exciting.' Jenna parroted the words, hoping she sounded more convincing than she felt. 'Life is full of possibilities.'

'Not stuck here, it isn't. Face it, Mum. It's crap.'

Ryan McKinley stood with his legs braced and his arms folded. His eyes stung from lack of sleep, he'd had no time to shave, and his mind was preoccupied by thoughts of the little girl with asthma he'd seen during the night. He dug his mobile out of his pocket and checked for missed calls and messages but for once there were none—which meant that the child was probably still sleeping peacefully. Which was what he would have been doing, given the choice.

As the ferry approached the quay, he slipped the phone back into his pocket, trying not to think of the extra hour he could have spent in bed.

Why had Evanna insisted that *he* be the one to meet the new practice nurse? If he hadn't known that the woman had a teenage daughter, he would have suspected Evanna of matchmaking. He'd even thought of mentioning his suspicions to Logan McNeil, his colleague and the senior partner in the Glenmore Medical Centre. If she was planning something, Logan would probably know, given that Evanna was his wife. Wife, mother, midwife and—Ryan sighed—friend. She was a loyal, caring friend.

In the two years he'd been living on the island she'd done everything she could to end his hermit-like existence. It had been Evanna who had dragged him into island life, and Evanna who had insisted that he help out when the second island doctor had left a year earlier.

He hadn't been planning to work, but the work had proved a distraction from his thoughts, as she'd guessed it would. And it was different enough from his old job to ensure that there were no difficult memories. Different had proved to be good. The shift in pace and pressure just what he'd needed. But, as grateful as he was to his colleague's wife for forcing him out of his life of self-imposed isolation, he refused to go along with her need to see him in a relationship.

There were some things that wouldn't change.

'Hi, Dr McKinley. You're up early—' A pretty girl strolled over to him, her hair swinging over her shoulders, her adoring gaze hopeful. 'Last night was fun, wasn't it?'

'It was a good night, Zoe.' Confronted with the realities of living as part of a small island community, Ryan chose his words carefully. This was the drawback of living and working in the same place, he mused. He was her doctor. He knew about her depression and the battle she'd had to get herself to this point. 'You looked as though you were enjoying yourself. It was good to see you out. I'm glad you're feeling better.'

He'd spent the evening trying to keep the girl at a safe distance without hurting her feelings in front of her friends. Aware that her emotions were fragile, he hadn't wanted to be the cause of any more damage—but he knew only too well how important it was to keep that distance.

'I wasn't drinking alcohol. You told me not to with those tablets.'

'Probably wise.'

'I—' She pushed her thumbs into the pockets of her jeans, slightly awkward. 'You know—if you ever wanted to go out some time—' She broke off and her face turned scarlet. 'I shouldn't have said that. Millions of girls want to go out with you, I know. Sorry. Why would someone like you pick a screwball like me?'

'You're not a screwball.' Ryan wondered why the most difficult conversations always happened at the most awkward times. The ferry was docking and he was doing a consultation on the quay, within earshot of a hundred disembarking passengers. And, as if that wasn't enough, she was trying to step over a line he never allowed a patient to cross. 'You're suffering from depression, Zoe, and that's an illness like any other.'

'Yes, I know. You made me see that.' Painfully awkward, she rubbed her toe on the hard concrete of the quay. 'You've been great, Dr McKinley. Really great. I feel better about everything, now. More able to cope, you know? And I just wondered if—'

Ryan cut her off before she went too far and said something that couldn't be unsaid. 'Apart from the fact I'm your doctor, and I'd be struck off if I said yes, I'm way too old for you.' Too old. Too cynical. 'But I'm pleased you feel like dating. That's good, Zoe. And, judging from the way the men of Glenmore were flocking around you last night, you're not short of admirers, so I think you should go for it. Pick someone you like and get yourself out there.'

Her wistful glance told him exactly who was top of her list, and she gazed at him for a moment before giving a short laugh. 'You're refusing me.'

'Yes.' Ryan spoke firmly, not wanting there to be any mistake. 'I am. But in the nicest possible way.'

Zoe was looking at him anxiously. 'I've embarrassed you—'

'I'm not embarrassed.' Ryan searched for the right thing to say, knowing that the correct response was crucial both for her self-esteem and their future relationship. 'We've talked a lot over the past two months, Zoe. You've trusted me with things you probably haven't told other people. It's not unusual for that type of confidence to make you feel a bit confused about your own feelings. If it would help, you can change doctors.'

'I'm not confused, Dr McKinley. And I don't want to change doctors. You've got such a way with words, and I've never known a man listen like you—I suppose that's why I—' She shrugged. 'Maybe I will date one of those guys.' She smiled up at him. 'That archaeologist who's hanging around this summer is pretty cool.'

'Interesting guy,' Ryan agreed, relieved that she didn't appear to be too heartbroken by his rejection.

'What about you, Dr McKinley? Why are you waiting for the ferry? Are you meeting a woman?'

'In a manner of speaking. Our new practice nurse is arriving today. Reinforcements.' And he had a favour to ask her. He just hoped that Jennifer Richards was a big-hearted woman.

'A new nurse?' There was a wistful note to Zoe's voice. 'Well, I know Nurse Evanna needs the help. So what's this new nurse like? Is she young?'

'She's coming with her teenage daughter.' Why had Evanna wanted him to meet her? That question played on his mind as he watched the ferry dock. It could have been an innocent request, but he also knew that his colleague was obsessed with matching people up. She wanted a happy ending.

Ryan felt the tension spread across his shoulders. He knew life didn't often offer up happy endings.

Zoe's face brightened. 'If she has a teenage daughter, she must be forty at least. Maybe even older.' She dismissed the competition. 'Well, the ferry is on time, so you're about to meet your nurse.'

Shaking the sleep out of his brain, Ryan watched as a patchwork of people flowed off the ferry. Businessmen in suits, families clutching bulging beach bags, toddlers in push-chairs. A slightly overweight, middle-aged woman puffed her way towards him carrying a suitcase.

He didn't know whether to be relieved that Evanna clearly hadn't been matchmaking or disappointed that their new practice nurse didn't look fit enough to work a hard day at the surgery. 'Jennifer?' He extended a hand. 'I'm Dr McKinley. Ryan McKinley. Welcome to Glenmore Island.'

The woman looked startled. 'Thank you, but I'm Caroline, not Jennifer. I'm just here for a week with my husband.' She glanced over her shoulder towards a sweating, balding man, who was struggling with a beach umbrella and an assortment of bags, one of which popped open, spilling the contents onto the quay.

'Oops. Let me help you—' A slim girl put down her own suitcase, stepped forward and deftly rescued the contents of the bag, her pink mouth curving into a friendly smile as she stuffed everything back inside and snapped the bag firmly shut.

Ryan's gaze lingered on that mouth for a full five seconds before shifting to her snaky dark curls. The clip at the back of her head suggested that at one time her hair had been fastened, but it had obviously made an escape bid during the ferry journey and was now tumbling unrestrained around her narrow shoulders. She was pale, and there were dark rings under her eyes—as if she hadn't had a decent sleep in months. As if life had closed its jaws and taken a bite out of her.

He recognised the look because for months he'd seen it in his own reflection when he'd looked in the mirror.

Or maybe he was imagining things. Plenty of people looked tired when they first arrived on the island. It took time to relax and unwind, but by the time they caught the ferry back to the mainland they had colour in their cheeks and the dark circles had gone.

Doubtless this girl had worked all winter in some grey, smog-filled city, saving up her holiday for a couple of bracing weeks on a remote Scottish island.

Eyeing the jumper looped around her shoulders, Ryan realised that she obviously knew that summer weather on Glenmore could be unpredictable.

He watched her for a full minute, surprised by the kindness she showed to a stranger. With no fuss, she helped rearrange his possessions into a manageable load, making small talk about the problems of packing for a holiday in a destination where the weather was unpredictable.

Having helped the couple, the girl stood for a moment, just breathing in the sea air, as if she hadn't stood still for ages while the man and his wife carted themselves and their luggage towards the two island taxis.

'The brochures promise you a welcome,' the woman panted, her voice carrying across the quay, 'but I didn't imagine that the island doctor would meet everyone personally. He even shook my hand! That *is* good service.'

A faint smile on his lips, Ryan watched them pile into a taxi. Then he stared at the ferry, resisting the temptation to take another look at the girl. He hoped the nurse and her daughter hadn't missed the boat.

A hand touched his arm. 'Did I hear you say that you're Dr McKinley?' The girl with the tumbling black hair was beside him, cases by her feet, her voice smoky soft and her eyes sharp and intelligent. 'I'm Jenna.'

Ryan looked into her eyes and thought of the sea. Shades of aquamarine, green and blue blended into a shade that was uniquely hers. He opened his mouth and closed it again—tried to look away and found that he couldn't. So he just carried on staring, and he saw something blossom in the depths of those eyes. Awareness. A connection. As if each recognised something in the other.

Something gripped him hard—something he hadn't felt in a long time.

Shocked by the chemistry, Ryan inhaled sharply and prepared himself to put up barriers, but she got there first.

Panic flickered across her face and she took a step backwards, clearly rejecting what had happened between them.

And that was fine with him, because he was rejecting it too.

He didn't even know why she'd introduced herself. Was every passenger going to shake his hand this morning?

Ryan knew he needed to say something casual and dismissive, but his eyes were fixed on the sweet lines of her profile and his tongue seemed to be stuck to the roof of his mouth.

She wasn't a girl, he realised. She was a woman. A young woman.

Mid-twenties?

And she looked bone tired—as if she was ready to collapse into a big comfortable bed and sleep for a month.

'Sorry. I must have misheard—' Flustered, she adjusted the bag that hung from her shoulder. 'I thought I heard you say that you're Dr McKinley.'

'I did.'

'Oh.' Her tone suggested that news was unwelcome. Then she stuck out her hand. 'Right, well, I'm Jennifer Richards. Jenna.' She left her hand hovering in the space between them for a moment, and then slowly withdrew it as he simply stared at her. 'What's wrong? Have I arrived on the wrong day? You look a bit…stunned to see me.'

Jennifer Richards? Stunned didn't begin to describe his reaction. Ryan cleared his throat and shook her hand, noticing that her fingers were slim and cool. 'Right day.' Wrong description. 'It's just that—my partner fed me false information. I was expecting a woman and her teenage daughter.' Someone about twenty years older. Someone who wasn't going to make his hormones surge.

'Ah—' She glanced towards the ferry, her smile tired. 'Well, I'm the woman, but the teenage daughter is still on the boat, I'm afraid. That's her, hanging over the side glaring at me. She's refusing to get off, and I'm still trying to decide how best to handle this particular situation without ruining my reputation before I even take my first clinic. I don't suppose you have any experience in handling moody teenagers, Dr McKinley?'

He cleared his throat. 'None.'

'Shame.' Her tone was a mixture of humour and weary acceptance. 'This is one of those occasions when I need to refer to my handbook on teenagers. Stupidly, I packed it at the bottom of the suitcase. Next time it's going in my handbag and if necessary I'll ditch my purse. I apologise for her lack of manners.' She flushed self-consciously and looked away. 'You're staring at me, Dr McKinley. You're thinking I should have better control over my child.'

Yes, he was staring. Of course he was staring.

All the men on Glenmore were going to be staring.

Ryan realised that she was waiting for him to say something. 'I'm thinking you can't possibly be old enough to be that girl's mother. Is she adopted?' Damn. That wasn't what he'd meant to say.

'No, she's all mine. I have sole responsibility for the behavioural problems. But it's refreshing to hear I don't look old enough. According to Lexi, I'm a dinosaur. And she's probably right. I certainly feel past it—particularly right now, when I'm going to have to get firm with her in public. Oh, joy.' The wind flipped a strand of hair across her face and she anchored it with her fingers. 'You're still staring, Dr McKinley. I'm sorry I'm not what you were expecting.'

So was he.

He wasn't ready to feel this. Wasn't sure he wanted to feel this.

Mistrusting his emotions, Ryan ran a hand over his neck, wondering what had happened to his powers of speech. 'You must have been a child bride. Either that or you have shares in Botox.'

'Child bride.' There was a wistful note to her voice, and something else that he couldn't decipher. And then she lifted her eyebrows as the girl flounced off the ferry. 'Well, that's a first. She's doing something I want her to do without a row. I wonder what made her co-operate. Lexi—' she lifted her voice slightly '—come and meet Dr McKinley.'

A slender, moody teenager stomped towards them.

Ryan, who had never had any trouble with numbers, couldn't work out how the girl in front of him could be this woman's daughter. 'Hi, there. Nice to meet you.'

Eyes exactly like her mother's stared back at him. 'Are you the one who gave my mum this job? You don't look like anything like a doctor.'

Ryan wanted to say that Jenna didn't look like the mother of a teenager, but he didn't. 'That's because I didn't have time to shave before I met the ferry.' He rubbed his fingers over his roughened jaw. 'I am a doctor. But I didn't give your mother the job—that was my colleague, Dr McNeil.'

'Well, whatever you do, don't put her in charge of family

planning. As you can probably tell from looking at me, contraception is *so* not her specialist subject.'

'Lexi!' Jenna sounded mortified and the girl flushed.

'Sorry. It's just—oh, never mind. Being in this place is really doing my head in.' Close to tears, the teenager flipped her hair away from her face and stared across the quay. 'Is there an internet café or something? Any way of contacting the outside world? Or are we using Morse code and smoke signals? Or, better still, can we just go home, Mum?'

Ryan was still watching Jenna. He saw the pain in her eyes, the exasperation and the sheer grit and determination. She looked like someone who was fighting her way through a storm, knowing that there was no shelter.

Interesting, he mused, that Glenmore so often provided a bolthole for the wounded.

He wondered what these two were escaping.

Sensing that Jenna was hideously embarrassed, he knew he ought to say something—but what did he know about handling teenagers? Nothing. And he knew even less about what to say to soften the blow of teenage rudeness. Assuming that something along the lines of *she'll be leaving home in another four years* wouldn't go down well, Ryan opted to keep his mouth shut.

He'd never raised a child, had he?

Never been given that option. Anger thudded through him and he stilled, acknowledging that the feelings hadn't gone away. He'd buried them, but they were still there.

Taking an audible breath, Jenna picked up their bags. 'We're renting a cottage at West Beach. Is there a bus that goes that way?'

'No bus. There are taxis, but before you think about that I have a favour to ask.'

'What favour can I possibly do you already?'

Ryan gently prised the suitcases from her cold fingers, sensing the vulnerability hidden beneath layers of poise and dignity. 'I know you're not supposed to officially start until tomorrow, but we're snowed under at the surgery. I'm supposed to exert my charm to persuade you to start early, only I was up three times in the night so I'm not feeling that charming. I'd appreciate it if you'd cut me some slack and say yes.'

'You do house-calls?'

'Is that surprising?'

'The doctors I worked with rarely did their own house-calls. It was the one thing—' She broke off and smiled at him, obviously deciding that she'd said too much.

'On Glenmore we can't delegate. We don't have an out-of-hours service or a local hospital—it's just the three of us.' He looked at her pointedly. 'Four now. You're one of the team.' And he still wasn't sure what he thought about that.

'Are you sure you still want me? You're sure you don't want to rethink my appointment after what Lexi just said?' Her tone was light, but there was vulnerability in her eyes that told him she was worrying about her daughter's comments.

Ryan was surprised that she was so sensitive to what others might be thinking. Out of the blue, his mind drifted to Connie. Connie hadn't given a damn what other people thought. She'd been so monumentally selfish and self-absorbed that it had driven him mad.

'Your qualifications are really impressive. We're delighted to have you here. And the sooner you can start the better.'

'I spoke to Evanna McNeil on the phone.' She turned her head and checked on her daughter. 'She's arranged for us to pick up the keys to the cottage this morning. I was going to spend the day settling in and start work tomorrow.'

'The cottage isn't far from here. And I know you were supposed to have today to settle in, but if there is any way I can persuade you to start work this morning that would be fantastic. There's a clinic starting at eight-thirty, and the girl who helps Evanna with the kids is off sick so she has to look after the children. I'd cancel it, but we're already overrun because we've been down a nurse for a few months.'

'But if the clinic starts at eight-thirty that's just half an hour from now.' Jenna glanced at her watch, flustered by his request, working out the implications. 'I want to help, of course. Normally I'd say yes instantly, but—well, I haven't made any arrangements for Lexi.'

'I'm not six, Mum. I'll stay on my own.' The girl looked round with a despairing look on her face. 'I'm hardly likely to get into danger here.'

Ryan had a feeling that the child would be capable of getting into trouble in an empty room, and Jenna was clearly of the same opinion because she looked doubtful.

'I'm not leaving you on your own until we've both settled in and found our feet. It's going to be OK, Lex.' Her gaze was fixed on her daughter's face and Ryan wanted to ask *what* was going to be OK. What had given her dark rings around her eyes? What was keeping her awake at night?

Why had she taken a job on a remote Scottish Island?

It didn't take a genius to sense that there was a great deal more going on than was revealed by their spoken communication. And he couldn't help noticing that no man had followed her off the ferry. If there was a Mr Richards, then he was keeping his distance.

With customary practicality, Ryan searched for a solution. 'Lexi can come too. The surgery is attached to the house. She can hang out with Evanna and the children. Evanna would be glad of the help, and it will give Lexi a chance to find out something about the island. And I can drive you over to the cottage at lunchtime. I'll even help you unpack to speed things up.'

'Mum!' Lexi spoke through gritted teeth. 'I'm not spending the morning looking after a couple of babies! I'd rather go to broken pottery camp, or whatever it's called!'

Ryan struggled to think like a teenager. 'Evanna has internet access, and the mobile signal is great from her house.'

Lexi gave a wide smile that transformed her face from sullen to stunning. 'Then what are we waiting for? Lead me to civilisation. Otherwise known as wireless broadband.'

CHAPTER TWO

'I NORMALLY see Nurse Evanna,' the old lady said, settling herself into the chair. 'She knows exactly what to do with my leg.'

Could today get any worse? Feeling mentally exhausted, Jenna scanned the notes on the screen.

Not only did her daughter not want her to be here, the patients didn't appear to want her either. And doubtless Dr McKinley was also regretting her appointment after that embarrassing scenario on the quay.

And to top it all, having not thought about sex for what seemed like the whole of her twenties, she'd looked into Ryan McKinley's cool blue eyes and suddenly started thinking about nothing but sex. She'd been so mesmerised by an alien flash of chemistry that she'd almost embarrassed herself.

Jenna cringed at the memory of just how long she'd stared at him. Who was she kidding? She *had* embarrassed herself. There was no almost about it.

And she'd embarrassed him.

Why else would he have been staring at her?

What must he have thought?

That she was a sad, desperate single mother who hadn't had sex for a lifetime.

He'd made all those polite noises about her looking too young to have a teenage daughter, but Jenna knew it was nonsense. People said that, didn't they? People said *You don't look thirty*, while secretly thinking you looked closer to forty. She shuddered, appalled at the thought that he might be sitting in his consulting room right now, formulating a strategy for keeping her at a distance. She needed to make sure he knew she didn't have designs on him—that a relationship with a man was right at the bottom of her wish list.

She was just trying to survive. Rebuild her life.

Knowing she couldn't afford to think about that now, Jenna concentrated on her patient. 'I understand that it's unsettling to have someone new, Mrs Parker, but Evanna has left detailed notes. If you see me doing anything differently, or anything that makes you feel worried, you can tell me.'

'You've a teenage daughter, I hear?' Mrs Parker dropped her bag onto the floor and slipped off her shoe. Her tights were the colour of stewed tea and twisted slightly around her ankles.

Jenna searched through the choice of dressings available to her, unsure what the surgery stocked. 'I only stepped off the ferry half an hour ago. Word travels fast.'

'Hard to have secrets on Glenmore. We're a close community.'

'That's why I chose to come here, Mrs Parker.' That and the fact she hadn't had much choice. She helped the woman onto the trolley. 'And I don't have any secrets.'

'Will your husband be joining you later?'

'I'm no longer married, Mrs Parker.' Jenna swiftly removed the old dressing, wondering why saying those words made her feel such a failure.

As if to reinforce those feelings, Mrs Parker pressed her

lips together in disapproval. 'I was married for fifty-two years. In those days we sorted out our differences. We didn't give up.'

Great. Just what she needed. A lecture. Still, she was used to those from her mother. She'd grown up seeing her failings highlighted in neon lights.

'I admire you, Mrs Parker. I'm just going to check your blood pressure.'

Mrs Parker sniffed her disapproval. 'I'm here to have the dressing changed.'

'I know that. And I've already picked out what I'm going to use.' Reminding herself that building relationships was essential to the smooth running of the practice, Jenna was patient. 'But it's important to check your blood pressure every six months or so, and I can see from your notes that it hasn't been done for a while.'

'I don't see what my blood pressure has to do with the ulcer on my leg.'

'Sometimes ulcers can be caused by bad circulation rather than venous problems. I want to do an ankle blood pressure as well as taking it on your arm.'

Mrs Parker relaxed slightly. 'You obviously know what you're doing. All right. But I haven't got all day.'

Jenna checked her blood pressure, reminding herself that she'd always known this move wouldn't be easy. Not for her, nor Lexi.

'So you fell pregnant when you were still in school, by the looks of you.' Mrs Parker's lips pursed. 'Still, everyone makes mistakes.'

Jenna carefully recorded the blood pressure readings before she replied. 'I don't consider my daughter to be a mistake, Mrs Parker.'

There was a moment of silence and then the old lady gave a chuckle. 'Capable of standing up for yourself, are you? I like that. You're obviously a bright girl. Why have you moved all the way up here? You could be in some leading city practice. Or are you running away?'

Jenna sensed that whatever she told this woman would be all over the island by lunchtime, so she delivered an edited version of the truth. 'My marriage ended. I needed a change. And this place has a good reputation. Logan McNeil has built a good practice.' She didn't add that she would have taken the job regardless, because it was as far from Clive and her parents as it was possible to get without leaving the country.

'Logan is a good doctor. So's Ryan McKinley, of course. But we all know he won't be around for long. He's a real high-flier. Used to work as one of those emergency doctors.'

Emergency doctor?

Confused, Jenna paused. 'How long has he lived here?'

'Came here two years ago and bought the old abandoned lighthouse that Ewan Kinaird had given up hope of selling. Too isolated for everyone. But not for Dr McKinley. Apparently isolation was what he wanted, and he paid a fair price for it. Didn't see him for most of that first year. Turned up occasionally in the village to buy supplies. Kept himself to himself. Never smiled. Some thought he was antisocial. Others thought he was recovering from some trauma or other. Certainly looked grim-faced whenever I glimpsed him.'

Jenna felt guilty for listening. Part of her wanted to cover her ears but she didn't want to be rude. And she was intrigued by Ryan McKinley. When she'd met him he hadn't seemed antisocial. Nor had he shown signs of trauma. He'd talked. Smiled. But she knew a smile often hid a secret. 'So how does he come to be working as a GP?'

'That was Evanna's doing. Won't let anyone be, that girl—especially not if they're in trouble. She coaxed him into helping out after the last locum left them in the lurch. She had baby Charlie, and Logan was managing the practice on his own. When he was needed, Ryan stepped up. But we all know he won't stick. He'll be off to some high-flying job before the tide has turned.' Mrs Parker took a closer look at her leg. 'What's your professional opinion of this, then?'

'I'm just taking a look now.' Jenna wondered what trauma had made a doctor qualified in emergency medicine buy a secluded lighthouse on an isolated island. 'How did you find out he was a doctor?'

'Oh, he kept it quiet.' Mrs Parker peered at her leg. 'But Fiona Grange crashed her car into a ditch in the middle of a storm and he happened to be passing when it happened. Some say he's the reason she's alive. Bones smashed, she was unconscious, and the air ambulance couldn't take off. And there was Dr McKinley, cool as a Glenmore winter, stopping the bleeding, extracting her from the car—shocked everyone, he did. Went from hermit to hero in the blink of an eye. But there was no hiding his profession after that. And he's been a good doctor, although he's private. Keeps himself to himself. Some think he's unfriendly. A bit cold.'

Unfriendly? Jenna thought about the man who had met her at the quay. He hadn't been unfriendly. Tired, definitely. Guarded, maybe. She would have described him as cool, but not cold.

'I'm going to take a proper look at your leg now.' Trying not to think about Ryan McKinley, Jenna washed her hands and opened the dressing pack. 'Your blood pressure is fine. How long have you had this problem, Mrs Parker?'

'I had it last summer and it went away. But then it came back.'

'Did you wear your compression stockings?' She glanced down at the tan stockings that had been placed neatly on the chair.

'Not as much as I'm supposed to.'

'They're not that comfortable, I know.' Jenna cleaned the wound and dressed it. 'That does look sore, you poor thing. Are you in a lot of pain?'

Mrs Parker relaxed slightly. 'I'm old. I'm always in pain. My bones ache every morning. The Glenmore winter is bitter. Like having your leg in the jaws of a shark.'

'I've only ever been here in the summer. My grandparents used to bring me. Tell me if this feels too tight.' Jenna bandaged the leg, applying most pressure to the ankle and gradually less towards the knee and thigh. 'Try and keep your leg up before you come and have that dressing changed next week. Have you tried putting a couple of pillows under your mattress? The aim is to let gravity pull the fluid and blood towards the heart. It will reduce the swelling. Can you move your ankle?'

'Yes. You've done a good job,' Mrs Parker said grudgingly. She stood up and put her stockings back on with Jenna's help. Then she reached for her bag. 'That dressing feels very comfortable, actually. But tell Evanna I'm sorry to have missed her.'

'I'll do that.'

Jenna watched as Mrs Parker walked slowly down the corridor, and then returned to the computer to type up the notes, sinking into the chair, exhausted. This was a huge mistake. She should have just bought a new flat in London, then she could have stayed in her job and Lexi could have stayed in her school.

Instead she'd chosen a small island where strangers were viewed with suspicion and where her life was going to be lived under a microscope.

She was an idiot.

Forcing herself to take several deep breaths, Jenna reminded herself that it was natural for the islanders to be wary of a new nurse. She just had to earn their trust.

Or maybe she should just buy another ferry ticket and get off this island as fast as possible. She sank her head into her hands, and then sat up quickly as she heard a rap on the door.

Ryan walked in. 'I owe you an apology. I had no idea Mrs Parker was your first patient. Talk about baptism of fire.'

Somewhere between meeting her on the quay and starting his surgery he'd shaved and changed. The faded jeans had been replaced by smart trousers and the comfortable tee shirt by a tailored shirt. In the confines of her consulting room he seemed taller. And broader. Suddenly she had no trouble imagining him as a high-powered consultant in a busy emergency department.

Her throat suddenly felt dry. 'Yes, she was my first patient.'

'You're still alive?'

Oh, yes. She knew she was alive because she could feel her heart banging hard against her chest. 'We did OK.'

'But now you want to resign?' His voice was dry. 'You're about to buy a return ferry ticket and run back to London?'

Jenna sat rigid, terrified that he'd guessed how bad she felt. 'No.' Her voice was bright. 'I'm not even remotely tempted to run away.'

His smile faded and his gaze sharpened. 'I was joking.'

'Oh.' She turned scarlet. 'Of course you were joking. Sorry. I'm a bit tired after the journey.'

'The last nurse we appointed lasted three days. Didn't Evanna tell you?'

'She did mention something. Don't worry, Dr McKinley. I'm not a quitter.' Jenna said it firmly, reminding herself of that fact. 'And Mrs Parker was fine.'

'I know Mrs Parker, so you must be lying.'

Yes, she was and it seemed that these days she spent her life lying. Even her smile was a lie. 'Mrs Parker was wary at seeing someone new, and that's normal—especially at her age. She doesn't like change. I understand that.' Jenna concentrated on the computer, thinking that she was finding change terrifying and she was several decades younger than Mrs Parker.

'That leg of hers is slow to heal.'

Jenna thought about the old lady—remembered how much had been said in a short time. 'I don't know her, but at a guess I'd say she doesn't really want it to heal. She's lonely. Her leg gives her a reason to come up here and interact with people.'

'That's possible.' His eyes narrowed thoughtfully. 'Despite your college-girl looks, you're obviously very sharp.'

Accustomed to thinking of herself as 'past it', his compliment made her feel strange. Or maybe it hadn't been a compliment. 'I'm interested in people. I like looking for the reasons they do things. It's why I do the job.' Even as she said the words she realised the flaw in that theory. If she was so interested in why people did what they did, why hadn't she spotted the signs that her husband was cheating on her? Maybe she wasn't so observant after all. Or maybe she hadn't wanted to see what was under her nose.

Feeling the tension erupt inside her, Jenna hit a button on the computer and exited Mrs Parker's file, wishing she could control her thinking. She had to stop asking 'what if?' She had to move on. That was what she was doing here, wasn't it? She was wiping out the past. 'Why do *you* do the job, Dr McKinley?' Would he tell her that he was an emergency specialist in hiding?

He was leaning against the wall, his broad shoulders threatening the safety of the asthma poster stuck to the wall. 'At the moment I can't remember. You'd better ask me that question again when I haven't been up for half the night doing calls. I'm always in a snarly mood when I get less than three hours' sleep.'

'That's understandable. Could you sneak off and sleep at some point today?'

'Unfortunately, no. Like I said to you on the quay—it's just the four of us. When we're busy, we're busy. We can't hand it over.'

'Who called you out last night? Locals or tourists?'

'One tourist with chest pains, a toddler with a febrile convulsion, and one of our own with a very nasty asthma attack.' He frowned. 'I called the mother a few moments ago to check on her and she told me the child is still asleep, but I'm going to call in later. I didn't like the look of her in the night. I gather you have an interest in asthma?'

'Yes. I ran a clinic in London.' Jenna was interested. 'Was there an obvious trigger? Did she have an infection or something?'

'They'd got themselves a dog from the rescue centre. I'm assuming it was that.'

'They didn't know that animal fur was a trigger?' Jenna pulled a face, understanding the ramifications of that statement. 'So is the dog being returned?'

'It's a strong possibility. They're thinking about it, but obviously the child will be upset.'

'It would be wonderful to have a dog,' Jenna said wistfully, and then sat up straight, slightly shocked by herself. A dog? Where had that thought come from? Why on earth would she want a dog?

'Maybe you could give this one a home?'

Jenna automatically shook her head. 'We can't have a dog. Cl—' She was about to say that Clive hated animals, but then she remembered that she wasn't married to Clive any more. His opinion didn't matter.

Glancing down at her left hand, she stared at the pale line on her finger that was the only remaining evidence that she'd once worn a ring. It still felt strange, seeing the finger bare. And it still brought a sting to the back of her throat.

'Something wrong?' His question made her jump.

'No. I was just thinking about your little asthma patient and the dog.'

'Right.' His gaze locked onto hers and she looked away quickly, thinking that Ryan McKinley was nothing like the men she usually met during her working day. For a start he was about two decades younger than the GPs she'd worked with in her last practice. She tried to imagine any of *them* extracting a seriously injured girl from the wreck of a car during a storm without the help of paramedics—and failed. Ryan McKinley was a different breed of doctor. And then there was the fact that he was indecently good-looking. Sexy.

A different breed of man.

'You look really stressed out.' Ryan spoke quietly. 'Is that Mrs Parker's doing? Or is it being thrown in at the deep end?'

'No! Not at all.' Oh, God, he'd noticed that she was stressed. And the one thing she absolutely couldn't afford to do was put a foot wrong in this job. 'I love being thrown in at the deep end. Anyway, I didn't ask why you were here. Did you want to talk to me? Is there something I can help you with, Dr McKinley?' Please don't let him say he'd changed his mind about hiring her.

'I wondered if you could take some bloods for me.' Ryan handed her a form, his eyes still on her face. 'Callum is fifteen and he's showing all the signs of glandular fever. I know you already have a full clinic, but I really need these results as soon as possible.'

'Of course you do.' As she took the form from him, Jenna's fingers brushed against his. She immediately snatched her hand away, feeling as though she'd touched a live wire. 'I'll do them straight away.' Without thinking, she rubbed her fingers, wondering whether she was doomed to overreact around this man.

'He's in the waiting room with his mum.' Ryan was looking at her fingers, and Jenna swallowed and dropped her hands into her lap.

'Fine. Great. I'll call him.'

'I appreciate it.' There was a tension about him that hadn't been there before. 'Your bikes have been delivered, by the way. I had them taken straight to the cottage. They'll be safe enough outside your front door.'

'Bikes?' Jenna had to force herself to concentrate. 'Bikes. Yes, of course. Evanna told me about this place that hires them for the summer, so I rang them. I thought it would be good for both of us to cycle.'

'I'm impressed. It's a good example to set to the patients.'

'So you'll try not to knock me off my bike when you're accelerating past in your Porsche?'

He gave a faint smile as he strolled towards the door. 'Are you accusing me of speeding or being a couch potato?'

'Neither. I'm sure you're very fit.' Her eyes slid to the hard muscle of his shoulders, clearly outlined by the smooth fabric of his casual shirt. Damn, she shouldn't have used the word *fit*. Wasn't that the word Lexi used when she found a boy attractive? 'I mean, you're obviously athletic—I mean, health-conscious—sorry, just ignore me…' Jenna had the distinct impression that he was laughing at her, but when she looked at him his expression was unreadable.

'Why would I want to ignore you?'

'Because I'm talking nonsense—' And he was super-cool, hyper-intelligent and nothing like the men she usually dealt with. She had no trouble believing Mrs Parker's assertion that he was a top doctor. He had an air of authority and command that she found mildly intimidating. 'The bikes will be great.'

'Does Lexi know you've ordered bikes?'

'Not yet.' She didn't know which impressed her more, the fact that he'd remembered her daughter's name or his uncannily accurate assessment of her character. 'Light the touch paper and stand well back. Which reminds me; I owe you an apology for her behaviour earlier.'

'What do you have to apologise for?'

'Lexi. She—' Jenna didn't want to reveal personal details, but she was unable to bear the thought he might think badly of her daughter. 'She's very mixed up at the moment. She didn't want to move from our home in London. It's been hard on her.'

He was silent for a moment, considering her words. She had a nasty feeling that he knew just how close to the edge she was. 'Glenmore has a very calming effect on people. It's a good place to escape.'

'Lexi didn't want to leave London.'

'Perhaps your needs are greater than hers at the moment,' he said gently. 'Does Lexi know you're living in a cottage on the beach?'

'No. There's only so much bad news that she can take at one time. She's going to hate me for not renting a house in the village.'

'That's not exactly a hub for entertainment, either.' He

opened the door. 'When you've finished your clinic, knock on my door. I'll take you and your luggage over there.'

'I don't expect you to do that. If you have any spare time, you need to sleep.'

'I'll give you a lift.' He hesitated, his hand on the door. 'Give it a few weeks before you buy that ferry ticket. I predict that in no time this place will feel like home.'

He knew.

He knew how bad she felt. She'd done a lousy job at hiding her feelings. He knew she was panicking and having second thoughts.

Horrified that he was clearly aware of how close she was to breaking, Jenna just sat there, not trusting herself to speak. Their eyes held, and then he gave a brief nod.

'Welcome to Glenmore, Jenna. We're very pleased to have you here.'

Ryan stood in front of his colleague, legs spread, hands dug in his back pockets. 'Tell me about Jenna.'

'Jenna?' Logan McNeil signed a prescription and glanced up, his expression interested. 'Why? Was it love at first sight? Your eyes met across a crowded ferry ramp?'

Remembering the flash of chemistry, Ryan rolled his shoulders to ease the tension. 'Just give me the facts, Logan.'

Logan put his pen down. 'She's been working as a practice nurse in England for the past six years, but I'm not holding that against her. Why are you asking? Has she killed a patient or something?'

'I'm worried about her.'

'Isn't that a little premature? She's been here for five minutes.'

And he'd been worried about her within thirty seconds of meeting her. She'd looked fragile and battered, as though she'd emerged from a terrible storm. 'Evanna asked me to meet her, remember? She looks as though she's holding it together by a thread.'

Suddenly Logan wasn't smiling. 'You're worried about her ability to do the job?'

'No. She handled Mrs Parker, which proves she's more than capable of doing the job. I'm worried about *her*!' Ryan shot him an impatient look. 'What do you know about her personal circumstances?'

With a sigh, Logan opened his drawer and pulled out a file. Scanning the papers, he paused. 'Divorced with a teenage daughter. That's all it says.'

Divorced.

Ryan prowled to the window of Logan's consulting room and stared across the fields. Remembering the white circle on her ring finger, he was willing to bet the divorce was recent. Was that why she was so pale and drawn? Divorce did that to people, didn't it? Was that why she jumped when a man touched her? 'Was her ex-husband abusive?'

'I have absolutely no idea. This is her CV, not a police statement. Are you sure you're not going a little over the top here? You seem very concerned about someone you only met a few hours ago.'

Ryan turned. 'She's a colleague,' he said evenly. 'It's in our interest to make sure she's happy here.'

'And that's all that's going on here?' Logan closed the file. 'You seem very interested in her.'

'I didn't say I was interested. I said it was in our interest to make sure she's happy.'

'Good. Then I'll leave it to you to make sure she is.' Logan pushed the file back in the drawer. 'Plenty of people get divorced, Ryan. It's a fact of life in our society. It doesn't mean she has problems. You could be barking up the wrong tree. Has she seen the cottage yet?'

'I'm taking her at the end of morning surgery.'

'Let's just hope she likes isolation, otherwise we'll be looking for a new practice nurse. Ted Walker has a flat vacant in the village if you think that would be better.'

'I know she's going to like the cottage.' He didn't know how he knew, but he did.

She was running—wounded—looking for a place to hide and recover.

And the cottage was the perfect place for her. Whether her teenager daughter would survive the isolation was another matter.

CHAPTER THREE

IT WAS the prettiest house she'd ever seen—one of four fishermen's cottages facing the sea, their front gardens leading straight down to a sandy beach.

The iron gate was rusty and creaked as she pushed it open, but Jenna felt a sudden feeling of calm and contentment. No more endless traffic jams and road rage. No more rush hour. No more litter on the streets and graffiti on the walls.

Just open space, fresh air, and the sound of the sea.

It was perfect.

Lexi gave a whimper of horror. 'This is it? It's the smallest house I've ever seen.'

Jenna felt the tension return to her stomach. 'Small, yes, but it's ours.' As long as she kept the job. The house came with the job. They had a home again. And it would be cheap to run.

Lexi was gaping at the tiny cottage. 'A whole summer here?'

'Yes.'

'You can't swing a cat.'

'We don't have a cat.' But they might have a dog. She'd been thinking about it ever since Ryan McKinley had mentioned the idea.

Lexi closed her eyes. 'Just kill me now,' she muttered, and Jenna searched for something to say that would cheer her up.

'Don't you think this is better than London?'

'Tell me that isn't a serious question—'

Jenna sighed. They'd come this far. They had to keep moving forward.

She walked up the path to the front door, her eyes scanning the pretty garden. She noticed a few weeds and her hands itched. It would be fun, she mused, to have a proper garden.

Lexi stared desperately at the house and then at the beach. 'Where's the nearest shop?'

'Walk straight down the road and you reach the harbour. If it's low tide you can walk along the beach.' Ryan strode up the path behind them, carrying both suitcases. He deposited them on the ground, gently removed the key from Jenna's hand and opened the door of the cottage.

'Sorry—I was miles away.' Jenna gave a smile of apology. 'It's so long since I had a garden. Our house in London just had a courtyard. I'm not used to so much outdoor space.' Enchanted, she stooped and touched some of the pretty pink flowers that clustered by the door. '*Armeria maritima.*'

Ryan raised his eyebrows, apparently amused. 'You're quoting the Latin names of plants at me?'

'My mother was a botanist. I grew up hearing Latin names. Some of them stuck.' She touched the flower with the tip of her finger. 'Sea pinks. They grow well in this climate, by the coast.'

Lexi rolled her eyes. 'Gosh, Mum, gripping stuff.'

Jenna flushed and stood up. 'Sorry. It's just so wonderful to have a garden.' Despite the knot in her stomach she felt better, and she was in no hurry to go indoors. Instead she breathed in the sea air and watched the plants waving in the breeze. The grass needed cutting, and there were weeds in the borders, but somehow that just added to the charm. She imagined herself lying on a rug on a warm Sunday morning, listening to the gulls and reading the paper.

When had she ever done that? Sundays were normally so busy, what with making a traditional Sunday roast for Clive and his mother, and then being expected to produce tea for the cricket club…

Aware that Ryan was watching her, Jenna flushed. She felt as though he could read her every thought, and that was disturbing because some of the thoughts she'd been having about him were definitely best kept private. 'When Evanna told me that the job came with a house, I never imagined it would be anywhere as perfect as this. I can't imagine why anyone would want to leave here. Who owns it?'

'Kyla—Logan's sister. Her husband, Ethan, was offered a job in the States. They'll be back at some point.'

But not soon. Please don't let it be soon.

A warm feeling spread through her, and for the first time since she'd left London Jenna felt a flicker of hope. Excitement. As if this might be the right decision after all.

She felt as if she belonged. She felt at home.

It's—so peaceful.' A gull shrieked above her and she laughed as she caught Ryan's eye. 'Well, not peaceful, perhaps, but the noises are different. Good noises. No car horns and revving engines. And everything is slow. I'm looking forward to just being still.' Realising that she probably sounded ridiculous, Jenna shrugged awkwardly. 'In London everything moves so fast. You get swept along with it so that sometimes you can't even take a breath—I hate the pace of it.'

'That's because you're so old, Mum.' Lexi fiddled with her phone. 'London was exciting. And our house was lovely.'

'London was noisy and smelly and our house was far too

big for the two of us.' It was what she'd told herself when she'd realised that their house had been sold and she and Lexi no longer had a home. It was the only way she had coped.

Pushing away that thought, Jenna stepped into the hallway of the cottage. They had a home now, and she loved it. Light reflected off the polished wooden floor, and through an open door she could see a bright, cheerful kitchen. 'We lived right next to an underground station and every three minutes the house shook.'

'Yeah, it was so cool.' Lexi tossed her hair away from her face, her eyes still on her mobile phone. 'I was never more than ten minutes from the shops.'

But Jenna wasn't thinking about shopping. It seemed far away. And so did Clive and the whole sordid mess she'd left behind. 'This place is wonderful. We can have our breakfast outside on that little table.' She turned to look at the pretty garden, eyes slightly misty, imagination running free. 'Lexi, you can go for a swim, or a run on the beach.'

How could this be a mistake?

Maybe she hadn't done the wrong thing. They could be happy here—she felt it.

Lexi shot her a look of incredulous disbelief and checked her mobile phone. 'No signal again. How do people function around here?'

'You can usually get a signal if you walk up the hill towards the castle.' Ryan lifted their suitcases into the hallway and Lexi gave an exaggerated sigh.

'Fine. If the only place I can use my phone is at the top of a hill then I'm going to have to walk up it!' Making a frustrated sound in her throat, she stalked away.

Jenna opened her mouth to say *be careful* and then closed

it again, leaving the words unspoken. She knew from experience that too much maternal anxiety was counterproductive.

But the guilt was back, eating away at her like acid, corroding her insides. She might have fallen in love with the cottage, but she knew this wasn't what Lexi wanted.

'It must be hard, letting them grow up.' Ryan was standing in the doorway, his thumbs hooked into the pockets of his trousers, a speculative look in his blue eyes as he watched her.

'You have no idea.' Keeping her tone light, Jenna walked past him into the garden, her gaze on Lexi as her daughter sauntered across the road and started up the hill. A dozen nightmare scenarios sped through her overactive maternal brain. To control them, she used black humour. *Say it aloud and it might not happen.* 'Are there any scary, dangerous individuals at large on Glenmore at the moment?'

'Well, you've already met Mrs Parker—they don't come much scarier or more dangerous than her. She's wanted in five counties.' His arm brushed against hers and Jenna felt her whole body tingle.

She stepped away from him, keeping her distance as she would from an electric fence. 'I was thinking more of axe-wielding murderers and rapists.'

'We had dozens of those last summer, but Mrs Parker saw them off. It's hard to commit a crime in a community that knows what you're planning to eat for supper.'

As Lexi's figure grew smaller, and then vanished from sight, Jenna felt a moment of panic. Catching his eye, she gave an embarrassed laugh. 'Yes, I know—I'm overreacting. It's hard to forget this isn't London. You must think I'm crazy. *I* think I'm crazy!'

'That isn't what I'm thinking.'

'It would be if you knew what was going through my

mind. It's taking all my will-power not to charge after her and follow her up that hill.'

His gaze shifted from her face to where Lexi had disappeared. 'I don't know much about teenagers, but at a guess I'd say that probably isn't the best idea.'

'Well, I'd have to be discreet, of course.' She made a joke of it. 'I'd probably start by sprinting up the hill and then drop to my stomach and crawl so that she couldn't see me.'

'You're going to have a hell of a job beating off an axe-wielding murderer if you're crawling on your stomach.'

'Never underestimate a mother protecting her young.'

'I'll remember that.' He had a deep voice. Deep and male, with a slightly husky timbre that made her think things she hadn't thought for a long time.

Jenna breathed in slowly and stared at the ridge, trying not to think about his voice. 'I can't believe she made it up there so quickly. Lexi isn't really into exercise. It's amazing what the lure of a mobile phone signal can do to cure teenage lethargy. I hope she'll be OK.'

Ryan turned to her, and she noticed that the passing hours had darkened his jaw again. 'She's crossed the only road and she's still alive. She'll be fine. I'm not so sure about you.'

Her gaze met his and their eyes held.

The rhythm of her heart altered and the oxygen was sucked from the air. The world shrank to this one place—this one man.

Everything else was forgotten.

Mesmerised by those blue eyes, Jenna felt her body come to life, like the slow, sensual unfolding of a bud under the heat of the sun. Not the sultry, languid heat of summer sunshine but the fierce, rapacious scorch of sexual awareness. Like a volcano too long dormant after centuries of sleep, it exploded violently—blowing the lid on everything she believed herself to be. Excitement ripped through her like a consuming, ravenous fire, and in her newly sensitised state she found staring longingly at the firm lines of his mouth.

If she wanted to kiss him, she could…

She was a free woman now.

The shriek of a seagull brought her to her senses and Jenna took a step backwards.

What on earth was she thinking? If she did something crazy, like kissing him, he'd fire her from her job, Lexi would have a nervous breakdown, and she'd be more of an emotional wreck than she was already. And anyway, if she hadn't been able to trust someone she'd known for fifteen years, what chance was there with someone she'd known for fifteen minutes?

Jenna straightened her shoulders. 'You're right. I worry far too much about her. I intend to work on that this summer. I'm hoping it will be easier here.' Unfortunately her bright, businesslike tone did nothing to dissipate the strange turbulence inside her. She needed to be on her own, so that she could undo whatever she'd just done to herself by looking at him. And she was sure he was desperate to escape from her, albeit for different reasons.

'Thanks so much for the lift, Dr McKinley. I'm sorry to hold you up.'

'You're not holding me up.' Instead of leaving, as she'd expected, he walked back towards the house. 'Do you have any caffeine?'

Pulling herself together, Jenna followed him. 'Pardon?'

'Caffeine. I'm feeling tired, and there's still most of the day to get through.' Suppressing a yawn, he walked through to the kitchen without asking for directions or permission. 'I need coffee. Strong coffee.'

'I thought you'd need to dash off somewhere—lunch, house-calls…' She had thought he'd be anxious to escape from her—the desperate divorcee…

'We try not to do too much dashing on Glenmore.' Concentration on his face, he pulled open a cupboard and rummaged through the contents. 'It's bad for the heart. Which do you prefer? Tea or coffee?'

'Either. I mean—I haven't had time to shop.'

'The kitchen should be stocked.'

'Oh.' Jenna was about to ask who could possibly have stocked the kitchen when the phone rang. She jumped. 'Who on earth can that be?'

'Why don't you answer it and see? Phone's in the hall.'

Jenna found the phone, answered it, and immediately wished she hadn't because it was her mother. 'Hi, Mum.' Oh, no, she absolutely didn't want to have this conversation with Ryan McKinley listening. Why, oh, why had she given her this number? 'No, everything is fine—' All her newfound tranquillity faded as her mother's cold disapproval trickled down the line like liquid nitrogen, freezing everything in its path. 'No, the doctors here don't care that I'm divorced.' She lowered her voice and turned away from the kitchen, hoping Ryan couldn't hear her above the hum of the kettle. 'No, the patients don't care, either—' She squeezed her eyes shut and tried not to think of Mrs Parker. 'And I'm not trying to ruin Lexi's life—it's kind of you to offer, but I don't think living with you would have been the best thing, Mum. I need to do this on my own—no, I'm not being stubborn—'

The conversation went the way it always went, with her mother stirring up every unpleasant emotion she could. Reminding herself to get caller ID, so that she could speak to her mother only when she was feeling really strong,

Jenna gripped the phone. 'Yes, I know you're very disappointed with the way things have turned out—I'm not whispering—'

By the time the conversation ended her throat was clogged and her eyes stung. Whatever magic the cottage had created had been undone. The knot was back in her stomach.

All she wanted was moral support. Was that really too much to ask from a mother?

Knowing that she wasn't capable of going back into the kitchen without making a fool of herself, Jenna stood for a moment in the hallway, still holding the phone to her ear. It was only when it was gently removed from her hand that she realised Ryan was standing next to her.

He replaced the receiver in the cradle and curved his hand over her shoulder, his touch firm. 'Are you all right?'

Jenna nodded vigorously, not trusting herself to speak. But the feel of his hand sent a warm glow through her body. It had been so long since anyone had touched her. She'd been divorced for months, and even during her marriage there hadn't been that much touching. Clive had never been tactile. More often than not he'd had dinner with clients or colleagues, which had meant she was in bed and asleep long before him. Even when they had made it to bed at the same time he'd been perfunctory, fumbling, as if making love to her had been another task on his 'to do' list and not something to be prolonged.

She was willing to bet that Ryan McKinley had never fumbled in his life.

His broad shoulders were there, right next to her, and Jenna had a powerful urge to just lean against him for a moment and see if some of his strength could be transferred to her by touch alone.

They stepped back from each other at exactly the same time, as if each had come to the same conclusion.

Not this. Not now.

'I found the coffee.' His voice was rough. 'We need scissors or a knife to open this.'

Blinking rapidly to clear the tears misting her eyes, Jenna saw that he was holding a packet of fresh coffee in his free hand. 'Great.' Appalled to realise how close she'd come to making a fool of herself, she took the coffee from his hand and walked back into the kitchen. Keeping her back to him, she opened the drawers one by one until she found a knife.

He followed her. 'Does a conversation with your mother always upset you like this?'

'How do you know it was my mother?'

'I heard you say, "Hi, Mum".'

'Oh.' If he'd heard that, then he'd heard everything—which meant that there was no point in trying to keep the messy details of her life a secret. Jenna stared down at the knives in the drawer. 'Stupid, isn't it? I'm thirty-three. She shouldn't have an effect on me, but she does. She has a talent for tapping into my deep-seated fears—exposing thoughts I'm having but would never admit even to myself.' She closed her fingers around the handle of a knife. 'She thinks I've made the wrong decision, coming here.'

'And what do you think?'

'I don't know any more.' The tears were back in her eyes, blurring her vision. 'I thought I was doing the right thing. But now I'm worrying that what's right for me might be wrong for Lexi. I've uprooted her. I've dragged her away from everything familiar. We had to leave our home, but I didn't have to come this far away—' Taking the knife from the drawer, Jenna turned, wishing she hadn't said so much. 'Sorry. You wanted a cup of coffee, not a confessional. My call has held you up. If you want to change your mind and get on with your day, I quite understand.'

It was mortifying, having your life exposed in front of a stranger.

'I'm not leaving until I've had my coffee. I'm not safe to drive.' He leaned against the granite work surface, thumbs hooked in his pockets. 'Why did you have to move?'

'I'm divorced.' There seemed no point in not being honest. Why keep it a secret?

It had happened. There was no going back. She had to get used to it.

The problem was that once people knew you were divorced, they inevitably wanted to know why.

Jenna stared at the coffee in her hand, trying not to think about the girl with the long legs and the blond hair who had been lying on her husband's desk having crazy, abandoned sex. When had *she* ever had crazy, abandoned sex? When had *she* ever lost control? Been overwhelmed—?

'Careful! You're going to cut yourself—' A frown on his face, Ryan removed the knife from her hand. 'In fact you have cut yourself. Obviously this isn't a conversation to have while you're holding a sharp object. Let me look at that for you.'

Jenna watched as blood poured down her finger. 'Oh!'

Ryan took her hand and held it under the tap, cleaned it and then examined the cut. 'We need to find a plaster. Call me traditional, but I prefer milk in my coffee.' He was cool and calm, but Jenna was thoroughly embarrassed, and she tugged her hand away from his, dried it in a towel and applied pressure.

'Stupid of me. I don't know what I was thinking.'

'You were thinking of your ex-husband. Perhaps I should clear the knives out of the cutlery drawer.'

'You don't need to worry about me. I'm fine.'

'Obviously not, or your hand wouldn't be bleeding now. And no one emerges from divorce completely unscathed.'

'I didn't say I was unscathed, Dr McKinley. I said I was fine.'

'Ryan—' He handed her another piece of kitchen roll for her finger. 'Call me Ryan. Round here we tend to be pretty informal. Do you always pretend everything is OK when it isn't?'

'I'm just starting a new job. I don't want everyone knowing I have baggage.' She pressed her finger hard, trying to stop the bleeding, exasperated with herself. 'It won't affect my work.'

'No one is suggesting that it would. Everyone has baggage, Jenna. You don't have to wrap it up and hide it.'

'Yes, I do. For Lexi's sake. I've seen couples let rip at each other through their kids and there is no way I'm going to let that happen. I refused to let it be acrimonious. I refuse to be a bitter ex-wife.'

'So you grit your teeth and shed your tears in private?' Ryan took her hand and strapped a plaster to her finger.

'Something like that.' She'd bottled up the humiliation, the devastation, the sense of betrayal—the sense of failure. All those years people had been waiting for her to fail. And she'd failed in spectacular style.

Feeling the familiar sickness inside her, Jenna snatched her hand away from his. 'Sorry. I'm talking too much. If you're sure you still want it, I'll make you that coffee.'

'I'll make it. You press on that finger.'

Watching him perform that simple task with swift efficiency, Jenna couldn't help comparing him with Clive, who had never made her a cup of coffee in all the years they'd been together. 'Do you live far from the practice, Dr Mc— Ryan?'

'In the old lighthouse, three bays round from this one. You can walk there in twenty minutes along the coast path.'

Jenna remembered what Mrs Parker had said about him living like a hermit. 'The views must be fantastic. If I had a lighthouse, I'd have my bedroom right in the top so that I could look at the view.'

'Then we think alike.' He poured fresh coffee into two mugs. 'Because I have a three-hundred–and-sixty-degree view from my bedroom.'

For some reason Jenna had a vision of Ryan sprawled in bed, and she felt a strange flutter behind her ribs, like butterflies trying to escape from a net.

'Lucky you.' Her image of leaning against his shoulder for comfort morphed into something entirely different. Different and dangerous.

She stood up quickly. 'Why don't we drink this in the garden?' The fresh air would do her good, and the kitchen suddenly seemed far too small. Or maybe he seemed too big. Something was definitely out of proportion.

'Why did you have to leave your home?' He followed her outside and put the coffee down on the wooden table. 'Couldn't you have bought him out?'

'He sold the house.' She felt her hair lift in the breeze and breathed in deeply, smelling the sea. 'He put it on the market without even telling me. I was living there with Lexi, and then one morning I woke up to find three estate agents on my doorstep.'

'Did you get yourself a good lawyer?'

'Clive *is* a lawyer,' Jenna said wearily. 'And I didn't want Lexi seeing her parents fighting. I wanted it to be as civilised as possible.'

'Civilised isn't sending round estate agents with no warning.'

'I know. But if I'd created a scene it would have been worse for Lexi. Apparently what he did was legal. I was only eighteen when we married—I didn't check whose name the house was in. I didn't check a lot of things.'

'Legal, maybe—decent, definitely not.' His tone was hard and there was a dangerous glint in his eyes. 'Does Lexi know he made you sell?'

'Yes. I told her the truth about that. I'm not sure if that was the right thing to do or not. She was already very angry with Clive for going off with another woman. And furious with me for choosing to relocate to Scotland.'

'Why *did* you choose Scotland?'

'Because it's a long way from London…' Jenna hesitated. 'Clive doesn't want Lexi around at the moment. He's living the single life and he sees her as a hindrance. I thought it would damage their relationship for ever if she found out he doesn't want her there, so I picked somewhere so far away it would be a logistical nightmare for her to spend time with him. I didn't want her having another reason to hate him.'

Ryan watched her for a long moment. 'No wonder you're exhausted. Lexi's a lucky girl, having a mother who cares as much as you do.'

'I don't know. Maybe I care too much. Maybe I'm protecting her too much. Or maybe I'm protecting myself. I don't want to admit that the man I was married to for fifteen years can behave like that. Anyway, this is a very boring for you.' Tormented by guilt, and depressed after the conversation with her mother, Jenna took a deep breath. 'Sorry. I'm lousy company, I know. Take no notice. I'm just tired after the journey. I'm sure you're really busy.'

'Why didn't your mother want you to come here?'

Jenna watched the sunlight spread across the pretty

garden. 'She wanted us to move in with her. She said it would save money.'

'Save money, but not your sanity. I gather you resisted?'

'Yes. I thought we'd be better off having a fresh start, away from everyone. Clive has another woman. Actually, it turned out he had several women throughout our marriage...' Her face was scarlet. 'I was the last person to know. That's another reason I wanted to get away. That and the fact that the girl he's started seeing is twenty-two. It was really difficult for Lexi.'

'And you, I should imagine.'

She didn't even want to think about how she'd felt. 'The hardest thing was seeing Lexi so hurt. I thought if we moved here we'd be right away from it. I thought it would be good— but at the moment she just hates me for dragging her away from her friends. She's worried no one here will speak to her. And I have no idea why I'm telling you all this.'

'Because I asked. And don't worry about no one speaking to her. This is Glenmore,' Ryan said dryly. 'There aren't enough people here for anyone to be ignored. It's a small community.'

'I hope she doesn't get into any trouble.' Jenna stared over her shoulder towards the grassy hill where Lexi had disappeared. 'I think she's very vulnerable at the moment.'

'If it's any consolation, there are not a lot of places to find trouble here. Mrs Parker aside, the crime rate on Glenmore is very low. When we do have trouble it's almost always tourists and nothing serious. Nick Hillier, the island policeman, has a pretty boring job. If there's a group of tourists drunk on the beach then it's an exciting day for him. You have nothing to worry about.'

'I'm a mother. Worrying yourself to death is part of the

package. It never changes. From the moment they're born, you're worrying. When they sleep you check them every five minutes to see if they're breathing. Once I even woke Lexi up in the night just to check she was alive. Can you believe that?'

His eyes amused, Ryan reached for his coffee. 'Our new mothers' group will love you. They talk about that sort of stuff all the time and I just nod sagely and say it's all normal.'

'But you're secretly thinking they're a bit odd?'

'Waking a sleeping baby? I have mothers tearing their hair out because the baby doesn't sleep, so, yes, it seems a bit odd to hear mothers worrying when the baby does sleep.'

'Once you have children you worry about everything, from sharp knives to global warming. And it doesn't stop.' Jenna shook her head, finding it a relief to talk to someone. He was a good listener. 'Will they fall off that bike they're riding? Will they remember to look both ways when they cross the road? You want them to be polite to people, and then you're worried they'll be too polite and might go off with some stranger because they don't want to give offence–'

'Jenna, relax! You're going to give yourself a nervous breakdown and you haven't even unpacked yet. You need to learn to chill.'

'Chill? What's that?' Jenna rolled her eyes in self-mockery. 'I don't know how to chill. But at work I'm sane, I promise. You must be wondering why on earth you gave me a lift. And a job.'

'Your job is safe. I can promise you that.'

'There's no such thing as safe.' She rubbed her finger over the table, following the grain of the wood. 'A year ago I had a husband, a home and a job. I lost all three.'

He was silent for a long moment. 'And now you have a home and a job again.'

There was something in his voice that made her look at him—made her wonder what personal trauma had driven him to this island.

'What I want is for Lexi to be happy.' Feeling calmer than she'd felt for ages, Jenna slipped off her shoes and curled her toes into the grass. 'I'm hoping that this will be a fresh start. I want it to feel like home.'

'If you need any help turning it into a home, give me a shout.' Ryan checked his watch and rose to his feet. 'I'm pretty good with a toolbox. Do you want any help unpacking? Is any of your furniture coming over?'

'No. No furniture.' Clive had claimed the furniture and all the belongings they'd collected over fifteen years of marriage. She hadn't had the strength to argue. She'd packed her clothes, a few books and not much else. 'I need to go shopping—oh, you said someone had stocked the place already?'

'When Evanna told the town meeting that you were coming, everyone from the village contributed.'

Jenna blinked. 'A group of people sat down and discussed my shopping list?'

'There's not a lot going on around here when the nightclubs are closed.'

'That's really kind.' Touched, Jenna made a mental note to thank everyone. 'Perhaps you could tell me the names. Then I can work out how much I owe everyone and pay them back.'

Ryan gave a faint smile, rolling up his shirtsleeves, revealing arms as strong as his shoulders. 'Oh, you'll pay. Don't worry about it. Everyone will claim a favour from you at some point. Usually at the most awkward, embarrassing moment, because that's how it works around here. One minute you're buying yourself a loaf of bread and the next you're giving an opinion on someone's rash.' He stood up. 'If we can do anything to help you settle in faster, let us know. The key to the back door is in the top drawer in the kitchen. It can be temperamental. If it jams, jiggle it slightly in the lock. And the shower turns cold if someone turns on a tap in the kitchen.'

'You know this house?'

'I stayed here for a few nights before I completed the sale on the lighthouse.'

'Oh.' Jenna had a disturbing image of him walking around the kitchen—showering in the bathroom. Naked.

Oh, God, she was losing it.

He raised an eyebrow. 'Are you all right?'

'Absolutely. How long should it take Lexi to get to the top and back? When do I start worrying?'

'You don't.' Ryan looked at the grassy ridge. 'She's on her way down now. I'll leave you to it. Surgery isn't until four. You can have a few hours to settle in. Spend some time together.'

'Yes.' Conscious that Lexi was approaching, Jenna lost her sense of calm. 'Thanks for the lift. And thanks for listening.'

He gave a brief nod and strolled out of her gate towards the sleek sports car that had transported her and her luggage from the surgery to the cottage. Without pausing in his stride, he exchanged a few words with Lexi as she sauntered past.

Watching anxiously from the garden, Jenna couldn't hear what he said, but whatever it was had Lexi smiling and that was an achievement in itself. Bracing herself for more complaints about her new home, she smiled at her daughter. 'Did you get a signal?'

'Yes, but everyone was out. Or maybe they're all still

asleep after a night clubbing. Lucky them.' Lexi glanced over her shoulder as the sports car growled its way up the road away from them. 'What was he doing here, Mum?'

'He gave us a lift, remember?'

'An hour and a half ago.'

An hour and a half? Was that how much time had passed? Startled, Jenna glanced at her watch. 'Well—we were talking.'

'About what?' Lexi stared at her suspiciously and Jenna felt herself blush.

'About work,' she said firmly. 'I'm new to this practice, remember?'

'Oh. Right. I thought for one awful minute you—' She broke off and Jenna stared at her, heart thumping.

'What?'

'Nothing.' The girl gave a careless shrug, but Jenna knew exactly what she'd been thinking— *That her mother had been showing interest in a man.*

Jenna walked back into the cottage, feeling the burden of responsibility settle on her like a heavy weight. Whatever happened, she mustn't do anything to make her daughter feel more insecure than she already did.

'Dr McKinley was telling me that he lives in a lighthouse.'

'Dr McKinley is really hot.'

'Lexi! You're fifteen years old.' Appalled, Jenna cast a look at her daughter, but Lexi had her head in the fridge.

'Nearly sixteen. Old enough to know when a man is hot. Don't worry—I don't expect you to understand. You wouldn't know a good-looking man if you fell over him.' She pulled some cheese out of the fridge and then noticed the empty mugs on the kitchen table. Suddenly the tension was back. 'You invited him in for coffee?'

No, he'd invited himself in for coffee. 'He was up all night with patients.' Jenna adopted a casual tone. 'He was tired. It was the least I could do after he'd helped us.'

'Oh, Mum—' Lexi rolled her eyes, visibly cringing. 'Poor guy, being trapped by someone desperate divorcee. I suppose he was too polite to refuse.'

Wondering if Ryan saw her as old and desperate, Jenna picked up the empty mugs and washed them by hand. 'Of course he was being polite.' She didn't need her daughter to tell her that. 'I'm going to spend a few hours unpacking before I do the clinic this afternoon. Come and see your bedroom.'

They wandered upstairs and Lexi stared into the pretty bedroom. It had been decorated in keeping with the beach setting, with white New England furniture. A rug with bold blue and white stripes sat in the centre of the white floorboards. 'This is mine?'

'Yes. We can put your duvet cover on the bed and—'

'Sorting out the bed isn't going to make this my home.'

'Home is where family is,' Jenna said softly, 'and I'm here with you.' She felt a pang as she saw the vulnerability in Lexi's eyes.

'Well, that doesn't mean anything does it?' Her tone was flippant. 'I mean—Dad just walked out. What's stopping you doing the same?'

'I'm not going to walk out, Lexi. Not ever.' Jenna sank onto the edge of the bed, wanting to reassure her daughter. 'I know how difficult this has been for you—'

'No, you don't! You haven't got a clue—you have no idea how embarrassing it is that my Dad is having sex with a girl not much older than me!' Her voice rose. 'It's gross!'

Jenna resisted the temptation to agree. 'I told you—adults have relationships, Lexi.'

'*You* were in a relationship,' Lexi hissed. 'With each other. Marriage is supposed to be for ever—isn't that what you taught me?'

Jenna bit her lip. 'Ideally, yes.'

'So why didn't you try and fix it with Dad?'

'He didn't want to fix it. And—' Jenna thought about everything that had happened. *The way he'd treated her*. 'Not everything can be fixed.'

'Well, don't tell me you know how I feel, because you have no idea.' Lexi flounced out of the room and locked herself in the bathroom.

Jenna flopped onto the bed, feeling wrung-out and exhausted.

It was will-power that drove her downstairs to fetch the suitcases. Will-power that made her unpack methodically, finding homes for her pathetically small number of belongings. Unfortunately her will-power wasn't strong enough to stop her from thinking about Ryan McKinley.

It was only when she was hanging her clothes in her wardrobe that she realised that they'd spent an hour and a half together and he'd told her nothing about himself.

Nothing at all.

CHAPTER FOUR

JENNA leant her bike against the wall near the quay, waving to Jim the ferryman.

'Morning, Nurse Jenna. Finished your morning clinic?' A grey haired lady with a stick ambled past her on the pavement and Jenna smiled.

'Yes, all done, Mrs Hampton. How's the hip?'

'It's a miracle. I've had my first good night's sleep for four years. I was dreading the operation, if I'm honest—probably wouldn't have gone ahead with it if Dr McKinley hadn't encouraged me.'

'Nurse Jenna?' Someone touched her arm. 'Sorry to bother you—'

The impromptu conversations continued, so that by the time she'd walked along South Quay and up to the row of terraced houses that overlooked the water she was ten minutes late.

Ryan was already there and glancing at his watch, a brooding frown on his handsome face.

Jenna quickened her pace and arrived breathless, although whether that was from rushing the last few metres or from the sight of him, she wasn't sure. After two weeks working alongside him she knew that her body did strange things when Ryan was near. It didn't matter that they kept every exchange strictly professional. That didn't alter the chemistry. She hadn't said anything, and neither had he, but they both knew it was there.

Funny, Jenna mused, that she could even recognise chemistry when she'd been with one man all her life. 'I'm so sorry I'm late—I was waylaid.'

'You did a clinic on the quay?'

'How did you guess?' Laughing, Jenna removed the clip from her hair. Smoothing her hands over her curls, she twisted it into a thick rope and secured it firmly. 'There was a strong wind on the coast road. I must look as though I've been dragged through a hedge backwards.'

His eyes moved from her face to her hair. 'That isn't how you look.'

Colour stung her cheeks and she felt a shaft of awareness pierce low in her pelvis. 'Did you know Abby Brown is pregnant? I saw her eating a double chocolate fudge sundae in Meg's Café to celebrate.'

Ryan gave a wry smile. 'Let's hope she doesn't keep that up throughout the pregnancy. Are you ready?' But before he could press the doorbell the door opened and a woman stood there, a baby in her arms and a harassed look on her face. 'Hello, Elaine.'

'Oh, Dr McKinley—come on in.' The woman stood to one side and almost tripped over the dog which was bouncing in the hallway. As his tail hit the umbrella stand flying, the woman winced. 'Whatever possessed me to say yes to a dog? Not only does he make Hope's asthma worse, he knocks everything over.'

'He's beautiful.' Jenna bent down and made a fuss of the

dog, and the animal leaped up and tried to lick her face, sensing an ally.

'Sorry—we've failed to teach him any manners.'

'I don't mind.' Giggling, Jenna pushed the dog down. 'What's his name?'

'We haven't decided—at the moment he's just called Black.'

Jenna tried to look stern. 'Sit!'

Black sat, and Ryan lifted an eyebrow. 'That's the first time I've seen that animal do as it's told.'

Elaine was astonished. 'You're so good with dogs! Do you have your own?'

'No.' Jenna stared at the black Labrador, who stared back, tongue lolling, tail wagging over the floor. It was a long time since anyone had looked at her with such adoration and un-questioning trust. 'I don't have a dog of my own.'

A family, she thought, didn't have to be a mother, a father and two children.

'You should think about getting one—you're obviously good with animals.' Elaine ushered them into the living room. 'Hope's on the sofa. She's had a much better night. We kept Black locked in the garden shed, and I vacuumed all the dog hairs this morning, but I haven't quite got my head round taking him back to the home.'

Jenna followed Ryan into the sitting room and noticed that the little girl's face brightened when she saw him.

'Dr Mac—I've been eating ice cream and jelly.'

'For breakfast?' Ryan pulled a face and sat down next to the child. He admired her doll, had a solemn conversation about which outfit she ought to wear for the day, and then pulled out his stethoscope. 'Can I listen to your chest?'

'It's all better.'

'So I hear. That's good. Can I listen?'

'OK.' With a wide smile, the little girl lay back on the sofa and waited.

His hands infinitely gentle, Ryan listened to her breathing, and watching him with the child made Jenna's breath catch. He focused entirely on the little girl, listening to every word she said as if she were the most important person in the room. 'I've been thinking about the attack she had, Elaine.' He folded the stethoscope and slid it back into his bag. 'You say she's using a normal inhaler, is that right?'

'Yes.'

'I think that might be the problem. I want to try her with a spacer—it's a device that relies less on technique, which is very useful for younger children. It makes sure they inhale the complete dose. To see you're taught to use it properly I've brought Nurse Jenna along with me.' Ryan gave a self-deprecating smile. 'I'm the first to admit that training children in inhaler technique probably isn't my forte, so I've called in the experts. Jenna used to do it all the time in her last job.'

Jenna removed the spacer from her bag and showed Hope's mother how it worked, explaining exactly what she had to do. 'It's really that simple.'

'She's due a dose now,' Elaine said. 'Could you check we do it right?'

Jenna watched, made a few suggestions, and explained to Hope exactly why it was important for her to take the drug.

'I breathe in that space thing every time?'

'Every time.'

'If I do that can I keep Black?'

Elaine sighed. 'No, sweetie. Black has to go.'

Hope's eyes filled with tears. 'But I love him. I can't send him back to that horrid place. I made him a promise. I promised him he had a home now.'

Feeling tears in her own eyes, Jenna blinked rapidly, feeling every bit of Elaine's anguish as a mother.

Elaine sank onto the sofa and shook her head. 'I have to take him back, Hope.' Her voice cracked. 'We can't keep him here. I can't risk going through what I went through the other night with you. I know it's hard, but we have no choice.'

'But I promised him he'd have a home and be loved.' Hope was sobbing now, great tearing sobs that shook her tiny body. 'I promised him, Mummy, and I can't break a promise. He'll be all on his own again. He'll think no one loves him.'

'I'll have him.' Jenna blurted the words past the lump in her throat and then stood in stunned silence, absorbing two things. Firstly, that she'd just got herself a dog, and secondly that making that decision had felt incredibly liberating.

For once she'd thought about herself. Not Clive. Not her mother. Herself.

Realising that everyone was looking at her, she shrugged. 'I'd like to have him. Really.' She looked at Hope. 'And I'll love him and give him a good home. So you won't have broken your promise…'

A tearful Elaine exchanged glances with Ryan. 'You want to take the dog?'

'I do.' Jenna spoke the words firmly, almost defiantly. Like a wedding ceremony, she thought with wry humour. *Do you take this dog…?* Only she knew without a flicker of doubt that the dog would never disappoint her. 'I really do. My daughter will be thrilled. And any time you want to come and see him, or meet up on the beach to throw a stick or two, you just bang on my front door…'

Ryan took a deep breath. 'Jenna, perhaps you should think about this—'

'I've thought about it for about thirty years. I've wanted a dog since I was a child.'

But her mother had said no. Then Clive had said no.

The advantage of being her own woman, in charge of her own life, was that there was no one to say no. And even if someone did say no, she wasn't sure she'd listen any more. She'd been weak, she realised. She'd allowed her own needs to come second. Her life had been about what Clive wanted. What Clive needed. And she'd been so busy keeping him happy, determined to keep her marriage alive and prove her mother wrong, that she'd stopped asking herself what she wanted.

Jenna straightened her shoulders and stood a little taller. 'If you wouldn't mind holding on to Black for one more day. I need to buy a book, check on the internet—make sure I know what I'm doing. A patient I saw last week breeds Labradors—I'd like to give her a ring and chat to her before I take Black.' Suddenly she felt strong, and the feeling was good—almost as if happiness was pouring through her veins.

Elaine gave a delighted laugh, relief lighting her face. 'If you're sure?'

'I'm completely sure.' And she had no need to ask Lexi what she thought. Lexi had wanted a dog all her life. 'I can take him with me on my visits—tie him to my bicycle while I go indoors. When I'm in clinic he can either play with Evanna's dog, or just stay in our garden. I'll find someone to build a fence.'

Elaine looked worried. 'Black rarely does what people want him to do.'

'That's fine by me.' Jenna stroked her hand over the dog's head, thinking of how often she'd disappointed her own mother. 'Maybe he and I have something in common. Welcome to rebellion.'

'That would be a good name,' Elaine laughed. 'Rebel. You should call him Rebel.'

'Just hope he doesn't live up to his name,' Ryan said dryly, closing his bag. 'There's a dog-training session every Thursday night in the church hall. You might want to book him in.'

'He ate your favourite shoes?' Laughing, Evanna leaned across the table and helped herself to more lasagne. 'You must have been mad.'

'With myself, for leaving them out.' Jenna was smiling too, and Ryan found it impossible not to watch her because the smile lit her face. He loved the dimple that appeared at the corner of her mouth, and the way her eyes shone when she was amused.

She was smiling regularly now, and the black circles had gone from under her eyes.

Extraordinary, he thought, how Glenmore could change people. 'What does Lexi think of him?'

'She adores him. She's the only teenager on Glenmore up at dawn during the summer holidays, and that's because she can't wait to walk him.'

Evanna cleared her plate and looked longingly at the food. 'Why am I so hungry? Do you think I could be pregnant again, Logan?'

It was only because he was looking at Jenna that Ryan saw her smile dim for a fraction of a second. Then she pulled herself together and joined in the conversation, her expression warm and excited.

'Do you think you could be? Charlie is two, isn't he? What a lovely age gap.'

Evanna agreed. 'I always wanted at least four kids.'

Ryan wondered if he was the only one who had noticed that Jenna had put her fork down quietly and was no longer eating.

Perhaps it was just that she found the whole happy family scene playing out in front of her emotionally painful. Or perhaps it was something else.

She'd been happy enough until Evanna had mentioned having more children.

Evanna lost the battle with her will-power and helped herself to more food. 'Weren't you tempted to have more children, Jenna?'

Sensing Jenna's tension, Ryan shifted the focus of the conversation away from her. 'If you're planning more children, you're going to have to build an extension on this house, Logan.'

'They can share a room,' Evanna said. 'If it's a girl, she can share with my Kirsty. If it's a boy, with Charlie.'

She and Logan spun plans while Jenna relocated her food from one side of her plate to the other.

It was the question about children that had chased away her appetite, Ryan thought grimly, reaching for his wine. And now he found himself wondering the same as Evanna. Why hadn't she had more children? She clearly loved being a mother.

Evanna heaped seconds onto everyone's plate except Jenna's. 'Aren't you enjoying it, Jenna?'

Jenna looked up and met Ryan's gaze.

They stared at each other for a moment, and then she gave a faltering smile and picked up her fork. 'It's delicious.' With a determined effort she ate, but Ryan knew she was doing it not because she was hungry, but because she didn't want to hurt Evanna's feelings. She was that sort of person, wasn't she? She thought about other people. Usually to the exclusion of her own needs.

He'd never actually met anyone as unselfish as her.

He felt something punch deep in his gut.

'Ryan—you have to fill those legs and wide shoulders with something.' Evanna pushed the dish towards Ryan but he held up a hand.

'Preferably not adipose tissue. I couldn't eat another thing, but it was delicious, thanks. I ought to be on my way.' Sitting here watching Jenna was doing nothing for his equilibrium.

Why had he accepted Evanna's invitation to dinner?

Over the past weeks he'd made sure he'd avoided being in a social situation with Jenna, and he had a feeling she'd been doing the same. And yet both of them had said yes to Evanna's impromptu invitation to join them for a casual supper.

'You can't go yet.' Evanna's eyes flickered to Jenna. 'Finish telling us about dog-training.'

It occurred to Ryan that the supper invitation probably hadn't been impromptu. Watching Evanna draw the two of them together, he had a sense that she'd planned the evening very carefully.

'The dog-training is a failure.' Jenna finished her wine. 'I really ought to go. Lexi was invited out to a friend's house, and she's taken Rebel, but she'll be back soon. I want to be there when they drop her home. I don't like her coming back to an empty house.'

Ryan poured himself a glass of water. 'I saw her eating fish and chips on the quay with the Harrington twins last week. She's obviously made friends.'

'Yes.' This time Jenna's smile wasn't forced. 'People have been very welcoming. There's hardly an evening when she's in.'

Which must mean that Jenna was often alone.

Ryan frowned, wondering how she spent her evenings. Was she lonely?

He realised suddenly just how hard this move must have been for Jenna. Her relationship with her mother was clearly strained and her husband had left her. She'd moved to an area of the country where she knew no one, taken a new job and started a new life. And her only support was a teenager who seemed to blame her for everything that had gone wrong. And yet she carried on with quiet dignity and determination.

Unsettled by just how much he admired her, he stood up. 'I need to get back. I have things to do.'

Like reminding himself that the worst thing you could do after a relationship went wrong was dive into another relationship. That was the last thing Jenna needed right now. As for him—he had no idea what he needed.

'You can't possibly leave now! I made dessert—' Evanna glanced between him and Jenna and then cast a frantic look at Logan, who appeared oblivious to his wife's efforts to keep the two of them at her table.

'If Ryan has things to do, he has things to do.'

'Well, obviously, but—I was hoping he'd give Jenna a lift.'

'I'll give Jenna a lift if she wants one,' Logan said, and Evanna glared at her husband.

'No! You can't do it, you have that—thing—you know…' she waved a hand vaguely '…to fix for me. It needs doing—urgently.'

'Thing?' Logan looked confused, and Ryan gave a half-smile and strolled to the door, scooping up his jacket on the way. If Evanna had hoped for help in her matchmaking attempts then she was going to be disappointed.

'I don't need a lift,' Jenna said quickly. 'I brought my bike. I'll cycle.'

She was keeping her distance, just as he was. Which suited him.

Unfortunately it didn't suit Evanna.

'You can't cycle! It's late. You could be mugged, or you might fall into a ditch.'

'It isn't that late, and if I don't cycle I won't be able to get to work tomorrow. My bike won't fit into Ryan's car.' Ever practical, Jenna stood up. 'I hadn't realised how late it was. Supper was delicious, Evanna. Are you sure I can't wash up?'

'No—the dishwasher does that bit…' Evanna looked crestfallen, but Jenna appeared not to notice as she dropped to her knees to hand a toy to Charlie, the couple's two-year-old son.

Catching the wistful look on her face, Ryan felt something tug inside him. He found her kindness as appealing as the length of her legs and the curve of her lips.

As she walked past him to the door he caught her eye and she blushed slightly, said another thank-you to Evanna and Logan and walked out of the house, leaving the scent of her hair trailing over his senses.

By the time Ryan had said his farewells and followed her out of the house Jenna was fiddling with her bike, head down. Something about the conversation had upset her, he knew that. He also knew that if he delved into the reason he'd probably upset her more. He strolled across to her, his feet crunching on the gravel. 'Are you sure you don't want a lift home?'

'Positive. I'll be fine, but thanks.' She hooked her bag over the handlebars and Ryan noticed that her movements were always graceful, fluid. Like a dancer.

'Mrs Parker was singing your praises this week.'

'That's good to hear.' Smiling, she pushed a cycle helmet onto her head and settled onto the bike. 'Under that fierce exterior she's a sweet lady. Interesting past. Did you know she drove an ambulance during the war?'

'No. Did she tell you that during one of your afternoon tea sessions?'

'She told you about that?' Jenna fastened the chin strap. 'I call in sometimes, on my way home. I pass her front door.'

And he had a feeling she would have called in even if it hadn't been on her way home. The fact that she had time for everyone hadn't gone unnoticed among the islanders. 'Her leg is looking better than it has for ages. I suspect it's because you're nagging her to wear her stockings.'

'It isn't easy when the weather is warm. She needs a little encouragement.'

'So you've been stopping by several times a week, encouraging her?'

'I like her.'

They were making conversation, but he knew she was as aware of him as he was of her.

Looking at her rose-pink mouth, he wondered if she'd had a relationship since her husband.

'Evanna upset you this evening.'

Her gaze flew to his. Guarded. 'Not at all. I was a little tired, that's all. Rebel sometimes wakes me up at night, walking round the kitchen. I'm a light sleeper.'

Ryan didn't push it. 'I walk on the beach most mornings. If you want help with the dog-training, you could join me.'

'I'll remember that. Thanks.' She dipped her head so that her face was in shadow, her expression unreadable. 'I'll see you tomorrow, Ryan.'

He was a breath away from stopping her. A heartbeat away

from doing something about the chemistry they were both so carefully ignoring.

What would she do if he knocked her off her bike and tumbled her into the heather that bordered Evanna's garden?

'Goodnight.' He spoke the word firmly and then watched as she cycled away, the bike wobbling slightly as she found her balance.

He was still watching as she vanished over the brow of the hill into the dusk.

CHAPTER FIVE

'Two salmon fillets, please.' Jenna stood in the fishmonger's, trying to remember a time when she'd bought food that wasn't shrink-wrapped and stamped with a date. And she'd never bought fish. Clive had hated fish.

Was that why she now ate fish three times a week?

Was she being contrary?

Eyeing the alternatives spread out in front of her, she gave a faint shrug. So what if she was? The advantage of being single was that you could live life the way you wanted to live it.

She had a dog and a garden, and now she was eating fish.

'Just you and the bairn eating tonight, then?' Hamish selected two plump fillets, wrapped the fish and dropped it into a bag.

'That's right.' How did anyone have a secret life on Glenmore? After only a month on the island, everyone knew who she was. And what she ate. And who she ate it with. Strangely enough, she didn't mind.

'How was your dinner with Dr McKinley?'

All right, maybe she minded.

Wondering if the entire island was involved in the match-making attempt, Jenna struggled for an answer. 'Dinner was

casual. With Evanna and Logan. Just supper—nothing personal.' She cringed, knowing she sounded as though she had
something to hide. 'How's Alice doing?' Changing the subject
quickly, she tried to look relaxed.

'Still rushing around. I say to her, "Rest, for goodness'
sake." But does she listen?' Hamish added a bunch of fresh
parsley to the bag. 'No, she doesn't. That's women for you.
Stubborn. Alice would die if it meant proving a point.'

'Well, I saw her in clinic yesterday and the wound was
healing nicely, so I'm sure she isn't going to die any time
soon.' Jenna dug her purse out of her bag. 'How much do I
owe you?'

'Nothing.' His weathered brow crinkled into a frown as he
handed over the bag. 'As if I'd take money after what you did
for my Alice. I said to her, "It's a good job you fell outside
Nurse Jenna's house, otherwise it would have been a different story." You sorted her out, fed her, had a lovely chat.' He
glanced up as the door opened behind her and a bell rang.
'Morning, Dr McKinley. Surf's up for you today. They had
the lifeboat out this morning—two kids in trouble on the
rocks round at the Devil's Jaws. Place is roped off, but they
climbed over.'

Jenna froze. He was behind her? She'd thought about him
all night—thought about the way he'd watched her across the
table. He'd made her so nervous she hadn't been able to eat.
And he'd noticed that she wasn't eating.

Adopting her most casual expression, she turned and looked.

He was standing in the doorway, a sleek black wetsuit
moulding itself to every muscular dip and curve of his powerful shoulders.

The bag of salmon slipped from her fingers and landed
with a plop on the tiled floor.

Hamish cleared his throat pointedly and Jenna stooped to retrieve her bag, her face as red as a bonfire. 'Good morning, Dr McKinley.' She turned back to the fish counter and developed a sudden interest in the dressed crab that Hamish had on display as she tried to compose herself. Over the past few weeks she'd had plenty of practice. In fact she was proud of how controlled she was around him.

They worked together every day, but so far she'd managed not to repeat any of the embarrassing sins she'd committed on her first day, like staring at his mouth. Even during dinner last night she'd managed to barely look at him.

And if she occasionally thought about how his hands had felt on her shoulders that day in her kitchen—well, that was her secret. A girl could dream, and she knew better than anyone that there was a world of difference between dreams and reality.

Jenna continued to stare at the crab. It was a shock to discover that, having thought she'd never trust a man again, she could actually find one attractive. But even if she could trust a man, the one thing she couldn't trust was her feelings. She knew she was hurt. She knew she was angry. And she knew that she was lonely for adult company.

This would be a bad, bad time to have a relationship even if one was on offer. Which it clearly wasn't—because, as Lexi was always telling her, she was past it. Why would Ryan want a relationship with someone like her?

'Thought I'd save you a journey and drop off that prescription.' Ryan handed it to Hamish. 'Did you know that crab personally, Jenna? You've been staring at him for the past five minutes.'

Jenna looked up, her inappropriate thoughts bringing the colour rushing to her cheeks. 'He has the same complexion as my first cousin.'

The corners of his mouth flickered. 'Yes? I can recommend a cream for that condition.'

She felt the breath catch in her throat because his smile was so sexy, and there was that unmistakable flash of chemistry that always occurred when they were together.

Imagining what it would be like to kiss a man like him, Jenna stared at him for a moment and then turned back to the crab, telling herself that even if things had been different she'd never have been sophisticated enough to hold a man like him. Ryan McKinley might be working on Glenmore, but she recognised a high-flier when she saw one. He was like one of those remote, intimidating consultants who strode the corridors of the hospital where she'd trained. Out of her league.

Hamish exchanged a look with Ryan and raised his eyebrows. 'You want to take a closer look at that crab?'

'No.' Flustered, Jenna pushed her hair out of her eyes. 'No, thanks— I— But it does look delicious.' Oh, for goodness' sake. What was the matter with her? Lexi was right—she was desperate. And she needed to leave this shop before she dropped her salmon a second time. Smiling at Hamish, she walked towards the door.

'Wait a minute, Nurse Jenna.' Hamish called after her. 'Has Dr McKinley asked you to the beach barbecue? Because if he hasn't, he's certainly been meaning to.'

Did everyone on Glenmore interfere with everyone else's lives?

Jenna looked at Ryan, who looked straight back at her, his expression unreadable.

Realising that Hamish had put them both in an impossible position, Jenna was about to formulate a response when Ryan straightened.

'It's on Saturday. In aid of the lifeboat. You should come.'

Knowing he'd only invited her because Hamish had pushed him, Jenna shook her head. 'I'm busy on Saturday.'

Hamish tutted. 'How can you be busy? Everything shuts early. Everyone on the island will be there. There's nothing else to do. Young thing like you needs a night out. You've done nothing but work since the day you stepped off that ferry.'

A night out?

When she finally felt ready for a night out it wouldn't be with a man like Ryan McKinley. When and if she did date a man again, she'd date someone safe and ordinary. Someone who didn't make her tongue knot and her insides turn to jelly. And preferably someone who didn't put her off her food.

He was watching her now, with that steady gaze that unsettled her so much. 'The islanders hold it every year, to raise funds for the lifeboat and the air ambulance. You're supposed to bring a dish that will feed four people. And wear a swimming costume.'

'Well, that's the end of that, then.' Somehow she kept it light. 'I can bring a dish to feed four people, but I don't own a swimming costume.'

'Swim naked,' Hamish said. 'Been done before.'

'And the culprits spent the night sobering up in one of Nick's four-star cells,' Ryan drawled, a sardonic gleam in his eyes. 'It's a family event. You can buy a costume from the Beach Hut, four doors down from here.'

Jenna had been into the Beach Hut twice, to buy clothes for Lexi. She hadn't bought anything for herself. 'Well—I'll think about it, thanks.'

Hamish scowled. 'You *have* to go. Isn't that right, Dr McKinley?'

Ryan was silent for a moment. 'I think Jenna will make her own decision about that.'

Jenna flushed. He wasn't going to coerce her. He wasn't going to tell her whether she should, or shouldn't go. He was leaving the choice up to her.

And that was what she did now, wasn't it? She made her own choices.

She decided whether she owned a dog and whether she was going to eat fish.

She shivered slightly, barely aware of the other customers who had entered the shop. She was only aware of Ryan, and the multitude of confusing feelings inside her. If she had to make a decision, what would it be?

She wanted to ask him whether he wanted her to go. She wanted to apologise for the fact that the islanders were match-making. She wanted him to know it had nothing to do with her.

Hideously embarrassed, she muttered that she'd think about it and walked out of the shop, her cheeks flushed.

It was crazy to feel this way about him, Jenna thought faintly. A man like him wasn't going to be interested in a divorced woman with a teenage daughter. And anyway, for all she knew he could be involved with someone. She couldn't imagine that a man like him could possibly be single.

Frustrated with herself, she hurried to her bike. She had to stop thinking about him. Even if he were interested in her, she wouldn't follow it through. For a start being with him would make her so nervous she wouldn't be able to eat a morsel, and to top it off Lexi was only just starting to settle into her new life. She could just imagine her daughter's reaction if her mother started seeing a man.

Thinking about Ryan occupied her mind for the cycle home, and she was still thinking about him as she propped her bike against the wall of the cottage and picked some flowers from the garden.

She walked into the kitchen to find Lexi sprawled on the kitchen floor, playing with Rebel.

Jenna put the flowers in a vase. 'How was the archaeology dig today?' Despite her complaints, it had taken Lexi only a matter of days to settle in and start enjoying herself. 'Did you have fun?'

'Yeah. Fraser found a piece of pot—everyone was really excited. I'm going to meet him for a walk on the beach later. I'll take Rebel. What time are we eating? I'm starving.'

Fraser? Lexi wanted to go for a walk on the beach with a boy?

'We're eating in about twenty minutes. So…' Retrieving the salmon fillets from her bag, Jenna tried to keep her voice casual. 'You haven't mentioned Fraser before. Is he nice?'

'He has a nose ring, five tattoos, long hair and swears all the time.' Lexi rubbed Rebel's glossy fur with her hands. 'You're going to love him—isn't she, Reb?'

With a wry smile, Jenna put the salmon under the grill. 'Lexi, you wait until you're a worried mother—'

'I'm not going to be like you. I'm going to trust my kids.'

Jenna sensed this was one of those moments when it was imperative to say the right thing. 'I trust you, Lexi,' she said quietly. 'You're a bright, caring, funny girl. But you're still a child—'

'I'm nearly sixteen—you're so over-protective.'

'I care about you. And you *are* still a child. Child going on woman, but still… I know all this has been hard on you. And being a teenager isn't easy.'

'What? You remember that far back?' But Lexi was smiling as she picked up Rebel's bowl. 'We're having fish again? I'm going to start swapping meals with the dog.'

'I thought you liked fish.'

'I do. But you never used to cook it in London. Now we have it almost every meal!'

'I didn't cook it in London because Dad hated it.' But Clive wasn't here now, and she was cooking what she wanted. And loving it, Jenna mused, mixing a teriyaki sauce to add to the salmon.

'Given that you're into all this healthy lifestyle stuff, I assume I *can* go for a walk on the beach with Fraser later?'

Jenna felt as though she was treading over broken glass. If she said no, she'd be accused of not trusting, and that could trigger a rebellious response. If she said yes, she'd worry all evening. 'Yes,' she croaked, washing a handful of tomatoes and adding them to the salad. 'All I ask is that you're home before dark.'

'Why? I can have sex in daylight just as easily as in the dark.'

Jenna closed her eyes. 'Lexi—'

'But I'm not going to. Credit me with some sense, Mum. You know I'm not going to do that. You've given me the sex, love, marriage talk often enough.'

'You've got it in the wrong order,' Jenna said weakly. 'And you've missed out contraception.' It was impossible not to be aware that Lexi was only a couple of years younger than she had been when she'd become pregnant.

Lexi rolled her eyes and then walked over and hugged her. 'Just chill, Mum.'

Astonished by the unexpected show of affection, Jenna felt a lump in her throat. 'That's nice. A hug.'

'Yeah—well, I'm sorry I was difficult about moving here. It's a pretty cool place. I didn't mean to be a nightmare.'

Jenna felt a rush of relief. 'You're not a nightmare, baby. I'm glad you're settling in.'

'It would be great if you could worry less.'

'It would be great if you could give me less to worry about.'

'OK. If I'm going to do something really bad, I'll warn you.'

'Lexi—about Fraser…'

'If you're going to talk to me about boys, Mum, don't waste your time. I probably know more than you anyway.'

Jenna blinked. That was probably true. She'd only ever had one boyfriend, and she'd married him at eighteen.

And he'd left her at thirty-two.

Lexi stole a tomato from the salad. 'We're just friends, OK? Mates. He's really easy to talk to. He really *gets* stuff. His dad—' She broke off and then shrugged. 'His dad walked out, too. When he was nine. That's why his mum came here.'

'Oh…'

What had happened to her had happened to millions of women around the world. She wasn't the only one in this situation. Lives shattered and were mended again, and she was mending, wasn't she? Slowly. She stared at the dog lying on her kitchen floor, and the bunch of flowers on her kitchen table. Life was different, but that didn't mean it wasn't good.

'You can go for a walk on the beach, Lexi.'

Lexi visibly relaxed. 'Thanks. We're just going to hang out, that's all. Fraser says there's really cool stuff on the beach once the tide goes out. He knows the names of everything. I feel like a real townie.'

'You'll have to teach me. Have they dug up anything else interesting at the castle yet?'

'Bits of stuff. They found these Viking combs—weird to think of Vikings combing their hair.'

'Perhaps their mothers nagged them,' Jenna said dryly, hugely relieved that Lexi appeared to be more like her old self. 'What's the castle like? I must go up there.'

'It's awesome. Fraser showed me this steep shaft into the

dungeons. He fell down it a few years ago and had to have his head stitched up.'

'It sounds dangerous.'

'Only to you. You see danger everywhere.'

'I'm a mother. Worrying goes with the territory.'

'Fraser's mother doesn't fuss over him all the time. She just lets him live his life.'

Jenna bit her lip, trying not to be hurt, well used to being told what other mothers did. 'I'm letting you live your life. I'd just rather you didn't do it in a hospital or an antenatal clinic. Wash your hands, Lex—dinner is nearly ready.'

'Do you want me to lay the table or do drinks or something?'

Hiding her surprise, Jenna smiled at her. 'That would be a great help. There's lemonade in the fridge—Evanna gave it to us as a gift.'

'It's delicious. I had some at her house.' Lexi opened the fridge door again and pulled out the bottle. 'She makes it by the bucketload, all fresh lemons and stuff. She's a good cook. I told her you were, too. Are we going to the barbecue on Saturday, Mum?'

Still reeling from the compliment, Jenna turned the salmon. 'How do you know about the barbecue?'

'Fraser mentioned it.'

Fraser, Fraser, Fraser—

Still, at least Lexi seemed happy. Relieved, Jenna put the salmon on the plates. 'Do you want to go?'

'Why not? Might be a laugh.' Her eyes narrowed. 'How did *you* hear about the barbecue?'

'In the fishmonger's.' Jenna omitted to say who she'd bumped into there. 'It's amazing to be able to buy such fresh fish.'

'It's amazing what old people find exciting.' Lexi suppressed a yawn as she picked up her plate. 'Let's eat in the garden. So how many lives did you save today? Did you see Dr Hot?'

'Dr who?'

'Dr Hot. Ryan McKinley. I bet women who are perfectly well make appointments just to spend five minutes with him. Fraser says he's brilliant.'

Even at home there was no escape, Jenna thought weakly, taking her plate and following her daughter out into the sunshine.

She wasn't going to think of him as Dr Hot.

She really wasn't.

'She was playing on the deck with a water pistol and she slipped and crashed into the fence—the bruise is horrendous. I'm worried she's fractured her eye socket or something.' The woman's face was white. 'I tried to get an appointment with one of the doctors, but Dr McNeil is out on a call and Dr McKinley has a full list.'

Jenna gave her shoulder a squeeze. 'Let me take a look at it. If I think she needs to be seen by one of the doctors, then I'll arrange it. Hello, Lily.' She crouched down so that she was at the same level as the child. 'What have you been doing to yourself?'

She studied the livid bruise across the child's cheekbone and the swelling distorting the face. 'Was she knocked out?'

'No.' The woman hovered. 'I put an ice pack on it straight away, but it doesn't seem to have made a difference.'

'I'm sure it helped.' Jenna examined the child's cheek, tested her vision and felt the orbit. 'Can you open your mouth for me, Lily? Good girl—now, close—brilliant. Does that hurt?' Confident that there was no fracture, she turned to Lily's mother. 'I think it's just badly bruised, Mrs Parsons.'

'But she could have fractured it. Sorry—it isn't that I don't trust you.' The woman closed her eyes briefly. 'And I know I'm being anxious, but—'

'I know all about anxious. You don't have to apologise.' Seeing how distressed the mother was, and sympathising, Jenna made a decision. 'I'll ask Dr McKinley to check her for you. Then you won't be going home, worrying.'

'Would you?'

'I'll go and see if he's free—just wait one moment.' Giving Lily a toy to play with, Jenna left her room and walked across to Ryan just as the door to his consulting room opened and a patient walked out.

She paused for a moment, conscious that she hadn't seen him since Hamish had embarrassed them both the day before.

'Ryan?' Putting that out of her mind, Jenna put her head round the door. 'I'm sorry, I know you're busy…' And tired, she thought, looking at the shadows under his eyes. He worked harder than any doctor she'd ever met.

Or were the shadows caused by something else?

'I'm not busy—what can I do for you?' The moment he looked at her, Jenna felt her insides flip over.

'I have a patient in my room—I wondered if you could give me your opinion. The little girl is six—she's slipped and banged her face. The bruising is bad, but I don't think there's a fracture—there's no flattening of the cheek.'

Work always helped, she thought. After Clive had left, work had been her healing potion. It had stopped her thinking, analysing, asking 'what if?' And she'd discovered that if you worked hard enough, you fell into bed dog-tired and slept, instead of lying awake, thinking all the same things you'd been thinking during the day.

'Flattening of the cheek can be obscured by swelling—'

'It isn't that swollen yet. It only happened half an hour ago, and her mum put an ice pack on it immediately. I can't feel any defect to the orbit, and she can open and close her mouth without difficulty.'

'It sounds as though you're confident with your assessment.' His long fingers toyed with the pen on his desk. 'Why do you need me?'

'Because the mother is so, so worried. I thought some reassurance from you might help. I know what it's like to be a panicking mother.'

'Who is the patient?'

'Parsons?'

Ryan stood up. 'Lily Parsons? That explains why you have a worried mother in your room. Little Lily had a nasty accident a couple of years ago—almost died. She fell in deep water in the quay and a boat propeller caught her artery.'

'Oh, no—' Jenna lifted her hand to her throat, horrified by the image his words created. 'How did she survive that?'

'My predecessor, Connor McNeil—Logan's cousin—was ex-army. Trauma was his speciality, otherwise I doubt Lily would be with us today. She went into respiratory arrest, lost so much blood—'

'Were you here?'

'No. It was just before I arrived, but Connor's rescue has gone down in island folklore. Apparently Jayne totally flipped. She witnessed the whole thing—blamed herself for the fact that Lily had fallen in. The child was watching the fish, and a crowd of tourists queuing for the ferry bumped into her and she lost her balance.'

'Poor Jayne!' To stop herself looking at his mouth, Jenna walked back towards the door. 'All the more reason why you should reassure her.'

Without arguing, Ryan followed her into the room, charmed Jayne, made Lily laugh, and then checked the child's eye with a thoroughness that would have satisfied the most hyper-anxious mother.

Jenna watched, wondering why someone with his own trauma skills would give up a glittering career to bury himself on Glenmore.

Something must have happened.

Life, she thought, had a way of doling out grim surprises.

'You're right that there is no flattening of the cheek.' He addressed the remark to Jenna, gave the little girl a wink and strolled across the room to wash his hands. 'Jayne, I'm happy with her, but that bruising is going to get worse before it gets better, and so is the swelling. I'm guessing your worrying is going to get worse before it gets better, too. I'll have a word with Janet on Reception so that she knows to slot you in if you feel worried and want me to take another look.'

'You don't want to X-ray her?'

'No. I don't think it's necessary.' Ryan dried his hands and dropped the paper towel in the bin. 'Look, why don't you bring her back to my surgery tomorrow morning anyway? That will stop you having to look at her every five minutes and decide whether you need to bring her back.'

Jayne Parsons gave a weak smile. 'You must think I'm a total idiot.'

'On the contrary, I think you're a worried mum and that's understandable.' Ryan scribbled a number on a scrap of paper. 'This is my mobile number. I drive past your house on the way to and from the surgery—just give me a call if you're worried and I can drop in. Take care, Lily.'

Mother and child left the room, more relaxed, and Jenna

stared at the door. 'Do you give your mobile number to every anxious patient?'

'If I think they need the reassurance, yes. Glenmore is an isolated island. It makes people more reliant on each other. They're in and out of each other's lives.' He gave a faint smile. 'As I'm sure you've noticed.'

She swallowed. 'I'm sorry about Evanna and Hamish—'

'Why are you sorry? None of it is your fault.' Ryan sat down at her desk and brought Lily's notes up on the computer screen. 'They just can't help themselves. Matchmaking is like eating and breathing to the people of Glenmore.'

'It happens a lot?'

'All the time—although I've pretty much escaped it up until now. That's one of the advantages of being a doctor. There are a limited number of people on this island who technically aren't my patients.'

'I expect they'll back off soon.'

'I wouldn't count on it.' Ryan typed the notes with one finger. 'Do you want a lift to the beach barbecue? I could pick you up on my way past.'

'I haven't even decided if we're going.'

'If you don't go, they'll come and get you. Come. Lexi would enjoy it. All the teenagers go. She seems to have made friends. Whenever I see her, she's smiling.'

'Yes.' Jenna was starting to wonder whether there was something more to her daughter's sudden change of attitude. 'What do you know about a boy called Fraser?'

'Fraser Price?' Ryan stood up. 'He lives near you. Just along the beach. His mum is called Ailsa—she's a single parent. Diabetic. Why are you asking?'

Jenna chewed her lip. 'Lexi seems to like him—'

'And you're worrying that he has unsavoury habits?'

'I'm just worrying generally. In London, Lexi started mixing with the wrong crowd. She made a point of doing all the things she thought would upset me…'

'Why would she want to upset you?'

Jenna hesitated. 'She blames me for not trying to fix my marriage.'

'Did you want to fix it?'

Jenna thought about Clive and the scene in his office that day. *Thought about what she'd learned about her marriage.* 'No. Some things can't be fixed.' She had an urge to qualify that with an explanation, but realised that there was no way she could elaborate without revealing that her husband hadn't found her sexy. Somehow that was too humiliating. She turned away and put a box of dressings back into the cupboard. 'There's nothing to talk about. My marriage ended. It happens to thousands of people every day.'

And thousands of people got on with their lives, as she had done. Picking up the pieces, patching them together again into something different.

'Did you think about buying him out so that you could stay in the house?'

It was a practical question, typically male. 'I'm a nurse, Ryan, not a millionaire. London is expensive. And anyway, I didn't want to stay in that house. It was full of memories I didn't want. I knew if I'd stayed there I'd always be looking back. I wanted to move forward. He offered me a sum of money and I took it.'

'I'm guessing it wasn't a generous sum.' His eyes darkened, and she wondered why he'd be angry about something that wasn't his problem.

'He completely ripped me off.' Only now, after almost a year, could she say it without starting to shake with emotion.

'I was really stupid and naïve, but in my own defence I was in a bit of a state at the time. I was more wrapped up in the emotional than the practical. I shouldn't really have been negotiating a divorce settlement so soon after he'd walked out. There were some mornings when I couldn't bear to drag myself from under the duvet. If it hadn't been for Lexi I wouldn't have bothered. I left it to him to get the valuations. And he took advantage.' She lifted her chin. 'He used his friends—fiddled with the numbers and offered me a sum that was just about plausible. And I took it. So I'm to blame for being a push-over.'

'You weren't a push-over. You were in shock, and I'm guessing you just wanted it to end.'

'I didn't want it dragging on and hurting Lexi. The whole thing was very hard on her.' Jenna rubbed her hands up and down her arms. 'And she was so angry with me.'

He took a slow breath. 'You did a brave thing, coming here. Was it the right thing to do?'

She considered the question. 'Yes. Yes, it was. We're healing.' The discovery warmed her. 'The best thing I did was to get Rebel. Lexi adores him. So do I. And we love living in the cottage. Having the beach on our doorstep is like heaven. And I'm relieved Lexi is happy, although I'm worrying that has something to do with her new friend.'

'I don't think you have to worry about Fraser. He's pretty responsible.'

'Well, if he's the reason Lexi is happy, then I suppose he has my approval.'

Ryan strolled towards the door. His arm brushed against hers and Jenna felt the response shoot right through her body. Seeing the frown touch his forehead, she wondered if he did, too.

'Our receptionist Janet was saying how smoothly every-thing is running since you arrived. The islanders love you.'

'Everyone has been very kind.' She wondered why she felt compelled to look at him all the time. If he was in the room, she wanted to stare. Every bit of him fascinated her, from his darkened jaw to his thick, lustrous hair. But what really inter-ested her was him. The man.

She wanted to ask why he'd chosen to come to Glenmore, but there was something about him that didn't invite personal questions.

Respecting his privacy, she smiled. 'We'll see you at the barbecue on Saturday.'

'Good.' He watched her for a long moment and she felt that look all the way down to her bones.

'Thanks for seeing Lily.'

He stirred. 'You're welcome.'

The sun was just breaking through the early-morning mist when she walked Rebel early the following day. The garden gate no longer creaked, thanks to a regular dose of oil, and Jenna paused for a moment to admire the pinks and purples in her garden before walking along the sandy path that led through the dunes to the beach. The stretch of sand was deserted and she slipped off her shoes and walked barefoot, loving the feel of the sand between her toes. Rebel bounded ahead, investigating pieces of seaweed and driftwood, tail wagging. Every now and then he raced back to her, sending water and sand flying.

Huge foaming breakers rolled in from the Atlantic, rising high and then exploding onto the beach with a crash and a hiss. Jenna watched as a lone surfer achieved apparently im-possible feats in the deadly waves. Admiring his strength and the fluidity of his body, she gave herself a little shake and turned her attention to the beach. After twenty years of not noticing men, suddenly she seemed to do nothing else.

Seeing a pretty shell poking out of the sand, she stooped to pick it up. The pearly white surface peeped from beneath a layer of sand and she carefully brushed it and slipped it into her pocket, thinking of the chunky glass vase in her little bathroom, which was already almost full of her growing collection of shells.

She was pocketing her second shell when Rebel started to bark furiously. He sped across the sand towards the water just as the surfer emerged from the waves, his board under his arm.

Recognising Ryan, Jenna felt her heart bump hard against her chest and she forgot about shells. She should have known it was him from the visceral reaction deep in her stomach. It wasn't men in general she was noticing. It was just one man.

Without thinking, she dragged her fingers through her curls and then recognised the futility of the gesture. She was wearing an old pair of shorts and a cotton tee shirt. Running her fingers through her hair wasn't going to make her presentable. For a moment she regretted not spending a few moments in front of the mirror before leaving her cottage. Thinking of herself doing her morning walk in lipgloss and a pretty top made her smile, and she was still smiling when he ran up to her.

'What's funny?'

'Meeting someone else at this time of the morning.'

He put his surfboard down on the sand. 'It's the best time. I surf most mornings, but I've never seen you out before.' The wetsuit emphasised the width and power of his shoulders and she looked towards the waves, trying to centre herself.

'Normally I'm a little later than this but I couldn't sleep.'

Because she'd been thinking about him. And then pushing away those thoughts with rational argument. But now those thoughts were back, swirling round her head, confusing her.

'You couldn't sleep?' His tone was amused. 'Maybe you were excited about the barbecue tomorrow.'

'That must have been it.' As Rebel bounded up to her, she sidestepped, dodging the soaking wet tail-wagging animal. 'Sit. *Sit!*' Ignoring her, Rebel shook himself hard and sprayed them both. 'Oh, you—! Rebel! I'm so sorry.'

'More of a problem for you than me. I'm wearing a wet-suit.' His eyes drifted to her damp tee shirt and lingered. 'Obviously the dog-training is progressing successfully.'

'It's a disaster. He obeyed me that day at Elaine's just to charm me into giving him a home. Since then he's been a nightmare.' Giggling and embarrassed, Jenna grabbed Rebel's collar and glared at him severely. 'Sit! Sit, Rebel. I said sit!'

The dog whimpered, his entire body wagging, and Ryan sighed.

'Sit!'

Rebel sat.

'OK—that's annoying.' Jenna put her hands on her hips. 'I've been working non-stop with him and you just say it once. What do you have that I don't?'

'An air of menace. You're kind and gentle. A dog can sense you're soft-hearted. Especially a dog like Rebel, who has had his own way for far too long.'

'You think I'm a push-over?'

'I don't see you as tough and ruthless, that's true.'

Her heart was pounding as if she'd run the length of the beach. 'I'll have you know I'm stronger than I look!'

'I didn't say you weren't strong.' The pitch of his voice had changed. 'I know you're strong, Jenna. You've proved your strength over and over again in the last month. You've dragged up your roots and put them down somewhere new. That's never easy.'

His eyes were oceans of blue, waiting to draw her in and drown her.

The want inside her became a desperate craving, and when his arm curled around her waist and he drew her towards him she didn't resist. Her thinking went from clear to clouded, and she waited, deliciously trapped by the inevitability of what was to come. She watched, hypnotised, as he lowered his head to hers. His mouth was warm and skilled, his kiss sending an explosion of light through her brain and fire through her belly.

It should have felt wrong, kissing a man. But it felt right—standing here with his lips against hers and nothing around them but the sound and smell of the sea.

Jenna dug her fingers into the front of his wetsuit, felt the hardness of his body brush against her knuckles. The fire spread, licking its way through her limbs until she was unsteady on her feet, and his grip on her tightened, his mouth more demanding as they kissed hungrily, feasting, exploring, discovering.

Rebel barked.

Ryan lifted his mouth from hers, his reluctance evident in the time he took. Dazed and disorientated, Jenna stared up at him for a moment and then at his mouth.

Now she knew how it felt…

Rebel barked again and she turned her head, trying to focus on the dog.

'What's the matter with you?' Her voice was croaky and Ryan released her.

'People on the beach.' His voice was calm and steady. 'Clearly we're not the only early risers.'

'Obviously not.' She knew she sounded stilted but she had no idea what to say. Were they supposed to talk about it? Or pretend it had never happened? 'I should be getting home. Lexi will be waking up…' Feeling really strange, she lifted a shaking hand to her forehead. The kiss had changed everything. Her world had tilted.

'Jenna—'

'I'll see you tomorrow.'

His gaze was disturbingly acute. 'You'll see me at the surgery today.'

'Yes—yes, of course I will. That's what I meant.' Flustered, she called to Rebel, who was nosing something on the sand, apparently oblivious to the fact that his owner's life had just changed.

Ryan seemed about to say something, but the people on the beach were moving closer and he shook his head in exasperation. 'I've never seen anyone else on this beach at this hour.'

'It's a very pretty place.' Babbling, Jenna backed away. 'You'd better go and have a shower—warm up—you can't do a surgery in your wetsuit—I really ought to be going—' She would have tripped over Rebel if Ryan hadn't shot out a hand and steadied her. 'Thanks. I'll see you later.' Without looking at him, she turned and almost flew over the sand after Rebel, not pausing until she was inside the cottage with the door shut firmly behind her.

'Mum? What's the matter with you?' Yawning, Lexi stood there in tee shirt and knickers.

'I've been—' Kissed, Jenna thought hysterically. Thoroughly, properly, deliciously kissed. '—for a walk. On the beach. With Rebel.'

Lexi threw her an odd look. 'Well, of course with Rebel—who else?'

'No one else. Absolutely no one else.' She needed to shut up before she said something she regretted. 'You're up early.'

'I'm going over to Evanna's to give the children breakfast before I go to the dig. She has that appointment thing today on the mainland so she took the first ferry.'

'Yes, of course. I know. I remember.' Her lips felt warm and tingly, and if she really concentrated she could still conjure up the feel of his mouth against hers. 'I have to take a shower and get ready for work.'

'Are you all right? You look—different.'

She felt different.

Up until today she'd felt as though she was surviving. Now she felt as though she was living.

Everything was different.

CHAPTER SIX

Too dressy.

Too casual.

Too cold—

Jenna threw the contents of her wardrobe onto her bed and stared at it in despair. Was it really that hard to decide what to wear to a beach barbecue? It was so long since she'd been out socially she'd lost her confidence. But she knew that the real reason she couldn't decide what to wear was because Ryan would be there and she wanted to look her best. Without looking as though she'd tried too hard.

Infuriated with herself, she reached for the first skirt she'd tried on, slipped it over her head and picked a simple tee shirt to go with it. The skirt was pretty, but the tee shirt was plain— which meant that the top half of her was underdressed and the bottom half was overdressed.

Looking in the mirror, Jenna scooped up her hair and piled it on top of her head. Then she pulled a face and let it fall loose around her shoulders. She gave a hysterical giggle. Maybe she should wear half of it up and half of it down.

'Mum?'

Hearing Lexi's voice, Jenna jumped guiltily and scooped the discarded clothes from the bed. She was just closing the wardrobe door on the evidence of her indecision when Lexi sauntered into the room.

'Are you ready?'

'Nearly.' Jenna eyed the lipgloss that she'd bought. It was still in its packaging because she hadn't decided whether or not to wear it. 'I just need to do my hair.' Up or down?

'Can I go ahead? I'm meeting Fraser.'

'We'll go together,' Jenna said firmly. With no choice but to leave her hair down, she grabbed a cardigan and made for the stairs. 'I'd like to meet him.'

'We're just mates,' Lexi muttered, sliding her feet into a pair of pretty flip-flops. 'We're not quite at the "meet the parents" stage.'

Jenna picked up her keys and the bowl containing the strawberries. 'This is Glenmore. On an island this size you have no option but to meet the parents. Everyone meets everyone about five times a day.' She wished she hadn't left her hair down. It made her feel wild and unrestrained, and she wanted to feel restrained and together.

'Are you all right, Mum?'

'I'm fine. Why wouldn't I be?'

'I don't know…' Her phone in her hand, Lexi frowned. 'You just seem jumpy. Nervous. You've been acting really weird since yesterday.'

'Nervous? I have no reason to be nervous!'

'All right, calm down. I realise it's a big excitement for you, getting out for an evening. Don't be too embarrassing, will you?'

Jenna locked the door because she hadn't got out of the London habit. 'I'm meant to be the one saying that to you.'

'Going out with your mother would never happen in London. Just promise me that whatever happens you won't dance.'

* * *

Ryan watched her walk across the sand towards him.

She'd left her hair loose, the way she'd worn it on the day she'd arrived on the island.

Feeling the tension spread across his shoulders, he lifted the bottle of beer to his lips, thinking about the kiss. He hadn't intended to kiss her but the temptation had been too great, and now he couldn't get it out of his mind.

He wondered why this woman in particular should have such a powerful effect on him. Not for one moment did he think it was anything to do with her gorgeous curves—he'd met plenty of women with good bodies and none of them had tempted him past the superficial. But Jenna…

Maybe it was her generous smile. Or her air of vulnerability—the way she was so painfully honest about the things that had gone wrong in her life when most people just put up a front. Or the way she put herself last. Either way, she was sneaking under his skin in a way that should have set off warning bells.

If his aim was to protect himself, then lusting after a recently divorced single mother with a teenage daughter was probably the stupidest thing he'd ever done.

She was clearly desperately hurt after her divorce, and any relationship she entered into now would be on the rebound.

But his body wasn't listening to reason and he felt himself harden as he watched her approach. She'd dressed modestly, her summery skirt falling to her ankles, her tee shirt high at the neck. But the Glenmore breeze was designed to mock modesty and it flattened the skirt to her legs, found the slit and blew it gaily until the soft fabric flew into the air, revealing long slim legs and a hint of turquoise that looked like a swimming costume.

Ryan saw her clutch at the skirt and drag it back into

position, her face pink as she pinned it down with her hand, defying the wind.

For a girl who was fresh out of the city, there was nothing city-slick about her. She was carrying a large flowery bag over one shoulder and she looked slightly uncertain—as if she wasn't used to large gatherings.

He was fully aware that she'd avoided him the day before at the surgery, going to great lengths to make sure they didn't bump into one another. Seeing her now, the emotion he felt was like a punch in the gut. He was attracted to her in a way he hadn't been attracted to a woman in years.

'She'd be perfect for you.' Evanna's voice came from behind him and he turned, keeping his expression neutral.

'You never give up, do you?'

'Not when I think something is worth the effort.' Evanna replied. 'Don't be angry with me.'

'Then don't interfere.'

'I'm helping.'

'Do you think I need help?'

'When you first came here, yes. You were so angry,' she said softly. 'I used to hear you sawing wood and banging nails. You swung that hammer as if you hoped someone's head was underneath it.'

Ryan breathed out slowly. 'I hadn't realised anyone witnessed that—'

'I came down to the lighthouse from time to time, trying to pluck up courage to ask you to join us for supper, but whenever I saw you your expression was so black and you were so dark and scary I lost my nerve.'

'I didn't know.' He'd been aware of nothing, he realised, but his own pain. 'So, have you become braver or am I less scary?'

Her smile was wise and gentle. 'You banged in a lot of nails.'

'I guess I did.' He respected the fact that she hadn't pushed him for the reason. She'd never pushed him. Just offered unconditional friendship. Humbled once again by the generosity of the islanders, he frowned. 'Evanna—'

'Just promise me that if I back off you won't let her slip through your fingers.'

'Life doesn't always come as neatly wrapped as you seem to think.'

'It takes work to wrap something neatly.' She stood on tiptoe and kissed his cheek. 'You've been here for two years. It's enough. Don't let the past mess up the future, Ryan.'

'Is that what I'm doing?'

'I don't know. Are you?'

Ryan thought about the kiss on the beach and the way he felt about Jenna. 'No,' he said. 'I'm not.'

He knew Jenna was nothing like Connie. And maybe that was one of the reasons he was so attracted to her.

'Is my wife sorting out your love-life?' Logan strolled over to them, Charlie on his shoulders.

'Who? Me?' Her expression innocent, Evanna picked up a bowl of green salad. 'Can you put this on the table, please? Next to the tomato salsa. I'm going to meet Jenna and make her feel welcome. She looks nervous. I'm sure she feels a bit daunted by the crowd.'

Ryan was willing to bet that her nerves had nothing to do with the crowd and everything to do with the kiss they'd shared. He'd flustered her.

He gave a faint smile. And he was looking forward to flustering her again.

'What does tomato salsa look like?' Logan's expression was comical as he steadied Charlie with one hand and took the salad from Evanna with the other. 'Is that the mushy red stuff?' Leaning forward, he kissed her swiftly on the mouth and Evanna sighed and kissed him back.

Watching them together, seeing the soft looks and the way they touched, Ryan felt a stab of something sharp stab his gut and recognised it as envy.

Even in the early days, his relationship with Connie had never been like that. They'd never achieved that level of closeness. They'd been a disaster waiting to happen. If he hadn't been so absorbed by his career maybe he would have picked up on the signs. Or maybe not. Connie had played her part well.

Lifting the bottle to his lips again, he watched as Evanna sprinted across the sand to meet Jenna—watched as she gave her a spontaneous hug and gestured with her hands, clearly telling her some anecdote. He had no idea what she was saying, but it had Jenna laughing, and her laugh was so honest and genuine that Ryan felt every muscle in his body tighten. He doubted Jenna had ever manipulated a man in her life. She wouldn't know how—and anyway, such behaviour would go against her moral code.

As they approached he could hear Evanna admiring Jenna's skirt, the conversation light and distinctly female in tone and content. Jenna responded in kind, handing over a bowl of rosy-red strawberries and chatting with the group gathered around the food table as if she'd been born and raised on the island.

It took less than a few seconds for him to realise that she was looking at everyone but him. Talking to everyone but him.

Aware of Evanna's puzzled expression, Ryan sighed. If he didn't do something, the situation would be taken out of his hands.

He strolled over to Jenna, who was busily sorting food on the long trestle table, carefully ignoring him.

'Where's Rebel?' Ryan felt the ripple of tension pass through her body and she carefully put down the bowl she was holding.

'Lexi has him on a lead. I thought all those sausages and steaks on the barbecue might prove too much of a temptation for a dog with a behavioural problem.'

'You could be right.' He noticed that her cheeks had turned a soft shade of pink and that she was making a point of not looking at his mouth.

No, he thought to himself. Jenna would never play games or manipulate. She was honest and genuine—surprisingly unsophisticated for a woman in her thirties.

Lexi strolled up to the table, earphones hanging from her ears, her iPod tucked into the back pocket of her jeans, her head bobbing to the rhythm. She was hanging on to Rebel, who was straining to run in the opposite direction. 'Hi, Ryan.'

Jenna looked embarrassed. 'Dr McKinley—'

'Ryan is fine.' He bent down to make a fuss of Rebel, who looked him in the eye and immediately sat.

'Mum, did you see that? He sat without even being told!' Lexi gaped at the dog. 'Given that he's behaving, you can hold him. I'm going to see my friends.' Without waiting for a reply, she pushed the lead into her mother's hand, took the cola Evanna was offering her with a smile of thanks and strolled across the sand to join a group of teenagers who were chatting together.

'I have a feeling it was a mistake to bring a dog—this particular dog, anyway—to a barbecue.' Gripping the lead until her knuckles were white, Jenna was still concentrating on Rebel. 'Hopefully your influence will prevail and he'll behave.'

'I think you may have an exaggerated idea of my power.'

'I hope not or I'm about to be seriously embarrassed.'

'I think you're already embarrassed.' Ryan spoke quietly,

so that he couldn't be overheard by the people milling close to them. Keeping his eyes on her face, he watched her reaction. 'And there's no need to be. Just as there was no need to run off yesterday morning and avoid me all day in surgery.'

She took a deep breath, her gaze fixed on Rebel. Then she glanced sideways and checked no one was listening. Finally, she looked at him. 'I haven't kissed, or been kissed, for a long time.'

'I know.' He watched as the tension rippled down her spine.

'I wasn't sure how I felt about it— I mean—' Her colour deepened. 'Obviously I know how I felt, but I wasn't sure what it all meant. I hadn't expected—'

'Neither had I.' Suddenly he regretted starting this conversation in such a public place. He should have dragged her somewhere private where he could have matched actions with words.

'Everyone is trying to pair us up.'

'I know that, too.'

'Doesn't that put you off?'

'I didn't kiss you because it was what other people wanted, Jenna. I kissed you because it was what I wanted.' And he still wanted it, he realised. Badly. Maybe two years of self-imposed isolation had intensified his feelings, but he had a feeling that it was something more than that.

'Is everyone watching us now?'

'Ignore them. What can I get you to drink?'

'What are you drinking?'

'Ginger beer,' he said dryly, 'but I'm on call. How about a glass of wine?'

She hesitated for a moment, and then something sparked in her eyes. 'Actually, I'd like a beer,' she said firmly. 'From the bottle. Don't bother with a glass.'

Hiding his surprise, Ryan took a bottle of ice-cold beer from the cooler and handed it to her. Maybe he didn't know her as well as he thought. She certainly didn't strike him as a woman who drank beer from a bottle.

'Thanks. Cheers.' Her grin was that of a defiant child, and she took a large mouthful and proceeded to spill half of it down her front. 'Oh, for goodness' sake!'

Struggling to keep a straight face, Ryan rescued her beer before she spilt the rest of it. 'You haven't done that before, have you?'

Pulling a face, she tugged her wet tee shirt away from her chest. 'What a mess! Everyone is going to think I'm an alcoholic.'

'Alcoholics generally manage to get the alcohol into their mouths, Jenna. I gather your husband was more of a wine in a glass sort of guy?' Ryan put their drinks down on the table and grabbed a handful of paper napkins.

'How do you know what my husband drank?'

'It's a wild guess, based on the fact you seem to be doing the opposite of everything you ever did with him.' He pressed the napkins against the damp patch, feeling the swell of her breasts under his fingers.

'Am I?'

'You got yourself a dog, you're drinking beer from the bottle for the first time in your life, you eat fish three times a week and you never used to eat fish—' He could have added that she'd kissed a man who wasn't her husband, but he decided it was better to leave that alone for now.

'How do you know how often I eat fish?'

'Hamish mentioned it.'

Her gasp was an astonished squeak. 'The islanders discuss my diet?'

'The islanders discuss everything. You should know that by now.'

'In that case you should probably let me mop up my own wet tee shirt.' She snatched the napkins from his hands, their fingers brushing. 'If we're trying to kill the gossip, I don't think you should be doing that.'

'Do you care about the gossip?'

'I care about Lexi hearing the gossip.'

'Ah—' He noticed the pulse beating in her throat and knew she felt the attraction as strongly as he did. He retrieved his bottle from the table. 'Can I get you something different to drink?'

'Absolutely not.' There was humour in her eyes. And determination. 'I'm not a quitter. If you can drink from the bottle without dribbling, then so can I.' She lifted the bottle carefully to her lips and this time didn't spill a drop.

His body throbbing, Ryan stood close to her. 'You were late. I thought you weren't coming.'

'I was working in the garden, and then Lexi had to change her outfit four times. And I wasn't sure if it was a good idea…' She paused, staring at the label on the bottle. 'This stuff is disgusting.'

'It's an acquired taste. And now?'

'I still don't know if it's a good idea. I've never been so confused in my life.'

Evanna was back at the table, rearranging salads and plates. Ryan saw the happy smile on her lips and ground his teeth. Suddenly he felt protective—Jenna ought to be able to get out and spread her wings socially without being made to feel that everything she did was being analysed and gossiped about.

He was about to intervene when Kirsty, Evanna's six-year-old daughter, sprinted across the sand and launched herself at Lexi. 'Lex—Lex, I want to show you my swimming.'

Ryan watched as the teenager stooped to pick the little girl up. 'Wow. Lucky me. I can't wait to see.' She was a million miles from the moody, sullen teenager who had dragged her feet off the ferry a month before.

The little girl's smile spread right across her face as she bounced in Lexi's arms. 'I can swim without armbands.'

'Really? That's cool.'

'Watch me.'

'Please would you watch me.' Evanna tipped dressing from a jug onto a bowl of salad leaves. 'Manners, Kirsty.'

'Pleeeease—'

Lexi grinned. 'Sure. But don't splash me. It took me ages to get my hair straight.' Her face suddenly turned scarlet, and Ryan glanced round and saw Fraser strolling across the sand towards them, a lopsided grin on his face.

'Hey, if it isn't the city girl.' He wore his board shorts low on his hips and carried a football under his arm. 'We were wondering when you were going to get here. You going to swim for us, Kirst?'

Ryan felt Jenna tense beside him and saw Lexi's shoulders stiffen.

'This is my mum—' She waved a hand awkwardly towards Jenna. 'This is Fraser.'

'Hi, Fraser.' Jenna's voice was friendly. 'Nice to meet you.'

'Hi, Mrs Richards.' With an easy smile Fraser pushed his sun-bleached hair out of his eyes and kicked the football towards his friends. 'Evanna, is it OK if we take Kirsty swimming?'

'You'd be doing me a favour.' Evanna didn't hesitate. 'Don't let her get her own way too often.'

With Kirsty still in her arms, Lexi slid off her shoes and walked barefoot across the sand with Fraser. Close, but not touching.

Watching Jenna sink her teeth into her lower lip, Ryan sighed. 'Relax.'

'Lexi isn't old enough to have responsibility for Kirsty. I'd better follow them.'

He wondered who she was worried about—Kirsty or her own daughter.

'She'll be fine,' Evanna said calmly. 'Fraser is very responsible. The beach here is pretty safe, and Ryan can keep an eye on them—he's the strongest swimmer round here.' Smiling, she gave Ryan a little push. 'Go on. You're on lifeguard duty.'

Ryan glanced at Logan, who was expertly flipping steaks on the barbecue.

'Your wife is a bully.'

'I know. I love a strong, forceful woman, don't you?'

It was a flippant remark, with no hidden meaning, but Ryan felt his jaw tighten as he considered the question. He liked a woman to be independent, yes. Strong? He had no problem with strong—he knew from experience that life dealt more blows than a boxer, so strong was probably good. But forceful? Was forceful a euphemism for selfish and single-minded? For doing absolutely what you wanted to do with no thought for anyone else? If so, then the answer was no—he didn't like forceful women.

The question killed his mood, and he was aware that Jenna was looking at him with concern in her eyes.

'I'll keep you company. You made me buy a swimming costume so I might as well use it.' She put her drink down. 'If you're really on lifeguard duty then you can come in the water with me. It's so long since I swam I'm probably going to need my own personal lifeguard.'

Wanting to escape his thoughts, Ryan put his drink down next to hers. 'All right.'

They walked across the sand and she quickened her pace to keep up with him.

'You seem upset.' She kept walking. 'Is something wrong?'

Startled by her insight, Ryan frowned, his eyes on the sea, where Lexi was dangling a shrieking Kirsty in the water. 'What could be wrong?'

'I don't know. I just thought—you seem very tense all of a sudden. I thought maybe you needed some space.' She took a deep breath. 'If you want to talk to someone, you can talk to me.'

Ryan turned his head in astonishment and she bit her lip, her smile faltering.

'I know, I know—men don't like to talk about their problems. But you've listened to me often enough over the past month— I just want you to know that the friendship works both ways.'

'Friendship?' He realised that he was looking at her mouth again, and the strange thing was he didn't need to look. He'd memorised everything about it, from the way her lips curved to the soft pink colour. 'Is that what we have?'

'Of course. I mean, I hope so. You've certainly been a friend to me since I arrived here.'

He stared down into her eyes and something shimmered between them. Something powerful. So powerful that if they hadn't been standing in the middle of a crowded beach with the entire population of Glenmore watching he would have kissed her again.

Unsettled by his own feelings, Ryan shifted his gaze back to the sea. 'I don't have any problems.' His tone was rougher than he'd intended and he heard her sigh.

'You've known me long enough to kiss me, Ryan,' she said quietly. 'Hopefully you've also known me long enough to trust me.'

He was about to say that it was nothing to do with trust, but he was too late. She was already walking ahead, her hair tumbling down her back, sand dusting her toes.

Wondering whether he'd hurt her feelings, Ryan followed her to the water's edge, relieved when she smiled at him.

Clearly Jenna Richards didn't sulk. Nor did she bear grudges.

Fraser and Lexi were either side of Kirsty, holding her hands and swinging her over the waves while she squealed with delight. All of them were laughing.

Ryan was about to speak when he caught the wistful expression on Jenna's face. Her eyes were on Kirsty, and she had that look on her face that women sometimes had when they stared into prams.

He wondered again why she'd only had one child when she was clearly a born mother. Patient, caring, and unfailingly loving.

Pain shafted through him like a lightning bolt and he watched as she lifted her skirt slightly and tentatively allowed the waves to lick her feet. With a soft gasp of shock she jumped back, her eyes shining with laughter as she looked at him.

'It's freezing! Forget swimming. I'll definitely turn to ice and drown if I go in there!'

Forcing aside his dark thoughts, Ryan strode into the waves. 'No way are you using that pathetic excuse.' He took her hand and pulled her deeper. 'You get used to it after a while.'

'After losing how many limbs to frostbite?' Still holding his hand, she lifted her skirt above her knees with her free hand. 'I'm not going to get used to this. I'm losing all sensation in my feet.'

'What are you complaining about?' He tightened his grip on her hand. 'This is a warm evening on Glenmore.'

'The evening may be warm, but someone has forgotten to tell the sea it's summer. My feet are aching they're so cold.' Her laughter was infectious, and Ryan found that he was laughing, too.

Laughing with a woman. That was something he hadn't done for a long time.

He intercepted Lexi's shocked stare and his laughter faded. She glanced between him and her mother, suspicion in her eyes.

Jenna was still laughing as she picked her way through the waves, apparently unaware of her daughter's frozen features.

'We wouldn't be doing this in London, would we, Lex?'

'Pull your skirt down, Mum,' Lexi hissed, and Ryan watched as Jenna suddenly went from being natural to self-conscious. The colour flooded into her cheeks and she re-leased the skirt. Instantly the hem trailed in the water. Flustered, she lifted it again.

'Lexi, watch me, watch me—' Kirsty bounced in the water, but Lexi stepped closer to her mother and dumped the child in Jenna's arms.

'Here you are, Mum. You take her. You're good with kids. Probably because you're old and motherly.'

Ryan was about to laugh at the joke when he realised that no one was laughing.

Old and motherly?

Was that how Lexi saw her mother? Was that how Jenna saw herself?

How old was she? Thirty-two? Thirty-three? She could have passed for ten years younger than that. She had a fresh, natural appeal that he found incredibly sexy. And, yes, she was different from Connie.

His jaw hardened. Connie wouldn't have paddled in the

sea—nor would she have appeared in public with a face free of make-up. And he couldn't remember a time when she'd giggled. But that might have been because Connie wasn't spontaneous. She was a woman with a plan and nothing was going to stand in her way. Certainly not their marriage.

'I can't believe you're brave enough to swim!' Jenna was beaming at Kirsty, as if the child had done something incredibly clever. 'I'm so cold I can barely stand in the water, let alone swim.' She sneaked a glance after her daughter, who was walking away from them, Fraser by her side.

'I swim with my daddy.' Keen to demonstrate her skills, Kirsty wriggled in Jenna's arms and plunged back into the water, thrashing her arms and kicking her legs.

Drenched and shivering, Jenna laughed. 'Kirsty, that's fantastic. I couldn't swim like that at your age. And never in sea this cold.' The water had glued the skirt to her legs and Logan looked away, forcing himself to concentrate on something other than the shape of her body.

A crowd of locals were playing volleyball, and he could see Evanna handing out plates of food. 'I smell barbecue,' he said mildly. 'We should probably go and eat something. Sausages, Kirsty?'

The child immediately held out her arms to Jenna, who scooped her out of the water and cuddled her, ignoring the damp limbs and soaking costume.

Ryan felt his body tighten as he watched her with the child.

It was such a painful moment that when the phone in his pocket buzzed he was grateful for the excuse to walk away.

'I'm on call. I'd better take this.' He strode out of the water and drew the phone from his pocket. Was he ever going to be able to look at a mother and child without feeling that degree of agony? He answered his phone with a violent stab of his finger. 'McKinley.' It took him less than five seconds to get the gist of the conversation. 'I'll be right there.' Even as he dropped the phone into this pocket, he was running.

Cuddling a soaking wet Kirsty, Jenna watched as Ryan took off across the beach. It was obvious that there was some sort of emergency. Knowing he'd probably need help, she waded out of the water as fast as her soaked skirt and the bouncing child would allow. Once on the sand, she put the little girl down and ran, holding the child's hand.

'Let's see how fast we can reach Mummy.' At least an emergency might stop her thinking about that kiss. Nothing else had worked so far.

They reached Evanna as she was handing Ryan a black bag.

'What's wrong?' Jenna handed Kirsty over to her mother. 'Is it an emergency?'

Ryan glanced at her briefly. 'Ben who runs the Stag's Head has a tourist who has collapsed. Logan—' He raised his voice. 'I'm going to the pub. Keep your phone switched on.'

'I'll come with you.' Jenna glanced across at Evanna. 'Lexi's walked off with Fraser—will you keep an eye on her for me?'

'Of course.' Looking worried, Evanna held toddler Charlie on her hip and a serving spoon in her other hand. 'I hope it turns out to be nothing. We'll hold the fort here, but if you need reinforcements call.'

Hampered by her wet skirt, Jenna sprinted after Logan and it was only when her feet touched tarmac that she realised she'd left her shoes back at the barbecue. 'Ouch!' Stupid, stupid. 'I left my shoes—'

The next minute she was scooped off the ground and Logan was carrying her across the road.

She gave a gasp of shock. 'Put me down! I weigh a ton!'

'You don't weigh anything, and it's good for my ego to carry a helpless woman occasionally.' He was still jogging, and she realised how fit he must be.

'I'm not helpless, just shoeless.'

'Cinderella.' With a brief smile, he lowered her to the pavement and strode into the pub.

Jenna followed, feeling ridiculous in a wet skirt and without shoes. But all self-consciousness faded as she saw the man lying on the floor. His lips and eyes were puffy, his breathing was laboured and noisy, and the woman next to him was shaking his shoulder and crying.

'Pete? Pete?'

'What happened?' Ryan was down on the floor beside the patient, checking his airway. His fingers moved swiftly and skilfully, checking, eliminating, searching for clues.

'One moment he was eating his supper,' the landlord said, 'and then he crashed down on the floor, holding his throat.'

'He said he felt funny,' his wife sobbed. 'He had a strange feeling in his throat. All of a sudden. I've no idea why. We've been on the beach all afternoon and he was fine. Never said a thing about feeling ill or anything.'

'Anaphylactic shock.' Ryan's mouth was grim and Jenna dropped to her knees beside him.

'Is he allergic to anything?' She glanced at the man's wife. 'Nuts? Could he have been stung? Wasp?'

The woman's eyes were wild with panic. 'I don't think he was stung and he's not allergic to anything. He's fine with nuts, all that sort of stuff—is he going to die?'

Ryan had his hand in his bag. 'He's not going to die. Ben,

call the air ambulance and fetch me that oxygen you keep round the back.' Icy calm, he jabbed an injection of adrenaline into the man's thigh, working with astonishing speed. 'Pete? Can you hear me? I'm Dr McKinley.'

Catching a glimpse of the role he'd played in a previous life, Jenna switched her focus back to the man's wife. 'What were you eating?' She looked at the table. 'Fish pie?'

'Yes. But he'd only had a few mouthfuls.'

'Are there prawns in that fish pie?'

'Yes.' Ben was back with the oxygen. 'But they were fresh this morning.'

'I'm not suggesting food poisoning,' Jenna said quickly, 'but maybe shellfish allergy?'

Covering the man's mouth and nose with the oxygen mask, Ryan looked at her for a moment, his eyes narrowed. Then he nodded. 'Shellfish. That's possible. That would explain it.' He adjusted the flow of oxygen. 'I'll give him five minutes and then give him another shot of epinephrine. Can you find it?'

Jenna delved in his bag and found the other drugs they were likely to need.

'Shellfish allergy?' The wife looked at them in horror. 'But—this isn't the first time he's eaten shellfish—can you just develop an allergy like that? Out of nowhere?'

'Jenna, can you squeeze his arm for me? I want to get a line in.'

'Actually, yes.' Jenna spoke to the woman as she handed Ryan a sterile cannula and then watched as he searched for a vein. 'Some adults do develop an allergy to something that hasn't harmed them before.'

'The body just decides it doesn't like it?'

'The body sees it as an invader,' Jenna explained, blinking

at the speed with which Ryan obtained IV access. Her fingers over his, she taped down the cannula so that it wouldn't be dislodged, the movements routine and familiar. 'It basically overreacts and produces chemicals and antibodies. Dr McKinley has just given an injection to counter that reaction.'

The woman's face was paper-white. 'Is it going to work?'

'I hope so. This is quite a severe reaction, so I'm giving him another dose.' Ryan took the syringe from Jenna. 'And I'm going to give him some antihistamine and hydrocortisone.'

'Air ambulance is on its way,' Ben said, and at that moment Jenna noticed something. Leaning forward, she lifted the man's tee shirt so that she could get a better look.

'He has a rash, Ryan.'

'I think it's safe to assume we're dealing with a shellfish allergy—when you get to the mainland they'll observe him overnight and then make an appointment for you to see an allergy consultant. Where do you live?'

'We're from London. We're just here for a holiday. We have another week to go.' The woman was staring at her husband's chest in disbelief. 'I've never seen a rash come on like that.'

'It's all part of the reaction,' Jenna said quietly. 'The drugs will help.'

'How long do you think they'll keep him in hospital?'

'With any luck they'll let you go tomorrow and you can get on with your holiday—avoiding shellfish.' Ryan examined the rash carefully. 'The hospital should refer you for allergy testing so you can be sure what you're dealing with. You may need to carry an Epipen.' He checked the man's pulse again. 'His breathing is improving. That last injection seems to have done the trick.'

'Thank goodness—' The woman slumped slightly and Jenna slipped her arm round her.

'You poor thing. Are you on your own here? Do you have any friends or family with you?' She tried to imagine what it must be like going through this on holiday, far from home, with no support.

'My sister and her husband, but they've gone to the beach barbecue.'

'I'll contact them for you,' Ben said immediately, taking the details and sending one of the locals down to the beach to locate the woman's family.

Once again the islanders impressed Jenna, working together to solve the problem in a way that would never really happen in a big city.

By the time the air ambulance arrived the man had regained consciousness and the woman had been reunited with her family. Jenna listened as Ryan exchanged information with the paramedics and masterminded the man's transfer. As the helicopter lifted off for the short trip to the mainland, she turned to him.

His face was tanned from the sun and the wind, his dark hair a surprising contrast to his ice-blue eyes.

Trapped by his gaze, Jenna stood still, inexplicably drawn to him. She forgot about the small stones pressing into her bare feet; she forgot that she was confused about her feelings. She forgot everything except the astonishing bolt of chemistry that pulled her towards Ryan.

She wanted to kiss him again.

She wanted to kiss him now.

Feeling like a teenager on her first date, she leaned towards him, melting like chocolate on a hot day. His hands came down on her shoulders and she heard the harshness of his breathing.

Yes, now, she thought dreamily, feeling the strength of his fingers—

'Mum!'

The voice of a real teenager carried across the beach, and Jenna jumped as if she'd been shot as she recognised Lexi's appalled tones. For a moment she stared into Ryan's eyes, and then she turned her head and saw her daughter staring at her in undisguised horror.

'What are you doing?'

Her heart pounding and her mouth dry, Jenna was grateful for the distance, which ensured that at least her daughter couldn't see her scarlet cheeks.

What *was* she doing?

She was a divorced mother of thirty-three and she'd been on the verge of kissing a man with virtually all the island-ers watching.

'We probably ought to get back to the barbecue…' Ryan's tone was level and she nodded, feeling numb.

'Yes. Absolutely.' If Lexi hadn't shouted she would have put her arms around his neck and kissed him.

And what would that have done for her relationship with her daughter, let alone her relationship with Ryan?

This was her new life and she'd almost blown it. If Lexi hadn't called out to her she would have risked everything. And all for what? A kiss?

'If they've eaten all the food, I'll kill someone.' Apparently suffering none of her torment, Ryan turned towards the steps that led down to the sand, as relaxed as if they'd been having a conversation about the weather. 'How are things, Jim?'

Jim?

It took Jenna a moment to realise that the ferryman was standing by the steps, chatting to another islander. Had he been that close all the time? There could have been a fire, a flood and a hurricane, and all she would have noticed was Ryan.

'Another life saved, Doc.' Grinning, Jim scratched the back of his neck and looked up at the sky, where the helicopter was now no more than a tiny dot. 'Another good holiday experience on Glenmore. They'll be coming back. I overheard someone saying on the ferry this morning that they'd booked a short break here just so that they could ask a doctor about a skin rash, because you lot always know what you're doing.'

Ryan rolled his eyes. 'I'll mention it to Logan. We obviously need to make more of an effort to be useless.'

Jenna produced a smile, pretending to listen, wondering whether she could just slink onto the ferry and take the first sailing back to the mainland in the morning. Maybe distance would make her forget the kiss, because nothing else was working—not even an emergency.

Lexi was waiting for them at the bottom of the steps. 'Mum? What were you doing?'

'She was debriefing with Dr McKinley,' Evanna said smoothly, and Jenna jumped with shock because she hadn't seen Evanna standing next to her daughter. Last time she'd looked Evanna had been serving sausages and salad. But somehow the other woman had materialised at the foot of the steps, Charlie in her arms. 'I gather everything went smoothly, Jenna? Rapid response from the air ambulance? Did things go according to plan?'

Grateful as she was for Evanna's focus on the professional, Jenna didn't manage to respond.

Fortunately Ryan took over. 'Things don't always go according to plan,' he said softly, 'but that's life, isn't it? Ideally

I would have liked to lose the audience, but you can't choose where these things happen.'

Jenna couldn't work out whether he was talking about the medical emergency or the fact she'd almost kissed him. They'd had an audience for both. and she was painfully aware that she'd embarrassed him as much as herself. These were his friends. His colleagues. No doubt he'd be on the receiving end of suggestive remarks for the rest of the summer. Yes, he'd kissed her on the beach, but that had been early in the morning with no one watching.

Because Lexi was still looking at her suspiciously, Jenna forced herself to join in the discussion. 'I—it was a bit unexpected. I'm not used to dealing with emergencies.' And she wasn't used to being attracted to a man. She'd behaved like a crazed, desperate woman.

'From what I've heard you were fantastic—a real Glenmore nurse.' Evanna was generous with her praise. 'We're expected to be able to turn our hands to pretty much anything. People are already singing your praises all over the island.' She tucked her hand through Jenna's arm, leading her back across the beach as if they'd been friends for ever. 'Word travels fast in this place. How are your feet?'

Jenna glanced down and realised that she'd forgotten she wasn't wearing shoes. 'Sore. I need to find my sandals.' Her face was burning and she didn't dare look round to see where Ryan was. Hiding, probably—afraid of the desperate divorcee who had tried to attack him. As for Lexi, she still wasn't smiling, but the scowl had left her features. Which presumably meant that Evanna's explanation had satisfied her.

'Your Lexi is so brilliant with the children.' Evanna led her back to the food and heaped potato salad on a plate. 'Logan—find something delicious for Jenna. She's earned it.'

Jenna accepted the food, even though the last thing she felt like was eating. She just wanted to go home and work out what she was going to say to Ryan next time she saw him on his own.

She had to apologise. She had to explain that she had absolutely no idea what had happened to her. Yes, she'd got a dog, she ate fish three times a week and she'd drunk beer from a bottle, but kissing a man in public…

Lexi flicked her hair away from her face. 'I'm off to play volleyball.' With a final glance in her direction, her daughter sauntered off across the sand towards Fraser, who was laughing with a friend, a can of cola in his hand. 'See you later.'

Jenna wanted to leave, but she knew that would draw attention to herself, and she'd already attracted far too much attention for one evening. Even without turning her head she was painfully aware of Ryan talking to Logan, discussing the air ambulance.

She wondered whether she should request that the air ambulance come back for her when they'd finished. She felt as though she needed it.

'Have a drink.' Clearly reading her mind, Evanna pushed a large glass of wine into her hand. 'And don't look so worried. Everything is fine. You and Ryan were a great team.'

Jenna managed a smile, but all she could think was, *Why am I feeling like this?*

She had to forget him. She had to forget that kiss.

Thank goodness tomorrow was Sunday and she didn't have to work. She had a whole day to talk some sense into herself.

CHAPTER SEVEN

10 reasons why I shouldn't fall in love with Ryan:
I've been divorced less than a year
I am too old
I'm ordinary and he is a sex god
Being with him puts me off my food
I have Lexi to think of
I need to act my age
I have to work with the man
He'll hurt me
I'm not his type

'MUM?'

Jenna dropped the pen before number ten and flipped the envelope over. 'I'm in the kitchen. You're up early.' Too early. Deciding that she couldn't hide the envelope without looking suspicious, Jenna slammed her mug of tea on it and smiled brightly. 'I was expecting you to sleep in.'

'I was hungry, and anyway I'm meeting the gang.' Yawning, Lexi tipped cereal into a bowl and added milk. 'You're up early, too.'

'I had things to do.' Like making a list of reasons why she shouldn't be thinking of Ryan.

Her head throbbing and her eyelids burning from lack of sleep, Jenna stood up and filled the kettle, bracing herself for the awkward questions she'd been dreading all night. 'You normally want to lie in bed.'

'That's only during term time, when there's nothing to get up for except boring old school.' Lexi frowned at her and then eyed the mug on the envelope. 'Why are you making tea when you haven't drunk the last one?'

Jenna stared in horror at the mug on the table.

Because she wasn't concentrating.

She'd been thinking about the kiss again.

Exasperated with herself, she picked up the half-full mug and scrunched the envelope in her hand. 'This one is nearly cold. And anyway, I thought you might like one.'

Lexi gaped at her. 'I don't drink tea. And why are you hiding that envelope? Is it a letter from Dad or something?'

'It's nothing—I mean—' Jenna stammered. 'I wrote a phone number on it—for a plumber—that tap is still leaking—'

Lexi's eyes drifted to the tap, which stubbornly refused to emit even a drop of water. 'So if there's a number on it, why did you just scrunch it up?'

'I only remembered about the number after I scrunched it up.'

Lexi shrugged, as if her mother's strange behaviour was so unfathomable it didn't bear thinking about. 'I won't be back for lunch. I'm meeting Fraser and a bunch of his friends up at the castle ruins at nine. We're making a day of it.'

'It's Sunday. Archaeology club isn't until tomorrow.'

'Not officially, but the chief archaeologist guy is going to show us the dungeons and stuff. Really cool.'

'Oh.' Still clutching the envelope, Jenna sat back down at the table, relieved that there wasn't going to be an inquisition about the night before. 'I was going to suggest we made a picnic and went for a walk on the cliffs, but if you're meeting your friends—well, that's great.'

Lexi pushed her bowl away and stood up. 'Do I look OK?'

Jenna scanned the pretty strap top vacantly, thinking that the blue reminded her of Ryan's eyes in the seconds before he'd kissed her on the beach. Had she ever felt this way about Clive? Was it just that she'd forgotten? And how did Ryan feel about her?

'Mum? What do you think?'

'I think he's a grown man and he knows what he's doing.'

'What?' Lexi stared at her. 'He's fifteen. Same age as me.'

Jenna turned scarlet. 'That's what I mean. He's almost a man. And I'm sure he's responsible.'

'But I didn't ask you—' Lexi shook her head in frustration. 'What *is* wrong with you this morning? Mum, are you OK?'

No, Jenna thought weakly. She definitely wasn't. 'Of course I'm OK. Why wouldn't I be? I'm great. Fine. I'm good. Really happy. Looking forward to a day off.'

Lexi backed away, hands raised. 'All right, all right. No need to go overboard—I was just asking. You look like you're having a breakdown or something.'

'No. No breakdown.' Her voice high pitched, Jenna pinned a smile on her face. She was good at this bit. Feel one emotion, show another. She'd done it repeatedly after her marriage had fallen apart. Misery on the inside, smile on the outside. Only in this case it was crazy lust-filled woman on the inside, respectable mother on the outside. 'Have a really, really nice day, Lexi. I'm glad you've made friends so quickly.'

Lexi narrowed her eyes suspiciously. 'What? No lecture? No "Don't go too near the edge or speak to strangers"? No

"Sex is for two people who love each other and are old enough to understand the commitment"? Are you sure you're OK?'

Back to thinking about Ryan, Jenna barely heard her. 'I thought you wanted me to worry less.'

'Yes, but I didn't exactly expect you to manage it!'

'Well, you can relax. I haven't actually stopped worrying—I've just stopped talking about it.' Still clutching the envelope, Jenna stood up and made herself another cup of tea. 'I've brought you up with the right values—it's time I trusted you. Time I gave you more independence and freedom to make your own mistakes.'

'Mum, are you feeling all right?'

No. No, she wasn't feeling all right.

She was feeling very confused. She was thinking about nothing but sex and that just wasn't her, was it? Had Clive's brutal betrayal left her so wounded and insecure that she needed affirmation that she was still an attractive woman? Or was it something to do with wanting what you couldn't have?

Lexi folded her arms. 'So you're perfectly OK if I just spend the day up at the castle, taking drugs and making out with Fraser?'

'That's fine.' Thinking of the way Ryan's body had felt against hers, Jenna stared blindly out of the kitchen window. 'Have a nice time.'

'OK, this is spooky. I just told you I'm going to use drugs and make out and you want me to have a *nice time*?'

Had she really said that? 'I know you wouldn't do that.' Jenna mindlessly tidied the kitchen. 'You're too sensible. You're always telling me you're going to have a career before children.'

'Sex doesn't have to end in children, Mum.' Lexi's voice was dry as she picked up her phone and her iPod and walked towards the door. 'One day, when you're old enough, I'll explain it all to you. In the meantime I'll leave you to your incoherent ramblings. Oh, and you might want to remove the teabags from the washing machine—you'll be looking for them later.'

She'd put the teabags in the washing machine?

Jenna extracted them, her cheeks pink, her brain too fuddled to form an appropriate response. 'Have fun. Don't forget your key.'

'You're acting so weird.' Lexi slipped it into her pocket, staring at her mother as if she were an alien. 'You know— last night, for a moment, I really thought—'

Jenna's breathing stopped. 'What did you think?'

'I thought that you—' Lexi broke off and shrugged. 'Never mind. Crazy idea, and anyway I was wrong. Thank goodness. What are you planning to do today?'

Chew over everything that had happened the night before; try not to spend the day thinking of Ryan; remind herself that she was too old to have crushes on men— 'Housework,' Jenna muttered, staring blindly at the pile of unwashed plates that were waiting to be stacked in the dishwasher. 'Catch up on a few things. The laundry basket is overflowing, and I need to weed the herbaceous border.' It all sounded like a boring day to her, but her answer seemed to satisfy Lexi.

Clearly Lexi had been reassured by Evanna's assertion that the two of them had been discussing the emergency they'd dealt with. Either that or she'd just decided that no man was ever going to be seriously interested in her mother.

'I'll see you later, then. Do you mind if I take Rebel?' Grabbing his lead, Lexi whistled to the dog and sauntered off to meet Fraser and his friends at the castle, leaving Jenna to face a day on her own with her thoughts.

And her thoughts didn't make good company.

Tormented by the memory of what had happened the night before, she pulled out one of the kitchen chairs and sat down with a thump. Then she smoothed the crumpled envelope she'd been clutching and stared at her list. She'd started with ten but there were probably a million reasons why it was a bad idea to kiss Ryan McKinley.

With a groan, she buried her face in her hands. She had to stop this nonsense. She had to pull herself together and act like an adult. She was a mother, for goodness' sake.

'You're obviously feeling as frustrated as I am.' His voice came from the doorway and Jenna flew to her feet, the chair crashing backwards onto the tiled floor, her heart pounding.

'Ryan!' The fact that she'd been thinking about him made the whole thing even more embarrassing—but not as humiliating as the fact that she was wearing nothing but her knickers and the old tee shirt of Lexi's that she'd worn to bed. Jenna tugged at the hem, until she realised that just exposed more of her breasts. 'What are you doing here?'

'Trying to have five minutes with you without the whole of Glenmore watching.' He strode across the kitchen, righting the chair that she'd tipped over. Then he gave her a wicked smile. 'Nice outfit.'

Too shocked to move, Jenna watched him walk towards her, dealing with the fact that a man was looking at her with undisguised sexual interest and he wasn't Clive. There was no mixing this man up with Clive. Her ex-husband was slight of build, with pale skin from spending most of his day in an office. Ryan was tall and broad-shouldered, his skin bronzed from the combination of wind and sun. When she'd looked at Clive she hadn't thought of sex and sin, but when she looked at Ryan—

He stopped in front of her. 'You have fantastic legs.'

A thrill of dangerous pleasure mingled with embarrassment. 'How did you get in?'

'The usual way—through the door.' Before she could say a word, he caught the front of her tee shirt in his hand, jerked her against him and brought his mouth down on hers. A thousand volts of pure sexual chemistry shot through her body and thoughts of sex and sin exploded into reality.

Jenna gripped his arms, feeling hard male muscle flex under her fingers. 'I've been thinking about you—'

'Good. I'd hate to be the only one suffering. You taste so good…' Groaning the words against her lips, Ryan sank his hands into her hair and devoured her mouth as if she were a feast and he was starving. His kiss was hot and hungry, and she felt her knees weaken and her heart pound. Flames licked through her veins and Jenna tightened her grip on his arms, grateful that she was leaning against the work surface.

Engulfed by an explosion of raw need Jenna wrapped her arms around his neck and pressed closer. His hands came round her back and he hauled her against him, leaving her in no doubt as to the effect she had on him. Feeling the hard ridge of his erection, Jenna felt excitement shoot through her body.

Dizzy and disorientated, she moaned against his mouth and he slid his hands under the tee shirt, his fingers warm against her flesh. She gasped as those same fingers dragged over her breasts, moaned as he toyed and teased. And still he kissed her. Mouth to mouth they stood, the skilled sweep of his tongue driving her wild, until she squirmed against him, the ache deep inside her almost intolerable.

Dimly, she heard him groan her name, and then he was lifting her tee shirt over her head and his mouth was on her bare breast. Jenna opened her mouth to tell him that it felt good, but the only sound that emerged was a faint moan, and her breathing became shallow as he drew the sensitive tip into his mouth. Her fingers sank into his thick dark hair as the excitement built, and suddenly she was aware of nothing but the heavy throb in her body and the desperate need for more. Every thought was driven from her mind, but one—

She wanted him. She wanted sex with him, and she didn't care about the consequences.

His mouth was back on hers, the slide of his tongue intimate and erotic.

Shaking now, Jenna reached for the waistband of his jeans and felt his abdomen clench against her fingers. She fumbled ineptly for a few moments, and then his hand closed around her wrist.

'Wait—God, I can't believe the way you make me feel.'

She moaned and pressed her mouth back to his, their breath mingling. 'I want to—'

With obvious difficulty he dragged his mouth from hers. 'I know you do, and so do I, but this time I really don't want to be disturbed—how long is Lexi out for? Is she going to be back in the next few hours?'

'Lexi?' Disorientated, Jenna stared at him for a moment, and then shook her head and rubbed her fingers over her forehead, trying to switch off the response of her body so that she could think clearly. 'Lexi.' She felt as though her personality had been split down the middle—mother and woman. 'She's out, but— What on earth am I doing?' Realising that she was virtually naked, Jenna quickly retrieved her tee shirt from the floor, but she was shaking so much that she couldn't turn it the right way round.

'I wish I hadn't said anything.' His tone rough, Ryan removed it gently from her hands, turned it the right way round and pulled it carefully over her head. 'I just didn't want her walking in on us.'

'No. And it's ridiculous. This whole thing is ridiculous— I'm— And you're—'

He raised an eyebrow. 'Is there any chance of you actually finishing a sentence, because I have no idea what you're thinking.'

'I'm thinking that this is crazy.' Jenna straightened the tee shirt and flipped her hair free. 'I'm thinking that I don't do things like this.'

'That doesn't mean you can't. You hadn't owned a dog or eaten fish until a month ago.'

She gave a hysterical laugh. 'Having sex is slightly different to getting a dog or eating fish.'

'I should hope so. If a few hours in my bed is on a par with eating fish or getting a dog, I'll give up sex.'

'That would be a terrible waste, because you're obviously very good at it.' Jenna slammed her hand over her mouth and stared at him, appalled. 'I can't believe I just said that.'

But he was laughing, his blue eyes bright with humour. 'I love the way you say what you think.'

'What I think is that I don't know what you're doing here with me.' With an embarrassed laugh, she yanked the tee shirt down, covering herself. 'I'm not some nubile twenty-year-old. I'm a mother and I'm thirty-three…' The words died in her throat as he covered her mouth with his fingers.

'You're incredibly sexy.'

Staring up into his cool blue eyes, Jenna gulped, still coming to terms with the feelings he'd uncovered. He'd had his hands on her, and as for his mouth… An earthquake could have hit and she wouldn't have noticed. In fact, she felt as though an earthquake *had* hit.

Everything about her world had changed and it was hard to keep her balance.

But she had to. She couldn't afford the luxury of acting on impulse. She wasn't a teenager.

Thinking of teenagers made her groan and close her eyes.

'Ryan, what are you doing here?' She jabbed her fingers into her hair, horrified by what could have happened. 'We could have— Lexi might have—'

'I saw her leave. And before you panic, no, she didn't see me. I stayed out of the way until she'd disappeared over the horizon. Given the way she guards you, I thought it was wise. She obviously doesn't see her mother as a living, breathing sexual woman.'

'That's because I'm not. I'm not like this. This isn't me.'

'Maybe it *is* you.' His eyes lingered on her mouth. 'Do you want to find out?'

Her heart bumped hard. 'I can't. I have responsibilities.'

'Talking of which, did she give you a hard time about last night?'

'She started to say something and then decided that she'd imagined it all. Thanks to Evanna. But—I'm sorry about last night. I was going to apologise to you.'

'Don't.' His mouth was so close to hers that it was impossible to concentrate.

'You must be furious with me for embarrassing you in public—'

His hand was buried in her hair, his lips moving along her jaw. 'Do I seem furious?' His mouth was warm and clever, and Jenna felt her will-power strained to the limit.

She put a hand on his chest, trying to be sensible. Trying to ignore the way he made her feel.

Then he paused and stooped to retrieve something from the

floor. It was her envelope. He would have discarded it had she not given an anguished squeak and reached for it.

'That's mine.'

'What is it?'

'It's nothing.' Jenna snatched at it but he held it out of reach, unfurling it with one hand.

'If it's nothing, why are you trying to stop me reading it?' He squinted at the crumpled paper. '"10 reasons why I shouldn't fall in love with Ryan—" Ah.'

With a groan, Jenna covered her face with her hands. 'Please, just ignore it—'

'No.' His voice was calm and steady. 'If you can make a list of ten reasons not to fall in love with me, I have a right to know what they are.' He scanned the list and frowned. 'I put you off your food? That's why you don't eat?'

Mortified, Jenna just shook her head, and he sighed and tucked the mangled envelope into the back pocket of his jeans.

'If you want my opinion, I don't think it matters that you've been divorced for less than a year, nor do I think your age has any relevance. The fact that I put you off your food might be a problem in the long term, but we won't worry for now. As for Lexi—' He stroked his fingers through her hair. 'I can see that might be a problem. That's why I stopped when I did. I didn't want her to walk in.'

'So you're not just a sex god.' She made a joke of it. 'You're thoughtful, too.'

'For selfish reasons. I want you, and you come with a daughter.'

Did he mean he *wanted her* body or he wanted her? She was afraid to ask and she found it hard to believe that he wanted her at all. 'Why do I always meet you looking my worst?' Jenna couldn't believe the unfairness of it all. He looked like a living, breathing fantasy and she was wearing Lexi's cast off tee shirt.

'I think you look fantastic.' Ryan slid his hand into her hair, studying each tangled curl in detail. 'Does your hair curl naturally?'

'Yes, of course. Do you think I'd pay to make it look like this?' She snapped the words, embarrassed that she was looking her worst when he was looking his best, and really, really confused by the way he made her feel.

'I really like it.' His smile was slow and sexy. 'You look as though you've had a really crazy night in some very lucky man's bed.'

Jenna couldn't concentrate. His fingers were massaging her scalp and she felt his touch right through her body. How did he know how to do that? Her eyes drifted shut and suddenly the impact on her other senses was magnified.

'As a matter of interest, what did you wear to bed when you were married?'

Jenna gulped. 'A long silky nightdress that Clive's mother bought me for Christmas. Why do you want to know?'

'Because I suspect this is another of your little rebellions. And now we've established that Lexi isn't coming back in the immediate future...' His voice husky, Ryan slid his hands under the offending tee shirt and she gasped because his hands were warm and strong and her nerve-endings were on fire.

'Ryan—'

His fingers slid down her back with a slow, deliberate movement that was unmistakably seductive. 'I hate to be the one to point this out, but I have a strong suspicion that neither Clive nor his mother would approve of your current choice of nightwear.'

'They'd be horrified—'

'Which is why you're wearing it.'

Jenna gave a choked laugh. 'Maybe. In which case I'm seriously disturbed and you should avoid me.'

Ryan lifted her chin so that she had no choice but to look at him. 'Is that what you want?'

All the pent-up emotion inside her exploded, as if the gates holding everything back had suddenly been opened. 'No, that isn't what I want! Of course it isn't. But I feel guilty, because I know I shouldn't be doing this, and confused because I've never lost control like that before. I'm angry with myself for being weak-willed, terrified that you'll hurt me—'

'Ah, yes—number eight on your list. Why do you assume I'll hurt you?'

Jenna thought about Clive. If Clive had found her boring, how much more boring would this man find her? 'I'm not very exciting. I'm sure I'm all wrong for you.'

'In what way are you wrong for me?'

'For a start I've never had sex on a desk,' she blurted out, and then paled in disbelief. 'Oh, no—I can't believe I said that—'

'Neither can I. You're saying some really interesting things at the moment.' To give him his due, he didn't laugh. But he did close his hands around her wrists and drew her closer. 'I'm guessing that statement has some significance—am I right?'

Jenna stared at a point on his chest. 'I walked in on them,' she breathed. 'She was lying on his desk.'

'And you think that's what was wrong with your marriage?'

'No. The problems in our marriage went far deeper than that. I wouldn't have wanted to have sex on a desk with Clive, whereas—' She broke off, and he was silent for a moment.

Then he lifted his hand and slowly dragged his finger over her scarlet cheek. 'Whereas you do want to have sex on a desk with me?'

'Yes,' she whispered. 'Well, I don't mean a desk specifically—anywhere... But that's crazy, because I'm just not that sort of person and I know I'm really, really not your type.'

'Number nine on the list. So what *is* my type, Jenna?'

'I don't know. Someone stunning. Young. You're disgustingly handsome and you're sickeningly clever.' She mumbled the words, making a mental note never to commit her thoughts to paper again. 'I may be naive, but I'm not stupid. You could have any woman you want. You don't need to settle for a mess like me. And now you ought to leave, because all I ever do when you're around is embarrass myself. I need to get my head together and think about Lexi.'

'Why do you want to think about Lexi? She's out enjoying herself.'

Jenna felt her heart bump against her chest. 'I don't want to hurt her.'

'Is it going to hurt her if you spend the day with me?' His head was near hers, their mouths still close.

'No. But it might hurt me. I find this whole situation scary,' she confessed softly. 'What if I'm doing this for all the wrong reasons?' She looked up at him. 'What if I'm trying to prove something? What if I'm just using you to prove to myself that someone finds me attractive?'

'That objection wasn't on your list.' His mouth was against her neck, his tongue trailing across the base of her throat. 'You're not allowed to think up new ones.'

'I can't think properly when you do that—'

'Sorry.' But he didn't sound sorry, and he didn't stop what he was doing.

Jenna felt her insides melt but her brain refused to shut up. 'What if I'm just doing this because I'm angry with Clive?'

With a sigh, Ryan lifted his head. 'You're suggesting that kissing me is an act of revenge?'

'I don't know. I have no idea what's going on in my head. What I'm thinking is changing by the minute.'

There was a trace of humour in his eyes as he scanned her face. 'When you kissed me were you thinking of Clive?'

'No! But that doesn't mean it isn't a reasonable theory.'

'Answer me one question.' His mouth was against her neck again and Jenna closed her eyes.

'What?'

'If Lexi wasn't part of the equation—if it were just you and me—what would you like to do now?'

'Spend the day together, as you suggested. But somewhere private. Somewhere no one will see us.' She sighed. 'An impossible request on Glenmore, I know.'

'Maybe not.' Stroking her hair away from her face, Ryan gave a slow smile. 'In fact, I think I know just the place.'

The lighthouse was perched on a circle of grass, and the only approach was down a narrow path that curved out of sight of the road.

'It's the most secluded property on the island.' Ryan held out his hand as she negotiated the stony path. 'Even Mrs Parker has never been down here.'

Jenna shaded her eyes and stared up towards the top of the lighthouse. 'It's incredible. I can't believe it's a house.'

'It used to be fairly basic, but I made a few changes.' Ryan opened the door and she walked through, into a beautiful circular kitchen.

'Oh, my!' Stunned, she glanced around her. It was stylish and yet comfortable, with a huge range cooker, an American fridge and a central island for preparing food. By the window overlooking the sea the owner had placed a table, ensuring that anyone eating there could enjoy the fantastic view. 'A few changes?'

'Quite a few changes.' Ryan leaned against the doorframe, watching her reaction. 'Do you like it?'

'I love it. I had no idea—from the outside it looks…' Lost for words, she shook her head. 'It's idyllic.'

'Do you want breakfast now, or after you've looked round?'

'After…'

'Oh, yes—objection number four.' He gave a faint smile and urged her towards an arched doorway and a spiral staircase. 'I put you off your food. I don't suppose you'd like to tell me why? I don't think I've ever made a woman feel sick before.'

She giggled. 'You don't make me feel sick. You make me sort of churny in my stomach.'

'Sort of churny?' He lifted an eyebrow at her description. 'Is that good or bad?'

'Good, if you're trying to lose weight.'

'Don't. I like you the way you are.' He was right behind her on the stairs and it was impossible not to be aware that it was just the two of them in the house.

'So no one overlooks this?'

'It's a very inhospitable part of the coast of Glenmore—hence the reason they built a lighthouse here originally. This is the living room.'

Jenna emerged into another large, circular room, with high ceilings and glass walls. It had been decorated to reflect its coastal surroundings, with white wooden floors, seagrass matting and deep white sofas. Touches of blue added colour and elegant pieces of driftwood added style. A wood-burning stove stood in the centre of the room. 'This is the most beautiful room I've ever seen. I can't imagine what it must be like to actually live somewhere as special as this.'

'It was virtually a shell when I bought it from the original owner.' Ryan strolled over to the window, his back to her. 'It took me a year to make it properly habitable.'

'Where did you live while you were renovating it?'

'I lived here. Amidst the rubble.'

'You did most of it yourself?'

'All of it except the glazing. I used a lot of glass and it was too heavy for one person to manipulate.'

Stunned, she looked around her. 'You did the building—the plumbing, electricity?'

'I'm a doctor,' he drawled. 'I'm used to connecting pipes and electrical circuits. Building a wall isn't so different to re-aligning a broken bone—basically you need the thing straight.'

Jenna shook her head in silent admiration and carried on up the spiral staircase. She pushed open a door and discovered a luxurious bathroom, complete with drench shower. Another door revealed a small guest bedroom. Deciding that she'd never seen a more perfect property in her life, Jenna took the final turn in the staircase and found herself in paradise.

The master bedroom had been designed to take maximum advantage of the incredible view, with acres of glass giving a three-hundred-and-sixty-degree outlook on Glenmore.

Speechless, Jenna walked slowly around the perimeter of the breathtaking room. Out of the corner of her eye she was conscious of the enormous bed, but she was also acutely conscious of Ryan, watching her from the head of the spiral staircase. The intimacy was unfamiliar and exciting.

Hardly able to breathe, she stared out across the sparkling

sea, watching as the view changed with every step. Far beneath her were vicious rocks that must have sent so many boats tumbling to the bottom of the ocean, but a few paces on and she had a perfect view of the coast path, winding like a ribbon along the grassy flanks of the island. A few more steps and she was looking inland, across wild moorland shaded purple with heather.

'It's like living outside.'

'That was the idea.'

'I can see everything,' she whispered, 'except people. No people.'

'Just beyond the headland is the Scott farm.' Ryan was directly behind her now, and he closed his hands over her shoulders, pointing her in the right direction. 'But everything here is protected land. No building. No people. Occasionally you see someone on the coast path in the distance, but they can't get down here because the rocks are too dangerous. The path we took is the only way down.'

'I've never been anywhere so perfect.' Acutely aware of his touch, Jenna could hardly breathe. He was standing close to her and she could feel the brush of his hard body against hers. Her heart racing, she stared up at the roof—and discovered more curving glass. 'It must be wild here when there's a storm. Is it scary?'

'It's tough glass. You'd be surprised how much sound it blocks out. Do you find storms scary?' He turned her gently, and suddenly she thought that what she was starting to feel for him was far scarier than any storm.

'I don't know.' Looking into his eyes, she felt as though everything in her life was changing. And not only did she not trust her feelings, she knew she couldn't have them. She had to think about Lexi. But Lexi wasn't here now, was she?

Maybe there was no future, but there could be a present. She was a woman as well as a mother.

His mouth was close to hers but he didn't kiss her, and she wondered whether he was waiting for her to make the decision.

Jenna lifted her hand to his face, the breath trapped in her throat. His jaw was rough against her fingers and she felt him tense, but still he didn't kiss her. Still he waited.

Consumed by the thrill of anticipation, she wrapped her arms around his neck and lifted her mouth to his, feeling her stomach swoop. It was like jumping off a cliff. As decisions went, this was a big one, and deep down in her gut she knew there would be a price to pay, but right now she didn't care. If she had to pay, she'd pay.

As her lips touched his she felt the ripple of tension spread across his shoulders—felt the coiled power in his athletic frame.

'Be sure, Jenna…' He breathed the words against her mouth, his hand light on her back, still giving her the option of retreat.

But the last thing she had in mind was retreat. She kept her mouth on his and he slid his hands into her hair and held her face still, taking all that she offered and more, his kiss demanding and hungry.

Someone groaned—her or him?—and then his arms came around her and he held her hard against him. The feel of his body made her heart race, and Jenna felt her linen skirt slide to the floor, even though she hadn't actually felt him undo it. And suddenly she was acutely aware of him—of the strength of his hands, the roughness of his jeans against the softness of her skin, the hard ridge of his arousal—

'Jenna—I have to—' His hands were full of her, stripping off her skirt, peeling off underwear until she was naked and writhing against him. And her hands were on him, too, on his zip, which refused to co-operate until he covered her hands with his. This time instead of stopping her, he helped her.

Hearts pounding, mouths fused, they fell to the floor, feasting.

'The bed is a metre away—' Ryan had his mouth on her breast and pleasure stabbed hard, stealing her breath. 'We should probably—'

'No—too far.' Terrified he'd stop what he was doing, Jenna clutched at his hair, gasping as she felt his tongue graze her nipple. Sensation shot through her and he teased, nipped and sucked one rigid peak while using his fingers on the other. The burn inside her was almost intolerable. Her hips writhed against the soft rug and she arched in an instinctive attempt to get closer to him. But she wasn't in charge. He was. Maybe there was some pattern to what he was doing, some sequence, but for her it was all a blur of ecstasy.

The words in her head died as his hand slid between her legs.

It had been two years since a man had touched her intimately, and even before that it had never felt like this. Never before had she felt this restless, burning ache.

'Ryan—' The slow, leisurely stroke of his skilled fingers drove her wild. 'Now.'

'I haven't even started...' His voice was husky against her ear, and his fingers slid deeper. Heat flushed across her skin and her breathing grew shallow. Her hand slid down and circled him and she heard him catch his breath.

'On second thoughts—now seems like a good idea...' He slid his hand under her bottom and lifted her, the blunt head of his erection brushing against her thigh.

Trembling with expectation, Jenna curved one thigh over his back and then groaned when he hesitated. 'Please...'

'Forgot something—' His voice hoarse, he eased himself

away from her, reached forward and grabbed something from the cupboard by his bed. 'Damn!' He struggled with the packet while he kissed her again.

Jenna was panting against his mouth. 'Just—can you please—?'

'Yeah, I definitely can.' He hauled her under him, dropping his forehead to hers. 'Are you sure?'

'Is that a serious question?' She was breathless—desperate—conscious of the press of his body against hers. 'If you stop now, Ryan McKinley, I swear, I'll punch you.'

His laugh was low and sexy, and her stomach flipped as she stared into those blue, blue eyes. And then she ceased to notice anything because the roughness of his thigh brushed against hers and then he was against her and inside her and Jenna decided that if sex had ever felt like this before then she must have lost her memory.

Heat spread through her body and she tried to tell him how good it felt, but the sleek thrust of his body drove thought from her brain. He kissed her mouth, then her neck, ran his hand down her side and under her bottom—lifted her—

She moaned his name and he brought his lips back to hers, taking her mouth even as he took her body, and the pleasure was so intense that she could hardly breathe. Her nails sank into his back and the excitement inside her roared forward like a train with no brakes—

'Oh— I—' Her orgasm consumed her in a flash of brilliant light and exquisite sensation and she heard him growl deep in his throat, surging deeper inside her as she pulsed around him. She sobbed his name, tightened her grip and felt him thrust hard for the last time. They clung, breathless, riding the wave, going where the pleasure took them.

With a harsh groan Ryan dropped his head onto her shoulder, his breathing dragging in his throat. 'Are you OK?'

'No, I don't think so.' Weak and shaky, Jenna stared up at the ceiling, shell shocked, stunned by the intensity of what they'd shared. 'It's never been like that before.'

'That's probably because you've never made love on a wooden floor.' Wincing slightly, Ryan eased his weight off her and rolled onto his back, his arms still round her. 'I need to buy a different floor covering. This was designed for walking on and aesthetic appearance, not for sex. Do you want to move to the bed?'

'I don't want to move at all.' She just wanted to lie here, with him, staring up at the blue sky and the clouds above them. It seemed a fitting view. 'It's perfect here.'

'Perfect, apart from the bruises.'

'I don't have bruises, and even if I do I don't care.' She turned and rested her cheek on his chest, revelling in the opportunity to touch him. 'This morning I was wondering whether I ought to kiss you again—'

'And what did you decide?'

'You interrupted me before I'd made my decision.'

'If you want my opinion, I think you should definitely kiss me again.' His eyes gleamed with humour and he lifted her chin with his fingers and kissed her lightly. 'And again.'

Jenna shifted until she lay on top of him. 'I've never done this before.'

He raised an eyebrow. 'You have a child.'

'I mean I've never been so desperate to have sex I couldn't make it as far as the bed—never lost control like that.' She kissed the corner of his mouth, unable to resist touching him. 'I've never wanted anyone the way I want you. Ever since I arrived on the island I've wanted you. I thought I was going crazy—'

'I was going crazy, too.' He sank his hands into her hair and kissed her. 'Believe me, you're not the only one who has been exercising will-power.'

'I wasn't sure this was what you wanted.' She was conscious that she still knew next to nothing about him, and suddenly a stab of anxiety pierced her happiness. 'Can I ask you something?' Through the open window she could hear the crash of the waves and the shriek of the seagulls, reminding her how isolated they were.

'Yes.'

'Are you married?'

He stilled. 'You think I'd be lying here with you like this if I were married?'

'I don't know. I hope not.'

'And I hope you know me better than that.'

'Now I've made you angry.' Suddenly she wished she hadn't ruined the mood by asking the question. 'I'm sorry— I shouldn't have—' She broke off and then frowned, knowing that her question was a valid one. 'You have to understand that I thought I knew Clive, and it turned out I didn't.'

'Jenna, I'm not angry. You don't have to talk about this.'

'Yes, I do. You thought it was an unjust question, but to me it wasn't unjust and I need you to understand that.' Her voice was firm. 'I lived with a man for sixteen years and I thought I knew him. I married him and had his child, I slept in his bed—we made a life together. And it turned out he had a whole other life going on that didn't involve me. He had three affairs over the course of our marriage, one of them with a friend of mine. I didn't find out until the third.'

Ryan pulled her back down into the circle of his arms. 'You have a right to ask me anything you want to ask me. And I'm not married. Not any more.'

'Oh.' Digesting that, she relaxed against him, trailing her fingers over his chest, lingering on dark hair and hard muscle. 'So it went wrong for you, too?'

'Yes.'

She waited for him to say something more but he didn't, and she lay for a moment, listening to his heartbeat, her fingers on his chest.

Obviously that was why he'd come here, she thought to herself. Like her, he'd found comfort in doing something, found a channel for his anger. He'd built something new.

Ryan sighed. 'I'm sure there are questions you want to ask me.'

But he didn't want to answer them; she knew that.

'Yes, I have a question.' She shifted on top of him, feeling his instant response. 'How comfortable is that bed of yours?'

'Fruit, rolls, coffee—' Ryan started loading a tray. 'How hungry are you?'

'Not very. You put me off my food, remember?' Having pulled on her linen skirt and tee shirt, Jenna sat on a stool watching him.

'You just used up about ten thousand calories. You need to eat.' Ryan warmed rolls in the oven, sliced melon and made a pot of coffee. 'This should be lunch rather than breakfast, but never mind.'

'Lunch? But we—' Her gaze slid to the clock on the wall and her eyes widened. 'Two o'clock?'

'Like I said—ten thousand calories.' And ten thousand volts to his system. He couldn't believe he wanted her again so quickly, but he could happily have taken her straight back to bed.

Ryan grabbed butter and a jar of thick golden honey and

then handed her some plates and mugs. 'You can carry these. I'll bring the rest.'

She stood still, holding the plates and mugs, staring at him.

Removing the rolls from the oven, he glanced at her. 'What's wrong?'

'Nothing.' Her voice was husky, and he frowned as he tipped the warm bread into a basket.

'Honesty, Jenna, remember?'

'It feels strange,' she admitted, 'being here with you like this.'

'Strange in a good way or strange in a bad way?'

'In a scary way. I was with Clive for sixteen years and he was my only boyfriend.'

Thinking about it, he realised he'd probably known that all along, but hearing it was still a shock. 'Your only boyfriend?'

'I met him when I was sixteen. I had Lexi when I was eighteen.'

Ryan wondered whether her selfish ex-husband had taken advantage of her. 'Does that have anything to do with why you have a difficult relationship with your mother?'

'I've always disappointed her.'

He frowned. 'I can't imagine you disappointing anyone.' But he could imagine her trying to please everyone, and her next words confirmed it.

'My parents had plans for me—which didn't involve me getting pregnant as a teenager.' Her head dipped and she pulled a pair of sunglasses out of the bag on her lap. 'Are we eating outside? I'll probably need these. It's sunny.'

He remembered the conversation she'd had with her mother. How distressed she'd been. 'So what did they want you to do?'

'Something respectable. I had a place lined up at Cambridge University to read English—my parents liked to boast about that. They were bitterly upset when I gave it up.'

'Did you have to give it up?'

'I chose to. Everyone thought I'd be a terrible mother because I was a teenager, and it made me even more determined to be the best mother I could be. I don't see why teenagers can't be good mothers—I'm not saying it's easy, but parenthood is never easy, whatever age you do it.' Tiny frown lines appeared on her forehead. 'I hate the assumption that just because you're young, you're going to be a dreadful parent. I know plenty of bad parents who waited until their thirties to have children.'

Ryan wondered if she was referring to her own. 'For what it's worth, I think you're an amazing mother.'

'Thank you.' Her voice was husky as she cleaned her sunglasses with the edge of her tee shirt. 'I don't think I'm amazing, but I love Lexi for who she is, not what she does. And I've always let her know that.'

'Who she is, not what she does…' Ryan repeated her words quietly, thinking that his own parents could have taken a few lessons from Jenna. In his home, praise had always revolved around achievement.

Jenna fiddled with her glasses. 'My parents were always more interested in what I did than who I was, and I was determined not to be like that. Clive worked—I stayed at home. Traditional, I know, but it was the way I wanted it.'

'Can I ask you something personal? Did you marry him because you loved him or because you were pregnant?'

She hesitated. 'I thought I loved him.'

'And now you're not sure?'

'How can you love someone you don't even know?' Her

voice cracked slightly and Ryan crossed the kitchen and dragged her into his arms.

'The guy is clearly deranged.' Dropping a kiss on her hair, he eased her away from him. 'So now I understand why you asked me that question. You must find it impossible to trust another man.'

'No.' She said the word fiercely. 'Clive lied to me, but I know all men aren't like that—just as not all teenage mothers are inept and not all boys wearing hoodies are carrying knives. I won't generalise. I don't trust him, that's true, but I don't want Lexi growing up thinking the whole male race is bad. I won't do that to her.'

Her answer surprised him. He'd met plenty of people with trust issues.

He had a few of his own.

'You're a surprising person, Jenna Richards.' Young in many ways, and yet in others more mature than many people older than her.

'I'm an ordinary person.'

He thought about the way she loved her child, the way she was determined to be as good a mother as she could be. He thought about the fact that she'd been with the same man since she was sixteen. 'There's nothing ordinary about you. I'm intrigued about something, though.' He stroked her hair away from her face, loving the feel of it. 'If you were at home with Lexi, when did you train as a nurse?'

'Once Lexi started school. I had a network of friends—many of them working mothers. We helped each other out. Sisterhood. They'd take Lexi for me when I was working, I'd take their children on my days off. Sometimes I had a house full of kids.'

He could imagine her with children everywhere. 'Can I ask

you something else? Why didn't you ever have more children? You obviously love them.'

'Clive didn't want more. He decided Lexi was enough.'

'Like he decided that you weren't going to have a dog or eat fish?'

She gave a shaky smile. 'Are you suggesting my final act of rebellion should be to have a baby? I think that might be taking it a bit far. And anyway, I couldn't do that now.'

'Why not?'

'Well, for a start, I'm too old.'

'You're thirty-three. Plenty of women don't have their first child until that age.'

She looked at him, and he knew she was wondering why he was dwelling on the subject. 'And then there's Lexi. If I had a baby now, it would be difficult for her.'

'Why?'

'Because there have been enough changes in her life. I suspect that at some point, probably soon, her father is going to have another child. I don't want to add to the confusion. I want her relationship with me to be as stable as possible. Why are you asking?'

Why *was* he asking? Unsettled by his own thoughts, Ryan turned his attention back to his breakfast. 'I'm just saying you're not too old to have a child.' He kept his voice even. 'Put your sunglasses on. You're right about it being sunny outside.'

CHAPTER EIGHT

IT WAS an affair full of snatched moments and secret assignations, all tinged with the bittersweet knowledge that it couldn't possibly last.

At times Jenna felt guilty that she was keeping her relationship with Ryan from Lexi, but her daughter was finally settled and happy and she was afraid to do or say anything that might change that.

She just couldn't give Ryan up.

They'd meet at the lighthouse at lunchtime, make love until they were both exhausted, and then part company and arrive back at the surgery at different times.

And, despite the subterfuge, she'd never been happier in her life.

'I actually feel grateful to Clive,' she murmured one afternoon as they lay on his cliffs, staring at the sea. Her hand was wrapped in his and she felt his warm fingers tighten. 'If he hadn't done what he did, I wouldn't be here now. I wouldn't have known it was possible to feel like this. It's scary, isn't it? You're in a relationship, and you have nothing to compare it to, so you say to yourself this is it. This is how it's supposed to feel. But you always have a sense that something is missing.'

'Did you?'

'Yes, but I assumed it was something in me that was lacking, not in my relationship.'

'Life has a funny way of working itself out.' He turned his head to look at her. 'Have you told Lexi about us yet?'

A grey cloud rolled over her happiness. 'No,' she said. 'Not yet.'

'Are you going to tell her?'

'I don't know.'

'You're afraid of her reaction?'

'Yes. She was devastated when Clive left. Horrified that he was involved with another woman. Apart from the obvious issues, teenagers don't like to see their parents as living, breathing sexual beings.'

And she didn't know what to say. *I've taken a lover…*

What exactly was their relationship? What could there be?

Ryan rolled onto his side and propped himself up on his elbow so that he could see her. 'I want to be with you, Jenna. I want more than lunchtimes and the occasional Sunday afternoon when Lexi is with her friends. I want more.'

Looking into his blue eyes, she felt her heart spin and dance. 'How much more?'

'I love you.' Ryan touched her face gently, as if making a discovery. 'I've loved you since you stepped off that boat looking like someone who had walked away from an accident.'

'You love me?' Jenna was jolted by a burst of happiness and he smiled.

He looked more relaxed than she'd ever seen him. 'Is that a surprise?'

'I didn't dare hope. I thought it might be just—' She was whispering, afraid that she might disturb the dream. 'I love you, too. I've never felt this way about anyone before. I didn't know it was possible.'

'Neither did I.' He kissed her gently, stroked her hair protectively with a hand that wasn't quite steady. Then he gave a shake of his head. 'You've never asked me about my marriage or why I ended up here. I'm sure there are things you want to know about me.'

'I assumed that if there was anything you wanted me to know, you'd tell me when you were ready.'

'You're a very unusual woman, do you know that? You're able to love me, not knowing what went before?'

'It's not relevant to how I feel about you.'

He breathed in deeply, his eyes never shifting from hers. 'I was married—to Connie. She was a very ambitious woman. Connie was born knowing what she wanted in life and nothing was going to stand in her way. We met when we were medical students. We were together briefly, and then met up again when we were both consultants in the same hospital. Looking back on it, we were a disaster waiting to happen, but at the time I suppose it must have seemed right.'

Thinking of her own situation, Jenna nodded. 'That happens.'

His laugh was tight and humourless. 'I think the truth is I was too busy for a relationship and Connie understood that. I was fighting my way to the top and I didn't need a woman asking me what time I'd be home at night. Connie didn't care what time I came home because she was never there to see. She was fighting *her* way to the top, too.'

Jenna sat quietly, letting him speak. She had an image in her head. An image of a beautiful, successful woman. The sort of woman she'd always imagined a man like him would choose. The cream of the crop. Bright and brilliant, like him. They would have been a golden couple. 'Was she beautiful?'

'No.' His hand dropped from her face and he sat up. Stared out across the sea. 'Physically I suppose she would be considered beautiful,' he conceded finally. 'But to me beauty is so much more than sleek hair and well-arranged features. Connie was cold. Selfish. Beauty is who you are and the way you behave. We were both very wrapped up in our careers. We worked all day, wrote research papers in what little spare time we had—our house had two offices.' He frowned and shook his head. 'How could I ever have thought that what we had was a marriage?'

'Go on…'

'I wanted us to start a family.'

'Oh.' It hadn't occurred to her that he might have a child. That was one question she hadn't asked. 'You have—?'

'I brought the subject up one night, about a week after I'd made Consultant. I thought it would be the perfect time.'

'She didn't agree?'

He stared blindly across the ocean and into the far distance. 'She told me she'd been sterilised.'

Jenna sat up. 'She— Oh, my gosh—and you didn't know?' She licked her lips, digesting the enormity of it.

'At medical school she decided she didn't ever want to have a baby. She wanted a career and didn't want children. In her usual ruthlessly efficient way she decided to deal with the problem once and for all. Unfortunately she didn't share that fact with me.' The confession was rough and hoarse, and she knew for sure he hadn't spoken the words to anyone else. Just her. The knowledge that he'd trusted her with something so personal was like a gift, fragile and precious, and Jenna tried to understand how he must be feeling, unwilling to break the connection between them by saying something that might make him regret his show of trust.

In the end she just said what was in her heart. 'That was wrong. Very wrong.'

'Some of the blame was mine. I made assumptions— didn't ask—I suppose I could be accused of being chauvinistic. I presumed we'd do the traditional thing at some point. It came as a shock to discover she had no intention of ever having a family.'

Jenna reached out a hand and touched his shoulder. 'She should have told you.'

'That was my feeling. I suddenly realised I'd been living with a stranger. That I didn't know her at all.' He gave a wry smile. 'But you know how that feels, don't you?'

'Only too well. I was living in this imaginary world— thinking things were fine. But Clive was living a completely different life. A life I didn't even see.' She looped her arms around her legs and rested her chin on her knees. 'I suppose part of the problem was that we just didn't communicate. We fell into marriage because I was pregnant and because it was what my parents expected. I made assumptions about him. He made assumptions about me.' Jenna turned her head and looked at him. 'So you told Connie you wanted a divorce?'

'Yes. I discovered that although I'd achieved what could be considered huge success in my professional life, my personal life was a disaster. I hadn't even thought about what I wanted, and suddenly I realised that what I wanted was the thing I didn't have—someone alongside me who loved me, who wanted to share their life with me. I wanted to come home at night to someone who cared about what sort of day I'd had. I didn't want our only communication to be via voicemail. And I wanted children. Connie thought I was being ridiculous—her exact words were, "It's not as if you're ever going to change a nappy, Ryan, and I'm certainly not doing it, so why would we want children?"'

'She didn't want a divorce?'

'I was flying high in my career and she liked that. I looked good on her CV.' There was a bitter note to his voice and his eyes were flint-hard. 'Being with me opened doors for her.'

'Did she love you?'

'I have no idea. If she did then it was a very selfish kind of a love. She wanted me for what I added to her, if that makes sense.'

'Yes, it makes sense. I don't know much about relationships…' Jenna thought about her own relationship with Clive '…but I do know that real love is about giving. It's about wanting someone else's happiness more than your own. If you care about someone, you want what's right for them.'

And that was the way she felt about Ryan, she realised. She wanted him to be happy.

Ryan put his arm around her shoulders and drew her against him. 'That's what you do with Lexi, all the time. You're lucky to have her. Lucky to have that bond.'

'Yes.' She melted as he kissed her, knowing that everything was changing. Once again life had taken her in a direction she hadn't anticipated, but this time the future wasn't terrifying. It was exciting. 'I'm going to talk to her. I've decided. I think maybe she's old enough to understand.' Strengthened by her feelings and his, she suddenly felt it was the right thing to do.

'You're going to talk to her about us?'

'Yes. This is what life is, isn't it? It's the happy and the sad and the unpredictable. It would be wrong to pretend anything different. Lexi needs to know that life is sometimes hard and that things can't always stay the same. She needs to know that change isn't always bad and that the unfamiliar can become familiar. And she needs to know that my love for her will never change, no matter what happens to the way we live.'

Ryan stroked his fingers over her cheek. 'You're the most selfless person I've ever met. When your husband walked out, who supported you? Not your mother, I assume. Your friends?'

'For a while. Then I discovered that they'd all known he was having the affair and that they'd known about his other affairs and hadn't told me.' Jenna pulled away from him. 'I found that hard. That and all the advice. "Turn a blind eye." "Dress like a pole dancer and seduce him back—"'

There was amusement in his eyes. 'Did you adopt that suggestion?'

'Of course—I went around wearing nothing but fishnets and a basque.' Pleased that she was able to make a joke about something she'd never thought would seem funny, she wound a strand of hair around her finger. 'To be honest, I didn't want him back. Not after I found out that he'd had a string of affairs throughout our marriage. But the worst thing of all was the way he behaved towards Lexi—it was as if he suddenly just washed his hands of her. His own daughter!' Humour faded and anger flooded through her, fresh as it had been on that first day. 'Whatever he felt about me, that was no excuse for cutting Lexi out of his life.'

'Forget him now.' His voice was rough as he pulled her back to him. 'He was your past. I'm your future.'

Jenna stared at him, silenced by the possibilities that extended in front of her. She wanted to ask what he meant. She wanted to ask whether the future meant a few weeks, or more than that, but she was terrified of voicing the question in case the answer was something she didn't want to hear.

He was watching her, absorbing her reaction. 'Jenna, I know this is soon, but—' There was a buzzing sound from his pocket, and Ryan swore fluently and dragged out his phone. 'Maybe there are some advantages to living in a city—at least someone else can carry the load when you want some time off.' He checked the number and frowned. 'It's Logan. I'd better take this—sorry.'

As he talked to the other doctor, Jenna gently extracted herself from his grip, wondering what he'd been about to say. It was obvious that she wasn't going to find out quickly, because Ryan was digging in his pocket for his car keys as he talked, the expression on his face enough for her to know that the phone call was serious.

He sprang to his feet. 'I'll get up there now.' His eyes flickered to hers. 'And I'll take Jenna with me—no, don't worry, we'll handle it together.'

Realising that she was supposed to help him with something, Jenna stood up and brushed the grass off her skirt.

Ryan was already striding towards the path that led up to his car. 'Have you done any emergency work?'

'Sorry?' Jenna jammed her feet into her shoes and sprinted after him, wondering how the tone of the afternoon could have shifted so quickly.

Glenmore, she thought, and its ever-changing moods.

Even the weather had changed. While they'd been talking the blue sky had turned an ominous grey and the sea a gunmetal-blue.

There was a storm coming.

'Did you ever work in an emergency department?' His mouth grim, Ryan was in the car and firing up the engine before she had time to answer the question.

'Yes. But it was quite a few years ago. What do you need

me to do?' Her head smacked lightly against the headrest as he accelerated along the empty road, and Jenna felt the power of the car come to life around her. She felt a shimmer of nerves mingled with anticipation. What if she wasn't up to the job?

To give herself confidence she cast a glance at Ryan, looking at his broad shoulders and strong, capable hands. He shifted gears like a racing driver, pushing the car to its limits as he negotiated the tight turns and narrow roads that led from the lighthouse. Even after a comparatively short time she knew he would be able to handle anything he encountered, and that knowledge gave her courage. 'Tell me what's happened.'

'Group of teenagers tombstoning on the Devil's Jaws. It's close to here.'

'Tombstoning?' Jenna rummaged in her pocket and found something to tie back her hair. 'What's that?'

'It's when they stand on the top of a cliff and jump into the sea.' Ryan slowed to take a sharp bend. 'The problem is the depth of the water changes according to the tide. Even when the tide is on your side it's a dangerous activity. And the Devil's Jaws is the most dangerous place you could wish for. It's narrow there—the cliffs have formed a tight channel, so not only can you kill yourself when you hit the bottom, if you get really lucky you can kill yourself on the way down.'

'Kids are doing that? Can't they fence the cliffs off or something?'

'It *is* fenced off. The place is lethal. No one is meant to go within a hundred metres of it, but you know teenagers.' He swung the car into a space at the side of the road and killed the engine. 'We have to walk from here. Are you afraid of heights?'

'I don't know. I don't think so.'

'Watch your footing. To add to the fun, the rocks are crumbling.' Ryan opened his boot and Jenna blinked as she saw the contents.

'You carry ropes in your boot?'

'I climb sometimes.' Without elaborating, he selected several ropes and started piling equipment into a large rucksack. Then he opened his medical bag and added another series of items, including drugs he thought he was going to need. His movements were swift and economical, brutally efficient.

Jenna focused on the drugs. 'Ketamine?'

'I prefer it to morphine. It doesn't produce respiratory depression or hypotension, and in analgesic doses it produces a mild bronchodilator effect.'

'Translate that into English?' A voice came from behind them and Jenna turned to see Nick Hillier, the island policeman. Only today he wasn't smiling.

'It means it controls the pain without affecting the breathing.' Ryan hoisted the bag out of the boot. 'Is it as bad as they say?'

'Worse. Two in the water—one trapped halfway down the cliff. They're right in the Jaws.'

'Of course they are—that's where they get the maximum adrenaline rush.'

'The one stuck on the cliff might be all right, as long as he doesn't let go, but he's getting tired. Coastguard helicopter has chosen today to have a technical problem—they're fixing it, but the cavalry isn't going to be arriving any time soon.' Nick sucked in a breath. 'I don't want anyone going near the edge. I don't want more casualties. We're going to wait and hope to hell they get that helicopter airborne in the next ten minutes. I think this is a rescue best carried out from the air or the sea.'

'I'll take a look at it. Then I'll decide.' Ryan lifted the rucksack onto his back and walked over the grass towards a gate. A sign warned the public that the area was dangerous. Dropping his rucksack onto the other side, Ryan vaulted the gate. Nick climbed over slightly more awkwardly, holding out a hand to Jenna.

She wondered who was going to have the last say on this one. The law or the doctor.

His mind clearly working in the same direction, Nick became visibly stressed. 'Ryan, you know how risky it is. A climber was killed abseiling from here earlier in the summer—the rocks sawed through his rope.'

'Then he didn't have his rope in the right place.' Ryan dropped his rucksack again, onto the grass a safe distance from the edge. 'There are injured kids, Nick. What do you expect me to do? Leave them?'

'My job is to make sure we rescue them with minimum further casualties—that doesn't involve you abseiling down a sheer, crumbling rock face.'

Listening to them, Jenna felt her heart race, and she wondered if she was going to be any use at all.

Yes, she'd worked in an emergency department for a short time, but working in a well-equipped department was quite different from giving pre-hospital care on a sheer cliff face.

She was so busy worrying about her own abilities that it was a few seconds before she noticed the teenager sitting on the grass. He was shivering and his face was white.

Focusing on his face, Jenna recognised Fraser and her stomach dropped. Suddenly everything seemed to happen in slow motion. She was aware of the guilt in Fraser's anguished glance, and of Ryan turning his head to look at her.

And those looks meant only one thing—

That it was Lexi who was lying in the grip of the Devil's Jaws.

Maternal instinct overwhelming everything else, Jenna gave a low moan of denial and stepped towards the edge, unthinking.

Ryan caught her arm in an iron grip.

'Don't take another step.' His hand was a steadying force and his voice was hard, forcing itself through the blind panic that clouded her thinking. 'Breathe. Up here, you don't run. You take small steps. You look where you're going and you make sure it's safe underfoot. I'll get her. I swear to you I'll get her. But I can't do it if I'm worrying about you going over the edge.'

Jenna stood still, held firm by the strength of his hand and the conviction in his voice.

Fraser struggled to his feet, his lips dry and cracked from the wind and the sun. 'You don't understand—she didn't jump. Lexi was trying to stop Matt doing it—we both were. But he did it anyway—he jumped at the wrong moment. You have to get it exactly right or you hit the rocks.' His voice shook. He was a teenager on the cusp of manhood, but today he was definitely more boy than man. 'Lexi went down there to save Matt. We could see him slipping under the water. He was going to drown. Jamie tried first, but he lost his nerve halfway down and now he can't move. I dunno—he just freaked out or something. So Lexi did it. She insisted. She was dead scared about getting down there, but she said she'd done first aid so she should be the one.'

'She climbed down?' There was a strange note in Ryan's voice and already he had his hands in his rucksack. 'Fraser, take this rope for me.'

'You should have seen her—she was amazing. Just went down slowly, hand and foot, hand and foot, muttering "Three points of contact on the rock face…" or something.'

'She did a climbing course last summer,' Jenna said faintly.

Last summer—just before everything had fallen apart. 'It was indoors on a climbing wall in London.'

Nowhere near greasy, slippery rocks or furious boiling sea.

Ryan's gaze met hers for a moment. 'I'd say that was money well spent.'

Fraser was sweating. 'I almost had a heart attack watching her. I'm not good with heights since I fell into that dungeon.' He looked at Jenna, shrinking. 'I'm really sorry. I tried to stop her…'

'It isn't your fault, Fraser.' Jenna's lips were stiff and her heart was pounding. 'Lexi is not your responsibility. She's old enough to make her own decisions.'

'She's as sure-footed as a goat.' There was awe in Fraser's voice. 'Matt was face-down in the water and she dragged him towards the rocks. She's been holding him, but he's too heavy for her to get him out by herself and the tide is coming in. The water level is rising. The ledge they're on will be under-water soon.'

That news made Jenna's knees weaken with panic, but Ryan was icy calm. When he spoke there was no doubt in anyone's mind who was in charge of the rescue.

'Fraser, I want you to stay here and act as runner. Is your mobile working?'

'Yes, the signal is good.'

'Keep it switched on. Dr McNeil is bringing equipment from the surgery. If the helicopter is delayed, then that will change the way we manage Matt's injuries.' Ryan stepped into a harness and adjusted it with hands that were steady and confident. 'Keep the phone line clear—if I need to talk to you, I'll call.'

Nick stepped forward and caught his arm. 'Ryan, for goodness' sake, man, I'm telling you we should wait for the helicopter.'

Jenna couldn't breathe. If Ryan agreed to wait for the helicopter then Lexi might drown. But if Ryan went down there—if he put himself at risk for her daughter and the two boys…

'You're wasting time, Nick.' His eyes flickered to hers and for a brief moment the connection was there. 'It will be all right. Trust me.'

And she did. Although why she should be so ready to trust a man she'd known for weeks when a man she'd known for years had let her down, she didn't understand. But life wasn't always easy to understand, was it? Some things happened without an explanation.

'What can I do?' Her mouth was so dry she could hardly form the words. 'How can I help?'

'You can stay there, away from the edge.'

Nick caught his arm. 'Ryan—'

'I'm going to abseil down, and I want you to lower the rest of my pack.' He adjusted his harness for a final time and held out his hand. 'Do you have a radio for me?'

Nick gave up arguing, but his face was white and his eyes flickered between the rising tide and the sky, obviously looking for a helicopter. Hoping.

Jenna felt helpless. 'I want to do something. If the boy is badly injured you'll need help. I can abseil down, too—'

Ryan didn't spare her a glance. 'You'll stay here.'

'It's my daughter down there.'

'That's why you're staying up here. You'll be too busy worrying about her to be any use to me.'

'Don't patronise me.' Anger spurting through her veins, Jenna picked up a harness. 'You need me down there, Ryan. Two of them are in the water, one of them injured, and one of them is stuck on the rock face. He could fall at any moment. You can't do this by yourself, and Lexi is just a child.'

Ryan paused. Then he looked over his shoulder, down at the jagged rocks. 'All right. This is what we'll do. I'll go down there first and do an assessment. If I need you, Nick can get you down to me. But watch my route. Have you abseiled before?'

Jenna swallowed, wishing she could tell him she'd scaled Everest four times without oxygen. 'Once. On an adventure camp when I was fifteen.'

'I love the fact that you're so honest. Don't worry—Nick can get you down there if I need you. Hopefully I won't.'

He went over the edge like someone from an action movie and Jenna blinked. Clearly there was plenty she still had to learn about Ryan, and the more she knew, the more she liked and admired him.

'I should have stopped him,' Nick muttered, and Jenna lifted an eyebrow because the idea of stopping Ryan doing something he was determined to do seemed laughable to her.

'How?'

The policeman gave a short laugh. 'Good question. Still, what Ryan doesn't know about ropes and climbing isn't worth knowing. I'm going to get this on you Jenna.' He had a harness in his hands. 'Just in case. I have a feeling he's going to need you. I can't believe I'm doing this.'

'If he's going to need me, why didn't he just say so?'

'Honestly? I'm guessing he's being protective. Either that or he doesn't want any of us to know how easy it is.' With a weak grin, Nick adjusted the harness and glanced at her face. Jenna wondered if he knew that there was something going on between them or whether he was matchmaking like the others.

Ryan's voice crackled over the radio. 'Nick, do you read me? I need you to lower that rope to me, over.'

'What he really needs is a miracle,' Nick muttered, lowering one end of a rope down to Ryan and securing the other end to a rock. 'That should keep the boy steady while Ryan finds out what's going on. I hope he does it quickly. There's a storm coming. Great timing. Can today get any worse?'

Only an hour earlier she'd been lying on the grass on Ryan's cliffs, bathed in sunshine and happiness.

Eyeing the rolling black clouds, Jenna approached the edge cautiously. Peering over the side, she caught her breath. Here, the cliff face was vertical. The rocks plunged downwards, the edges ragged and sharp as sharks' teeth, ready to razor through the flesh of the unwary. Her stomach lurched, and the sheer terror of facing that drop almost swallowed her whole.

'I can't believe they thought they could jump down there,' she said faintly, biting her lip as she saw Ryan attaching the rope to a boy clinging halfway down. Then her gaze drifted lower and she saw Lexi's small figure, crouched on an exposed rock at the bottom. The girl had her arms around a boy's shoulders, holding him out of the water, straining with the effort as the sea boiled and foamed angrily around them, the level of the water rising with each incoming wave.

Watching the waves lick hungrily at her daughter, Jenna felt physically sick. 'That boy is going to be under the water in another few minutes. Lexi isn't strong enough to pull him out. And she isn't going to be strong enough to keep herself out.' Feeling completely helpless, she turned to Nick. 'Get me down there now. Don't wait for Ryan to talk to you. He has his hands full. I can help—I know I can.'

'I'm not risking another person unless I have to. It's bad enough Ryan going down there, but at least he knows what he's doing. You have no cliff rescue skills—'

'I'm her mother,' Jenna said icily. 'That counts for a great deal, believe me. Get me down there, Nick.'

He slid his fingers into the collar of his jacket, easing the pressure. 'If someone has to go it should probably be me.'

'You need to stay up here to co-ordinate with the coast-guard. I don't know anything about that—I wouldn't have a clue.' Jenna glanced down again and saw that Ryan had secured the boy and was now abseiling to the bottom of the cliff. He landed on shiny deadly rock just as another enormous wave rushed in and swamped both teenagers.

Instantly Ryan's voice crackled over the radio. 'Get Jenna down here, Nick. It's an easy abseil—'

Easy? Torn between relief and raw terror, Jenna switched off her brain. To think was to panic, and she couldn't afford to panic. Her daughter had climbed down there, she reminded herself as she leaned backwards and did as Nick instructed. All the same, there was a moment when her courage failed her and she thought she was going to freeze on the black forbidding rock.

'Just take it steady, Jen.' Ryan's voice came from below her, solid and secure. 'You're nearly there.'

To stop would be to disappoint him as well as risk lives, so Jenna kept going, thinking to herself that if he genuinely thought this was easy she wouldn't want to do a difficult abseil. The cliff fell away sharply and she went down slowly, listening to Ryan's voice from below her, thinking of Lexi and not of the drop, or of the man who had died when his rope was severed. As her feet finally touched the rocks strong hands caught her. Ryan's hands.

He unclipped the rope and the sea immediately swamped her feet. If he hadn't clamped an arm around her waist she would have stumbled under the sudden pressure of the water. As it was, the cold made her gasp. Above her the cliff face towered, blocking out the last of the sunshine, revealing only ominous clouds in the chink of sky above. Here, in the slit of the rock, it was freezing.

She guessed that if the helicopter didn't manage to get to them soon, then it would be too late. The weather would close in and make flying impossible.

And then what?

'The tide is coming in—Ryan, I can't hold his head any longer—' Lexi's voice came from behind them and Jenna turned, her stomach lurching as she saw the blood on her daughter's tee shirt.

'It's not mine.' Lexi read her mind and gave a quick shake of her head. 'It's Matt's. His legs—both of them, I think. He jumped in and hit rock under the surface. I didn't know what to do—he's too heavy. Mummy, do something!'

Mummy. She hadn't heard 'Mummy' since Lexi was about six, and it sent strength pouring back through her rubbery legs.

'Just hold on, Lexi.' Her voice was firm and confident, and Ryan gave her a brief smile and released her, checking that she was steady on her feet before crossing the rocks to the two teenagers.

'You're a total star, Lexi. I just need you to hold on for another minute. Can you do that?' He ripped equipment out of the rucksack as he spoke, and Jenna saw Lexi swallow as she stared up at him.

'Yes.'

'Good. We're going to get him out of the water now, and you're going to help.' Ryan had a rope in his hand. 'Just do everything I say.'

Jenna saw the fierce light of determination in her daughter's eyes—saw the faith and trust in her expression as she looked at Ryan.

Gone was the child who moaned when she couldn't get a mobile phone signal.

Jenna's flash of pride lasted only seconds as she saw another huge wave bearing down on them.

She saw Ryan glance at Lexi and then back towards her, trying to make a decision.

Jenna made the decision for him. 'Hold onto the children!' She slithered towards the rock face and managed to get a grip just as the wave rose in height and started to break. With a ferocious roar it crashed onto the rocks with an explosion of white froth, as if determined to claim its prize. Jenna clung, feeling the water pull at her and then retreat.

Wiping salt water from her face, she looked over her shoulder and saw that Ryan had his hands on Lexi's shoulders, holding her. As soon as the wave receded he turned his attention to Matt. The boy was moaning softly, his body half in and half out of the water.

'My legs—I can't put any weight—'

'Yeah—we're going to help you with that.' Ryan glanced around him, judging, coming up with a plan. 'If we can get him clear of the water and onto that rock higher up, that should give us at least another ten minutes before the tide hits us again. Enough time to check the damage and give him some pain relief.' He spoke into the radio, telling Nick what he was doing and listing the equipment he needed. 'While they're sorting that out, I'm going to get a rope on you, Matt.'

'Just leave me.' His face white with pain, the boy choked the words out. 'I don't want anyone to drown because of me.'

'No one is drowning today.' Ryan looped the rope under the boy's shoulders and secured it to a shaft of rock that jutted out of the cliff. Then he did the same to Lexi. 'The rope is going to hold both of you if another wave comes before we're done. We're going to get you out of the water, Matt. Then I'm going to give you something for the pain.' He questioned the boy about the way he'd landed, about his neck, about the movement in his limbs.

Jenna wondered why he didn't give the boy painkillers first, but then she saw another wave rushing down on them and realised that the boy was only minutes from drowning. Rope or no rope, if Ryan couldn't lift him clear of the water the boy was dead.

As the wave swamped all four of them Jenna held her breath and gripped the rock tightly. The tide was coming in. They didn't have much time.

'What can I do?'

'Do you see that narrow ledge just under the waterline? Stand on it. I need you to hold his body steady so that we move him as little as possible.' As a precaution, Ryan put a supportive collar around Matt's neck.

Jenna stepped into the water, gritting her teeth as the ice-cold sea turned her legs numb. If she felt this cold, how must the children be feeling? She steadied Matt's body, her hands firm. 'I'm ready.'

'I'm going to lift—try not to let his legs drag against the rocks.'

Using nothing but brute strength and hard muscle, Ryan hauled the boy out of the water. Matt's screams echoed around the narrow chasm, bouncing off the rocks and adding to the deadly feel of the place.

Her heart breaking for him, Jenna gritted her teeth, wanting to stop but knowing they couldn't. They had to get him clear of the water. He'd already been in there too long. Even as Ryan lifted him she saw the terrible gashes on the boy's legs and knew they were dealing with serious injuries. Blood mixed with the water, and as they laid him flat on the rock Matt was white-faced, his lips bloodless.

'Shaft of femur—both legs.' Now that he could see the damage, Ryan worked swiftly, checking for other injuries and then examining the wound. 'Jenna, we need to control the bleeding on his left leg and cover that wound. Get me pads and a broad bandage out of the rucksack. I'm going to give him some Ketamine. Matt, this will help with the pain.'

Matt groaned. 'I'm going to die. I know I am—'

'You're not going to die.' Seeing Lexi's horrified look, Jenna spoke firmly, and Ryan gave the boy's shoulder a quick squeeze.

'No one is dying on my shift,' he said easily, and Matt made a sound that was halfway between a sob and a moan.

'If the pain doesn't kill me, my mum will.'

Jenna closed her hand over his, checking that Lexi was safely out of the water. 'Your mum won't kill you,' she said huskily. 'She's just going to be relieved you're OK.'

Ryan's gaze flickered to hers and she read his mind.

Matt was far from OK. He had two fractured femurs and he was still losing blood. Knowing that she had to help, Jenna let go of the boy's hand and dug into the rucksack, finding what she needed. Thinking clearly now, she ripped open the sterile dressings and talked to her daughter. 'Lexi? Do you have your digital camera with you?'

'What?' Soaked through and shivering, Lexi stared at her mother as though she were mad. 'Matt's bleeding half to death here and you want me to take a photo of the view?'

'He's not bleeding to death.' Taking her cue from Ryan, Jenna kept her voice calm. 'I don't want you to take the view. I want you to take a picture of Matt's legs. It will help the ER staff.'

'Good thinking.' Ryan injected the Ketamine. '*Do* you have your camera, Lex?'

'Yes—yes. But…' Baffled, Lexi cast a glance at Matt and rose to her feet, holding the rocks so that she didn't slip. She was wearing jeans, and the denim was dark with seawater. 'In my jacket pocket. What do you want me to do?'

'Take several pictures of the wounds. I'll do it, if you like.' Jenna was worried about her daughter seeing the extent of the injuries, but Lexi just gritted her teeth and pointed her digital camera. She took several photos and checked them quickly.

'OK. It's done.'

'Good.' Now that the pictures were taken, Jenna covered the wounds. 'It saves the receiving team in the hospital from removing the dressings from his legs to see what's going on.'

'Oh. I get it.' Several shades paler than she'd been a moment earlier, Lexi nodded. 'What else can I do?'

'Stay out of reach of the waves,' Ryan said immediately, his hands on Jenna's as they packed the wound, using a bandage to hold it in place. 'Any change—tell me. Jen, I'm going to splint both legs together.'

They worked as a team, Jenna following his instructions to the letter. It didn't matter that she'd never done anything like this before because his commands were clear and precise. Do this. Do that. Put your hands here—

Later, she'd look back on it and wonder how he could have been so sure about everything, but for now she just did as she was told.

Checking the pulse in both Matt's feet, she nodded to Ryan. 'His circulation is good in both legs.'

'Right. Lex, take this for me.' Ryan passed his radio to Lexi, freeing up his hands. Then he turned back to the boy. 'Matt, you've broken both your legs. I'm going to put a splint on them because that will reduce the bleeding and it will help the pain.' He looked towards Lexi. 'Logan should be up there by now. Make contact and tell Nick I need a towel.'

A towel? Glancing at the water around them, Jenna wondered if he'd gone mad, and then reminded himself that everything he'd done so far had been spot-on.

Worried that all this was too much for Lexi, Jenna was about to repeat the instructions but Lexi was already working the radio. Doing everything she'd been asked to do, she talked to Nick and relayed messages back and forth, copying the radio style she'd heard Ryan use.

'Dr McNeil is there. He wants to know what you need.'

'I'll have a Sager splint, if he has one, otherwise any traction splint, And oxygen. And ask Nick if we have an ETA on the helicopter.'

'Sager?' Jenna handed him a Venflon and Ryan slid the cannula into the vein in Matt's arm as smoothly as if he was working in a state-of-the-art emergency unit, not a chasm in the rocks.

'It's an American splint. I prefer it.'

'They're lowering it down now. I'll get it.' One eye on the waves, Lexi picked her way across the slippery rocks like a tightrope walker and reached for the rucksack that had been lowered on the end of a rope.

Watching the boiling cauldron of water lapping angrily at her daughter's ankles, Jenna prayed that she wouldn't slip. Pride swelled inside her and she blinked rapidly, forcing herself to concentrate on her part of the rescue. 'Is it possible to apply a splint in these conditions with just the two of us?'

'I can do it in two and a half minutes, and it will make it easier to evacuate him by helicopter.' Ryan took the rucksack Lexi handed him and opened it. Using the towel, he dried

Matt's legs and then opened the bag containing the splint. In a few swift movements he'd removed, unfolded and assembled the splint. 'OK, that's ready.' He positioned it between Matt's legs, explaining what he was doing.

Hearing the sound of a helicopter overhead, Jenna looked up, relief providing a much-needed flood of warmth through her body. 'Oh, thank goodness—they're here.'

Ryan didn't look up. 'They can take Jamie off first. By the time they have him in the helicopter Matt will be ready.' He wrapped the harness around the boy's ankles. 'Lexi, tell Nick.' He was treating the girl like an adult, showing no doubt in her ability to perform the tasks he set.

Without faltering Lexi spoke into the radio again, obviously proud to have something useful to do.

Jenna helped Ryan with the splint. 'How much traction do you apply?'

'Generally ten per cent of the patient's body weight per fractured femur.' Eyeing Matt's frame, Ryan checked the amount of traction on the scale. 'I'm making an educated guess.'

The noise of the helicopter increased, and Jenna watched in awe as the winchman was lowered into the narrow gap between the cliffs. In no time he had a harness on Jamie and was lifting him towards the helicopter.

'At least there's no wind.' Ryan secured straps around Matt's thighs until both legs were well supported.

Staggered by the speed with which he'd applied the splint, Jenna took Matt's hand. 'How are you doing?'

'It feels a bit better,' Matt muttered, 'but I'm not looking forward to going up in that helicopter.'

'You're going to be fine. They're experts.' Ryan watched as the winchman was lowered again, this time with a stretcher. 'We're going to get you on board, Matt, and then I'll give you oxygen and fluid on our way to hospital. Once we're on dry land, we can make you comfortable.'

Jenna looked at him, his words sinking home.

Ryan was leaving them.

She gave herself a mental shake. Of course he had to go with the casualty. What else? But she couldn't stop the shiver, and her palms dug a little harder into the grey slippery rock as she kept hold.

Ryan helped the winchman transfer Matt onto the stretcher. They had a conversation about the injury, the loss of blood— Jenna knew they were deciding whether it was best to have a doctor on board. The winchman was a paramedic, but still—

She watched as Matt was lifted slowly out of the narrow gap between the rocks, the winchman steadying the stretcher.

Once he was safely inside the helicopter, Ryan turned to Jenna.

Seeing the indecision on his face, she didn't hesitate.

'You should go! He might need you. You have to leave us here while you get him to hospital.'

Ryan's face was damp with seawater, his hair soaked, his jaw tense. 'I can't see any other way.' Already the winchman was being lowered for the final time.

Jenna lifted her chin. 'You're wasting time. We'll be fine, Ryan. We'll climb a little higher and the helicopter will be back for us soon. They're ready for you.' She watched, dry-mouthed, as the winchman landed on the rocks. 'Go.' To make it easier for both of them, she turned away and picked her way over the rocks to Lexi.

The girl was shivering, although whether it was from the cold or shock, Jenna didn't know.

She was shivering, too.

'They'll be back for us ever so quickly. You did so well,

Lexi. I was so proud of you.' She wrapped her arms around her daughter and rubbed the girl's back, trying to stop the shivering. 'Oh, you're soaked through, you poor thing. How long have you been in that water? You must be freezing.'

'Is Matt going to die, Mum?' Lexi's teeth were chattering and her long hair fell in wet ropes around her shoulders. 'There was so much blood—'

'That's because the seawater made it seem like more.' Jenna's protective instincts flooded to the surface as she heard the fear in Lexi's voice and decided this was one of those times when it was best to be economical with the truth. 'He isn't going to die. He is seriously injured, and he's going to be spending quite a bit of time in hospital, but he'll be all right, I'm sure. Largely thanks to you. How did you do it, Lexi? How did you climb down here?' Her stomach tightened at the thought.

'He was just lying there, Mum. I had to do something.'

Jenna hugged her tightly. 'You saved his life.'

'Not me. Ryan.' Lexi hugged her back. 'Did you see him come down that cliff face, Mum? It was like watching one of those special forces movies. Commandos or something.'

'Yes, I saw.' Jenna closed her eyes, trying to wipe out the image of her daughter negotiating those deadly, slippery rocks without a rope.

'And he knew exactly what to do—'

'Yes.'

Lexi gave a sniff and adjusted her position on the rock. 'He's so cool. And you were good, too, Mum. I've never seen you work before. I didn't know you were so—I dunno—so great.'

Jenna smiled weakly. 'It's amazing what you can do when the tide is coming in.'

'You and Ryan get on well together. You look like—a team.'

Jenna stilled. Had Lexi guessed that her relationship with

Ryan had deepened into something more? 'We are a team. A professional team,' she said firmly, and Lexi lifted her head.

'Do you like him, Mum?'

Oh, no, not now. 'Of course I like him. I think he's an excellent doctor and—'

'That wasn't what I was asking!' Lexi's teeth were chattering. 'He was really worried about you. You should have seen the look on his face when he had to decide whether to hang onto me or you. He never took his eyes off you. If you'd been swept into the water he'd have been in there after you. What's going on?'

This was the perfect time to say something.

Jenna licked her lips. 'Do you like Ryan, sweetheart?'

'Oh, yes. And I like Evanna and the kids, and Fraser. Loads of people, actually. I never thought this place would be so cool.' Lexi clung tighter. 'I've got used to it here, Mum. I like Glenmore. And do you know the best thing?'

Ryan, Jenna thought. He was the best thing. 'Tell me the best thing for you.'

'The fact that it's just the two of us. I love that.'

Just the two of us.

Jenna swallowed down the words she'd been about to speak. How could she say them now?

Lexi buried her face in Jenna's shoulder. 'Dad was awful to you. I see that now. He didn't even tell you stuff face to face. He just let you find out.'

'I expect he did what he thought was best.' Burying her own needs, Jenna watched as the sea level rose. 'Don't think about it now.' They needed to climb higher, she thought numbly, glancing upwards with a sinking feeling in her stomach. Now that the immediate crisis was over, the impossibility of it overwhelmed her.

'I want to talk about it, Mum!' Lexi seemed to have forgotten her surroundings. 'You're always protecting me, but I want the truth.'

Shivering, wet, chilled to the bone, Jenna tried to stop her teeth from chattering as she searched for the right thing to say. 'Dad— He— Actually, Lex, I don't know what happened with your dad. The truth is that sometimes the people we love disappoint us. But I'm not going to do that. I will always be here for you. Always. You'll have a home with me always.' She smoothed the girl's soaking hair. 'Even when you're off at university, or travelling the world, you'll still have a home with me.'

If they survived.

If they didn't both drown in this isolated, godforsaken gash in the cliff face.

'Dad just acted like he didn't have a family—' Lexi's voice jerked. 'I mean, he made you sell the house so that he could have the money, and he didn't even want me to go and stay with him this summer. That's why we came up here, isn't it? You made it impossible for me to get back there, so I wouldn't find out the truth. But when I rang him he told me it wasn't convenient for me to come—he didn't want me around, and that's why we came up here.'

Jenna stroked her daughter's soaking hair, smoothing it away from her face. 'I don't know what's going on in your dad's head right now, sweetheart, but I do know he loves you. You need to give him time to sort himself out.'

'He loves me as long as I don't mess up his new life.' Lexi scrubbed tears away with her hand. 'I'm sorry I was so difficult. I'm sorry I made it hard for you.'

'You didn't. It always would have been hard. Having you is what's kept me going. Having you is the best thing that ever happened in my life.' With a flash of relief, Jenna saw the helicopter and drew Lexi back against the rock face. 'Right. They're going to get us out of here. You go first.'

Lexi clung to her mother. 'I don't want to leave you here—'

'I'll be right behind you, I promise.'

As Lexi was clipped onto the rope and lifted into the helicopter Jenna had a few moments alone on the rock.

Looking at the swirling, greedy sea, she knew that she was facing the most difficult decision of her life. She thought back to the moment when Ryan had been forced to choose between holding her and holding her daughter and the injured boy. That was life, wasn't it? It was full of tough decisions. Things were rarely straightforward and every decision had a price.

If she told Lexi about her relationship with Ryan, she'd threaten her daughter's security and happiness. And what could she offer Ryan? He wanted a family. Babies. Even if she was able to have more children, how could she do that to Lexi?

There was no choice to make because it had already been made for her.

Clinging to the rock, Jenna watched Lexi pulled to safety inside the helicopter, the seawater mingling with her tears.

CHAPTER NINE

OVERNIGHT, Lexi became a heroine.

As word spread of her daring climb down the cliffs to save Matt, Jenna couldn't walk two steps along the bustling quay without being stopped and told how proud she must be feeling. Every time she opened her front door there was another gift lying there waiting for them. Fresh fruit. Cake. Chocolate. Hand-knitted socks for Lexi—

'What am I expected to do with these? They're basically disgusting!' Back to her insouciant teenage self, Lexi looked at them in abject horror. 'I wouldn't be seen dead in them. Who on earth thinks I'll look good in purple and green? Just shoot me now.'

'You'll wear them,' Jenna said calmly, and Lexi shuddered.

'How to kill off your love-life. If I'd known there was going to be this much fuss I would have let Matt drown.' She grabbed a baseball cap and pulled it onto her head, tipping the brim down. 'If this is how it feels to be a celebrity, I don't want any of it. Two people took photos of me yesterday, and I've got a spot on my chin!'

Jenna smiled at the normality of it. It helped. There was an ache and an emptiness inside her, far greater than she'd felt after Clive had left. One pain had been replaced by another. 'Ryan rang.' She kept her voice casual. 'He thought you'd want to know that Matt's surgery went well and he's definitely not in any danger. The surgeons said that if he'd lost any more blood he might have died, so you really are the hero of the hour.'

'It wasn't me, it was Ryan.' Obviously deciding that being a heroine had its drawbacks, Lexi stuffed her iPod into her pocket and strolled towards the door. 'I'm meeting Fraser on the beach. At least that way I might be able to walk five centimetres. And, no, I'm not wearing those socks.'

'You can wear them in the winter.'

'Any chance of us moving back to London before the weather is cold enough for socks?' But, despite the sarcasm, there was humour in her eyes and Lexi gave Jenna a swift hug and a kiss. 'What are you doing today?'

'Nothing much. Just pottering. I might go for a walk.' To the lighthouse, to tell Ryan that their relationship had to end.

Jenna watched as Lexi picked up her phone and strolled out of the house, hips swaying to the music which was so loud that Jenna could hear it even without the benefit of the earphones.

Her daughter was safe, she thought. That was all that mattered. Safe and settled. And as for the rest—well, she'd cope with it.

Ryan was standing on the cliffs, staring out over the sea, when he heard the light crunch of footsteps on the path. Even without turning he knew it was her. And he knew what she'd come to say.

Bracing himself, he turned. 'I didn't think you'd be coming

over today. I assumed you'd be resting—that's why I rang instead of coming round.'

'We appreciated the call. We've both been thinking about Matt all night.' She was wearing jeans and her hair blew in the wind. She looked like a girl, not a mother. 'Lexi has gone for a walk and I wanted to talk to you.'

He wanted to stop her, as if not giving her the chance to say the words might change things. But what was the point of that? Where had denial ever got him? 'Are you all right after yesterday? No ill effects?'

'No. We were just cold. Nothing that a hot bath didn't cure. Ryan—'

'I know what you're going to say, Jenna.'

'You do?'

'Of course. You want to end it.'

She took so long to answer that he wondered if he'd got it wrong, and then she made a sound that was somewhere between a sigh and a sob. 'I have to. This just isn't a good time for me to have a new relationship. I have to think of Lexi. She's found out just how selfish her dad has been—she feels rejected and unimportant—if I put my happiness before hers, I'll be making her feel as though she matters to no one. I can't do that. She says she likes the fact that it's just the two of us. Our relationship is her anchor. It's the one thing that hasn't changed. I don't want to threaten that.'

'Of course you don't.' Ryan felt numb and strangely detached. 'I love you—you know that, don't you?'

'Yes.' Her feet made no sound in the soft grass as she walked towards him. 'And I love you. And that's the other reason I can't do this. You want children. You deserve children, Ryan. I'm thirty-three. I have no idea whether I can even have another child. And even if I could—and even if Lexi accepted our relationship in time—I couldn't do that to her. She'd feel really pushed out.' The hand she placed on his arm shook. 'What am I saying? I'm talking about children and a future and you haven't even said what you want—'

'I want you.' It was the one question he had no problem answering. In a mind clouded with thoughts and memories, it was the one thing that was shiny and clear. 'Have you talked to Lexi about it at all?'

'No. No, I haven't.'

'Maybe you should.' Refusing to give up without a fight, he slid his hands into her hair and brought his mouth down on hers. The kiss was hungry and desperate, and he wondered if by kissing her he was simply making it worse for them both. He tasted her tears and lifted her head. 'Sorry. That wasn't fair of me.'

'It isn't you. It isn't your fault.' She scrubbed her palm over her cheek. 'But we're grown-ups. She's a child. This whole situation is terrible for her, and I'd do anything to change it, but I can't. The one thing I can do is not make things worse.' Her voice broke. 'She is not ready for me to have another relationship.'

'Are you telling me that you're never going to have another relationship in case it upsets Lexi?'

'One day, maybe. But not yet. It's just too soon. I won't do anything that makes this whole thing worse for her. I suppose I could hide our relationship, but I don't want to. I don't want to sneak around and live a lie. We deserve better.' Jenna lifted her fingers to her temples and shook her head. 'This is ridiculous. I may be thirty-three but I feel seventeen. And I never should have started this. I never should have hurt you—'

'You've always been honest with me, and that's all I ask.'

The hopelessness of it made the moment all the more intense, and their mouths fused, their hands impatient and demanding as they took from each other. Urgent, hungry, they made love on the grass, with the call of the seagulls and the crash of the sea for company.

Aferwards they lay on the grass in silence, because there was nothing more to say.

When Jenna stood up and walked away he didn't stop her.

The following day Jenna was half an hour late to surgery because everyone had kept stopping her to ask her for the details or give her another bit of gossip. Feeling numb inside, she'd responded on automatic, her thoughts on Ryan. 'Thank you—so kind—yes, we're both fine—no permanent damage—Matt's doing well—'

The effort of keeping up a front was so exhausting that she was relieved when she finally pushed open the glass doors to the Medical Centre. Hurrying through Reception, she was caught in an enormous hug by a woman she'd never met before.

'Nurse Jenna—how can I thank you?'

'I—' Taken aback, Jenna cast a questioning glance at Janet, the receptionist, who grinned.

'That's Pam. Matt's aunt. He has four aunts living on the island, so there's going to be more where that came from.' Janet handed a signed prescription to one lady and answered the phone with her other hand. 'There's a crowd waiting for you here, Jenna.'

Matt's aunt was still hugging her tightly. 'It's thanks to your lass that our boy's alive. I heard she climbed down—and then you went down that rope after her.'

'Lexi was brave, that's true—I'm very proud of her. And

Ryan. But I didn't do anything.' Embarrassed by the fuss, desperate to be on her own, Jenna eased herself away from the woman, but people still crowded around her.

'Can't believe you went down that rope—'

'Lexi climbed down without any help—'

'Anyone who says today's teenagers are a waste of space has never met a Glenmore teenager—'

'Devil's Jaws—'

'Been more deaths there than any other part of Glenmore—'

Jenna lifted a hand to her throbbing head. 'Maybe I'd rather not hear that part,' she said weakly, remembering with horrifying clarity the moment when she'd stepped over the edge of the cliff. 'I'm just so pleased Matt's going to be all right. Dr McKinley rang yesterday and the hospital said surgery went well.' After a summer on Glenmore she knew better than to bother worrying about patient confidentiality. If she didn't tell them what was going on they'd find out another way, and the information would be less reliable. 'I'm just sorry I'm late this morning. If everyone could be patient…'

'Don't give it a thought.' Kate Green, who ran the gift shop on the quay, waved a hand. 'Won't kill any of us to wait. Anything we can do to help? We're sorting out a rota to make food for Matt's family when they're back from the mainland. They won't want to be fussing with things like that.'

Jenna looked at them all—looked at their kind faces, which shone with their eagerness to support each other in times of crisis. It was impossible not to compare it to the surgery she'd worked at in London, where patients had complained bitterly if they were kept waiting more than ten minutes. In London everyone led parallel lives, she thought numbly. Here, lives were tangled together. People looked left and right instead of straight ahead. They noticed if things weren't right with the person next to them. They helped.

Someone pushed something into her hand.

Jenna opened the bag and saw two freshly baked muffins.

'My mum thought you might not have had time for breakfast. We made you these.' The child was no more than seven years old, and for Jenna it was the final straw. Too emotionally fragile to cope with the volume of kindness, she burst into tears.

'Oh, now…' Clucking like a mother hen, Kate Green urged her towards the nearest chair.

'Shock—that's what it is. It was her lass who stayed with Matt. Saved him, she did. That's a worry for any mother.'

'Tired, I expect…'

'I'm so sorry.' Struggling desperately to control herself, Jenna rummaged in her pocket for a tissue. Someone pushed one into her hand. 'Just leave me for a minute—I'll be fine.' Oh, God, she was going to crack. Right here in public, with these kind people around her.

Evanna hurried out of her clinic, alerted by Janet. 'Jenna? Are you all right?'

Jenna blew her nose. 'Just being really stupid. And making my clinic even more behind than it is at the moment.'

'Then perhaps we can get on with it? I'm first.' Mrs Parker's crisp voice cut through the mumbling and the sympathy. 'And I've been standing on this leg for twenty minutes now. I'm too old to be kept waiting around. It isn't the first drama we've had on Glenmore and it won't be the last.'

Even the gentle Evanna gritted her teeth, but Jenna stood up, grateful to be forced into action.

'Of course, Mrs Parker. I'm so sorry. Come with me. The rest of you—' she glanced around the crowded waiting room '—I'll be as quick as I can.'

Following Mrs Parker down the corridor to her room, Jenna braced herself for a sharp rebuke and a lecture.

Instead she was given a hug. 'There, now…' Mrs Parker's voice shook slightly, and her thin fingers rubbed Jenna's back awkwardly. 'Those folks think they're helping, but they're overwhelming, aren't they? I've lived on this island all my life and there are times when I could kill the lot of them. You must feel like a crust of bread being fought over by a flock of seagulls.' With a sniff she pulled away, leaving Jenna with a lump in her throat.

'Oh, Mrs Parker—'

'Now, don't you get all sentimental on me, young lady.' Mrs Parker settled herself in the chair. 'Sentimental is all very well once in a while, but it doesn't solve problems. I'm guessing those tears have nothing to do with that foolhardy rescue or lack of sleep. Do you want to talk about it?'

Jenna blew her nose again. 'I'm supposed to be dressing your leg—'

'You're a woman. Are you telling me you can't talk and bandage a leg at the same time?'

Jenna gave a weak smile and turned her attention to work. Washing her hands, she prepared the equipment she needed. 'It's just reaction to yesterday, I'm sure. And I am a little tired. Really.'

'I'm old, not stupid. But not so old I don't remember how it feels to be confused about a man. You came here as a single mother. I'm guessing you're rethinking that now.'

Jenna's hands shook as she removed the bandage from the old lady's leg. 'No. No, I'm not rethinking that. Lexi and I are a team.'

'So you're going to let a strong, impressive man like Dr McKinley walk away from you?'

Jenna stilled. She thought about denying it and then re-alised it was useless. 'Does everyone know?'

Mrs Parker sighed. 'Of course. This is Glenmore. What we don't know is why you're not just booking the church. The Reverend King is quite happy to marry you, even though you've been divorced. I asked him.'

'You—?' Jenna gulped. 'Mrs Parker, you can't possibly—you shouldn't have—'

'You have a daughter. You need to keep it respectable. One bad marriage shouldn't put you off doing it again.' Mrs Parker glared at her. 'What? You think it's right, teaching that girl of yours it's all right to take up with whoever takes your fancy? You need to set an example. If you like him enough to roll around in his sheets with him, you like him enough to marry him. And he certainly likes you. There's a bet going on down at the pub that he's going to ask you to marry him. You'd better have your answer ready.'

'It would have to be no.'

Mrs Parker looked at her steadily, her customary frown absent. 'As we've been drinking tea together for almost two months now, perhaps you'd do me the courtesy of explaining why you'd say no to a man most women would kill to be with.'

Jenna didn't pause to wonder why she was talking to this woman. She needed to talk to someone, and Mrs Parker had proved to be a surprisingly good listener. 'Because of Lexi.'

She blurted it all out. Everything she was feeling. The only thing she didn't mention was Ryan's past. That wasn't hers to reveal.

Mrs Parker listened without interrupting. Only when Jenna had finished and was placing a fresh dressing on the wound did she finally speak. Her hands were folded carefully in her lap.

Age and wisdom, Jenna thought, wondering what secrets Mrs Parker had in her past. She was a girl once. A young woman. *We see them as patients, but they're people.*

'Tell me something.' The old lady looked at her in the eye. 'Do you plan to try and shield your daughter from everything that happens in life?'

Jenna swallowed. 'If I can.' Then she gave a sigh. 'No, of course not. Not everything, but—I love her. I want her to be happy.'

'Has it occurred to you that she might like a new man around the house?'

'I think it would unsettle her.' Jenna finished the bandage, concentrating on the job. 'Is that comfortable?'

Mrs Parker put her weight on her leg. 'It's perfect, as usual.' Her voice calm, she picked up her handbag. 'You're not the only one who can love, you know. And if love is wanting someone else's happiness, maybe Lexi should be thinking of yours. Maybe you should give her the chance to worry about you for a change. I want you to think about that.'

'Mrs Parker—'

'Just think about it. I'd hate to see you turning your back on something special. I'll send the next person in, shall I? Don't forget to drop in for tea when you're passing.' With a quiet smile, the dragon of Glenmore opened the door. 'I happen to know that Rev King has a date free in December. I always think a winter wedding is romantic. And I expect an invitation. I have a particularly nice coat that I haven't had reason to wear for at least two decades.'

'He rolled in a pile of something gross and now he stinks—Mum, are you listening to me? Basically, the dog is rank.' A frown on her face, Lexi helped herself to crisps from the cupboard and waved them under her mother's nose. 'Junk food alert! Time to nag!'

Her mind miles away, Jenna stared out of the window, trying to find the right way to say what needed to be said.

'On my fourth packet—' Lexi rustled the bag of crisps dramatically. 'Might add some more salt to them just to make them extra yummy—'

'Lexi…' Her strained voice caught her daughter's attention. 'What? What's wrong?'

'I—there's something I need to talk to you about. Something very adult.'

'Is it about the fact you're having sex with Ryan? Because honestly, Mum—' Lexi stuck her hand in the crisp packet '—I don't want to know the details. I mean, I love you, and I love that we talk about stuff, but I don't want to talk about that. It would feel too weird.'

Stunned, Jenna felt her face turn scarlet. 'You— I—'

'Don't get me wrong. I'm basically cool with it, Mum. I'm pleased for you.' Grinning, Lexi nibbled a crisp. 'It's nice for someone of your age to have some excitement.'

Jenna moved her lips but no sound came out.

Lexi squinted out of the window. 'Better pull it together fast, Mum, lover-boy is strolling up the path. I'll go and let him in, shall I?' She sauntered towards the door, crisps in her hand. 'Hi, Ryan. I'm glad you're here, because Mum so needs a doctor. She's acting weird. I've waved, like, five packets of crisps under her nose and she hasn't even reacted. Normally she'd be freaking out and going on about too much salt, too much fat. Today—nothing. What's the matter with her?'

'Perhaps you'd better leave us for a moment.' Ryan dropped his car keys on the table, but Lexi shook her head and plopped onto a chair by the kitchen table.

'No way. I'm fed up with being the last person to know stuff around here. If you want to get rid of me you'll have to kick me out, and that will be child abuse.'

A smile flickered at the corners of Ryan's mouth. 'Presumably that wouldn't be a good start to our relationship.'

Lexi looked at him thoughtfully. 'You've got a thing for my mum, haven't you?'

Ryan winced, and Jenna came to her senses. 'Lexi!'

'It's too late for discipline. I'm already full of crisps.' Lexi folded her arms. 'It would be great if someone around here would give me a straight answer for once. I know you like my mum, so there's no point in denying it.'

'That isn't quite how I'd describe it,' Ryan said carefully, and Jenna felt the pulse beat in her throat.

Lexi didn't pause. 'What words would you use?'

'I love your mum.' Ryan spoke the words calmly, with no hint of apology or question. 'I love her very much. But I realise that the situation is complicated.'

'What's complicated about it? She's divorced, and you—' Lexi frowned. 'Are you married or something?'

'No. I was in the past.'

'So, basically, you're free and single?' Lexi grinned cheekily. 'I missed out the "young" bit, did you notice?'

'I noticed. Remind me to punish you later.' A sardonic smile on his face, Ryan sat down at the table. 'I'm not sure what order to do this in. If you want to be part of a family that already exists, do you propose to the woman or the daughter?'

'Don't waste your time proposing to me,' Lexi said casually. 'You may be hot, but you're way too old for me. How old *are* you?'

'Thirty-six.'

Lexi shuddered. 'You'd go and die, or something, while

I was still in my prime. Mind you, that has its advantages. Are you rich?'

'Lexi!' Jenna finally found her voice. 'You can't—'

'Actually, I am pretty rich. Why does that matter?' Ryan's long fingers toyed with his keys. 'Are you open to bribery and corruption?'

'Of course. I'm a teenager. The art of negotiation is an important life skill.' Lexi grabbed a grape from the fruit bowl and popped it in her mouth. 'So how big a bribe are we talking about? If I let you marry my mum you'll buy me a pink Porsche?'

Ryan grimaced. 'Not pink. Please not pink.'

Glancing between the two of them in disbelief, Jenna shook her head. 'Can we have a proper conversation?'

'We are having a proper conversation.' Lexi looked at Ryan speculatively. 'What music do you like?'

'I have eclectic tastes.'

'In other words you'll pretend to like anything I like.'

'No. But I'm sure there would be some common ground.'

'If I let you marry my mum, will you teach me to abseil?'

Jenna felt faint. 'Lexi—Ryan—for goodness' sake—'

'I don't see why not.'

'And surf?'

'Your balance was pretty impressive on those rocks, and you don't seem to mind being swamped by seawater.' Ryan gave a casual shrug and a smile touched his mouth. 'Looks like I'm going to be busy.'

'And you promise not to tell me what time to go to bed or nag me about my diet?'

'You can eat what you like and go to bed when you like.'

Lexi fiddled with his car keys. 'Do I have to call you Dad?'

'You can call me whatever you like.'

'I never thought about having another father.'

There was a long silence, and then Ryan stirred. 'How about another friend? Have you thought about having another one of those?'

Lexi gave a slow smile and stood up. 'Yeah,' she drawled huskily, 'I could go with that. I'll leave you two alone now. The thought of watching a man kiss my mum is just a bit gross. I'm taking Rebel down on the beach to wash off whatever it is he's rolled in. I reckon it's going to take me at least two hours to get him clean, and I'm going to bang the front door really loudly when I come back.' Grinning wickedly, she scooped up the lead and then walked over to Jenna. 'Say yes, Mum. You know you want to.' She glanced over her shoulder to Ryan. 'And he's pretty cool—for an older person. We're going to do OK.'

Jenna couldn't find her voice. 'Lex—'

'You're almost too old to have another baby, so you'd better not waste any time,' Lexi advised, kissing Jenna on the cheek.

Sensing Ryan's eyes on her, Jenna swallowed. 'Lexi, we won't—'

'I hope you do. Think of all the money I'd earn babysitting.' Lexi grinned. 'How much would you pay me to change nappies? I'll think about a decent rate while I'm scrubbing Rebel. See you later.' She sauntered out of the house, leaving the two of them alone.

Aware of Ryan still watching her, Jenna opened her mouth and closed it again.

He stood up and walked across to her. 'I had an unexpected visitor this morning.'

'You did?'

'The Reverend King.' There was a gleam of humour in his

eyes. 'He wanted to know exactly what time we wanted the church on Christmas Eve. Apparently it's been reserved provisionally in our name. His suggestion was just before lunch, so that the entire island could then gather for food at our expense. I wondered what you thought.'

Jenna swallowed. Then she turned her head and stared into the garden, watching as Lexi put Rebel on his lead and led him through the little gate towards the beach. 'I think that life sometimes surprises you,' she said huskily. 'I think that just when you think everything is wrong, it suddenly turns out right. I think I'm lucky. What do you think?'

Ryan closed his hands over her shoulders and turned her to face him. 'I think we only have two hours before Lexi comes home.' His fingers were strong, and he held her as though he never intended to let her go. 'We should probably make the most of it. Especially if we want to make a baby before we're both too old.'

She made a sound that was somewhere between a laugh and a sob and flung her arms around his neck. 'What if I can't? What if I *am* too old? What if I can't give you a family?'

His hands gentle, he cupped her face and lowered his mouth to hers. 'Marry me and you will have given me all the family I need. You. Lexi.'

'But—'

'Sometimes we don't begin a journey knowing where it's going to end,' he said softly, resting his forehead against hers as he looked down at her. 'Sometimes we don't have all the answers. We don't know what the future holds, but we do know that whatever it is we'll deal with it. Together. The three of us. And Rebel, of course.'

The three of us.

Holding those words against her like a warm blanket, Jenna lifted her head. 'The three of us,' she whispered softly. 'That sounds good to me.'

DR DROP-DEAD GORGEOUS

BY
EMILY FORBES

MILLS & BOON

First published in Great Britain 2010
Harlequin Mills & Boon Limited,
Eton House, 18-24 Paradise Road, Richmond, Surrey TW9 1SR

© Emily Forbes 2010

ISBN: 978 0 263 87902 5

Harlequin Mills & Boon policy is to use papers that are natural, renewable and recyclable products and made from wood grown in sustainable forests. The logging and manufacturing process conform to the legal environmental regulations of the country of origin.

Printed and bound in Spain
by Litografia Rosés, S.A., Barcelona

Emily Forbes is the pseudonym of two sisters who share both a passion for writing and a life-long love of reading. Beyond books and their families, their interests include cooking (food is a recurring theme in their books!), learning languages, playing the piano and netball, as well as an addiction to travel—armchair travel is fine, but anything involving a plane ticket is better. Home for both is South Australia, where they live three minutes apart with their husbands and four young children. With backgrounds in business administration, law, arts, clinical psychology and physiotherapy they have worked in many areas. This past professional experience adds to their writing in many ways: legal dilemmas, psychological ordeals and business scandals are all intermeshed with the medical settings of their stories. And, since nothing could ever be as delicious as spending their days telling the stories of gorgeous heroes and spirited heroines, they are eternally grateful their mutual dream of writing for a living came true.

They would love you to visit and keep up to date with current news future releases at the Medical™ Romance authors' website at: http://www.medicalromance.com

Recent titles by the same author:

A FATHER FOR HER TWINS
THE PLAYBOY FIREFIGHTER'S PROPOSAL
EMERGENCY: WIFE WANTED
WEDDING AT PELICAN BEACH

To my very own Drop-Dead-Gorgeous husband
and romantic inspiration, James,
and our two gorgeous boys, Ned & Finn—
it is the most amazing feeling to have your support
and to know how proud you are of my writing.

You are the most precious people
in the world to me and this book is for you
with my thanks and love.

CHAPTER ONE

'JULIET! Can you hear me? Stay with us, Juliet.'

Maggie woke with a start. She was in strange surroundings, curled up and cramped in an armchair. She rubbed her neck with one hand as she tried to work out where she was. The room came into focus. A drip stand, an overway table, white sheets on a single bed—a hospital room.

She remembered where she was. She was waiting for her sister to come out of Theatre.

She looked around, searching for the person whose voice had woken her. A man's voice, she was sure of it. He'd been talking loudly but the room was quiet now; she was alone.

Had she been dreaming?

Her heart was thumping in her chest—she put her hand over it, as if she could slow it down. She had been dreaming; she could recall it now. She'd been dreaming about Juliet's operation. Juliet's heart had stopped and the doctors had been using cardiac paddles to get it going again. That was what had woken her so abruptly. That was why her heart was racing—it was as though she'd felt the shock of the charge going through her own chest.

Something had gone wrong and she needed to find out what it was.

She jumped out of the chair.

How long had she been sleeping? She checked her watch, quarter past two. Juliet should have been out of Theatre by now. Someone must know something.

Maggie needed information; she needed to know what had happened and she needed to know if Juliet was OK.

She made her way to the nurses' station. The nurse sitting at the desk was the one who'd come to take Juliet to Theatre. Maggie was relieved there hadn't been a change of shift yet. She had no time for pleasantries or to explain who she was.

'Carol, do you know if Juliet is out of Theatre yet?'

The nurse looked up and must have recognised her. 'I haven't heard anything. Would you like me to check?'

'Please. I thought she'd be finished by now.' Maggie tapped her foot impatiently.

Carol picked up the phone and punched in the extension number, frowning as the call went unanswered. 'There's no answer but if they're busy they don't always pick up.'

Maggie knew that was true but she immediately wondered what was happening in Theatre or Recovery that would make the phone go unanswered. Was Juliet all right?

'I'll try again in a minute and come and find you. Will you wait in Juliet's room?' Carol waited for Maggie to nod before returning her attention to her paperwork.

Maggie made a pretence of returning to her sister's room but there was no way she'd be able to sit and wait. She walked past the door and headed for the lift to take her up to Theatres and Recovery.

She paced around the confines of the lift as it carried her to the top floor. She exited the lift and followed the signs, hurrying along the corridor to the recovery suites and pressing the call button by the door. She pressed it twice before a nurse responded.

Maggie barely waited for the nurse to ask what she wanted before she spoke. 'I'm Juliet Taylor's sister. Can you tell me how she is?'

The nurse's eyes widened and Maggie's eyes narrowed in response as she tried to work out what was bothering the girl. Was she surprised to find a stranger hovering by the door or was she trying to formulate an answer? Maggie suspected that something had happened and that this nurse didn't want to be the one to tell her about it.

'What happened? Is she OK?'

The nurse continued to stand there, mute.

Maggie recognised the nurse's expression now. Something unexpected had happened in Theatre and Maggie had been right to come barging up here to find out what. Something had happened to Juliet.

There was a flurry of movement behind the nurse. Maggie peered over her shoulder and saw a patient being wheeled into Recovery. She shoved her foot in the doorway to prevent the nurse from closing her out and waited, trying to catch a glimpse of the patient on the barouche. Was it Juliet? She couldn't relax until she saw her sister with her own eyes.

There was quite a crowd surrounding the bed, fussing about as they connected the patient to various monitors. It was difficult to see who was lying there but as the nurse backed away Maggie had a strong suspicion the patient was Juliet. She wasn't waiting any longer—somebody must be able to tell her something. She looked around for someone, anyone, who didn't appear to be busy.

She saw the nurse she'd spoken to approach one of the

other theatre staff—a man—and saw her point at the doorway, at Maggie. Maggie focused on her as she directed her comment to the room in general.

'Excuse me, I'm Juliet Taylor's sister. Could someone please tell me what's going on?'

The man looked in her direction, issued what seemed to be instructions to the other staff and started towards her.

There was no hesitation on his part. He walked confidently. He looked as if he was used to being in control; he looked like a man who could avert a disaster.

Something in his walk told Maggie that even if there had been a problem, he'd solved it. He didn't walk like a man who was about to deliver bad news. Maggie felt herself relax; she could breathe normally again.

'You're Juliet's sister?'

Maggie nodded. 'I'm Maggie Petersen.'

'Ben McMahon, Juliet's plastic surgeon.' He held out his hand, offering to shake hers. His grip was warm and strong. Comforting, Maggie thought as she put her hand in his and felt her heart stop its crazy hammering and return to its normal rhythm, calmed by this man's touch.

'Is she OK?'

'Yes, she's going to be fine but there were some complications.'

'What sort of complications?' Maggie's heart skipped a beat and she took a deep breath, willing herself to stay calm, willing her heart to beat normally. Juliet had cheated death once before—could she be lucky a second time?

'Let's find somewhere to sit down.' He led her around a corner to a room with several recliner chairs lining the walls. It was obviously used for day-surgery patients but at the moment it was vacant.

Ben waited for her to sit in one recliner, then he sat on the edge of the next one facing her. It looked as though he was trying to work out how to phrase his words gently and Maggie didn't have the patience for that. 'I'm a nurse—just tell me what happened.'

He jerked back a little, perhaps surprised by her abruptness, but he recovered quickly and answered Maggie's question without hesitating. 'Juliet's reconstructive surgery went well—I was pleased with that aspect—but as the anaesthetist was about to reverse the anaesthetic Juliet's blood pressure plummeted. You saw her in recovery—' he waited for Maggie to nod in assent '—so you know she's pulled through but her heart did stop and we had to resuscitate her.'

Maggie recalled her dream—maybe it hadn't been as strange as it seemed. Her voice was tight as she forced her next question out. 'She's fine now?'

'We'll keep a close eye on her, of course, but so far she's fine.'

'How long did it take to revive her?' Maggie needed facts.

'About ninety seconds.'

Within safe time limits, Maggie knew. 'What triggered the drop in BP?' she asked.

'The anaesthetist suspects it might have been a reaction to the antinausea drug. That's not uncommon but it's reassuring to know that in patients who've experienced this reaction there have been no long-term after-effects.'

Maggie could hear what Dr McMahon was telling her—Juliet would be fine—but she'd had a sense of unease about this surgery from the beginning and now she wondered what else could go wrong. She hadn't been convinced that Juliet had needed this surgery but it hadn't been her decision and there'd been no way of stopping Juliet once she'd made up her mind. That had been the case their whole lives. Juliet didn't wait for other people to make her decisions. She didn't leave it up to fate either. Juliet did what Juliet wanted and when.

This operation was a perfect example, Maggie thought. Juliet had been diagnosed with breast cancer twelve months ago. She'd undergone a bilateral mastectomy even though the cancer had been in one breast only. When she found out that, due to a faulty gene, she had a high chance of getting cancer in her other breast she'd very quickly decided to have both removed. Now she had just completed the first step of breast reconstruction. Maggie hadn't seen the point of a reconstruction but, as Juliet had pointed out, it wasn't her body, and Juliet had been adamant that was what she was going to do. And now it had nearly killed her.

Maggie had always thought the surgery unnecessary and now it had almost cost Juliet her life. A life she'd fought so desperately to save just twelve months earlier. Maggie sighed, knowing that even this latest drama wouldn't stop Juliet from going after what she wanted.

'Are you OK?'

Dr McMahon's hand on her arm startled Maggie out of her reverie. She'd forgotten she wasn't alone. She lifted her head. He was looking at her with concern. Worried she was about to collapse too? She was quite OK. The only thing upsetting her equilibrium was Dr McMahon—he was seriously gorgeous and sitting far too close. She just remembered to nod in reply to his question even as she registered that his eyes were the exact same blue as his theatre scrubs.

'Come with me—I'll take you in to see for yourself. She's going to be fine. Trust me.'

And for some reason she couldn't explain, Maggie did

trust this man. This man she'd only just met. Somehow she believed if he said everything would be fine, it would be.

She followed him along the corridor, back to Recovery. His back filled her field of vision. He was more than six foot by a couple of inches, Maggie guessed, solidly built, not fat but fit. He filled out his scrubs nicely—broad shoulders, narrower hips with his trousers tied loosely around them. Maggie was well aware just how unflattering theatre clothes could be but somehow, despite this, he managed to pull off the look. Some people would look good in a sack and Maggie suspected this man was one them. He could be a poster boy for tall, dark and handsome men.

Maggie stayed beside her sister, keeping one eye on the monitors that displayed her blood pressure, heart rate and oxygen levels, and one eye on the gentle rise and fall of the sheets as Juliet breathed in and out. Ben had been telling the truth—Juliet seemed fine. There was nothing for Maggie to do except watch. Watch and think. She thought about the past two years, about what Juliet had been through, but she also thought about Dr Ben McMahon. He'd left Recovery after checking on Juliet's status but Maggie could very easily recall his turquoise gaze and his calm and confident aura. She was glad he'd been there; she felt reassured.

She stayed until she was sure Juliet was OK, until she was certain she could go home and tell Juliet's children their mother was fine.

Maggie felt as though she'd barely slept for two nights. She was staying at Juliet's house to look after the children but they were unsettled and missing their mother and Maggie's nerves were stretched. She was tired and stressed, worried about her sister's recovery. Each time she woke during the night she rang the hospital to check on Juliet. Her recovery had been unremarkable and, just as Dr McMahon had predicted, there'd been no more dramas and everything seemed back to normal.

Juliet was expecting to be discharged today. She'd asked Maggie to get to the hospital as early as possible, anticipating going home. She was obviously feeling better—she was certainly pushing to be discharged—but nothing much had ever slowed Juliet down.

Maggie had just managed to get Juliet's children ready and to school on time before she returned to the hospital. She'd showered but hadn't had time to wash her hair. She'd pulled it back into a ponytail and thrown on a pair of old jeans and a jumper but no make-up. She thought she probably looked worse than Juliet.

Juliet had been moved out of HDU into a private room after twenty-four hours but she'd spent most of yesterday sleeping and she looked surprisingly good. I *do* look worse than her, Maggie decided.

She walked over to the bed, leaning over to kiss Juliet's cheek. 'Hi. How are you feeling?'

'A bit tired and sore but otherwise fine, surprisingly enough.'

'Ready to go home, do you think?'

'Definitely. I'm just waiting for the surgeon to come and discharge me.'

That would be Ben. Maggie's heart flip-flopped in her chest. She hadn't seen him yesterday when she'd visited Juliet, but she didn't want to admit she'd felt disappointed. 'Did he explain to you what happened?'

'They think I had a reaction to the antinausea drug but there don't seem to be any ongoing problems and they certainly don't seem to be expecting any,' Juliet replied.

'Do you remember anything? Were you scared?'

Juliet shook her head. 'Not at all. It was the strangest experience though. It was just like I've heard people describe it. The light. That floating sensation. How safe you feel. Everything.' She paused and then continued. 'Steven was there.'

'My Steven?'

Juliet nodded.

'Did you see him?' Maggie didn't doubt her sister's recollection. Maggie was a theatre nurse; she'd heard plenty of these tales before, too many for her to rule them all out as nonsense.

'No, I couldn't see anything up there. The light was beautiful but it concealed everything. I could look down, I could see the operating theatre, I could see myself—but I couldn't see Steven. I just heard him.'

'What did he say?'

'He told me it wasn't my time. He sent me back. Told me my babies needed me.' Juliet paused. 'Do I sound crazy?'

Maggie shook her head. 'I've had patients tell me similar things before,' she answered honestly. 'Did Steven say anything to me?'

The question was out before she could wonder why she'd even asked it.

What was she hoping to hear? Did she want a message or not? Would it matter either way?

When Steven first passed away Maggie would have given anything for one more chance just to touch him, one more chance to have him hold her, one more chance to hear him whisper her name. But that had been ten years ago and she'd come to terms with her loss. Even though she hadn't found anyone to take Steven's place his absence was no longer a gaping hole in her life—it was just a part of her. A part of her she'd become used to living with.

So why had she asked the question?

Curiosity, she decided. That was the answer.

Juliet shook her head. 'No, sorry, Mags.'

She shrugged; it didn't matter. What had she expected him to say? Only what she imagined she'd want to hear. 'Be happy. I miss you. I love you'?

Did she still love him? She loved him but she couldn't still be *in love* with someone who'd been dead for ten years. That wasn't realistic. It didn't matter that there'd been no message. A message wouldn't change the fact that she was a widow and her life had moved on.

She picked up the chart at the end of the bed and flicked through it, looking for a change in topic. The monitors said Juliet was fine and the charts agreed. The medical staff had checked and double-checked everything and there was nothing untoward going on. Nothing that required further discussion.

'Morning, ladies.'

Maggie looked up from the chart at the sound of Ben's voice. It was rich and deep and she could feel it reverberate through her body. She hurriedly replaced the chart only to realize he was focused on Juliet and apparently not at all concerned about her activities. She silently reprimanded herself for being so foolish. Just because she felt a spark of attraction didn't mean anything. He was obviously just a man doing his job.

'Juliet, how are you?' he asked.

'Great. Packed and ready to go home. Ben, this is my sister, Maggie.'

'Yes, we met.' He glanced in her direction before returning his attention to Juliet. His focus was definitely on his patient, and Maggie swallowed her pride. 'How's your chest?'

'A bit sore but better than yesterday, and otherwise I'm fine.'

Maggie stepped away from the bed, giving Ben space to

examine Juliet. She thought putting some distance between them would give her a chance to recover her nerve but all she did was stand there and study him while his attention was focused elsewhere.

His thick dark hair was cut short but it looked as though it would curl if left to grow longer. His jaw was square and firm, perfectly symmetrical. He smiled at something Juliet said and creases appeared in the corners of his eyes. He was leaning over Juliet now, checking her wounds, and his trousers moulded around his buttocks. Maggie felt herself blush and quickly moved her attention a bit higher, away from temptation. From behind him she couldn't see his eyes but she remembered the colour—turquoise blue.

She noticed a few flecks of silver in his hair and guessed him to be in his late thirties or early forties, about her age. The silver did nothing to detract from his looks—he really was gorgeous. But, she supposed, given that he was a plastic surgeon, he *should* be gorgeous. She wondered if he'd had any work done.

He'd finished examining Juliet and was standing in profile now; this allowed Maggie to study his nose, which, for the record, was a perfect Roman nose, narrow and straight. He turned to face her. 'Is something wrong?'

Had he felt her staring at him? Normally she would have blushed and looked away—normally she would be mortified to have someone catch her staring—but she found herself unable, or unwilling, to break his gaze.

'Your nose.'

Ben reached up, rubbing his nose with one hand as if expecting to find something distasteful there. 'Is that better?' he asked.

'No, no, there wasn't anything wrong with your nose—that was what I was wondering, whether you'd had it fixed.'

'Maggie!' Juliet exclaimed.

'What?' Maggie looked at her sister, relieved to find she was actually able to break Ben's gaze after all.

'You can't ask that.'

'Why not? If I can't ask a plastic surgeon about plastic surgery, who can I ask? Besides, you know I've always hated my nose so if I see a nice nose and I find out it's been surgically assisted I might consider getting my own done.'

'Thank you,' Ben responded. 'I think that was a compliment, but my nose is one hundred per cent natural, sorry.'

Maggie looked back at him. He was smiling at her, and she immediately forgot what she'd been talking about. If he was gorgeous before, he was now twice as gorgeous. His teeth were perfect, straight and white—what she always thought of as American teeth, the sort all sitcom actors had—but when he smiled she could see a streak of mischief in him that you wouldn't have noticed at first. Not smiling, he was the epitome of a clean-cut, college-educated Aussie male, but when he smiled, she knew he wasn't as wholesome as he first appeared. There was more to him than met the eye—he had a definite larrikin streak, which by no means diminished his appeal. If anything, it made her wonder even more about him. What was he thinking about that could make him smile like that?

His blue eyes sparkled. 'Just out of interest, what's wrong with your nose?'

Maggie touched the bridge of her nose. 'I hate this bump in the middle.'

'That's a hard thing to guarantee to fix, you know. Think of it as giving you individuality.' Ben delivered his verdict with a wink before turning his attention back to Juliet.

Maggie stood, stuck to the spot as strange sensations

flooded through her. This man was disturbing her equilibrium in a major way.

She'd met plenty of attractive, intelligent men in her time but Ben seemed so down-to-earth, with no signs of an over-inflated ego. He seemed normal, charming. Or at least he was charming her! But it didn't seem deliberate on his part. It seemed natural. And Maggie was definitely not immune. Her mouth was dry and her hands were shaking; her pulse was racing. She put a hand to her stomach, trying to settle her nerves. Don't be ridiculous, she told herself.

'So, can I go home? Maggie's a nurse—I'll be in good hands.'

Hearing her name brought her attention back to the matter at hand, getting Juliet home. She realized she'd missed most of Ben and Juliet's conversation as she'd tried to get her wayward thoughts under control.

Ben addressed her now. 'That's right—you told me that the other day, didn't you? What sort of nurse?'

'I work in Theatre.'

'Can you handle patients who are conscious?' Ben's accompanying smile made Maggie's skin tingle. It was the strangest sensation, as if her skin had a life and mind of its own.

'I'll be fine,' she said, smiling back at him, or at least hoping she was smiling and not grinning like a half-crazed woman.

Ben turned his focus back to Juliet. 'In that case I'll discharge you and see you in a fortnight. Have you got your appointment?' Juliet nodded and Ben continued. 'Any concerns, ring me. And remember, no heavy lifting or strenuous housework—that includes shopping for groceries and hanging up washing.'

Both sisters watched him leave the room and once he was supposedly out of earshot Juliet spoke up.

'Told you he was fabulous, didn't I?'

Had she? Maggie couldn't remember. She'd be surprised

if Juliet hadn't said something—it wasn't every day you came across someone as striking as Ben—but she could barely remember right now what her own name was let alone whether Juliet had mentioned her handsome plastic surgeon. Silently she did agree that he seemed fabulous but she wasn't sure whether her mind was really processing things properly so she chose to keep her own counsel.

'Pity he's my specialist,' Juliet continued talking, apparently unaware that Maggie hadn't answered her.

'You wouldn't!' Maggie gasped.

'Wouldn't what? Jump into bed with him if I got the chance?' Juliet laughed. ''Course I would. I'm divorced, not dead. I've survived twice now, first breast cancer and then being brought back from death's door two days ago, and I intend to make the most of being alive. Just wait until I get my new boobs—there's more life in this old girl and I intend to enjoy some of it.'

Maggie laughed but also wondered what Juliet would say if she told her that was exactly how she felt!

Her first response hadn't been wrong—Ben was seriously attractive, and she definitely wasn't immune to his physical qualities. The small space of Juliet's hospital room hadn't been able to contain his energy and charisma, and Maggie was just as aware of his appeal today as she had been two days earlier. But, while she could appreciate Ben's attributes, unlike Juliet, she couldn't imagine being with him any more than she was sure he could imagine being with her.

As much as she'd consider the idea in theory she couldn't imagine it ever eventuating in real life. What would a gorgeous, successful, charming man who, she imagined, could have any woman he wanted see in her—a skinny, forty-two-year-old widow with a flat chest and a bump in her nose!

CHAPTER TWO

THE next fortnight passed in a blur for Maggie. Despite Juliet's insistence that she felt one hundred per cent well Maggie knew she was still far from fully recovered. Juliet's ex-husband was away on a training exercise with the Australian navy and being a single mother was hard enough when you were fit and healthy, let alone when you were re-covering from surgery. Maggie understood that and it was why she was in Melbourne, to take some of the pressure off her sister. Juliet's children were at school but it was their extra-curricular activities that had Maggie run off her feet, and by the time nine-year-old Kate and six-year-old Edward were in bed Maggie was looking forward to putting her feet up and enjoying a glass of wine. Maggie's niece and nephew were a lot younger than her own children and she'd forgotten how much time got eaten up just doing the basics for a young family. She'd forgotten how exhausting it could be.

'Here's to tomorrow, the start of my new life.' Juliet raised her wine glass in a toast to the future and waited for Maggie to join her. As Maggie's glass clinked against hers Juliet went on. 'And here's to a fresh start for you too.'

'What do you mean?'

'I've discovered there's nothing like coming face to face with your own mortality to make one stop and assess their life. There're still so many things I want to see and do so I'm putting the past two years behind me and putting my energy into my future.' Juliet sipped her wine. 'But thinking about my future got me wondering about yours too. I've been trying to work out where you're headed as well.'

'I'm not sure I'm headed anywhere.'

'That's my point,' Juliet replied. 'You should be. I think you need to take stock of your life too. I think everyone should. We should all have a five- or ten-year plan.'

'What ten-year plan?'

'The one we're going to work out tonight. Your kids are adults now and they'll be busy with their own lives. You should have a list of a thousand things you've always wanted to do but never had time for. Now's your chance to start on that list—you just have to work out what to do first.'

'I've been thinking about doing some courses, taking up a hobby,' Maggie admitted.

Juliet snickered.

'What?' Maggie asked.

'I was thinking more of long-term things, more about your life for the foreseeable future, not just the next few months.'

'You asked what was on my list.'

'Maybe I should have been more specific. Who do you want to do those things with? You're forty-two—you could potentially live for another forty years. You're not going to spend those years alone, are you?'

Juliet must be feeling better, Maggie decided; she was back to her bossy self! 'You could be in the same position, you know. Merry widow, gay divorcée—either way we're both single,' she retorted.

'Don't think I haven't thought about that,' Juliet said. 'Leaving Sam was one of the hardest things I've ever done but I haven't accepted that I'll never find love again. And I hate to think of *you* spending the rest of your life alone.'

'I thought I could move in with you. Once your kids have flown the nest we could be two old-maid sisters living out their last days in peace and quiet,' Maggie joked.

'Speak for yourself—*I* don't intend to spend my twilight years alone. It's too soon for me but I think *you* need to start dating.'

'I've been on dates.'

'When was your last date?' Juliet asked.

'Just before I came down to Melbourne.'

'How many third dates have you had?'

Maggie was silent—third dates were few and far between. Most of the time a second date was as far as things went before she decided there was no chemistry, attraction or even the possibility of intelligent conversation and called it quits.

'Thought so,' Juliet responded, interpreting her silence. 'And when was the last time you had sex?'

'I don't remember.'

Juliet threw her hands up into the air, almost spilling her wine in the process. 'That's my point exactly—you should remember. It should have been recent and it should have been fantastic. You need to get out more.'

Maggie twirled her wine glass in her hands. 'Do you want to know why I don't date? For the first twelve months after Steven died no one knew what to do with me. I didn't get invited anywhere. Everyone assumed I needed time to deal with my grief but what they didn't realize was that the lack of invitations meant I had more time than I knew what to do with, more time to think about what I'd lost. When I finally got invited out again I got the feeling that half the women thought I'd be after their husbands. It made me uncomfortable. It was easier not to go to some things.'

'Don't you meet people at work?'

'I don't want to date people from work,' Maggie replied. 'It's too complicated.'

'What about people you meet *through* work?'

'Like who? Patients?' She laughed. 'I work in Theatre, remember? I only see patients for a few minutes before they go under anaesthetic and then they're off to Recovery before they really wake up. Not much opportunity to start chatting, other than telling them to count backwards from twenty!' Maggie shook her head. 'I'm not against the idea of romance or even a simple roll in the hay but in my opinion dating takes too much effort. A hobby would be much easier.'

'Back to that!' Juliet sighed. 'You know you don't necessarily have to date if all you want is a bit of romp.'

But that wasn't really how Maggie operated. She knew she was someone who wanted the whole experience—attraction, romance, a strong connection both emotionally and physically. That was exactly why she was still on her own, why she didn't often go on third dates. She was still waiting for the perfect man to sweep her off her feet, just as Steven had done more than twenty years ago. But was Juliet right? Was she being too fussy? Was she looking at spending the next forty years alone?

Working and being a sole parent for the past ten years had drained her, but when she thought of Juliet's life hers seemed blessed in comparison. Juliet had been through a divorce, a malignant breast lump, chemotherapy, a double mastectomy and then a near-death experience. Just one of those things would be more than most people could cope with, Maggie thought, let alone all of them.

'You deserve to have some fun after the past two years you've had,' she said to Juliet.

'What about you? Don't you want to have fun?'

'I'm happy as I am.' Was that true? What was her definition of happy? Her own children made her happy—most of the time, she thought with a smile. Her extended family. Her work. But was that enough?

'Don't you think you could be happier?' Juliet wanted to know.

Maggie shrugged. She wasn't sure this was a conversation she wanted to have.

But Juliet wasn't finished yet. 'I have a suggestion for you. I know you've come to Melbourne to help me but you don't need to stay home twenty-four hours a day on my account. If I can introduce you to some decent single men, would you go out on a date?'

'Why?'

'Because you might have fun! I'm not ready to get out and about yet but that doesn't mean we both have to sit at home. I'm quite happy to live vicariously through you for the time being. Nobody in Melbourne knows you and your story—it's a good chance to relax and enjoy yourself.'

'Who are these single men you have in mind?' Maggie wasn't about to agree to Juliet's plans without more information.

'You can choose.'

'Me?'

Juliet nodded. 'I know a few single men. Besides, I have an ulterior motive. If I can find you someone perfect you might end up staying in Melbourne, close to me,' she said with a grin.

'Why am I not surprised?' Maggie said. 'There's always a grand plan with you!'

'Tell me your idea of a perfect man and I'll see what I can do,' Juliet prompted.

Maggie decided she really didn't have anything to lose by agreeing to Juliet's plan. If nothing else, it would keep Juliet off her back, and Maggie had learned a long time ago that letting Juliet think she was winning a battle was one way of ensuring a quiet life. So what would her perfect man look like these days?

Tall and solid, but fit rather than fat. A protector. Someone dependable. Dark hair. Blue eyes. Turquoise blue. An image of Ben McMahon flashed before Maggie's eyes. Tall, dark, gorgeous and obviously intelligent—was it any surprise he sprang to mind?

'Who is it?' Juliet badgered. 'You must have someone in mind—you're daydreaming.'

'I don't know if he's perfect—he seems too good to be true.'

'Sounds interesting. Who?'

'Ben McMahon.'

'Mmm. Good choice. He's pretty close to perfect. Smart, sexy and single.'

'Single?' She hadn't actually expected him to be single. 'So *that's* what's wrong with him.' Maggie sighed.

'What?'

'He's gay.'

Juliet laughed. 'Not as far as I know but why don't you test that theory?'

'How?'

'Ask him out.'

'Hang on a minute—I thought *you* were finding me a date.'

'He wasn't on my list,' Juliet argued, 'but I'm sure we can work something out. Why don't you try flirting with him at my appointment tomorrow, then we'll find out if he's interested.'

Maggie got embarrassed at the *thought* of flirting with Ben. She couldn't possibly do it for real without making a complete spectacle of herself, could she?

'Are you sure he's not married?' she clarified. That would be too humiliating and just her luck.

'Trust me, he's single and he's straight.'

'How do you know?'

'He's always in the social pages—his family is Melbourne high society—and he's always with a different woman in every photo. I'm sure that's not just camouflage, and if he had a wife I'm certain she wouldn't be putting up with that!'

'What do you mean, 'high society'?' Maggie's curiosity was piqued.

'His father's family owns a publishing company and his mother runs the McMahon Foundation. Even in Sydney you would have heard of them, surely?'

'He's one of *those* McMahons?'

Juliet nodded and Maggie felt sick at the thought of trying to have a normal conversation with Ben now, let alone flirt with the man. He would have women throwing themselves at him at every opportunity, and she didn't want to put herself in that same category. 'I don't know. He's way out of my league.'

'Don't be ridiculous, you need to stop thinking like that right now. You're good enough for anyone. Besides, I'm only asking you to flirt with the guy—he doesn't need to propose.'

But appreciating a fine example when it crossed her path was one thing; drawing attention to herself was another thing entirely.

As she rinsed out the wine glasses and got ready for bed she reflected on what she'd just agreed to. Juliet wanted to have fun; Maggie wanted to be happy.

She didn't want to be lonely but she very much doubted

that Ben McMahon held the key to her happiness. She shrugged her shoulders. She supposed she had nothing to lose by flirting a little. What was the worst that could happen?

Maggie hesitated over applying make-up the next morning as she got ready to take Juliet for her first post-op appointment with Dr McMahon. Ben.

She wasn't as completely out of practice as Juliet might think. It had been years after Steven had died before she'd even contemplated dating but she had been on a few dates in the past five years. It was just that she hadn't enjoyed them particularly. When that was the case she couldn't see the point of continuing to date, of waiting to see if she 'grew to like them'. She knew she wouldn't, so while she *had* dated, it could certainly be said she hadn't had a proper relationship since Steven had died.

She reminded herself that the aim of today wasn't to get Ben to ask her out on a date; she just needed to make a little light conversation, just to show she was trying. She didn't necessarily want to draw attention to herself but she decided a bit of make-up might help her feel more in control of the situation.

Her hand shook as she tried to apply her lipgloss. She was as nervous as she could ever remember being. All because she was supposed to flirt with a gorgeous man! She ignored the eyeshadow, thinking it would be overkill for a morning appointment, and just put some eye drops into her eyes to dull any traces of red. She brushed her dark hair until it shone and debated over whether to tie it up but in the end she left it down, falling over her shoulders. The brushstrokes were relaxing but she was still terrified she'd embarrass herself despite Juliet's assurances that men would either be flattered by, or ignorant of, her methods.

Maybe if she failed spectacularly Juliet would let her off the hook. She thought she might prefer being lonely to being terrified.

But she needed to at least look as though she was trying. And she was still a woman—she still wanted to see if she could catch a man's eye, even if she wasn't quite sure what she wanted to do next. Everyone's ego needed a boost now and then; she wasn't really any different to the next person. She decided to make an effort.

She searched through her clothes looking for a bra that wasn't more than three years old and that managed to lift her boobs back up to somewhere close to where they used to be. She pulled a dress out of the wardrobe, holding it in front of her—too fancy for a doctor's appointment she decided. Jeans? Too casual. She swapped the jeans for a skirt that gave a little bit of shape to her boyish figure and put on a fitted T-shirt—white—to make it look as if her boobs were bigger than they really were. That looked better. Finally she was ready.

Maggie sat in the waiting room, convinced everyone could hear her heart hammering in her chest. She wiped her clammy hands on her skirt and looked for something to distract her.

'What do you think of these?'

Maggie glanced at the photograph in the magazine her sister was holding.

'Pamela Anderson! Is that what you chose?' Maggie knew her younger sister had gotten the flamboyant gene whereas she'd inherited the conservative one but, even so, she hadn't expected her to choose to be quite so out there. 'You're not serious! I thought you wanted to look like the old you?'

Juliet grinned at her. 'You're right, classy, not brassy. I picked out boobs that look more like Kate Winslet's.' Juliet turned back a page and showed Maggie another photo.

'Huh!'

'What?' Juliet asked.

'I didn't realise when you said the "old you," you really meant the "young you." Kate's boobs look like yours did in your teens, not what they looked like in your thirties after a couple of kids!' Maggie couldn't resist teasing her sister; some light-hearted banter was just what she needed to distract her from Juliet's 'mission.'

'You think her boobs are too good for me?'

'Not at all, it's just that they're not at all saggy.'

Juliet took the magazine back and had another look at the photo, her forehead creasing a little as she studied it. 'Why is that, do you think? She's had two kids as well.' She paused, tilting her head slightly to one side. 'Could be a flattering angle or a good bra.'

'Or she could have had work done,' Maggie said.

'That does it, I'm definitely getting boobs like hers, then— particularly if they look natural and they're not! Not much point in saggy new boobs.'

Maggie glanced down at her own chest. She'd never been more than a B-cup and she'd never considered being anything else—as long as everything worked, that was all that mattered, as far as she was concerned. But even though she wasn't about to change her own body, which had served her well for forty-two years, she could see Juliet's point. 'I suppose, if you're going to have a breast reconstruction, you might as well get what you want.'

'My thoughts exactly.' Juliet chuckled.

'Come through, Juliet.' Ben appeared in the waiting room

and Maggie was surprised by the pull of attraction she felt. He was wearing a white shirt with no tie; his collar was open at his throat, and as Maggie stood she could see a smattering of dark hair below his collarbones. 'You sound in good spirits.'

'Just showing Maggie which boobs I've ordered.' Juliet gestured towards her sister. 'You remember Maggie, don't you?'

'Of course. Are you feeling the pressure of providing a second opinion?' His eyes met hers, holding her attention. There was something in the way he looked at her that made her go weak at the knees. She got the feeling he could read her mind, could see into her soul. Her heartbeat increased its pace.

She couldn't do this! She knew she'd get flustered and make a fool of herself. There was an energy that surrounded him, and she was much too attracted to him to flirt comfortably. In the two weeks since she'd seen him she'd forgotten just how good-looking he was.

But he was waiting for her response. She said the first thing that popped into her head. 'Someone had to make sure Juliet didn't end up looking like Pamela Anderson.' She went for levity in her reply in an attempt to break the spell Ben seemed to have over her. If she could crack a joke maybe she'd be able to breathe again and maybe her heart would be able to return to its normal rhythm.

So far, so good. Her voice sounded normal, no squeaks or breathlessness.

He smiled. There was a definite sparkle in his eyes and that was all it took for her heart to start racing again. 'That was an option?' he asked as he led them through to his office.

She answered quickly while his back was turned, before he had another opportunity to throw her off kilter. 'Not for long!'

'Don't tell fibs, Mags,' Juliet said as she sat in one of the chairs in front of Ben's desk and placed the magazine on the table, tapping a photograph. 'I'd like to look like Kate Winslet, please.'

Ben picked up the magazine. 'Kate Winslet? What do you think, Maggie?' He lifted his gaze to hers, his blue eyes focusing on her and making her stomach somersault. If he kept looking at her like that she'd never be able to answer.

She tore her gaze away, concentrating on the photograph. 'Far more suitable than Pamela,' she replied.

'Pamela might have been fun though,' Juliet said.

'I'm sure you'd find those boobs more annoying than fun after a while, not to mention the backache.' That was better. She should concentrate on Juliet; she could talk to her like a normal person!

'Oh, Mags, you're such a sensible older sister.'

'Be nice or I'll get Ben to give you the saggy version of Kate.'

'You wouldn't dare!'

Maggie stuck out her tongue and Ben laughed. The sound washed over Maggie. She'd made him laugh and it was the nicest sound she'd heard in a long time. Deep and rich, he laughed like a man who enjoyed himself, like a man who laughed often and easily.

'Sorry, girls, I'd prefer not to do saggy and I wouldn't give Juliet "Pammy" breasts either. Neither option would be good for my reputation.'

Ben's comment took Maggie by surprise. She thought all men would choose Pamela Anderson if they got the chance. And he looked as if he'd prefer American-type women. Blonde, blue-eyed, white teeth and big boobs—cheerleaders.

What was she doing? Why was she even considering what type of women he'd like? His taste in women was of no concern to her, although she'd bet his taste didn't lean towards skinny, small-breasted, brunette Aussie women!

Stop it—who cares? she thought, knowing, even as she asked herself the question, that she did.

This flirting thing was going to end in disaster unless she got her hormones under control.

Ben was talking to Juliet now, the consultation under way, leaving Maggie time to settle her nerves. 'A good C-cup will suit you perfectly Juliet, as we've discussed. That's assuming the tissue expander stretches enough over the next few weeks to allow me to put C-cup implants in. Have you had any soreness or noticed any redness over the past few days?'

'No, everything's settled down well.'

'Excellent. If you're ready to get started I'll get you to go behind the screen, slip your shirt off and lie down on the bed. There's a sheet there to put over you.'

Juliet disappeared behind the privacy screen, and Ben went to the sink to wash his hands before pulling on a pair of disposable gloves.

Maggie could hear him explaining the process to Juliet as he worked. She listened to him while she studied his office.

'Everything looks good. I'm planning to inject about ninety millilitres of saline into the tissue expander today if I can. Remember, the whole process will take six to eight weeks as each injection stretches the expander a little more until we can replace it with the implants. How many weeks exactly will depend on how easily your skin stretches.'

Maggie scanned the artwork on the walls. There had been a definite African theme to the pictures in the waiting room and that continued in Ben's office where several stunning photographs were displayed on the walls. She told herself she was interested in the photos for art's sake but she knew the truth. The truth was she was looking for clues about Ben, about his life outside of work. She was snooping. But the artwork told her nothing except that he seemed to have an interest in Africa.

'I'll do the left side first. It won't hurt—there are no nerve endings so you won't feel the saline going in. It goes straight into the expander through the skin valve. You might feel a little stretching but that should be about it.'

Maggie's gaze travelled to the desk. There were a few pieces of African art—sculptures and the like on his desk and bookshelf—but no photos, particularly no photos that could be of a wife, or ex-wife, and children.

So Juliet was right...Ben was single?

'OK, almost done. You might find it gets a little uncomfortable over the next twenty-four hours or so as the muscles stretch. Take some mild analgesics if you need to.'

Maggie heard Ben snap his gloves off and then he reappeared from behind the privacy screen.

'Are you able to help Juliet for the next twenty-four hours, Maggie? I'd like her to avoid driving, heavy lifting and raising her arms above chest height for the next day, just to help prevent any additional soreness.'

'Yes, I'm still staying at her house.'

'Great,' he said as Juliet joined them in front of the screen. 'I'll see you both next Friday, then?'

'Definitely,' Juliet said, jumping in before Maggie had a chance to reply.

Ben opened the door for them but didn't follow them out.

'There you go—that wasn't so hard, was it?' Juliet asked as they returned to the reception desk to confirm her remaining appointments. 'And he sounds like he's looking forward to seeing you next week too.'

'I'm sure he's just making polite conversation.'

'Time will tell,' Juliet said with a grin.

Maggie sensed she had more to add but fortunately they were now back in the waiting area and Juliet seemed to decide not to share her opinion with the rest of Ben's patients, or his staff. But Juliet's comment got Maggie thinking as she waited for the receptionist to confirm the next appointment—did she want Ben's remark to be genuine? She was sure it had been said with sincerity—she didn't doubt that—but did she want him to be looking forward to seeing her again specifically? That thought made her equally nervous and excited and she found herself replaying his words many times over the course of the evening before finally deciding it was what it was—a polite comment with no hidden agenda! As much as she hated to admit it, disappointment accompanied that realisation.

CHAPTER THREE

IT WAS a busy Saturday morning in Hawthorn and Maggie was feeling a little frazzled after trying to find a car park around Glenferrie Oval, where vacant spots were as rare as the proverbial hen's teeth.

'OK, champ, let's get in the line to hand in your registration,' she said to Edward as they joined the queue stretching around the perimeter of the oval.

It was her nephew's first football-coaching clinic and Maggie had offered to bring him as Juliet was still feeling tender and sore following the tissue expander procedure the day before.

There seemed to be hundreds of six-year-olds running amok all over the oval and dozens of footballs were whizzing through the air in all directions. The grass was a mass of brown and gold as most children were wearing miniature versions of the local football team's tops.

'Can you do it, Auntie Maggie? My friends are over there kicking the footy.' Edward pointed across the oval and looked up at her with his best pleading expression.

What should she do? If it were her own child she'd say yes in a flash but Maggie didn't know Edward's friends and didn't really know what today's procedure was.

'Please?' he begged.

'Which friends?'

'Jake and Rory.' He pointed at a group of children, all in brown-and-yellow football jerseys. Maggie couldn't tell one from the other, but she remembered meeting one of Juliet's friends, Anna, who had a son called Jake. She could only assume that was who Edward was talking about.

The oval was fenced and Edward didn't seem bothered. In fact, he seemed rather keen to run off. Maggie shrugged. 'I guess that's all right but just listen when they call you in for the start of the session, OK? I'll sit in the grandstand and watch.'

Edward nodded his head and disappeared, leaving Maggie to stand in line to register before she could make her way to the old grandstand.

'Morning, Maggie.'

She had just sat down in the front row of the grandstand where she could bask in the autumn sun when she heard the greeting. She hadn't expected anyone to recognise her here. She certainly hadn't expected to know anyone herself, but that voice was instantly recognisable.

'Ben! What are you doing here?' A thousand questions raced through Maggie's mind in the space of a few short seconds. The questions seemed to be keeping time with her heartbeat. And as quickly as her heart had begun racing it stopped and sank in her chest as she realised why he was here. 'Do you have children here?'

He shook his head. 'A nephew. You?'

Her heart leapt back up to its rightful spot. 'Same. I brought Juliet's son.'

'Are you staying to watch the session?' he asked and when Maggie nodded he continued. 'Can I get you a coffee? I was just on my way for one.'

A warm glow spread through her. She wouldn't say no to Ben's company. Juliet's plan sprang to mind and while she certainly couldn't call this a date it did involve striking up a conversation. Who knew, maybe she *could* flirt with him. And let's face it, she told herself, if she couldn't flirt with someone who literally made her toes curl with desire there wasn't much hope for her, was there?

'That would be lovely, thank you.'

'Cappuccino, latte, flat white?'

'You don't suppose they'd make a hot chocolate?' she asked.

He smiled at her—yep, her toes were curling—and said, 'I'll see what I can do,' before he headed off towards the coffee van.

'One hot chocolate,' he said on his return, handing her a takeaway cup and a paper bag, 'and a blueberry muffin. I'm eating so I took a chance on your preference.'

Maggie peeked into the bag, 'Looks great, thanks.'

'Here, let me hold the muffin while you take the lid off your drink.' Ben's fingers brushed against her hand as he took the bag from her, and she almost dropped the cup when a trail of heat raced up her arm. Her hand shook as she removed the lid to allow her drink to cool down but Ben seemed oblivious to her sudden bout of nerves. 'Which one is your nephew?' he asked.

Maggie shielded her eyes with one hand as she sought out Edward. She'd left her sunglasses in the car. The day had started off grey and bleak, and she'd forgotten how rapidly Melbourne weather changed.

'Is the sun bothering you? Did you want to move further back in the grandstand?' Ben asked.

'No. I'm enjoying the sun. I'm finding Melbourne mornings a bit chilly, to be honest. I need some sunshine to warm me up.'

'Are you not from here?'

'I'm from Sydney. I've just come down to help Juliet with the kids while she was having surgery.'

'Did you grow up here or there?'

If she'd had a thousand questions when she'd first seen Ben this morning it seemed as though he had more! 'Sydney, born and bred,' she replied. 'Juliet moved here with her ex-husband. He's in the navy and she stayed when they split up. Kate, her daughter, was settled in school and Juliet figured that was easier than moving.'

'How long are you here for?'

'I've taken some long service leave and I might go back and forward a bit until she's had the implants. It sort of depends on how she goes with the procedures.' She held his gaze. 'I guess it's up to you a bit, isn't it?'

'Maybe I should take my time,' he said. 'Give you a chance to enjoy our hospitality.' He smiled and his blue eyes sparkled, reminding her of the ocean on a sunny day.

She couldn't believe it—was he flirting back? Maybe his farewell after Juliet's appointment hadn't been simply polite rhetoric? Before she had time to work that out Ben had moved on in the conversation.

'Speaking of Juliet, how is she going?'

She decided she didn't have the skills to work out whether or not Ben was flirting so she stuck to the script. 'She's a bit sore today. She says she feels as though she's done too many push-ups, so I guess it's muscular soreness she's describing.'

'She hasn't had any other side effects?'

'Physically or emotionally?'

'Either.'

'Not really. I expected her to be a bit tired from the surgery and the near-death experience but she seems to have bounced back with more energy than ever. She's even more determined to make the most of every moment now. She's been a bit like that since she finished chemo after the mastectomy but it's more noticeable now. She would have come with me today except she's taken her daughter to a ballet class.' Ben opened his mouth to speak out but Maggie guessed what he was about to ask and added, 'Don't worry, she didn't have to drive. It's walking distance.'

'So she doesn't seem worried about what happened in Theatre?'

'No, she seems fine, quite calm about the whole thing considering.'

'Considering what?'

'The fact she says she heard my husband's voice.'

Husband? Ben's eyes flicked to Maggie's left hand. She was wearing a wedding ring. He'd noticed her; how had he not noticed her wedding ring?

'Is it possible she could have heard him?' His mind was buzzing but somehow he managed to formulate a reply.

She shrugged. 'It's not impossible. He died ten years ago.'

So she was widowed. Had she remarried? Was that why she was wearing a ring? Questions whirled around in his head. While newly single women were definitely fair game in his opinion, married women definitely were not. But when had he put Maggie in his sights? He knew the answer to that. Yesterday—when he'd spent too much time thinking about her when he should have been writing reports. He was supposed to have been entering details of Juliet's procedure into her file but his mind had kept drifting, not aimlessly but rather definitely, to Maggie.

She was a stunning woman. As a plastic surgeon he was trained to notice bone structure and Maggie had a perfect oval face and fabulous cheekbones. Even the bump in the bridge of her nose, that she apparently hated, gave her face character. He'd been honest when he said he wouldn't change it.

Her eyes were a startling blue, and as he looked into them now he could picture her in Theatre. Gowned, masked, capped—covered up except for her eyes. He wondered how the other staff kept focused.

He shook his head to clear his mind and ran back over the events in his theatre. He couldn't remember everything—it had all happened very quickly—but some things were clear. 'Was his name Steven?'

'Yes.' Maggie's brow creased with concentration as she looked at him, or was it confusion? 'How did you know that?'

'When we'd revived her I asked her if she could hear me and she called me Steven. At least, I thought she was talking to me.'

Maggie shook her head. 'She thinks she was talking to my husband.'

'You're a nurse, a theatre nurse, you said?' He waited for her confirmation. 'Do you think there's something to these "near-death experiences," for want of a better term?'

'I've heard too many reports to be able to discount them completely.'

'Really? You've had other patients report similar things? Firsthand experiences?'

Maggie nodded. 'Three or four times, I reckon. And there have been plenty of similarities between them. The light, the feeling of peace and tranquillity, hearing loved ones.'

'So what's your opinion, then?'

'I've often wondered about it, from both sides—the emotional and the physiological. I can see the scientists' point of view—they say it's all chemical reaction and nerve synapses—but when Juliet said she'd heard Steven's voice, that all made sense too. But maybe she just confused someone else's voice with his, maybe it was you she could hear. Do you remember what you said? If you can remember it could explain whether she heard you or not.'

He shook his head. 'I don't remember anything specific, it was all rather frantic. I was more interested in trying to save her life than in paying attention to what I was saying. I would have been talking to her, trying to get her to hold on, but more than that I couldn't say. I've never had one of my patients flatline before. I was more concerned about saving her.'

'Well, I'm very glad you did. I don't think I could bear to lose Juliet, not after all she's been through.' Maggie smiled at him as she spoke but her smile was tinged with sadness, and Ben knew she was thinking of more than just Juliet's close call. Maggie had lost someone she loved before, and he wondered if she had found love again. 'And, as for near-death experiences, I'd like to think they're real.'

'The white light and the voices… You think people are waiting to guide us to heaven?'

She shrugged her shoulders and her dark hair shone as the sunlight bounced off it showing up shades of red and gold amongst the predominantly dark waves. 'I don't know about heaven but I believe there's another life waiting for us after this one. I think it's likely to be very different but I need to believe there is something. Even if it's just a place where souls can meet again. But that's just my opinion. I'm still not sure if Juliet's recollection gives any more weight to my theory.'

'It's a nice idea though.'

'Yes, it is.' Maggie's eyes met his and for a moment neither of them spoke. He understood her need to believe in an after-life, in whatever form it came. As a doctor he'd seen that belief get people through some horrendous situations. This sharing of opinions forged a connection between them that didn't need words. He kept eye contact, amazed again at just how blue her eyes were, their unusual colour accentuated by her dark eyelashes. Other than the bump in her nose her features were remarkably symmetrical and gave her a slight ethereal quality.

'Thank you for listening.' Maggie put a hand on his arm. It was an unconscious gesture on her part—he'd swear she was completely unaware of the movement—but the touch of her palm on his bare forearm sent a surge of desire through him that took him by surprise.

She was an attractive woman—physically not more so than a dozen others he knew—but this spark that zipped through him was unusual. There had to be some scientific reason for it; in his mind there was a scientific reason for everything. Even near-death experiences, in his opinion, were simply a by-product of a person's wiring. Not that he'd pushed that idea on Maggie; he'd been too interested in her thoughts. But chemistry between two people, two strangers, that was stuff of fiction. The spark must simply be due to ions in their bodies or the humidity in the air. Something simple. Something scientific.

'Look what I got, Uncle Ben.'

An unexpected voice startled him. His nephew was standing in front of him, proudly displaying a bright yellow football and a backpack.

'Rory! Has the clinic finished?' He hadn't noticed the session coming to an end.

'Rory is your nephew?' Maggie said. 'My nephew Edward's friend? Why didn't you say something?'

He turned to Maggie—he must have missed some information along the way. 'I didn't know there was a connection,' he admitted. 'I know that my sister, Gabby, recommended me to Juliet but I didn't think to ask how they knew each other. It must be through the boys' school.' He paused, wondering if this information gave him licence to take another step, before deciding there was only one way to find out. 'We're going to have a milkshake now, why don't you join us?'

'Thank you, we'd love to but we can't. I made a deal with Juliet that if she wanted to walk Kate to ballet I'd pick her up afterwards. We'll have to get going.'

That was OK—she hadn't knocked him back. 'Maybe next week, then.'

'Will you be bringing Rory again?'

'More than likely. My sister and her husband travel quite often for their business, and I help my parents out with Rory on weekends when I can.'

'That's very good of you.'

'Not at all, I think I get more out of it than Rory. He's great company.'

'So, next Saturday, then?' she said with a smile which he found ridiculously satisfying.

He nodded, pleased she seemed keen to join him, and as he watched her walking away, a slim figure in faded jeans, he tried again to work out what it was about her that appealed to him. He thought back over their conversation. She'd been very open and honest; he guessed there'd be no game playing with her. Perhaps that was her point of difference—she was genuine. Could it be that simple?

As he caught the last glimpse of her as she and Edward left

the oval he realised he was already looking forward to next week. She intrigued him, he decided, and he couldn't recall the last time he'd been able to say that about someone.

Maggie listened to Edward recount the morning's activities to Juliet as she heated soup for lunch and prepared sandwiches. He didn't mention Ben, but then why would he? Football had been the big attraction for him.

'Was it as much fun as Edward thinks?' Juliet asked her when she came into the kitchen. 'It didn't drag on for too long?'

'Not at all,' Maggie answered. The time had passed in the blink of an eye.

'Did you have to help out?'

Maggie shook her head. 'No, there were plenty of official helpers. It was pretty well organised.'

'What did you do for an hour, then?'

'Ben McMahon was there,' Maggie said, hoping she sounded calm despite her sizzling nerves. 'I chatted to him.'

Juliet squealed. 'What did you talk about?'

My dead husband, Maggie thought, knowing that Juliet would have a fit if she admitted this had been a topic of conversation; that was surely a no-go zone in the 'art of flirting.' She decided to keep that to herself and went with, 'This and that—the kids. Ben said that Rory's parents are away—something to do with their work?' She changed the subject.

'I'd forgotten they're interstate. They run a rather successful art gallery in St Kilda and they focus on indigenous art, Aboriginal and other cultures. They travel a lot.' Juliet paused and Maggie could almost see the wheels turning in her head. 'You should get Ben to show you their gallery.'

'I think he'd have better things to do.'

'You'll never know until you ask.'

Maggie could have told Juliet then all about their conversation but she knew it was too complicated to explain how she'd immediately felt comfortable in Ben's company. How it hadn't felt strange to talk to Ben about Steven or about such a controversial subject as life after death and people's perceptions of heaven.

Talking to Ben she'd felt as though her opinion mattered, as though it was worth something. She was an intensely private sort of person, much more so than Juliet, so to have such a revealing conversation with a virtual stranger must say something about Ben. Or maybe it said more about her feelings towards Ben, and she wasn't ready to share those yet. Not even with Juliet.

Nor was she about to mention the plans for next weekend. She wanted to hug that to herself for a little longer. It felt too precious, and she knew that sharing the news would diminish that. So she just shrugged and concentrated on making lunch and steered the conversation back to Juliet's morning and then onto their plans and schedule for the following week. It had been a while since her own children had depended on her for everything, and Maggie wanted to make sure she had a handle on what needed to happen in order for Juliet's household to run smoothly. The kids had had enough upheaval, and Maggie wanted to make things easy for everyone. Focusing on what everyone else needed also meant she didn't have time to examine her own feelings too closely.

But over the next week Maggie's thoughts kept returning to Ben with rather alarming frequency. Folding laundry, washing dishes, chatting to Juliet, driving the children around town—no activity was immune and it was a strange sensation to have her mind wandering off on its own tangent.

Her reaction to Ben scared her a little; she barely knew the man. How was it he could have such a strong impact on her?

'I missed you at Juliet's appointment yesterday.'

Maggie was standing at the edge of the football oval, having just sent Edward to join his training group, and she turned at the sound of Ben's voice, a smile already on her face.

Her breath caught in her throat as she met his eyes. He hadn't shaved this morning and his square jaw was darkened by stubble and the blue of his eyes was heightened by the shadow of his beard. He was seriously gorgeous. He was holding two takeaway coffee cups, and her eyes were drawn to his hands as he offered her a cup. The cups looked small in his grasp but although his hands were large they weren't chunky. His fingers were slender, his nails clean and nicely shaped. 'One hot chocolate for you.'

'Thank you,' she replied, touched he'd remembered her order. She'd spent countless hours over the previous week rehearsing what she'd say to Ben when she saw him next, running through all the topics one might consider suitable for conversation—work, movies, books, sport. The only trouble was she wasn't working, she hadn't had time to go to the movies or read, and she really knew nothing about football—and to admit that to a Melbournian was social suicide. Maybe Ben could teach her about football? In the meantime she'd have to stick with talking about the children. 'I couldn't make Juliet's appointment yesterday,' she explained in reply to his initial comment. 'I went to school assembly instead. Kate's class was doing a presentation.'

Ben nodded. 'Juliet told me.'

Ben had asked Juliet where she was? A thrill of excitement snaked its way through Maggie's stomach at the thought.

'She also told me that you enjoyed last week's football clinic so much you'd volunteered to come again today,' Ben continued.

Maggie could feel the heat suffusing her cheeks and cursed her fair skin as the blush spread across her face. She made a show of looking out across the oval, pretending to watch the children chasing after footballs, anything to avoid looking directly at Ben and letting him see how embarrassed she was. 'What else did she tell you?'

'That you don't need to rush off after today's session. Which means you and Edward are free to join us for a milkshake.'

She smiled, pleased the invitation was still there. 'We hadn't forgotten.'

'Is Juliet here as well?' he asked as, in silent agreement, they made their way up the stairs of the grandstand to sit in the same seats as last week.

Maggie shook her head. 'No, she said it was too cold this morning. She's at home.' Maggie silently wondered whether Juliet had deliberately used the weather as an excuse but then realised she didn't care. She was actually pleased to have Ben's company to herself. She'd promised herself she'd try to have a more cheerful conversation this week though—no talk of dead husbands or gruesome hospital tales—and she intended to remain full of good news and optimism. She was about to ask him how his week had been when her mobile phone rang, interrupting her train of thought.

As Maggie excused herself to answer her phone Ben grabbed the chance to study her. He hadn't been surprised to hear that Maggie had enjoyed his company last Saturday— without being conceited he knew he could be good company when he chose—but he had been surprised to find how pleased he was to hear that information. Surprised to realise how much he was looking forward to seeing her again too.

'Everything OK?' he asked when Maggie returned. He hoped Juliet wasn't calling her home for something.

'Fine. That was Sophie, my daughter,' Maggie explained as she sat beside him.

Her daughter? Had he known she had a daughter? He couldn't remember any being mentioned. 'Who's looking after her while you're here?'

Maggie smiled. 'They're OK on their own.'

'What?' She had more than one child? 'They're on their own?'

She was smiling at him; his confusion seemed to be amusing her. 'Sophie is almost twenty-one. James is nineteen.'

How old?

'Are they your stepchildren?' he asked.

'Stepchildren?'

The conversation seemed to be spoken in riddles. 'You can't possibly have children that old.' He looked at her wedding ring. 'You're wearing a ring—I assumed you'd remarried.'

'I haven't remarried.'

She was twisting her wedding ring around on her finger. Ben wanted to ask her more but she was looking out across the oval, not meeting his eyes, and he knew now wasn't the time. He'd ask her about her children instead—in his experience all mothers loved to talk about their kids.

'What do your children do? Are they working, studying, travelling?'

'James is doing vet science and Sophie's— Oh, no!'

Ben followed Maggie's gaze. She was watching Edward's group as they were doing marking practice. Edward was sliding along the ground to scoop up a ball in his arms. It was a difficult catch, one Ben thought he'd managed well—until he couldn't stop his slide. Edward overshot the edge of the oval and crashed into the boundary fence right in front of the grandstand. His head collided with the metal post in the wire-mesh fence. Ben saw his forehead split open like a ripe tomato and blood pour from the wound.

Maggie was rooted to the spot. Ben pushed past her and raced down the grandstand steps, clearing the low boundary fence with a quick jump. Edward was sitting up, holding his hands in front of him and staring silently at the blood as it ran from his forehead and into his hands. Ben knelt beside him, pushing the hair from Ed's forehead to inspect the damage. There was a nasty gash about three inches long running down the centre of his forehead.

He pulled a clean handkerchief from his pocket and pressed it against the wound. He looked around, looking for an extra pair of hands, looking for assistance, looking for Maggie. She was standing behind his left shoulder.

'Maggie.'

She didn't answer.

'Maggie,' he repeated. 'Can you find me a first-aid kit?' She was staring back at him but her gaze was blank. He needed her to focus but he couldn't get her attention.

Several other parents had gathered around and one of them spoke up. 'I'll find someone for you.'

Ben nodded in acknowledgement before turning his attention back to Ed. He'd worry about Maggie later.

'Edward, can you look at me?' he asked.

Edward lifted his head and looked up. Ben checked his eyes, looking to see if his pupils were equally dilated.

'Do you know where you are, Ed?'

'At footy.'

'Can I get through? I've got the first-aid kit.' One of the clinic organisers pushed through the throng of kids who were standing around, mesmerised by the gory scene in front of them.

'Pass it to me, I'm a doctor.' Ben took the kit; he wasn't about to relinquish control to someone who possibly had only basic first-aid training. 'Can someone find me a blanket too?' He issued instructions before addressing the children who were still gathered around. 'It's OK, kids, heads bleed a lot. It looks worse than it is.' Now that Ben had stemmed the flow of blood all the kids, other than his nephew, Rory, drifted back to football training, which was obviously more interesting.

Ben kept pressure on Edward's head with one hand as he flicked open the first-aid box with the other.

'Has he got a parent with him?' asked the first-aid officer.

Ben pointed at Maggie with his free hand. 'That's his aunt. Can you ask her to give me a hand? She's a nurse.'

Maggie was standing less than two feet from Ben but if the first-aid officer thought it was odd that Ben didn't ask Maggie himself she didn't comment. Ben needed someone to get Maggie to focus.

'Are you his aunt?' Ben heard the woman ask Maggie. She didn't get an immediate response. She touched Maggie's arm. 'Excuse me, are you with this child?'

Maggie heard her this time but Ben thought she looked surprised to find someone standing in front of her addressing her. Maggie nodded.

'He's asked if you could give him a hand.' The woman indicated Ben. 'You are a nurse?' The uncertainty was clear in her tone.

Ben saw Maggie look down at him.

'Maggie, do you think you could find some sterile pads for

me?' He could have asked the first-aid officer to help but he thought Edward might prefer familiar faces. He wondered what the matter was with Maggie. He was worried she'd gone into shock, although the accident seemed too minor to have caused such a reaction.

Maggie knelt beside him and rummaged through the first-aid kit. She found pads and ripped the packets open, holding them out for Ben to take. Her hands were shaking but she was at least able to follow instructions, although she still hadn't spoken.

Ben worked quickly, completely focused on the task at hand, but still managing to talk in a calm, quiet voice to Edward, explaining what he was doing.

Someone passed Maggie a blanket, and she wrapped it around Ed's shoulders.

Rory was still standing behind Ben, watching the proceedings. 'Is he going to be OK?' he asked. A huge lump had appeared on Edward's head, and the gash was like a red mouth in the middle of the egg.

'He'll be fine,' Ben answered, 'but he'll need a few stitches.'

'Shall we call an ambulance?' the official asked.

'I can stitch it, I'm a plastic surgeon. I know Edward's mother.' He turned to Maggie. 'Will Juliet be happy for me to do it?'

Maggie couldn't imagine Juliet would have any objections. She nodded.

'OK, then, let's get this held together as best we can for the moment and then we'll take him to my rooms. Can you open some Steri-Strips for me?'

Having a task to do helped Maggie to focus, and she passed Ben the closures for him to tape across Edward's wound, holding the edges together. A dressing followed and Maggie then wrapped a bandage around Edward's head while Ben held the dressing in place. They worked in sync, Maggie simply following Ben's instructions and somehow managing not to get in his way, until Edward was sufficiently patched up and able to be moved.

'All set,' Ben said as he stood, gathering Edward into his arms. 'Let's get to my surgery and I'll stitch you up properly.'

Maggie quickly packed unused items back into the first-aid kit and balled the rubbish up inside a clean surgical glove and handed it to the official. She did these tasks without thinking, her movements automatic. Now that Ben had got things under control Maggie found her skills returning. As she stood she noticed Rory, still standing beside Ben.

'What about Rory?'

Ben frowned. 'He'll have to come with us.'

'I can take him home with me if you like.'

Maggie looked up and recognised Jake's mum, Anna.

Anna continued to organise the logistics. 'I'll drop the boys off with my husband and then I'll pick Juliet up and bring her to your rooms.'

'If you could take Rory that would help.' Ben turned to his nephew. 'Is that OK, mate? You can go home with Jake and I'll pick you up later?' Ben waited for confirmation from Rory before turning back to Anna. 'We'll ring Juliet and tell her what's happened. I won't take long to patch him up so we'll bring Edward home. I'd be finished before you'd get back with Juliet.'

Maggie followed Ben from the oval, pulling her mobile phone from her bag. She pressed the speed dial to call Juliet, hoping her nerves had settled enough to make it sound as though she had things under control. She knew she'd panicked earlier—thank God Ben had been there.

She knew she'd frozen; despite her years of nursing experience her mind had been a complete blank. As a nurse she should be able to cope with an emergency but she also knew she wasn't good with trauma, especially not if it involved a head injury and a family member. She was a theatre nurse in a private hospital that specialised in elective orthopaedic surgery; emergency medicine was not her speciality, and Ben's presence had been a huge comfort. She was deeply indebted to him.

At the surgery Maggie was amazed at how well Edward coped with the situation. Once again, Maggie knew that was thanks to Ben's composed demeanour. Edward had remained quiet and still while Ben stitched his forehead with tiny, perfect subcutaneous stitches before closing the wound with glue to minimise the scarring. Even when Ben injected the local anaesthetic Edward had barely complained.

Ben had chatted away to Edward while he worked, asking him about the footy clinic and his week at school, and Maggie had been greatly relieved when his answers were accurate and valid. Ed remembered crashing into the fence and also remembered catching the ball just prior to that, which was a good sign. He had a headache but his speech wasn't slurred. His memory seemed fine and his movements appeared normal. As Ben drove them home Maggie tried to make herself relax.

Juliet was waiting in the driveway when Ben and Maggie arrived. She opened the door to cuddle Edward but as she began to lift him out of the car Ben stopped her.

'Hold on, Juliet. I'll carry him. He's too heavy for you after your procedure yesterday.'

Ben lifted him easily, and Maggie marvelled again at how small Edward looked against Ben's bulk. She trailed behind them all as Ben carried Ed to his room, explaining what had happened, and what he'd done, to Juliet on the way.

'He's had some analgesia—he'll probably need a sleep but wake him in an hour or so just to check. He didn't lose consciousness and was lucid so I expect he'll just have a sore head. And a good story.'

'Thanks, Ben. We were so lucky you were there.' Juliet turned to Maggie. 'Can you get Ben something to eat or drink while I see to Ed?'

'Thanks, but I can't stay. I need to pick up Rory.'

Disappointment flooded through Maggie. She walked him out to his car, trying to keep up a normal conversation while she tried to figure out why she was so affected by him.

'Are you positive you don't have kids of your own? You're so good with them.'

Ben held up his three middle fingers, pressing his little finger down with his thumb. 'I haven't got any hidden away somewhere, Scouts' honour.'

'I don't know what I would have done if you hadn't been there—my mind went completely blank.' She knew why she'd panicked but she couldn't explain that to Ben just yet. 'You were brilliant. How can I thank you?'

'You can have dinner with me.'

'Dinner?'

Ben nodded.

'Why?' Her surprise made her sound far less enthusiastic than she felt!

'It might be a pleasant way to end the day. If you think Juliet can manage without you, then I think you've earned a night out.'

'Is this dinner, as in a date?' Maggie wasn't sure whether to trust her ears and hated to think she might read something into Ben's invitation that wasn't there.

He nodded.

Still she hesitated; was she brave enough?

'Do you like Italian food?'

'It's my favourite.' She wondered briefly if Juliet had told him that, before dismissing the thought as silly. She wasn't important enough for them to have discussed her likes and dislikes.

'Perfect. There's a fabulous Italian restaurant in Carlton I'll take you to. It's nothing fancy but the food is superb. I'll pick you up at eight.'

'You want to go tonight?'

'Yes, is that a problem?'

'I'd love to have dinner with you but I can't, not tonight. Can I take a rain check?'

Ben looked at her; he was obviously waiting for more of an explanation but how could she explain that she was too frightened to leave Edward? He seemed fine, he wasn't her son and Juliet was home, but Maggie knew she'd be poor company tonight. She needed to stay close to Edward for her own peace of mind.

To his credit, Ben didn't question her further. 'Sure, you must be exhausted. We can do it another time,' was all he said, making a perfect excuse for her.

As he drove away she wondered if he let her off the hook so easily because he had plenty of other options. There were sure to be plenty more fish in his sea. Maggie experienced a momentary pang of regret but it wasn't enough to get her to leave Edward's side.

Curiosity had gotten the better of him. He'd seen Maggie in stressful situations twice now, once after Juliet needed reviving on the operating table and once today. Juliet's was surely the more confronting of the two dramas, yet Maggie had been remarkably calm then, in comparison to today. She was a nurse—she was used to dealing with stressful situations—so he couldn't understand why she'd gone to pieces today over a cut forehead. His curiosity had gotten the better of him and he wanted to know why someone whom he thought was calm, confident and rational had struggled to cope with Edward's injury. Having dinner together might have given him a chance to work her out, to satisfy his curiosity, but now it would have to wait.

CHAPTER FOUR

'MUMMY, Mummy, my head hurts.'

Maggie opened her eyes, waking at the sound of Ed's voice. It was still dark outside, just the faint signs that dawn was coming.

'I'm here, darling, what's wrong? It's Auntie Maggie.' Maggie threw back the quilt and sat up, her senses on full alert. She'd been up and down all through the night checking on Ed and had eventually pulled the trundle bed out, grabbed her quilt and fallen asleep next to Edward's bed. She'd been too worried to sleep soundly though, waking at every little noise.

'I can't move my head.'

She flew out of the trundle bed, anxious to check him. She bent over her nephew, who was sitting up in bed. He looked dreadful—his eyelids were bruised purple and his forehead was swollen and misshapen with a sticky dressing plastered across the middle of it. The dressing had started off white but was stained orange with Betadine and his fringe was matted with blood that Juliet hadn't been able to wash out. He resembled a character from a horror film.

She moved around the bed and saw Edward follow her path with his eyes—just his eyes, his neck was stiff and immobile.

'Does it hurt to move your neck?'

'No. My head is sore but my neck is just stuck.'

Maggie frowned. Could he have fractured or displaced a vertebra yesterday when he'd collided with the fence? What if they'd missed it?

'See if you can slowly turn your head to look out the window?'

Edward turned to face the window but he turned his whole body, twisting from the waist. He moved the way people suffering from a wry neck moved, and Maggie wondered whether he had simply slept awkwardly. He could move his thoracic spine well enough; perhaps he just had some muscle spasm or inflammation in his neck muscles.

Juliet entered the room then; their voices must have woken her. 'What's going on?'

'Ed's neck is stiff, I'm just checking it out,' Maggie explained as she sent her sister a warning glance, telling her not to panic or say anything that might alarm Edward. Maggie was worried enough for both of them. 'Jules, would you get me a torch. Ed, can you open and close your hands for me?'

Maggie watched with relief as Edward did this without difficulty.

'Where does your head hurt?'

Edward reached one hand up towards the bump on his forehead but didn't touch it. 'Where I hit it.'

Juliet had turned on the light before leaving the room and it seemed as though bright light wasn't bothering him but Maggie needed to know for sure. 'You can see OK?' she asked Ed as Juliet came back into the bedroom and handed her a small torch.

'Yeah.'

'I'm just going to check your eyes to make certain. Can

you close them both for me and then I'll open one at a time and quickly shine the torch in. I need to see what your eyes do in bright light, OK?'

Maggie was relieved to see both pupils were still reacting equally but that didn't rule out a neck injury, just confirmed that Ed probably hadn't suffered any trauma to his brain.

'That all seems fine,' she said to Juliet. 'I hope it's just muscle spasm—it could be the way he slept. I could palpate his neck but I'm not sure I know what to look for and pressure in the wrong spot might make matters worse.' She was thinking out loud. 'I might just ring Ben and see what he thinks.' She was proud of herself that she hadn't fallen apart this morning, unlike yesterday, but she still wanted Ben's advice. She found the card he'd given her and punched his number into the phone.

'Ben McMahon.' He answered on the third ring but his voice sounded groggy, and she realised she'd woken him. She'd been so focused on Edward she hadn't stopped to think of the time.

'Ben, it's Maggie. Sorry to wake you but I'm worried about Edward.'

'What's the matter?'

She could hear in his voice now that he was awake and giving her his full attention. 'He can't move his neck. I think it might be muscular but I want to get him checked out just in case. Could you tell me where I should take him?'

'What are his other symptoms?'

'He's got a bit of a headache, frontal, over the wound site but his pupils are reacting normally and he's got normal movement and sensation in his extremities. He can turn his thoracic and lumbar spine—he just can't turn his neck.'

'It would be pretty unusual to fracture a vertebra when you

hit something front on unless there was a whiplash effect. A fall onto the top of his head or a blow to his neck would be more likely to cause a fracture.' Ben immediately picked up on Maggie's concern but his reckoning made sense and eased Maggie's worries slightly. 'Can you get him to the Hawthorn Sports Medicine Clinic? That will be the closest place for X-rays. You should be all right to drive him, just support his head. I'll meet you there. Can you do that or do you want to call an ambulance?'

'We'll manage, thanks, Ben. We'll see you soon.' Just the fact that he was happy to make decisions, relieving her of some of that burden, helped to set her at ease.

She disconnected the call and went back to the bedroom. 'Ben will meet us at the Hawthorn Sports Medicine Clinic. Do you know where that is?' Juliet nodded. 'What about Kate—do you need to wake her up to come with us?'

'She went to a friend's for a sleepover. She won't be home till lunchtime.' Maggie had forgotten that Kate had gone out; that made things a little easier. 'What do I need to do?' Juliet asked. Maggie balked for a second but of course Juliet would expect her to direct proceedings now; she was the nurse.

'Let me get dressed, and if you can get me a towel I'll use that to support Edward's neck. Leave him in his pyjamas, there's no need for him to get changed.' The less Edward moved around the better, as far as Maggie was concerned.

Within ten minutes they had carried Ed to the car and were on their way. Maggie had fashioned a cervical collar from the bath towel and she sat with Edward in the back, helping to support his head, while Juliet drove to the clinic. Ben had phoned ahead and the radiographer was expecting them. She had a wheelchair waiting for Ed and whisked him straight into

X-ray, with Juliet following, leaving Maggie in the waiting area, pacing the floor, unable to settle.

She counted the squares in the linoleum, a small grey-and-white chequerboard pattern. Five squares to a pace, five paces across the room; twenty-five squares there, another twenty-five back. As she turned for the seventh trip, after one hundred and fifty squares, Ben arrived.

He stopped just inside the door and Maggie ceased her pacing. The room shrank until it felt as though they were the only two in the space.

He was wearing jeans, a black T-shirt and a black leather jacket, and she had never seen anyone look better. He looked capable, strong and comfortable—all the things she wanted to be.

He also looked far hotter than anyone should look at this hour on a Sunday morning. He looked as if he'd just rolled out of bed, which she knew was the case, and she felt a pang of unexpected jealousy as she wondered whether anyone had shared his bed.

His eyes met hers and she felt the pull, the irresistible magnetic force that joined her to him. Suddenly it didn't matter if he'd had company; he was here now, with her.

'Any news?' he asked as he crossed the floor and came to her side.

'No, they've just gone through.'

'I'm sure he's fine. There was nothing to indicate any problems yesterday.'

Maggie knew that was true but that didn't stop her from worrying, although Ben's words were spoken so calmly and confidently that she almost believed him. How had he guessed how worried she was? Was she that transparent or was he just able to read people well? And how had she come to rely on him for reassurance so quickly?

'I know, but there's a part of me that can't relax.'

Ben looked at her, his turquoise eyes studying her carefully, and she felt he could read her thoughts. 'It's OK.'

'You must think I'm a complete nervous Nellie. First Edward's accident yesterday and now, panicking over a stiff neck.'

'It's no problem. Between Juliet's medical history and now Ed you've had a lot happening. It's understandable if you're on edge. Most people would be.'

'There's more to it than that. I'd like to explain if you'd like to hear?' Maggie felt she owed him an explanation. Maybe he didn't need to hear it—he certainly seemed to be in tune with her and could probably guess why she was so paranoid—but she wanted to offer him something in return for the consolation and comfort he was giving her.

Ben nodded. 'Wait here, I'll be right back,' he said as he sat her gently in a chair beside the door. He went to the desk and spoke briefly to the clerk before returning to Maggie. He took her hand. 'Let's get some fresh air. The receptionist will ring me when Juliet comes out.' Ben guided her outside, out of earshot of everyone else in the waiting room, and it was only then that Maggie became aware that other people had arrived at the clinic.

'Would you like to walk or sit?' There was a bench just outside the clinic door but across the road was a small park.

'Let's walk,' she said, knowing she'd find it easier to launch in to her story if she were moving. She wasn't normally this forthcoming with stories about herself but she found she wanted to tell Ben, wanted to explain to him, wanted him to understand. But she wasn't brave enough to sit still and tell him; she wasn't brave enough to keep eye contact. He could already read her too well, and she didn't want him deducing things she wasn't ready to talk about.

They crossed the road, entering the park through a pair of old iron gates. The park was empty at this hour of the morning and as they walked along the winding gravel path she began to talk. 'I never used to be quite so nervous about things. As a nurse you get desensitised to a lot of things, but when something affects you personally, that's different.' The path they took was in sunlight, but the sun was weak at this time of the year and the air was cool. Maggie tied her jacket more tightly to keep the breeze out. 'I need to tell you about my husband. Steven was a policeman. Most of the time that didn't bother me. A lot of their work isn't dangerous—usually it's pretty routine, sometimes even downright boring—but every now and then there'd be something that was a little out of the ordinary, something that did put them at risk. But Steven always managed to come through unscathed and, while I worried, I never thought anything really serious would happen.'

The path narrowed slightly and she stepped closer to Ben. She was conscious of his arm brushing against hers, their steps in sync.

'But one day things changed. It was the summer holidays and Sydney was sweltering in the middle of a heat wave. Tempers were fraying and general violence was escalating among tired, bored, uncomfortable Sydneysiders. One day a fight broke out at the beach between two different ethnic groups, and the police were called in to break it up. The beach was part of Steven's beat.

'It was quite brutal and the situation got very ugly very quickly. There were men with knives and those without were using anything they could lay their hands on as weapons— breaking wooden slats off benches, hurling rubbish bins, chairs and empty bottles. Steven, of course, was right in amongst it, all the police were. At some point Steven hit his head. He couldn't remember if he'd been hit with something and had then fallen or whether he'd fallen after being pushed or even if he'd just tripped, and naturally, no one had seen anything.

'He had a big lump on the back of his head but initially he said he was fine. He'd been taken to hospital and discharged home but by night time he was complaining of a headache. He took some painkillers and went to bed but the headache got worse. He woke me up during the night, saying he'd never felt such bad pain before.'

The path meandered under a large Moreton Bay fig tree that blocked the pale sunlight. Maggie shivered and Ben wrapped his left arm around her shoulders and rubbed her arm. Maggie wasn't sure whether his gesture was intended to comfort her or simply to warm her but either way it helped ease the pain of this memory. She leant against him and continued to talk. 'His left pupil was dilated and fixed—earlier it had been fine—so I took him back to the emergency department. Being a police officer he didn't wait—the doctors saw him immediately. A CT scan showed a blood clot in his brain. It was after midnight by now and the neurosurgeon had to be called in. The clot dislodged before he got there.' She took a deep breath, steeling herself for the next sentence. 'Steven didn't make it.'

Ben stopped walking then and turned her towards him, pulling her tight against his chest. He felt warm and safe, and she could have happily stayed there all day but she hadn't finished her story yet. She lifted her head, pulling her chest away just a fraction but not enough to break the circle of his arms. 'So now, whenever someone hits their head, even in a minor way, I have a tendency to panic. I know I do but I can't help it. I know how easily it can happen. That's why I froze when Ed hit his head—the worst-case scenario always springs to mind now.'

A strand of hair had fallen across her cheek. Ben lifted one hand and tucked it behind her ear, his fingers grazing her face. 'Why didn't you insist on a scan for Edward yesterday? Would that have helped?'

Maggie's heart was pounding. She always found this topic highly emotional, and Ben's touch was sending her hormones into overdrive, stirring her emotions even further. She was surprised to find she could still speak. 'I know I panic and I've tried to teach myself to be logical. Not every bump on the head is going to result in a blood clot.'

'Edward's was a bit more than a little bump.'

'I know, but you were checking his pupils, and he had no memory loss or motor dysfunction. His headache went with pain relief. There really wasn't any reason to panic but I did anyway. I was awake most of the night checking him. I ended up sleeping in his room so I'd hear if he called out, and when he couldn't move his neck this morning I started to worry all over again.'

'You had perfectly good reasons to worry. I'd worry too if I'd lived your story, but I'm sure he's fine.' If he had anything further to add he was distracted as his phone beeped in his pocket. Ben retrieved it. 'OK, thanks. We're on our way.' He closed his phone.

'Is everything OK?'

'Seems to be. They've just finished with the doctor.'

Maggie spun around and headed back to the Sports Medicine Clinic with Ben matching her stride.

'So any other phobias I need to know about?' he asked her. 'Spiders, fear of flying, anything like that?'

'I do have some bravado,' she replied, nudging him with her elbow as he held the door for her.

Juliet and Edward were in the waiting room when Ben and Maggie returned. Ed had a cervical collar around his neck and the sight of him made Maggie stop in her tracks and she felt her shoulders tense with worry. All OK, Ben had said! But why was Edward in a neck brace?

Maggie felt Ben's arm around her again, and his reassuring touch calmed her nerves a bit. 'Come on, look at the big grin on his face. I reckon he's OK,' he said.

Maggie noticed then that her nephew was smiling. Ben was right—he didn't look like a kid with serious injuries.

Juliet was watching them, and Maggie saw her register Ben's arm around her shoulders. Her sister's knowing smirk was enough to mobilise her. She stepped forward, out of Ben's embrace, determined to stay in control of her emotions this time.

'What did the X-rays show?' she asked.

Juliet stood as she answered. 'Nothing. He's been seen by the radiologist and the orthopod, and they think it's just severe muscle spasm. There doesn't appear to be any bone damage, no fractures in the neck or skull and no sign of any internal bleeding. The orthopod doesn't think there's any underlying damage. He says it's probably just a result of yesterday's trauma.' She was stroking Edward's head as she spoke. 'He's given him some mild muscle relaxants and wants him to wear the brace to support his head and hopefully give his neck muscles a chance to relax.'

'So he's been given the all-clear? He can come home?'

Juliet nodded. 'He'll be off school for a day or two and he has a physio appointment for tomorrow but the doctor expects it all to settle fairly quickly.'

'But what if my black eyes are gone by the time I go back to school?' Edward asked.

Juliet rolled her eyes and looked at Maggie and grinned. 'If you need any more proof that he's fine, there it is!' She turned to her son. 'I'm sure you'll still be able to see some of the bruises and I'll take a photo of you just in case, OK?'

'Good news, then,' said Ben.

'Yes,' Juliet replied, adding, 'thank you for staying—you didn't need to.'

'I thought Maggie could use the company.'

Juliet raised an eyebrow and looked questioningly at Maggie. Fortunately Ben had turned to face her too and missed Juliet's look. Maggie kept quiet.

'I'll call you later to make sure all your patients are OK,' Ben said to her, 'but ring me before then if you're worried about anything. Doesn't matter what it is.'

He squeezed her shoulder before he left, raising a hand in farewell to Edward and Juliet. 'Go home and rest, both of you,' he said, directing his comment to Juliet. 'Doctor's orders.'

'Yes, sir!' Juliet replied as Maggie wondered how long it would take before the questions would begin.

It took longer than she expected.

They were in the car and Maggie was driving before Juliet started her cross-examination. Had she waited until she had a captive audience? Maggie remembered using the same tactic on her kids when they were teenagers. If you talked to them while they were in the car you didn't need to keep eye contact, so they felt more comfortable but they couldn't get away!

'So what did you two do while you were waiting?'

'We went for a walk in the park.'

'And?'

'And what?' Maggie stalled for time.

'What did you do there?'

Maggie shrugged. 'Nothing. We talked.'

'What about?' Juliet asked. Maggie kept her eyes fixed on the road ahead and kept her lips closed. 'You know I'll drag it out of you eventually. You might as well just tell me,' her sister added.

Maggie sighed. 'Steven.'

'What! You told him about Steven?'

Maggie knew why Juliet was so surprised. She didn't talk about Steven to anyone who hadn't known him. It was her story and hers alone. She still couldn't explain why she felt it was important for Ben to know. She certainly didn't have to tell him as much as she had, although she still hadn't told him everything.

'Technically, *I* didn't tell him about Steven, you did.'

'Me?' Juliet was frowning. 'When?'

'In Theatre. You mentioned Steven when they were resuscitating you. Ben thought you were talking to him until I explained who Steven was.'

'How much does he know?'

'Most of it.' Even with her gaze focused on the road Maggie could feel Juliet's raised eyebrows. 'You didn't see me when Ed hit his head. I wanted Ben to understand why I freaked out over the accident,' she explained.

'Wow. He must really be something.'

Maggie shrugged her shoulders. 'I like him.'

Juliet laughed. 'That's pretty obvious. What is it that you like exactly?'

'He's pretty easy on the eyes,' Maggie said with a smile. 'But I like the way he makes me feel. When I'm with him I don't feel like a skinny forty-two-year-old with small boobs and a bump in my nose. I feel feminine and desirable. I feel special. And he's easy to talk to. He's a good listener but it's more than that. Most of the time he just gets me. He seems to know me. There are no preconceptions like there are with people in Sydney. To him, I'm just Maggie. I'm not someone's widow or someone's mother. He doesn't know me through work or through the kids. He's not a girlfriend's ex-husband who's either trying to hit on me or terrified I'll hit on him and make things difficult with his ex.' She shrugged again. 'He's good company.'

And, although she didn't say it, when she was with Ben she didn't feel alone any more.

Which probably explained why, when Ben phoned later that day as promised and invited her again to have dinner with him, she agreed. Edward was recovering well and Maggie's concerns were dissipating. Dinner with Ben was immensely appealing.

CHAPTER FIVE

BELLA'S Restaurant was tiny and intimate, and Maggie felt enormously conspicuous as she walked in with Ben and discovered he was a regular patron. Marco and his wife, Isabella, were perfect hosts and obviously knew him well. They greeted him by name and also with a kiss on both cheeks, European style. Maggie smiled at the picture of Ben almost bending himself in half so the two Italians could reach him. They were polite and welcoming to Maggie also but she couldn't help but wonder how she compared to Ben's past companions.

The restaurant was on Lygon Street, a street renowned for its cafés and restaurants, but Bella's was already almost full. The dining room was wider than it was deep and divided down the centre by a bar. Three large, communal dining tables filled one side of the room, and there were seven smaller tables on the other side, seating two to four guests each. Marco showed Ben and Maggie to a table set for two in the window.

Ben held her chair for her, and she ran her eyes over him again as she lowered herself into her seat. He looked fabulous. He was wearing dark jeans and a pale grey shirt that made his eyes look more grey than blue. Smouldering.

Maggie was wearing a pale pink top—a colour she knew suited her—but now, amongst the trendily dressed European-looking crowd, she felt decidedly out of place. She fidgeted with her neckline.

'Are you too hot?' Ben asked.

'No. Just wishing I'd worn something else. Something black.'

Ben laughed. 'I'm glad you didn't. Melbournians seem to all wear black. You have no idea how nice it is to see something different. And that colour suits you.'

Suddenly it didn't matter what she was wearing—Ben thought she looked good.

'Thank you.' She smiled at him, her confidence restored. 'Do you always know the right thing to say?'

'I'd like to think so—years of practice, you see.' He winked at her and Maggie didn't doubt he'd had just that—years of practice. She wondered what else he'd learnt.

'Do tell.' She said but as the words left her mouth she wondered if she was actually game to hear.

'What would you like to know?'

Where did she start?

He must have thought she was never going to answer because he said, 'Why don't I get us a drink from the bar while you think of what you want to know most? Shall I order you a glass of pinot grigio?'

'That would be lovely, thanks.' As Ben moved to the bar Maggie realised she wanted to know everything. How old was he? How many siblings did he have? Why had he become a doctor? Had he been married? Why didn't he have children? What was his favourite movie?

But which of these questions was appropriate for a first date?

When he returned with their drinks she went with, 'What made you choose plastic surgery as your specialty?'

'It's plastic and reconstructive surgery technically,' he said with a grin as he took his seat opposite her. 'Haven't you looked me up on the internet?'

'No.' Was he serious? 'I never even thought of it. Are you that important that I'd find you on the web.'

'Apparently.'

'My kids would look you up, I'd rather have a conversation. Call me old-fashioned but I wouldn't even know where to start.'

'An old-fashioned girl—that's something you don't find every day.' Ben smiled at her and Maggie immediately relaxed, knowing instinctively that he didn't think old-fashioned meant boring. 'Let me order and then you can ask me anything you like. Do you want to choose something or do you trust me?'

'I trust you to order.'

Ben called Marco over to the table. 'We'll have the mushroom ravioli and the gnocchi followed by veal scaloppine and linguine marinara. Thanks, Marco.'

'That sounds like a lot of food.'

'You won't be sorry. Isabella is the best cook I know, and don't think I haven't noticed your caveat on trusting me.'

'What do you mean?'

'You said you trust me to order—do I take it you don't trust me on other things?'

'You make me nervous,' she admitted.

'Really?' Ben's raised eyebrows suggested that wasn't the reply he'd expected.

'I'm not sure why you invited me to dinner.' There, that was the big question she'd wanted to know the answer to since the start of the evening.

'You want to know what my motives are?'

'Something like that.'

He paused and Maggie's nerves returned as she wondered what his answer would be. 'You never say what I expect you to say—I find that intriguing. I find *you* intriguing,' he answered.

'Me?'

'Yes. You wouldn't believe how refreshing it is to meet someone who isn't afraid to have a proper conversation. Or should I say, who knows *how* to have a proper conversation. And I think you've had a very interesting life. The circle I move in is very small. I've known many of the people for years, and the women spend most of their time talking about the latest club, the best tanning salon and their next vacation spot.'

'There must be *some* interesting women?'

'Most definitely. But they're all married and most of them won't have dinner on their own with me.'

'So I'm not the only one who doesn't trust your motives?' she joked as she sipped her wine.

He laughed and held up a hand in mock protest. 'I promise I've never made a move on a married woman.' He paused. 'Not deliberately anyway.'

Marco delivered their entrées and Ben placed the ravioli in front of Maggie. She waited until he'd started on his gnocchi before asking her next question, using her meal as an excuse to avoid looking at him as she nosed her way into his private life. 'Have you ever been married?'

If Ben was surprised by the question he didn't show it. He shook his head as he swallowed his food. 'No. I'm not the settling-down sort. I don't want children so there's no point really.'

'You don't want children?'

'No, I'm a career person.'

Maggie couldn't believe it; having seen him interact with

both Rory and Edward in vastly different situations she couldn't imagine him not wanting a family of his own. She raised her eyebrows, silently asking him to elaborate.

'Believe me, I know how much time and effort it takes to raise a family—I see that with Rory—and I don't think I can do justice to children and my career. I don't think there are enough hours in the day. I travel a lot and I've seen things that aren't right—children suffering from sickness, war, hunger—and I don't think raising a family is for me.'

Maggie remembered all the African art. 'The photos in your office, did you take those?'

Ben nodded. 'I travelled to Uganda last year to work in a hospital there, doing reconstructive work. It was an amazing experience, confrontational at times but also immensely rewarding.'

'How long where you there?'

'Eight weeks. I'm going again in a few weeks' time, once I've raised a bit more money.'

'You pay to work there?' she asked.

'Not exactly but I don't get any financial benefit from that work. Some of my income here goes towards equipment, medical supplies, that sort of thing, but there's a lot of fund-raising as well to pay for nurses, drugs, hospital administration, general expenses. Most of my surgeries in Uganda aren't life-or-death situations but rather reconstructive, to improve patients' quality of life. They can't afford to pay for it so I have to work out ways to fund everything. To be fair, my family's foundation contributes a lot financially towards my hobby.'

'It sounds like more than a hobby.' She wondered if he'd notice she didn't question him about the foundation. Would that give her away—tell him she knew more about him than she was letting on? She decided she couldn't be bothered about that, not when he was divulging other such personal information.

'Yes, it's my dream, to be honest, and finally getting there last year was a culmination of years of work.'

'What made you choose to work there?' As someone who had only experienced health care in a first-world country she found the subject fascinating.

'My sister and I were brought up to believe that having money doesn't make you a better person—it's what you do with that money. And in Africa the work of one person can make an enormous difference. To me, it's an incredible feeling to be able to help people, children, who are disfigured, some through war and others with congenital defects. Africa and her people have really got under my skin. Most of these people have nothing, so to be able to give them something, to help to give them a better life, is such a privilege. Africa is an amazing place. Have you ever been there?'

'I've never been overseas. I was a child bride, remember—babies followed soon after, and then, as a single mother, overseas holidays weren't really on the agenda.'

'What about now? Do you have a desire to travel?'

Maggie sensed he wanted to change the topic, steer it away from himself. She could oblige even though she wanted to hear more about Ben's dreams. 'I've always wanted to see Paris.'

'What's stopping you?'

'Now you *sound* like a man who doesn't have a wife and children. It's not that easy to sneak off. There always seems to be someone who needs me.'

'Is that how you see it? Sneaking off?'

Maggie shrugged. 'I guess I must. Obviously my priority isn't getting away,' she said with a smile.

'Maybe it's time you did something for yourself.'

'I am. Having dinner with you is the most selfish thing I've done with my time in a long while.'

'I better make it worth it, then.'

Ben looked at her with such intensity it was all she could do to stop herself from reaching out to touch him. A warm glow spread through her which she recognised as desire. She hadn't felt that good in a long time. 'It already is.' Goodness, how forward she sounded—where had that come from?

She was so comfortable with Ben's company. The conversation was easy, and it felt as though they were the only two in the room. Immersed in their own little world the conversation didn't lapse into any uncomfortable silences as Maggie found herself falling under Ben's spell.

She'd started the evening thinking he was charming, intelligent and handsome. By the time they'd eaten their main courses she was adding generous, considerate and thoughtful to Ben's list of attributes.

There had to be something wrong with him. He didn't want commitment, that was obvious, but even his lack of desire to have children couldn't be seen as a negative. He had valid reasons for that decision, and while she couldn't imagine not having her own children she knew that not everyone shared her point of view.

Eventually they were the only two remaining in the restaurant.

'Do you think Marco and Isabella would like us to go home now?' Maggie asked, reluctant to end the evening but knowing it couldn't last forever.

Ben looked around the restaurant, and Maggie could swear

he hadn't noticed that all the other patrons had gone. Had he been as engrossed in her company as she was in his? Could she dare to think that?

'I'm like family to them but perhaps we'd better go before I get asked to help with the dishes.' He laughed.

She added down-to-earth to her list which, at the beginning of the night, would have surprised her given his family tree but now, after listening to his story, she could see how that was possible.

Ben went to pay their bill and thank Marco and Isabella before returning to help her up from her chair. Marco and Isabella came with him to farewell them both, kissing Maggie on both cheeks too now, and she was touched to be included in their ritual.

She left the restaurant on a high, and when Ben took her hand as they walked along Lygon Street she didn't hesitate or resist. It just felt right.

It wasn't late, still well before midnight, and there were plenty of people wandering along the footpaths or sitting having coffee at the sidewalk tables, sheltered from the chill of the evening by clear café blinds and warmed by the outdoor gas heaters.

Ben pointed out the landmarks from a recent television drama that had been filmed in and around Melbourne. Lygon Street had featured frequently as the site of the meeting places of the real-life 'underworld' figures on whom the telemovie had been based. The drama had been a huge ratings success with its, mostly, accurate storylines of sex, drugs, money and violence—stories people would never have believed if they hadn't been based on real events.

Ben and Maggie had walked less than two blocks when a loud explosion split the air. Maggie jumped, frightened by the unexpected noise. Ben's stories and the sound combined to conjure up threatening images, and she imagined a gun being fired. She paused in her tracks.

A second explosion followed the first and a faint scent of gunpowder carried to them on the evening breeze.

'What was that?' she asked as she moved slightly closer to Ben, pressing against his side, taking comfort in his bulk.

'It's OK, I think it's just firecrackers,' he replied, seeming nonplussed.

Maggie breathed out and moved forward again, walking with Ben. As they reached an intersection a crowd of young men surged around the corner. They surrounded the two of them, separating Maggie from Ben. Maggie was jostled and bumped. The men smelt of beer and cigarettes. They were loud and rough.

Maggie crossed her arms over her chest, tucking her bag against her, and searched frantically for Ben. The crowd continued to swarm around her. There were too many people to fit on the sidewalk, and they overflowed onto the street and brought traffic to a standstill. Their voices were raised, yelling and shouting. Unfriendly voices which reverberated through Maggie.

She tried to push across the flow of the crowd, tried to get out of the stream of people, but it was impossible to break through. She felt herself starting to get swept along, carried back down Lygon Street towards Bella's Restaurant. She couldn't control her direction; she was at the mercy of the crowd. She tried to call out for Ben but her voice got stuck in her throat. She started to shake; she was struggling for air. She was more than afraid…. She was terrified.

Where was Ben? How could she lose sight of someone as big and tall as him?

Two men were arguing as they walked in front of her, swearing at each other, tempers building. One man pushed the other, deliberately provoking him. Maggie didn't want to be here, caught in the middle of this anger, alone.

The second man retaliated, pushing back against the first. Both of them stopped in their tracks, blocking her path. The first man threw a punch as the crowd behind her continued to push forwards. Maggie was trapped and in a moment she'd be in the middle of the brawl herself.

She felt someone's arms grabbing her from behind. She found her voice; she screamed and struggled, fighting against the hold.

'Maggie, it's me, Ben. It's OK, I've got you.'

His voice washed over her. She stopped struggling and instead relaxed into his hold. She was safe. He'd found her.

She felt him pick her up as if she weighed no more than a child. His arms were wrapped around her as he carried her away from the crowd. The masses parted for Ben as he moved forwards across the footpath towards the buildings. For her the mass of bodies had been impenetrable but now it was as if Ben was Moses parting the Red Sea.

He reached a doorway and gently stood Maggie down. Her knees were shaking so badly Ben was unable to let her go completely. If he had she would have collapsed in a quivering mess at his feet. He held her, shielding her from the crowd.

'You're safe. We're back at Bella's,' he said.

Maggie recognised the restaurant through the window; they were standing in the doorway. Ben reached over her shoulder and pushed the door. It swung open and he ushered her inside. He called out to Marco, letting him know they were back before locking the door.

'What's happened?' Marco asked as he emerged from the kitchen.

'We got caught up in the middle of some soccer fans. Unfortunately they weren't all barracking for the same team and things got a little out of control.'

Marco glanced out the window where hoards of people continued to stream past. 'No matter. You wait here for as long as you like—we're just cleaning up.'

'Why don't we help you in the kitchen?' Maggie offered.

Ben saw Marco register Maggie's ashen face and the slight wobble in her voice. 'No, no, you sit here—' Marco indicated a table at the back of the room '—and I'll bring you a coffee. Maybe some grappa too.'

Marco disappeared into the kitchen. Maggie still looked visibly distressed and she moved away from the large front windows towards the table Marco had indicated. She slid onto the couch that ran along the back wall of the restaurant and served as a seat. Ben waited, taking the coffee from Marco, before sitting next to Maggie on the small couch.

Ben was confident they were in no danger but Maggie still seemed quite nervous and she jumped when someone thudded into the window. He put one hand on her thigh, surprised to find she was trembling.

'Hey, it's OK, you're safe here.'

'I hate big crowds. I'm never quite sure what's going to happen but I always expect the worst.'

Ben moved his hand from her thigh and put it around her shoulders, pulling her in close. 'I don't think we're in any danger in here. We'll stay put until everything's calmed down,' he said, attempting to reassure her.

She nodded and Ben watched her as she picked up her coffee cup; her hand was shaking so badly she spilt her coffee.

'Sorry,' she said as she grabbed a serviette and started to mop up the mess she'd made.

Ben took the serviette from her and wiped up the coffee as Marco came over and poured them each a glass of grappa. 'Here, drink this instead while your coffee cools down,' he said, passing her a glass.

Maggie's hand was still shaking as she held the glass so Ben covered her hand with his, helping her to hold the glass to her lips as she drank. She finished the small glass in a couple of mouthfuls and it seemed to do the trick. She relaxed.

'Is that better?' he asked.

She nodded. His left arm was still around her shoulders, and as she looked up at him their faces were only inches apart. Her blue eyes were enormous in her pale face, her freckles clearly visible across the bridge of her nose.

He could see her breasts rising and falling with each breath, could feel them pushing against his chest as she remained tucked against his side. Their gazes were locked, neither one aware of what was happening outside the restaurant any longer. Both of them were immersed in the small, imaginary bubble that was just big enough for the two of them.

Maggie's pupils were dilated, her breathing rapid. He could feel her breath on the side of his neck. Her tongue darted out as she licked her lips, giving Ben a brief glimpse of dark pink between small white teeth. He couldn't resist— he had to know what Maggie's lips would feel like, what she would taste like. He closed his eyes as he bent his head, capturing her mouth with his, feeling her lips under his. He hadn't stopped to think, hadn't been able to think.

Her lips were soft and tasted like grappa. She smelt of orange blossom.

Her lips opened; her tongue met his, joining him in the kiss.

He cupped her face, holding her close to him, deepening the kiss. Maggie moaned and he felt her hands slide around behind his head, sending shivers of anticipation down his spine as her fingers brushed the nape of his neck.

Her lips moved under his as she nipped at his lip with her teeth, pulling his lip into her mouth. She pressed closer to him, removing a hand from behind his head and running it down his chest, leaving a trail of heat in her wake.

Her hand was on his thigh now, and it was all he could do to retain some sense of composure. He was consumed with desire; he had to regain control.

He pulled back. They were both breathing in short, rapid bursts, their hearts beating with a staccato rhythm. Her left hand was still resting on his thigh. He covered it with his and felt the warm band of metal under his fingers.

Her wedding ring.

She must have felt his fingers connect with the band and she looked down.

He expected her to move away. She didn't but she did remove her hand.

What had he been thinking? What was *she* thinking? he wondered.

He felt a brief pang of guilt—had he taken advantage of her in her distressed state? He started to apologise. 'Maggie…'

She put her hand on his chest, stopping his apology. 'Don't. It's OK, I needed a distraction.' She smiled, her blue eyes sparkling. She was relaxed, happy even.

The guilty feeling vanished when he remembered she'd kissed him back, and he knew he'd kiss her again if he had another opportunity.

'You're sure you're OK?' Ben was puzzled. He'd thought Maggie was close to going into shock and now she'd bounced back?

She nodded. 'Yes, I am now, but I'm glad you found me when you did. I don't think I would have coped much longer.'

'I'm sorry it took me that long to reach you. I could see you but I couldn't get through.'

She shook her head, her chestnut hair grazing her shoulders. 'It's not your fault.' She paused. 'I actually didn't tell you everything this morning. I have a bit of a problem with crowds as well.' He thought she was going to leave the conversation there but she continued. 'I was at the beach the day the brawl broke out, the day Steven died.' Her voice faltered. 'He wasn't supposed to be working. We'd gone to the beach for a family outing with the kids but when the fight started Steven took us to the police station. His station. He got us to safety but then he went out, joining his mates, trying to diffuse things. He got us to safety but not before I'd seen things I'd rather forget.' That explained her vivid description of the day, Ben realised. Maggie had been part of it. 'That was the day my life changed, and I've never been able to handle volatile situations since then.'

That explained a lot. Under the circumstances Ben was amazed she'd held it together for as long as she had today.

'Maggie, I'm so sorry I put you in that situation.'

'You weren't to know.'

'No, but it hasn't been a great weekend for you on a scale of one to ten, has it?'

'It hasn't been all bad,' she said with a smile.

He grinned back at her. She really was an amazing woman. He was constantly surprised by people's resilience. He'd seen it many times in his patients, but for Maggie to not only get through tonight but to be able to finish the evening with a smile on her face was incredible. He wanted to work out what made her tick. He wanted to kiss her again but he'd have to choose the right moment. It wasn't now.

The street was silent again; the crowd had moved on. It was time to leave the sanctuary of the restaurant. 'I'll fetch the car and bring it back here to collect you.' He didn't want to risk taking Maggie back out into the neighbourhood.

Maggie didn't bother arguing. She wasn't keen on braving the streets again, and if Ben was prepared to fetch the car she was prepared to wait, pleased to have a chance to reflect on what had just transpired between them. 'Thank you.'

'My pleasure. I'll just let Marco know.' Ben stood but not before he gave her another light kiss on the lips, a much gentler, softer kiss but one that she still felt burn through her body from her lips to her toes. Her stomach was tumbling with desire and her legs were like jelly. Maggie knew her legs wouldn't be able to support her for some time and that had nothing to do with the earlier crowds and everything to do with Ben. She sank back into the couch, pleased to have a chance to collect her thoughts.

Ben left via the front door, and as she watched him go she decided to add sexy to her list of attributes for him and then wondered if she shouldn't add dangerous as well. Now she knew what the expression 'to be swept off your feet' meant. With Steven it hadn't really been a case of being swept off her feet. They'd practically grown up together at high school, and she'd always known they belonged together but she couldn't remember ever experiencing such a strong and un-expected rush of desire.

She pushed Steven to the back of her mind. She'd made a con-scious decision to have dinner with Ben and she certainly hadn't resisted his kiss. Now was not the time for thoughts of the past.

She fiddled with her wedding ring, twisting it around her finger. She'd never taken it off, not because she still felt married but because there'd never been any need to. She had no idea where things were headed with Ben but for the first time she wondered if there would come a day when she might want to remove her wedding ring.

A shadow fell across the table, and she looked up to see Marco standing beside her.

'Do you mind if I join you?' he asked.

'Of course not,' she said as Marco pulled out a chair opposite her.

'He is a nice man, no?'

'Very nice,' Maggie agreed with a smile, thinking she'd just come to the same conclusion. Marco and his wife were obviously very fond of Ben, and she was intrigued by their relationship. 'How is it that you know him?'

'Ahh, he operated on our grandson. He was born with a cleft palate. My daughter was so upset but Ben fixed it. *Perfecto*.' Marco emphasised his point by putting his thumb and forefinger together in a circle before raising them to his lips and kissing them with a flourish. 'He is lovely man. And now,' he said with a shrug, 'he is family. He eats with us often and it's always good to see him. We owe him a huge debt.'

As Marco finished speaking Ben pulled his car into the curb.

'Ah, here he is.' Marco stood, waiting for Maggie to stand as well. 'It was lovely to meet such a beautiful lady. We hope to see you again soon,' he said as he took Maggie's hands in his and kissed her again on both cheeks before accompanying her to the door where Ben was waiting.

'Beware of this man, Maggie,' Ben said, winking at her as he held the door open. 'Casanova was an Italian, remember.'

Maggie just beamed, happier than she could remember being for some time.

'The ladies didn't complain, Ben. Casanova must have done something right.' Marco managed to get the last word in as Ben closed the door for Maggie.

The trip home was quiet as Maggie reflected on the night's events. She took a deep breath, surprised to find she felt remarkably calm. Her heart rate was back to normal. No thanks to Ben.

She was still stunned by the intensity of her feelings, the response he was able to evoke from her. Where had that come from? She'd completely lost herself in his kiss; time and place had no meaning.

What had she been thinking?

She knew she hadn't been thinking—she hadn't been capable of thinking. Only feeling. When his fingers had felt her wedding ring she realised then that wearing the ring was a habit; she was used to it being on her finger. Her reaction to Ben's kisses certainly hadn't been one of a woman who still felt married.

She lay in bed later, replaying the evening in her mind.

When she was caught in the crowd, trapped and terrified, she thought that feeling would haunt her for a long time, but Ben's kiss had eradicated everything else from her mind. How was that possible? He'd rescued her from the crowd, carried her to safety and then wiped all memory of that event with his kiss. Almost all she could recall from the evening was the feel of his hand on her face, his fingers on her cheek and the first touch of his lips on hers, the sweet taste of his mouth. He'd set her senses on fire.

Ben had kissed her again when he pulled up in front of Juliet's house. Or did she kiss him? She'd had no idea she could be so forward but she didn't doubt that she'd been as much the instigator of another kiss. There had been no discussion, yet somehow they were kissing again, making out in the car like a couple of teenagers.

Ben's kisses had transported her to a different place, a world away from her everyday life, and once she'd tasted him she couldn't get enough. She was like a hummingbird drawn to the sweet smell of nectar and she knew she could easily become addicted. She tried to remember how she'd felt when Steven had kissed her. They'd been so young and inexperienced when they first got together. She laughed—she was still inexperienced. It wasn't as if she had a lot of notches in the bed post.

She lay with her left hand on her chest as she twisted her wedding ring around on her finger. What would Steven think of Ben?

For the first time Maggie realised that it didn't matter what Steven would have thought. Her life was her own now. The kids were adults, living their own lives; she was entitled to live hers. And as Juliet said, she was entitled to have some fun.

So that was exactly what she planned to do.

The next five days went past in the blink of an eye. Maggie knew it was because she was busy but by Friday all she could remember about the week were the moments which had included Ben. He had phoned the house several times to check on Edward's progress and had called in unexpectedly after work one evening. He'd said it was to check on his young patient but he'd invited Maggie to a movie and she accepted. Juliet had all but pushed her out the door.

Maggie knew she was floating on air but Ben was such

good company. She could scarcely wait until Juliet's next appointment. She'd begun to count the hours until she saw Ben again, as pathetic as that made her feel.

Finally Friday dawned and Maggie drove Juliet to her appointment, but parking spaces were scarce so she dropped Juliet at the door and then looked for an empty spot. By the time she got into the waiting room Juliet was already in with Ben. Disappointment flooded her as she realised she wouldn't see him now. There was no need for her to be in the consulting room; she'd have to sit and wait with all the other patients.

'Mrs Petersen?' Ben's receptionist called across the waiting room to Maggie. 'Dr McMahon asked for you to be sent down when you got here.'

Maggie leapt to her feet; she was going to see him after all! She almost ran down the corridor and just remembered to stop and knock on the door before she burst into the room.

'Good, you're here,' Ben said as Maggie came to a stop in the middle of the room. He was washing his hands, as calm as ever, in stark contrast to Maggie's flustered demeanour.

She tried to regain some control. 'Is everything all right?'

'Everything's fine. Juliet's skin is stretching nicely. Everything is progressing as expected. I wanted to know if you've decided to accompany me to the art exhibition tomorrow night.'

'What exhibition?' Juliet chimed in as she reappeared from behind the privacy screen, shrugging into her jacket as she walked.

'Gabby and Finn are having an exhibition of my photographs at their gallery. It opens tomorrow and I invited Maggie to come with me. She hasn't given me an answer yet.'

'*Your* photographs?'

'These are Ben's photos,' Maggie said as she gestured to the photos hanging on the walls of Ben's office.

Juliet scanned the pictures. 'Yours! Wow.'

Ben shrugged. 'It's a hobby but Gabby is kind enough to put some on display, and the proceeds go towards my medical work in Africa.'

'Do you sell a lot?'

'Surprisingly, yes.' He was so self-deprecating, a trait Maggie found totally endearing. 'Why don't you come to the opening as well?' he asked Juliet. 'Maybe then Maggie will accept my invitation.'

'I'd love to but I don't think I'd find a babysitter at such short notice. You should go though, Mags. You haven't got anything else on, have you?'

Maggie frowned at her sister. She knew jolly well Maggie had a free schedule. What would she have to do on a Saturday night?

'Great. I'll pick you up at seven. Don't wear black.' Ben smiled at her as he added the condition, and Maggie knew he was thinking of her outfit dilemma from their dinner date at Bella's. A warm glow spread through her. With three words Ben was able to make her feel as though she had his full attention even though he was in the middle of a consulting list and Juliet was in the room with them. He had enough charm for ten men, she thought as she smiled back and nodded before following Juliet out of the room.

'Why didn't you say yes straight away?' Juliet asked as they left the building and returned to the car.

'We've been to dinner and a movie. This will be our third date.'

'Why is that a problem?'

'That's the point where it starts to get complicated. Is it

going to go any further? What do we do next? If we take the next step, what does that mean?'

'You're overthinking things. Don't worry about what happens next, just have fun.'

But Maggie couldn't just continue to 'have fun.' For her the third date was always a turning point, the time when she stopped and thought about what she wanted. And, in Ben's case, she knew exactly what she wanted but she also knew that if she took the next step it would be almost impossible to get him out of her system. A third date was a big deal for her and that was why she'd hesitated.

'You're only going to an art gallery with him—you're not eloping,' Juliet continued, taking advantage of Maggie's silence to dish out more advice. She looked Maggie up and down as she unlocked the car. 'What you need is a confidence-boosting dress and a killer pair of high heels. I think we should go shopping.'

'Don't you need to go home and rest?' Maggie asked hopefully. She didn't love shopping, especially not for herself.

'Nope, I'm feeling good. I think I'm getting used to these expander sessions. Let's shop,' Juliet said as she pulled her seat belt on.

The factory outlet shops in Richmond were between Ben's East Melbourne office and Juliet's house, and after trying several different shops and many different outfits Maggie managed to pick up a gorgeous deep-purple wrap dress by a well-known designer for a fraction of the normal retail price.

She took it home and hung it on the wardrobe door, and every time she looked at it over the next twenty-four hours she vacillated between third-date nerves and excitement at seeing Ben again. She hoped the dress was going to be as confidence boosting as Juliet proclaimed.

When it finally came time to get ready Juliet and Kate both helped to dress and accessorise her. The dress hugged Maggie's figure and for once she was glad she didn't have much padding—the fabric of the dress would have emphasised every bulge. Juliet produced a wide black belt that she fixed around Maggie's waist, helping to create the illusion of curves beneath the wrap dress, and Maggie completed her outfit with a pair of black knee-high boots that Juliet had insisted she buy during their shopping spree. Unlike the dress, the boots had not been on sale and the price had nearly made Maggie's eyes pop out of her head. But she had to admit, looking at her entire ensemble, that the boots really made a statement. Juliet had been right. Maggie felt confident, feminine and sexy, and more importantly, ready to meet Ben's family.

Kate brushed Maggie's chestnut hair until it shone and begged to paint her nails. Maggie relented and chose a black nail polish from Juliet's stash, removing her boots to let her niece colour her toenails. If she was going to be a vamp, she figured she might as well embrace it wholeheartedly.

Even if no one would see her toenails?

Even so, she decided. She would know and that knowledge would give her more confidence.

'What about your make-up?' Juliet asked as they waited for Maggie's nails to dry. 'What shall we emphasise, eyes or lips?'

Maggie had no idea what lipstick she should wear to complement a purple dress. 'Eyes, I think.'

'OK,' Juliet said as she got to work adding eye make-up and blush to Maggie's base of foundation. 'You can do your lips now. I promised the kids dessert—I'd better go and do that,' Juliet said when she finished.

Maggie applied a pale lipgloss, something that wouldn't

clash with her dress, and sat down to put her boots back on. As she zipped them up her wedding ring caught her eye. She slid it off her finger and looked at the white line marking where it had sat for twenty-two years.

She held the ring in her right hand, the metal pressing into her palm. Should she leave it off? Could she?

She sat on the bed and stared at her left hand. It didn't look like hers any more. It looked empty. She'd taken her engagement ring off years ago but now her hand was completely bare and it was a strange feeling.

She took the ring from her palm and held it between her thumb and forefinger. Was she being premature, taking it off? Should she put it back on?

She was still staring at the ring when she heard Kate's voice yelling from the hallway.

'He's here!'

Decision time.

On or off?

Adrenalin coursed through her system in anticipation of the evening ahead. She could feel every beat of her heart as though she had a miniature drum inside her chest counting the seconds until she saw Ben.

On or off?

Her hands were shaking as she put the ring into her handbag, zipping it into the inside pocket.

She wanted to be free to make her own choices as far as Ben was concerned. For the first time in twenty-two years she wanted to feel like a single woman.

Off.

CHAPTER SIX

THE exhibition was fabulous. Within half an hour of the scheduled start the gallery was packed with guests, all sipping champagne and sampling the cocktail food while they perused the artworks and chatted.

The gallery was in the beachside suburb of St Kilda. The front two rooms were large and airy and faced directly onto the street. The walls were painted white and in the daytime the rooms would be flooded with natural light spilling through the enormous floor-to-ceiling windows that also afforded the passing foot traffic good views of the artwork on display. St Kilda was a popular tourist haunt and Gabby and her husband, Finn, had dedicated one front room to Aboriginal art, leaving the other front room available for exhibitions—in this case African art, including Ben's photographs. Displayed on stands around the room were African carvings and beadwork that Ben had sourced for his sister to import.

Ben had some unofficial duties to attend to that involved making sure those guests who were likely to part with their money were given the proper amount of attention. Maggie had expected this and while he had introduced her to a number of the guests she was quite happy to move about the gallery on her own. The noise level was quite high and it was relatively easy in a group as large as this for Maggie to blend in.

She had spent some time in the African room and was amazed by the quality of Ben's photographs. In contrast to the landscapes and animal shots that adorned his office walls there were a large number of portraits on display here. Maggie wished several of the portraits could talk; she would have loved to listen to their stories.

As the crowd grew larger she wandered into one of the smaller rooms at the rear of the gallery. She had the space to herself for a little while before she felt someone enter the room behind her. She knew it was Ben—her senses immediately went on high alert whenever he was nearby, making her nerves tingle and raising goose bumps on her skin.

He came up behind her and wrapped his right arm around her waist. He whispered into her ear and his breath was warm on her cheek. 'Have I told you how gorgeous you look in purple?'

She turned her head slightly to look at him, aware as she did that their mouths were now inches apart. 'You could always tell me twice,' she replied.

'You look gorgeous.' Maggie felt herself blush. 'Purple suits you. And it's much easier to find you in a crowd if you're not wearing black.' He grinned. 'Are you hungry?' He brought his left hand around in front of her, offering her a plate piled high with nibbles. 'I brought a selection. I wasn't sure what you'd want.'

Maggie chose a prawn skewered on a stalk of lemongrass. 'You've managed to pull quite a crowd,' she said as she removed the prawn by its tail, separating it from the lemongrass.

'I don't know that I can take all the credit. Gabby and Finn work hard promoting these events, and I never underestimate the benefit of having the McMahon Foundation associated with it,' Ben said before popping a caviar blini into his mouth.

'I'd better get back to the main gallery,' he said when he finished eating. 'There'll be people wondering where I am. Are you OK in here or would you like to come with me?'

'I'm fine, thanks,' she said, touched by his attentiveness. 'I'll have a look in the other rooms for a bit and then come back to the front.'

'Don't be long,' he said as he leant forward to kiss her cheek. 'I'll see you in a minute.'

Maggie had to stop herself from following him immediately. She needed to show some restraint even if his kiss had her shaking in her new boots. She forced herself to wander through the rest of the gallery before returning to the African room. Almost instantly Finn appeared by her side with a refill for her drink.

'Thank you,' she said as he topped up her champagne, 'but please don't feel you have to look after me. I'm quite all right.' She felt surprisingly comfortable wandering about on her own, and she knew that was because each time she would catch a glimpse of Ben as he worked the room he'd have one eye on her and send her a wink or a smile. Just knowing he was aware of where she was made her feel confident. Confident enough to be brave in a room full of strangers. That plus the fact that either he or Finn would appear by her side at regular intervals to top up her champagne!

'I'm not doing this because I have to. I'm happy to look after you.' Finn's Irish accent was pronounced against the backdrop of Aussie twangs.

'Really? Ben didn't ask you to keep an eye on me?'

'No.' Finn paused before sending a cheeky grin her way. 'He didn't have to—Gabby got in first. She didn't want you to feel we were subjecting you to the Spanish Inquisition so she decided she'd leave you to me. She thought I'd be less threatening!'

'Well, I appreciate the attention, thank you.'

'Had to make sure you're enjoying yourself. Are you?'

'Very much.'

'And you like the art?'

'I do, but to be honest I'm having just as much fun watching the people.'

'Ahh, I could tell you a few stories about some of these people.'

'I don't doubt it.' She smiled at him. Maggie had taken an instant liking to Ben's brother-in-law. He had a quick, dry sense of humour and a laid-back charm. He was one of those people who, after spending five minutes with them, you felt as if you'd known them for years. She could easily imagine how Gabby, as a young art student studying in Paris, had been swept off her feet by the amusing Irishman. 'Could Ben tell some stories too?'

'Aye, he could. Different to mine, of course. There's a few hearts he's broken in this room.' Finn was nodding his head as he looked about the room but Maggie resisted the temptation to follow his gaze. 'Don't let that bother you. It's not from broken promises. It's just that they want more than Ben is prepared to give. That'll all change when he finds true love, you can bet on it.'

'Has he ever been in love?' The question popped out of Maggie's mouth before she knew what she was saying.

'That's not my story to tell, I'm afraid, but if you want my opinion, he's still looking for true love—he just doesn't know it.' Maggie looked across the room towards Ben. Finn was watching her closely. 'Be patient with him.'

Was that true? Was Ben looking for true love? She supposed deep down it was true of most people. But why then hadn't Ben found it already? Was there something she didn't know?

That was a ridiculous question; there must be a hundred things she didn't know about Ben. Finn could probably give her a lot of the answers. She turned to ask him but he'd already darted away, off to chat with another guest. He had been blessed with the Irish gift of the gab, that was for sure.

Her gaze settled instead on Ben and she watched him as he worked the room. He was so incredibly sexy, moving fluidly through the crowd, charming the men and women alike. He was taller than most of the guests, and as he bent his head to listen she could see the faces of the female guests gazing adoringly up at him. Every now and again he'd touch someone lightly on the arm, and the women, young and old, would bask in the attention. To Maggie's eyes seeing their pleasure was the equivalent of watching someone win the lottery.

She expected to feel slightly jealous as she watched other women lap up his attentions but she found his charm was an incredibly powerful aphrodisiac. Plus he was still keeping an eye on her; a slight tilt of his head or a quick wink at regular intervals let her know he knew her whereabouts.

Her feet, in her new high-heeled boots, were beginning to complain so she perched on a zebra-skin ottoman in the centre of the room. She ran her hand over the fabric, hoping it was fake, then hoping that it was actually made for sitting on. Was she sitting on the artwork? She quickly checked for any sign of a description or price and was relieved to find nothing.

She looked up and saw Ben crossing the room towards her, and neither the artwork nor the furniture could possibly hold her attention then.

She loved the way he walked. It wasn't a swagger—describing it that way would make him sound conceited—but he definitely walked with confidence, with an air of someone who was used to being respected. Not for who he was but rather for what he did. He was comfortable in his own skin, and that confidence was obvious in the way he held himself. Even in a room as spacious as this one Ben looked larger than life. He was stopped several times by guests wanting to chat but those conversations were brief, and she knew he was coming for her. Her heartbeat increased its pace with every step he took towards her.

He sat beside her, his knees relaxed and apart, one thigh resting against hers.

'How are you holding up? Are you getting bored?'

She could hear the concern in his voice and allayed his fears. 'Not at all. My feet just need a rest.'

He glanced down at the floor. 'I'm not surprised in those heels.' He leant a little closer, his voice soft in her ear. 'I'd be happy to massage your feet for you later.'

Maggie smiled. 'I'd be happy to let you.' A foot massage was her idea of heaven. She looked at his hands—they were large but his fingers were delicate and seemed capable of giving a very good massage. 'Can I ask you a question?'

'Of course, but you should know I've never had any complaints about my massages.'

Maggie laughed and deliberately pushed against him, enjoying the feeling of her shoulder pressing into his arm. 'It's not about your massages. You have so many fabulous portraits on display here, why don't you have any in your office?'

'I can't have photos of people in the waiting room, it's too confronting.'

Maggie frowned. 'Why? Do you think the world should be full of perfect people?'

'People who look perfect, you mean?'

She nodded.

'No. That's exactly what I don't want.' He paused and glanced around the room. 'Tell me, which is your favourite photo?'

Maggie pointed at a black-and-white photo of an old African woman in profile. She had her head turned slightly and was watching some young children playing in the distance.

'This one.'

'Why?'

'It looks like she's looking back at her past, back at what her childhood was like, and it makes me want to know about her life, because she doesn't look sad that she's old now and those days are long gone. She looks content. I want her to tell me her story.'

'Exactly. She looks like she has a story to tell. People with lines, scars, even regrets, who've learned to live with all that, look comfortable in their skins, and that shows through in the photographs. The best ones are of people with character, and that's what I want to preserve in my patients. I want them to preserve their character. I don't want to turn them into someone else. That's why I don't have photos of people on the wall. I don't want them to say to me, "Make me look like that." I want them to look like themselves.'

'So no Pamela Anderson or Kate Winslet?'

Ben shook his head. 'I want people to be happy with how they look after I finish with them. I don't want them to be comparing themselves to anyone else. Not everyone can look like Angelina Jolie, and people shouldn't want to. But if I put photos of people on display, patients will compare themselves to those pictures. They might do it subconsciously but they'll all do it—it's human nature. If something needs fixing I'm happy for people to show me pictures they've chosen them-selves. It gives me an idea of what my patients want the finished results to resemble. As long as they realise it's unlikely to be a perfect match and if it's going to look ridiculous—'

'Like Pammy's boobs on Juliet?'

'Yes, then I'll talk them out of it. But we have to start some-where. So, they can give me a general idea as long as it's *their* idea.'

'So you want your patients to still look like themselves.'

'Yes. A person's face is the window to their soul and should be able to express the life they've led. You shouldn't be a blank canvas, nor should you aspire to look like someone else either because of who they are or just because you like the way they look. I want people to love their own face. I want to make it possible for people to live and love and express themselves without fear of ridicule or embarrassment. Most of my work is in reconstructive surgery, very little of what I do is purely cosmetic. If I have photos of beautiful people in the waiting room it reminds patients of their perceived flaws, and sometimes those flaws are what make them special. It's my job to mend deformities, for appearances' sake, or to improve quality of life, or for some other medical reasons, but I don't want people believing they need to change every little thing about themselves that might be considered less than perfect.

'So I could hang photos like this one you like but I think it's better not to have portraits at all. I don't want people to be influenced by my artwork. There's enough external influ-ence. I want them to feel comfortable with what they're asking me to do and I want them to feel like it's their decision. I want to be able to read about a person in their face.'

She wondered about Finn's comment. About Ben looking

for love and what might have happened to him in his past. What would she be able to read in Ben's face in another thirty years? What would she see in Ben's eyes?

'Sorry, that was a rather long-winded answer to your question. Are you ready to go? I think we could make an escape now.' Had he mistaken her silence for boredom? 'What shall we do next?' he asked.

'Before the foot massage, you mean?'

He grinned. 'Before that.'

'Could we get something to eat? You and Finn have been plying me with champagne all night, and I think I should have eaten a bit more.'

'I have plenty of food at my place. Can I interest you in a midnight snack?' Ben winked at her as he issued his invitation and his expression was so full of innuendo that Maggie nearly melted in a pool of desire at his feet.

She nodded, knowing she was agreeing to more than a late-night supper. He stood, holding out one hand to help her off the zebra-skin ottoman, and at the touch of his palm on hers the tingle of anticipation that had been building in her all night exploded in a dozen different directions through her body.

He pulled her to her feet and bent her elbow so she was standing almost pressed against his chest. 'Are you sure about this?' he asked. If he hadn't been holding her she knew she couldn't have supported herself—adrenalin was racing through her body, making her knees shake. Her heart leapt against her ribs and desire thrummed in her veins.

She licked her lips; her mouth was dry, so dry she could barely speak. 'Positive.'

He kept hold of her hand as they said goodnight to Gabby and Finn, and Maggie was barely aware of leaving the gallery—all she was conscious of was Ben's touch.

They'd arrived in a chauffeured car, and Ben had kept it waiting, citing parking difficulties and lack of taxis as his excuse. Maggie had thought it extravagant but now she was extremely grateful she didn't have to wait in the cold night air. She was also aware, as she sank back into the soft leather seats, that having the car waiting for them meant she didn't have time to think about what she was doing. She just followed her hormones—her brain had shut down a long time ago.

The chauffeur delivered them to a converted three-storey house in South Yarra, overlooking the river. Ben's apartment took up the entire top floor and had stunning views across the Yarra River to the city but Maggie wasn't interested in the view outside the windows.

He'd taken his jacket off as soon as they'd come inside and now he loosened his tie, letting it hang around his neck as he undid the top two buttons of his shirt. Maggie watched his fingers as he manipulated the buttons. She was tempted to reach out to touch the hollow at the base of his throat, to run her fingers along his collarbone and under his shirt.

'What can I get you? I have cheese, fruit, smoked salmon. Champagne.'

She dragged her eyes back to his face, away from the bare skin of his throat, and wondered if he'd stocked the fridge in anticipation of having company or if he was always prepared. 'I'd really like some toast with Vegemite.'

Ben laughed. 'I'm not sure how well that goes with champagne. Tell you what—if you stay the night I'll make you Vegemite toast for breakfast.'

The words fell so smoothly from his lips, and she could feel herself falling further under his spell. Knowing he'd had plenty of practise at seducing women didn't make it any easier to resist him. And she didn't want to. She wanted to be here; she wanted to be under his spell.

He poured her a glass of champagne, and she reached for it with her left hand, but instead of handing her the drink Ben put the glass on the benchtop and took her hand in his. He turned it over. 'Where is your wedding ring?'

'I took it off.'

'Why?' He ran his thumb over the white line her ring had left on her finger. His fingers were nestled in her palm, and Maggie could barely speak because of the sparks of desire that were shooting from her palm to her chest.

'I didn't want to look like a married woman tonight. I didn't want Gabby and Finn to get the wrong idea.' She wasn't ready to tell him her real reasons, the reason she was standing here in his kitchen. She wasn't ready to tell him how she'd been imagining what his body looked like under his clothes, imagining how his hands would feel on her bare skin. What if their relationship went no further? She would have made a complete fool of herself.

Ben took a step towards her until he was standing only a few inches away. He lifted her hand, bringing it up to his mouth. 'And what would that idea have been?' he asked as he kissed her fingertips. This time the sparks of desire shot straight to her breasts. Maggie felt her nipples harden as Ben lips melted her fingers. She leaned back against the bench, needing its bulk to hold her up, and this time she really couldn't speak. Ben answered his own question. 'The idea that I wanted to bring that woman home with me and watch her drink champagne so I could taste it from her lips afterwards?'

He lowered her hand and leaned forward a fraction more. Maggie tilted her head up, expecting to be kissed, but Ben just brought his mouth to her ear and whispered, 'Have I got the general idea?'

Maggie nodded again; it was all she was capable of.

'It seems to me you're in need of a champagne, then,' he said as he reached behind her and picked up the two champagne glasses in one hand. He handed her one glass, clinking his against it in a silent toast.

Maggie sipped her champagne, deliberately maintaining eye contact and watching Ben's eyes follow the movement of her mouth, watched his lips part as his breathing deepened. He moved towards her, closing the distance, but she sidestepped him. She wanted to savour this moment; she wanted to tease him a bit more.

She took his hand and led him to the couch. Her wrap dress slipped as she took her seat, revealing one thigh. She pulled the fabric of the skirt across to cover her legs.

'Don't.' Ben reached for her hand, removing it from her lap. The fabric slipped off her leg again, and he ran his hand over her skin, grazing the inside of her thigh.

Waves of desire washed over Maggie and it took all her concentration to remember just to breathe. The touch of his fingertips on her bare skin sent a buzz of anticipation straight to her groin and she felt as though she was on fire. She closed her eyes, relishing the sensation as Ben's touch brought her body to life. She'd forgotten who was teasing who.

She felt him remove her champagne flute from her grasp and opened her eyes to see him offer it to her for another sip before putting it on the coffee table. He leant towards her, his face inches from hers, his lips close enough to lick. He was so close she could feel her breasts brush against his shirt each time she breathed in. She parted her lips, breathing in deeply, savouring his smell. He reached for her, two fingers under her chin, tipping her face up to his. About to taste the champagne from her lips as promised.

Maggie leant back into the sofa and heard herself moan as he kissed her. Kissed her hard. She parted her lips, welcoming his tongue into her mouth. Letting him explore her and taste her as she tasted him.

He reached down and lifted her right foot, unzipping her boot and pulling it off before doing the same with the left one. He brought her legs into his lap and ran his fingers up the inside of her calf and underneath the hem of her dress, stroking her knee. He bent his head and kissed her again, the promised foot massage forgotten by them both.

His hand left her knee and teased at the neckline of her dress, and the crossover front of the wrap dress offered no resistance to his inquisitive fingers. Maggie gasped as his fingers brushed over her breast and she felt her nipple harden in expectation as his fingers slipped inside her bra. He found her nipple, stopping to tease it, running his fingers around it and over it, sending electric shocks through her body.

He loosened her belt and her dress fell open, revealing black lace underwear. He pushed the lace of her bra aside, freeing her breast. He was in control and Maggie was incapable of doing anything except succumbing to his touch. She moaned again as he ran his fingers over first one nipple, then the other.

He trailed a line of kisses down her neck to her breasts and ran his tongue across one nipple, turning Maggie dizzy with desire before he took her other breast into his mouth, sucking it and making her writhe in ecstasy. She raised her hips off the couch, unable to lie still, pushing them towards Ben.

She needed him to touch her. Needed to feel his hands on her. She couldn't think beyond where his fingers might land next. Where she might next feel his mouth on her skin. She was consumed by need. By passion.

She reached for him now, her hands reading her mind, tugging at his shirt. She pulled it free from his pants, running her fingers up inside the shirt, over his skin, feeling the heat radiating from him.

She undid his belt and her fingers fumbled with the button on his waistband. He lifted her legs from his lap and, with one hand, pushed his trousers off his hips and onto the floor. He lay beside her on the couch, one hand still between her thighs, as he moved his mouth back to cover hers, kissing her deeply.

Maggie knew where this night would end—there was no denying that, just as there was no denying she wanted it as badly as she'd wanted anything in her entire life. As far as she was concerned she was Ben's for the taking.

His hand parted her thighs and he lay one of his legs across hers, pinning her to the couch. His hand moved higher until he found the place where her legs joined, until his hand covered her most sensitive spot. A place that felt like the centre of the universe. Her universe. He slid his hand under the elastic of her underpants, and she could feel the moisture coming from her, preparing her for the next progression.

He slid one finger inside her, and Maggie closed her eyes, almost unable to bear the waves of desire crashing through her. Heat flooded through her and she was desperate to feel Ben's skin on hers. She tugged his shirt over her head until they were lying chest to chest, skin to skin. His fingers continued to work their magic; he was bringing her to a peak of pleasure. She threw her head back as she thrust her hips towards him, and just when she thought she was about to explode he paused.

She opened her eyes and she saw the question in his face.

She didn't want him to stop; there was only one conclusion she could bear to have. She pushed his underpants down over his hips, freeing him, and her hand closed around his shaft. He was fully aroused, firm and warm in her hand, and as she ran her fingers up his shaft and across the sensitive tip she heard him gasp with pleasure.

She wanted him unable to resist, she wanted him at her mercy and she wanted him inside her.

She pulled his head down to her and kissed him hard, wondering at what point she had become the leader. She broke away, biting his lip gently between her teeth and making eye contact. She wanted to watch him, wanted to see his expression as she took control.

She pushed him backwards slightly, adjusting her hips before she brought him back to her and guided him inside. She welcomed him in and wrapped her legs around him to keep him close. He closed his eyes and a sigh of pleasure escaped his lips. Maggie lifted her hips, pushing him deeper inside her and closed her eyes too as she listened to him moan in delight. She concentrated on the rhythm of movement, the sensation of their bodies joined together as he thrust into her.

But he wasn't to be outdone. He found a gap between their hips and with one hand he found the source of her pleasure. His fingers moved in small, soft circles that almost brought her undone.

She heard his name on her lips as he thrust inside her, as his fingers continued their magic, bringing her to a peak of excitement.

'Now, please,' she begged for release. She couldn't hold on any longer. Her head was thrown back and Ben dropped his head to her breast, sucking on a nipple. She lifted her hands to his head, holding onto his hair, keeping his head down as he brought her to a climax. Her entire body shuddered and as she felt her orgasm peak she felt Ben's release too. Complete and fulfilled.

They collapsed in each other's arms, spent and satisfied.

She was nestled against his chest now, wrapped in his arms, slight and warm, a perfect fit. Her eyes were closed and he could feel her body relax against him, smell the fresh scent of orange blossom that he knew would forever remind him of her. He ducked his head and kissed her eyelids and was surprised to find they tasted salty. He looked more closely, studying her face in the faint light. There were tears on her cheeks.

'Oh, God, Maggie, what's wrong? Did I hurt you?'

She shook her head and smiled.

'You're all right?'

She nodded. 'I'm great. In fact, I haven't felt this good in years.'

'But you're crying.' He brushed a strand of hair from her cheek, surprised to see her smiling up at him.

'Don't worry, they're happy tears. Tears of release, I think. I'd forgotten how great good sex feels.'

Ben prided himself on his understanding of women. He thought he was usually pretty attuned to their desires and needs but tears were the one thing he'd never managed to master. Happy tears were a bizarre concept to him but he was prepared to believe her. She certainly looked happy enough.

'In that case,' he said, choosing to take her at her word, 'shall we move to the bedroom and try it again? Make sure it gets imprinted on your memory this time so you don't forget too easily.'

Maggie followed him to his room and they made love

again in his bed, taking their time, exploring each other and finding their rhythm. Ben revelled in Maggie's lack of self-consciousness. He was used to women finding fault with their own bodies and over the years he'd come to find ways of praising them and making them feel good about themselves, but Maggie accepted her body—other than the bump in her nose, he thought with a smile—and she was happy to share it with him. Her confidence was both enticing and illuminating.

Eventually they fell asleep, completely exhausted and completely relaxed. She was wrapped in Ben's embrace, and they barely moved until the morning sun disturbed them, hours later.

He woke first and lay still, waiting for the familiar flutter of panic that always came the first time he woke up with a new woman in his bed. There was always a moment when he wondered what he would say and how he would feel. Sometimes the women talked enough for them both, sometimes they continued on from the night before, having no need for words, and sometimes things were awkward, stilted, forced. He lifted his head to watch Maggie as she lay sleeping and knew things would be OK. He wanted her to be there. She looked good in his bed; she looked calm and peaceful and there was no need to disturb her.

He was able to breathe deeply. His breaths came easily; panic wasn't squeezing his lungs. He covered Maggie with the sheet as he slid out of bed. He'd let her sleep while he kept his promise from last night.

She was still sleeping when he returned from the kitchen but she stirred as he sat on the edge of the bed. She opened her eyes and her pupils shrank in the light and contrasted with the brilliant blue of her irises.

He leant forwards, kissing her. 'Good morning. Did you sleep well?'

She smiled. 'Morning. I slept like a baby. No, I slept better than a baby.'

'Are you hungry?'

'Starving.'

'I made you toast, with Vegemite, as promised.'

Maggie rolled onto her side and grinned up at him as she reached for the plate in his lap and pinched a slice. 'You're a star,' she said as she bit into the toast.

'I don't know about that but I like to think I'm a man of my word.'

Maggie sat up and moved across to the other side of the bed. 'Are you hopping back in?' The sheet had fallen to her waist but she made no effort to pull it back up to cover her nakedness. She lay back on the pillows, eating toast and looking completely relaxed. He didn't need to be asked twice. They lay in his bed, both completely naked, and ate toast while they talked.

The next two weeks were some of the happiest of Maggie's life.

She and Juliet had a routine worked out and the kids were settled. Edward's wound had healed and he was back at the football clinics, a bit of a local hero with the remnants of his black eyes. Maggie and Ben took the boys to football as it was precious time they could spend together, and a couple of nights a week Maggie would sneak out, once she'd helped Juliet with the kids, and have dinner or see a movie with Ben or just spend the evening at his place, in his bed.

At the end of the two weeks Maggie's daughter, Sophie, had flown down to Melbourne for the weekend to watch

Kate's ballet recital. Despite knowing she'd miss him terribly, even if it was only for a couple of days, Maggie had given Ben a leave pass. She hadn't expected him to meet her daughter but he'd insisted and he'd charmed Sophie, just as he'd charmed her.

Maggie was happy and content. She knew this time with Ben wasn't going to last forever. In fact, the end was near as he was leaving for Uganda in seven days, but while she didn't want to think about her life post-Ben she did feel as though she'd be able to tackle any challenges that came her way. She felt strong.

And at times she also felt as though there were two of her. The responsible Maggie—the mother, the sister, the aunt— and the Maggie that appeared when she was alone with Ben. The fun Maggie.

She'd found herself again. Ben's company was good for her. Ben was good for her.

But she was realistic enough to know this situation couldn't last forever. Realistic enough to know his departure for Uganda would be their conclusion. They were two people, meeting by chance, who happened to form a strong connection but one that would almost certainly be broken once circumstances changed, once geography came into play. It was ridiculous to think this could last any longer than the next few days so Maggie was going to enjoy it until then.

CHAPTER SEVEN

FOUR days to go. Just enough time to still be counting in days but not enough time to ignore the fact Ben would soon be gone.

Juliet was in hospital again. Ben had done the breast reconstruction and, fortunately, with this surgery, there had been no dramas, but it did mean that Maggie's routine underwent some minor adjustments. Her time wasn't quite so free now as she became the primary carer for Juliet's children again.

Her time was divided between the hospital, the school, the children's extra-curricular activities, the supermarket and the house. If she was lucky and everything went according to the new plan she might be able to spend some time with Ben over the weekend but that was still two days away.

Maggie was leaving Juliet's room after her morning visit as Ben came down the hospital corridor. The unexpected meeting instantly set her pulse racing.

'Hey, there.' He grinned broadly at her, his blue eyes shining. 'I was hoping I'd run into you. Have you got a second? There's something I need to ask you.' He opened the door of the room opposite Juliet's.

Maggie frowned as he pulled her inside, closing the door

behind them. The room was empty. 'How did you know this room wasn't being used?'

'I have my sources.' He winked at her as he pulled her in close and kissed her hard. Maggie didn't resist. She'd learnt over the past three weeks that her resistance when it came to Ben McMahon was fairly pathetic. 'Have you got time to see me over the weekend? I leave for Africa in four days.'

Maggie couldn't resist teasing him just a little. 'Juliet tells me you're planning on discharging her tomorrow.' She raised an eyebrow in question—Ben knew she'd be needed to look after Juliet and her kids.

'Damn. I guess you'll be busy. I didn't plan that very well.'

He looked genuinely disappointed and Maggie took pity. 'Actually, Juliet's ex-husband is coming to town to help with the kids. He's got shore leave so I should have some free time once we all get sorted. He gets in tonight.'

'You're kidding? You can spend the whole weekend with me?'

That had been part of Maggie's plan. 'Most of it, I hope, depending on how Sam goes.' She grinned at Ben. 'Once Sam and I get Juliet home and settled, I'm all yours.'

'Fantastic.' Ben stepped forward, moving Maggie backwards a pace or two, and she felt the edge of a hospital bed behind her thighs. Ben reached behind him and pulled the privacy curtain around the bed, screening them from the small window in the door. He bent his head down and kissed her again. She leant backwards and her top pulled away from her jeans. She felt Ben's hand slip underneath her shirt, warm against her waist, and she held her breath as his hand rose higher. 'It's a pity these doors don't have locks on them,' he said as his thumb teased her nipple, sending a wave of desire through her.

'You'd better make sure you pack tonight. You won't have time to do that on the weekend,' she said before kissing him back. She couldn't believe how wanton she'd become. Ben had reignited her libido, and she'd embraced it wholeheartedly. 'But you'd better get back to work before someone comes looking for you.' It took all her strength to resist the sensations exploding through her, to resist him, but somehow she managed it. 'I'll see you on Saturday. I'll get away as soon as I can.' She kissed him again, quickly, before pushing him out the door. She gave herself a few moments to straighten her clothing before she followed, floating on a cushion of excitement and expectation as she thought ahead to the weekend.

Ben had been pacing backwards and forwards between his kitchen and living room for the best part of an hour. Maggie had hoped she'd be able to get away from Juliet's house after lunch, and even though she hadn't been specific he'd been restless ever since the clock had struck two.

This was completely out of character for him. To plan to spend a weekend with someone was not his normal style. That wasn't to say he hadn't done it—it had happened often but he'd never planned it in advance. He'd never wanted to make a habit of spending that much time with one woman and he definitely never extended an invitation in advance.

Yet here he was, keeping a vigil near the front door, waiting for the bell to chime. Waiting for this moment.

The doorbell buzzed and he made himself count to ten before opening the door, testing his self-control.

She was holding a small overnight bag. She was here to stay. He waited for the familiar feeling of panic to hit his chest. But nothing happened. Knowing Maggie was going to be in his house, in his bed, for the weekend didn't scare him at all. He had to admit he was quite excited by the prospect.

He took her bag from her hand and dropped it in the hallway before pulling her inside and closing the door. He knew their time together was running out fast now, and it took enormous restraint just to get them to the bedroom before he undressed her.

At six o'clock Maggie's stomach began to grumble. She put her hand over it in an attempt to dampen the noise but the sound was unmistakable and made them both laugh. They'd spent the whole afternoon in bed and food had been the last thing on their minds.

'The fridge is almost empty,' he said. He hadn't bothered to go shopping, knowing he was leaving for Africa on Monday. 'We'll have to go out to eat or get takeaway. What do you feel like? Italian, Asian, Greek, seafood? Any preference?'

'Can we go to Bella's again?'

He hesitated; Maggie was only the second woman he'd ever taken to Bella's; normally he went on his own or with Gabby, Finn and Rory. He told himself it was a chance to catch up with family, and he included Isabella and Marco in that collective. In reality, it was because the one time he'd taken a girlfriend Isabella had told him off. She'd said, in no uncertain terms, that neither she nor Marco were interested in meeting everyone he dated and unless he was serious about the girl he shouldn't bring her to their restaurant. And he hadn't. Until Maggie. And now she wanted to go again.

The look on Marco's face as Ben arrived with Maggie was enough to have him squirming. Isabella had looked like the cat who'd gotten the cream, and Ben wasn't brave enough to deny their satisfied grins. He wasn't brave enough to put a label on his feelings. Not for himself and definitely not for anyone else.

He ignored the questions in their expressions and quietly took the table they offered. He decided he could last another couple of days, and then he wouldn't have to think about this relationship with Maggie and what it meant to him. He'd be on the other side of the world. Safely on the other side of the world.

But knowing their time together was going to come to a natural end wasn't filling him with the usual sense of anticipation. Normally he'd be ready for the next adventure, the next woman, but he found himself almost regretting the fact he was bound for Uganda. Almost wanting to delay the inevitable. Almost.

'Thirty-six hours left,' he said as he polished off the remains of his lasagne.

'Thirty-five,' Maggie said with a smile.

He tried to smile back but it felt forced. How could this be? 'Thirty-five,' he agreed.

'How should we spend our final hours?' Maggie asked.

'Are they?' Hearing her description he realised he wasn't ready for the end.

Maggie frowned. 'Are they what?'

'Our final hours.'

'We come from—' she paused, seeming to collect her thoughts '—not two different worlds exactly but two different places. It's impossible to think we can have more than this.'

'Plenty of people have long-distance relationships—it's not uncommon,' he said.

'No, but it's silly. I understand that sometimes people do

it because they have to. One partner has to go away for work, that sort of thing, but ultimately people have to live in the same place for it to succeed. Most long-distance relationships fail.' She reached across the table and took his hand. He felt her trying to soften her blows but they continued to land on him, pummelling his heart. 'You have your life, I have mine. There were never any promises. I don't deny it will be hard to say goodbye but we always knew this would come to an end.'

'It doesn't have to.'

She didn't answer immediately. He thought she was thinking things over. It turned out she was looking for a way to let him down gently. 'Don't feel you owe me a commitment. I'm a big girl. I've been on my own before.'

Her words were like a knife through his gut. He hadn't expected her to be prepared to walk away like this. He had to give it another shot. 'I know but I'd like to see you again—when I get home.' He could scarcely believe these words were spilling from his lips. He never pleaded, yet here he was, almost begging someone to wait for him, to see him again.

He put his wine glass down; perhaps he'd better stick to water.

She shook her head. 'I'm not the one you're looking for. I've been married, I've had my kids. You've got all that ahead of you.'

'I don't want to do those things.'

'One day you'll understand. You're almost forty. There will come a time when you wonder what you've been working so hard for, what the point of your life is. You'll fall in love with a girl—she'll probably be very different from all your past girlfriends and probably ten years younger than you—and you'll want to marry her. You'll want her to be the mother of your children. And you should. You'd be a terrific father. You'd be surprised how happy you could be.'

I'm happy now, he wanted to say. But the words got stuck in his throat.

'Please, let's not make any promises tonight. I would like to see you again but there's nothing worse than promises that can't be kept, and this way we have no expectations,' she said.

She was giving him an escape clause, making it easy for him. He didn't want her to make it easy. He didn't want to listen.

She smiled at him, a smile that left no doubt in his mind about where her thoughts lay. 'Why don't we skip dessert and make the most of the few hours we have left?'

Knowing she wasn't completely immune to his charms soothed his wounded ego. She didn't need to ask him twice. He paid Marco and tried to ignore his friend's perceptive glances.

He thought he'd try to have the conversation again when they got home but Maggie had other ideas.

'No more talking,' she said. She slid his jacket from his shoulders. 'We've got thirty-three hours left—' she undid the buttons on his shirt '—and I've got plans for you. I hope you took my advice and packed already.' One by one she slipped the buttons through the buttonholes until she could lay her hands on his bare chest. She ran one thumb over his nipple, caressing it until it hardened. 'My plans don't involve talking or watching you pack and I'll warn you now,' she said as she ran her hand down his stomach and loosened his belt, 'you might not get time to sleep either.'

He closed his eyes as her hand travelled lower. He focused on the pressure of her fingers on his skin, lost in the shivers he felt flowing through his body. He heard her whisper, 'You can sleep on the plane.'

He opened his eyes. Her gaze was unwavering and he watched, entranced, as she parted her lips and licked them with the tip of her tongue.

He groaned, giving in to his desire, giving in to hers. He wrapped one arm around her back, buried his other hand in her hair and pulled her to him, kissing her hard.

She was dangerous. He couldn't afford to lose control, he knew that, but this was too much. He couldn't resist her, couldn't fight it. He was only a man. A powerless man. The world ceased to exist except for Maggie.

Nothing else mattered.

There *was* nothing else.

He felt her move her hand on his chest, felt it brush over one nipple. Felt a rush of blood to his groin. He breathed her name and that was the last coherent thought he had. With one arm he scooped her up, holding her against his chest, pressing her to him. He turned, pinning her back to the wall, searching for her mouth. He felt her legs wrap around his waist, pinning him to her. Her hands were in his hair. He had one hand around her back, the other pressed hard against the wall, afraid if he let go his legs wouldn't have the strength to support them.

Then Maggie pushed her hips against his and his resistance crumbled. She pushed him back a step, unwrapping herself from his waist, and pulled him by the hand to his room. He followed—what else could he do?

In silence, she pushed him onto his bed. They had no need for words; she had successfully eradicated all thoughts of conversation from his mind. He lay where she put him, powerless, as she lifted her arms to remove her top. He reached for her but she wasn't finished. She pulled his belt from its loops and undid his trousers, releasing him from their constraints before lifting her skirt and stepping out of her underwear. Only then did she let him take her hand and pull her onto his lap, her legs straddling him.

He cupped her breast in his hand, teasing the nipple with his thumb, making her moan. She leant forwards, offering herself to him, and he took one breast in his mouth, sucking hard. Maggie gasped and writhed in his arms. He felt her hand close around him, heard his own moan in reply.

There was no thought of abstinence. He only just remembered protection before she guided him into her, urgently, unable to hold back. There was nothing gentle in their lovemaking. It was fuelled by pure desire. Desperate, all-consuming desire.

They clung together, making love as though it might be the last time. Maggie rocked her hips and moved lower, pressing her bottom into his groin as she slid him into her warmth before she rose up again, exposing the length of his shaft to the air, then lowering herself once more to take him inside her. Up and down she moved, faster and faster, until she brought him undone and they climaxed together.

Completely spent he gathered her to him, holding her close, reluctant to let her go. He held her as their heart rates slowed and their breathing returned to normal. He wanted to savour this moment. Who knew what their future held? Each moment had to be appreciated. Each moment deserved to be enjoyed.

He lay there and listened to the sound of her breathing, enjoying the weight of her as she lay across his chest. Her hair was fanned out and he could smell the faint trace of orange blossom, the scent of her shampoo, the scent he'd come to associate with her. He wasn't ready to say goodbye; he wasn't ready to give her up, but what other option did he have? She was right, long-distance relationships invariably failed.

They'd made no promises and they'd embarked on this affair knowing their time was finite. Could he offer more than a continuing long-distance affair?

He knew he wouldn't. As much as he wanted to he wasn't brave enough to take that step. He would leave for Africa and she would return to Sydney. He would have to let her go.

He felt her breath as it brushed his chest, and it was almost enough to bring him undone, almost enough to make him try one last time, almost enough to make him beg her for one last chance. Almost.

But when he boarded his flight to Entebbe International Airport via Sydney and Johannesburg the status quo remained. He and Maggie had gone their separate ways, and all he had to take comfort in was a vague promise that they would see how they felt when he returned in eight weeks.

Bidding goodbye to Maggie had taken the gloss off returning to Africa. He'd never felt less like leaving.

The two weeks since Ben had left couldn't have felt more different to Maggie than the weeks they'd shared prior to his departure. Saying goodbye had been one of the hardest things she'd ever done but she hadn't been able to see any other option. She couldn't see how they would make the relationship work when they lived nearly a thousand kilometres apart and she wasn't sure that they even wanted the same things.

She didn't even know what *she* wanted any more, and it was easier to walk away sooner rather than later, before she got in much deeper. She didn't think she'd find it so easy if they continued.

One of them had to be strong. It had to be her.

Maggie had returned to Sydney but she'd come home with a gastro bug that was proving difficult to shake off. She was listless and drained and lacked her usual energy and spark. It was as though Ben had taken that with him when he left.

She was back at work but when she got home at the end of a shift she collapsed onto the couch, exhausted. Her children were virtually fending for themselves, and although they were adults and the three of them usually shared household chores Maggie normally did most of the grocery shopping and cooking. She was feeling guilty about her lack of contribution but the thought of shopping and cooking made her stomach churn, thanks to the gastro bug.

She was resting on the couch when the phone rang. She always found enough energy to answer just in case it was Ben. The phone lines weren't that reliable in Uganda, and Maggie didn't want to miss an opportunity to talk to him. He'd rung her a few times and even though they usually had to talk over some dreadful static and cope with the line dropping out Maggie knew that some form of conversation was better than nothing at all.

This time though the call was from Juliet.

'Hi, Mags. Sorry, did I wake you?'

'I was just having a catnap. I'm still so tired from this gastro thing.'

'You're still not better?'

'Not a hundred per cent.'

'Are you eating again?'

'No, I can't stand the thought of eating yet. Toast is about as much as I can handle.'

'Tired, no appetite—two weeks is a long time to take to get over a gastro bug. Are you sure it's not something else?' Juliet asked.

'Like what?'

'Menopause.'

Maggie felt her eyes widen at the thought. 'You're kidding, aren't you?'

'You've got some of the symptoms.'

'I have not!'

'Well, either that or you're pregnant.'

That made her laugh, 'God, I hope not.' Somehow that idea was more entertaining than it was horrific. 'No, no, I'm pretty sure it's not that. I'm sure I'll feel better eventually. So how are you?'

'Good. I saw Dr Clark, Ben's offsider, and he's really pleased with me.'

'And Sam? How's everything going?'

'We haven't been arguing, so that's a good start.'

Juliet sounded happy and Maggie was pleased for her. She was a naturally positive person but during the past couple of phone calls she really sounded as though she was getting her zest for life back. Maggie wondered if any of that was due to her ex-husband's presence.

They chatted for a while and after Juliet hung up Maggie pondered her sister's relationship with her ex. She was busy wondering if Juliet and Sam would try to rekindle their relationship when another wave of nausea hit her. She hadn't mentioned this continuing nausea to her sister—there wasn't anything she could do to help when she was almost a thousand kilometres away in another city—but Maggie wondered whether Juliet could have accurately diagnosed her condition via a phone call.

She couldn't be pregnant, could she?

She tried to remember when she'd had her last period. She'd had one when Juliet was first in hospital, when she'd almost died. Had she had one since?

She must have been due again around the time Ben left

for Africa—maybe the week before that? But it hadn't come. Had she missed one because she was sick or was there another reason? Had she missed a period because she was already pregnant?

Absentmindedly she pressed on her boobs. They were tender but they usually were just before her period. Maybe she'd just miscalculated. There was plenty going on; it would be understandable if she were distracted.

But her boobs were always tender when she was pregnant too.

She couldn't be, could she?

There was only one way to know for sure.

Maggie walked around to the local pharmacy and bought a home pregnancy-test kit. She couldn't believe she was doing this. Walking home she felt as though everyone she passed could see through the paper bag, see the test kit she carried, and she was sure they all thought, Foolish old woman, what do you think you're doing?

Nearing home her steps got slower and slower as she approached her front door. She was terrified of doing the test. What if it was positive? What would she do, a forty-two-year-old single mother with an already grown family? She couldn't go back to those days.

She sat on her bed, staring at the box and reading the instructions at least five times. Most of it didn't sink in but she already knew the basics. Wee on the stick, wait ten minutes and check the results. One pink line would show the test was working but that would be all—everything normal, no pregnancy, no reason to panic.

Two pink lines would mean trouble.

Eventually she summoned up enough courage to go to the bathroom but then stage fright set in. The instructions said to wee on the stick mid-stream. How did the manufacturers expect a mature woman, who'd already had a couple of babies years ago, to be able to control her wee well enough to wee, hold, put the stick in the right place, then start to wee again? It was a recipe for disaster, in her opinion.

She tore open the packet and removed the stick. Enough procrastinating.

She managed to follow the instructions, just. Wee, stop, hold stick, wee again, then wait.

One pink line, the test was working.

How long before the second line would show up?

She checked the instructions again. Ten minutes.

She put the stick on the edge of the basin and flushed the toilet, closing the lid.

As she sat, waiting for the second line, she asked herself what she was wishing for.

Did she want to see the second line or not?

Not.

I don't want to be pregnant, do I? A single mother at the age of forty-two?

No.

She waited well past the ten minutes the instructions advised.

She closed her eyes and turned her head towards the basin, towards the stick. Slowly, hesitantly, she opened one eye and peered at the stick.

She couldn't see well enough; her vision was blurry.

She opened both eyes.

One line only. Negative.

She had her answer.

She threw the stick in the bin, a slight pang of disappointment in her chest. Would it have been so awful to be pregnant? To be carrying Ben's baby?

Maggie let her imagination run down that track, just for a

moment. In a way the idea was vaguely exciting. Not as terrifying as it should be.

She pulled herself together. What was wrong with her? What was she doing contemplating pregnancy at her age?

Besides, Ben had made no secret of the fact he didn't want children, and she didn't want to do the single mother thing again—she'd had her family. No, it was just as well she wasn't pregnant.

She supposed she'd have to make a doctor's appointment now. She really wasn't feeling great, and the physical symptoms were getting a bit hard to ignore. She could pretend it was heartache but she really needed to get to the bottom of it.

It was three days before she could get an appointment with her doctor. She could have said it was an emergency but it wasn't really. She wasn't feeling any worse—she just wasn't feeling any better.

'Morning, Maggie. What can I do for you?' Dr Ebert had been Maggie's GP since her children were small. She'd seen her through some tough times after Steven's death and also when Juliet was diagnosed with breast cancer, and Maggie knew she wouldn't dismiss her symptoms as trifling. If she thought there was reason to investigate her symptoms Maggie knew she would, and if she thought there was nothing that a bit of rest wouldn't take care of, then Maggie was happy to take her advice.

Maggie took a seat and tried to describe her ailments as best she could. 'I've been feeling flat for the past three weeks but it's nothing that I can really pin down. It started with what I thought was a case of too much red wine but the next day I still felt nauseous. I had a slight temperature and I thought maybe I'd picked up a gastro bug but while I felt queasy I wasn't actually vomiting. I still feel a bit off-colour but I can't make my symptoms fit one particular box.'

'Are your symptoms getting better or worse?'

'Neither really. I'm not getting worse—I just don't feel a hundred per cent.'

'Let's start with the basics, then, shall we?' Dr Ebert said as she fastened the blood pressure cuff around Maggie's arm. 'Are you on any medication?'

'No, an occasional paracetamol.'

'Headaches?'

Maggie thought about that question for a moment. 'Not currently.'

'Are you sleeping OK?' she asked as she popped the thermometer in Maggie's ear.

'I'm really tired. I think I'm asleep before my head hits the pillow and I wake up during the night to go to the loo but I can usually go back to sleep. No different to normal, I don't think.'

'You're not going to the toilet more often than normal?' asked the doctor. 'Your BP is fine but your temperature is a bit raised. You don't think you could have a UTI?'

Maggie shook her head. 'I might be going to the toilet a little more frequently but there's no discomfort.'

'How are your children and the rest of your family?' Dr Ebert asked as she checked the glands in Maggie's neck. 'Are they all well?'

'Pretty good. I've just been down to Melbourne to stay with Juliet while she had her breast reconstruction surgery.'

'How did that go?'

'Good. She had a few dramas initially but she's managing well now and her ex is in town for a while too, giving her a hand.'

'What sort of dramas?'

'She had a reaction to the anaesthetic when she was having the expanders put in initially. She had to be resuscitated but there were no after-effects.'

'And you're OK with that? You don't feel stressed at all?'

'No, I know what I'm like when I'm stressed—this isn't it.' Lonely maybe, she thought, but loneliness didn't manifest as physical symptoms, did it?

'I think I'd better run some blood tests, see if that shows anything. Check your hormone levels. You haven't experienced any hot flushes?'

'I feel slightly feverish but that's fairly constant, nothing I'd actually call a hot flush—no night sweats or palpitations.'

Dr Ebert tightened the tourniquet around Maggie's upper arm. 'Squeeze your fist for me.' She slid a needle into Maggie's vein and filled some small vials with blood as she continued her questioning. 'Do you know how old your mother was when she went through menopause?'

'Not you too?' Maggie moaned. 'Juliet suggested that. She said I was either menopausal or pregnant.'

'Is there a chance you could be pregnant?' Dr Ebert capped the last test tube and released the tourniquet as Maggie put pressure over the puncture site.

'I guess so. Technically. But I did a pregnancy test last week and it was negative.'

'When was your last period?

'Six weeks ago.' Maggie had actually sat down and calculated it properly before coming to this appointment.

'Let's do another test just in case.' Dr Ebert took the cotton-wool ball from Maggie and taped over the puncture wound in her elbow before handing her a specimen jar. 'Can you go out to the bathroom and bring me back a sample?' Maggie pulled a face; she hated these little jars. Dr Ebert saw her expression and added, 'There has to be some reason for your symptoms. You've got to admit, pregnancy fits.'

'Surely there are other possibilities?'

'Yes, some less than desirable ones like ovarian cancer. What would you rather choose?'

'A nasty gastro virus, which is what I thought this was,' Maggie sulked.

'We'll eliminate the options one by one, shall we? Starting with the easy ones. Off you go.' Dr Ebert smiled and waved her out the door.

Maggie did as she was told and handed back the jar on her return, waiting nervously as Dr Ebert tested the sample.

'You said you couldn't make your symptoms fit any one box. I think that's because you stopped looking too soon.'

Maggie frowned. 'What are you saying?'

'I'm saying this test is positive. Congratulations! You're pregnant.'

CHAPTER EIGHT

'WHAT?' Maggie stared at her doctor.

'You're pregnant.'

Maggie rubbed her face as the diagnosis sunk in. She covered her mouth with her hands and she took a deep breath. She really wasn't prepared for this news and she'd bet Ben wasn't either.

Dr Ebert ran through some more details with her, and by the time Maggie walked out of the medical clinic her head was spinning. No more hypotheticals; she really was pregnant. She had the test result and the referral letter to her obstetrician in her handbag to prove it.

She needed to let Ben know. She felt nauseous and she knew that feeling couldn't be blamed on the pregnancy this time. It was purely and simply nervousness.

He knew she was going to the doctor today; she'd told him that much during their last phone call. Would he ring to find out what had happened?

What would he say?

She knew all too well his thoughts on fatherhood. But when confronted with the probability instead of the possibility would he change his opinion?

She checked her watch. Uganda was seven hours behind Sydney so that made it only four in the morning there. Even if he managed to ring her today it wouldn't be for a few hours. She had at least three hours to get through, and spending that time trying to imagine what his reaction would be would do her head in. She needed to find another distraction.

Maggie went home via the bookstore. Her last experience of pregnancy was almost twenty years ago and she thought, hoped, antenatal care would have changed since then, particularly as she was now, according to Dr Ebert, going to experience a 'geriatric' pregnancy. Dr Ebert had been teasing but Maggie didn't find it that amusing. She hoped reading would help pass the time, help to keep her mind occupied and focused on something other than Ben's reaction.

She wondered if there were books that were written specifically for 'geriatric' mothers. She perused the bookshelves and found a couple. She bought one, figuring she might as well be properly informed, and left the store.

Early morning was Ben's favourite time of the day in Kampala, before the humidity and temperature made conditions hot, sticky and uncomfortable. The air smelt clean and fresh just after sunrise and the traffic hadn't yet polluted the city. The Ugandan capital was a lush, vibrant place, surrounded by hills and with numerous parks and gardens—plants flourished in the tropical conditions.

Ben preferred to walk to the hospital, and most mornings he wandered through the food market near the hotel to buy his breakfast. He usually purchased local Ugandan produce, banana or pawpaw, but today the scent of oranges was heavy in the air. The smell was irresistible, instantly reminding him of Maggie and the fragrance of her hair.

He was missing her, more than he'd expected to. He missed the smoothness of her skin, the taste of her lips and the way she laughed—she laughed like someone who really meant to and her laugh was infectious. He missed the freckles scattered over the bump in her nose and he missed the way she ate Vegemite toast when he made it for her, as if she hadn't eaten in a week. She said it tasted better when someone else made it, and breakfast in bed, made by him, had become their morning ritual. He missed seeing her smile but most of all he missed her fragrance, the fresh orange-blossom scent of her.

He stood in the middle of the market surrounded by memories. Usually he found himself totally immersed in Africa—it was all-consuming and there was usually no room in his head for thoughts of home—but the memories kept coming, forcing their way into his consciousness. It was a strange experience, to have his two worlds collide like this.

He paid for the oranges, holding them up to his nose and inhaling deeply, thinking about Maggie. He could almost picture her here, wide-eyed and fascinated.

He remembered she had a doctor's appointment today. It was unusual for someone who was normally fit and healthy to have a virus that dragged on this long, and he hoped that a virus was all that was wrong. He started walking—he'd call her as soon as he got to the hospital and find out how she was.

He peeled and segmented the oranges as he dialled her number. She answered on the fourth ring but an annoying echo on the line made conversation difficult. Although a clearer line wouldn't have changed anything—either way the conversation was not what he'd expected.

'Pregnant? Are you sure?'

The interference on the line must have been worse than he thought—surely he'd misheard?

'I went to the doctor today. I'm sure.'

'What about this gastro bug you thought you had?'

'Turns out it wasn't gastro.'

'Pregnant.' He tried to process the information, tried to make it fit with what he knew, but pieces were missing. 'There's no mistake?'

'No.'

'What are you going to do?' Ben felt as though he'd been winded; he could barely breathe.

'I have no idea. I'm still waiting for the news to sink in. I thought we'd work this out together.'

'Together?' The oranges, which before had tasted so sweet, turned sour in his stomach.

'Yes, I thought we could—'

'Maggie?'

Ben heard the echo of his own voice coming back along the line. *Maggie?* There was no accompanying answer. He repeated her name—still nothing. He slammed the receiver down when it was clear the line had completely dropped out and cursed under his breath. What a phone call to have from halfway around the world! He'd never felt so unable to control things.

What a bloody mess.

Pregnant!

Of all the scenarios he'd envisaged that hadn't been one of them. He'd imagined them carrying on their affair without any changes. Continuing on where they'd left off, continuing to have fun. He hadn't anticipated having to deal with a pregnancy. Not with Maggie. She'd had her family.

This was so not what he'd envisaged.

He debated about whether to try dialling her again and decided against it. He needed time to clear his mind, to get his thoughts in order. He still felt as though the wind had been knocked out of him.

Conversation could wait; it was time for damage control.

Ben gave the taxi driver the address and then put his head back and closed his eyes, hoping he could trust the cab driver to get him safely to his destination. He was exhausted.

His head snapped forwards, startling him, as the taxi stopped abruptly. He must have fallen asleep. He checked his watch, hoping the few minutes he'd had were enough to sharpen his senses that had been dulled by the long plane flight.

He paid the fare and retrieved his hand luggage from the boot before opening the front gate and negotiating the flagstone path to the front door. It was a pleasant winter's evening but the air was chilly after the warm African temperatures he'd gotten used to over the past few weeks.

He stood by the front door, wondering if turning up unannounced was the right thing to do. He should have called from the airport—he knew that—but he'd chosen not to. He should have asked the taxi to wait while he made sure she was home.

His thought processes hadn't been that clear for the past four or five days. Since he'd last spoken to Maggie. Since she'd dropped her bombshell. He had called before leaving Uganda but hadn't managed to speak to her again.

He banged the heavy brass door knocker and heard it echo down the hallway.

He heard footsteps. Their rhythm was familiar.

The door opened.

She looked smaller than he remembered. Thinner.

'Ben!' She stepped straight into his arms.

He'd been planning on keeping his distance when he got here, physically as well as emotionally, but what could he do? Seeing her looking so small and wan and feeling her against his chest, it was a natural reflex to wrap his arms around her and hold her tight. Hugging her felt right. But it shouldn't. It couldn't. He dropped his arms and stepped back.

'What are you doing here?' He heard the excitement in her voice and hated himself for what he was going to do.

'We need to talk. And it wasn't a conversation I thought we could have over the phone, especially when we're likely to get disconnected halfway through.'

'So, what, you just flew back from Uganda?' She reached out one hand and touched him on the arm, almost as though she was checking he was really there. Her fingers were warm and soft and oddly comforting.

He lifted his arm, pretending to scratch his head but really just wanting to break the contact. No, not wanting to, needing to. He couldn't think straight when she was touching him. He nodded. 'I just landed.'

'You came straight here.' She was looking up at him, her blue eyes shining, the dusting of freckles across her nose dark against the pallor of her skin.

He shrugged and broke eye contact. 'There didn't seem much point in going anywhere else.'

She smiled. He could tell she thought his appearance was a positive thing and, coward that he was, he let her think that, for a little longer anyway. He didn't want to have this conversation on the front doorstep. He wanted to be inside, behind closed doors.

'You'd better come in,' she said as she stepped backwards, into the hall. 'Sorry, I'm so surprised I'm not thinking straight.'

He knew the feeling. Nothing was making sense. He'd been so certain of mind during the plane flight home, so sure he knew what he had to do and so sure his plan was the right one, but seeing Maggie again, feeling her touch, hearing her voice, was confusing him. He remembered how he'd missed her. Missed the softness of her skin, the smell of her hair, how the scent of oranges at the market in Kampala had reminded him of her.

He followed her down the hall. Her walk was still so familiar to him.

He remembered the plans that had been forming in his mind when he left. Plans for him and Maggie. But those plans had centred around the two of them, not around the two of them and children.

There were complications now, he reminded himself, the playing field had changed.

He followed her to the back of the house, to a living room adjacent to the kitchen. He was conscious of a sense of calm, a feeling of security, in her house but his mind was focused on things other than Maggie's living arrangements.

'Have a seat. I'll put the kettle on.'

'You haven't got anything stronger, have you?' He hated asking but he didn't think he could handle this conversation on a cup of tea, not after a twenty-four-hour trip.

'I've probably got some whiskey, would that do?' she asked from the kitchen.

'Perfect.' He was too keyed up to sit still so he wandered around the room while he waited. The room wasn't large—there wasn't really anywhere to go—but there were plenty of photographs displayed on the bookshelf and mantelpiece. He found himself studying those but then wishing he hadn't. They were mostly of Maggie's children but there were also several family shots. He knew she was a great mother but seeing these photographs really reinforced the bond she shared with her children. And seeing the photographs didn't ease his conscience.

'Here you go.' Maggie returned and handed him a drink. 'Let's sit down.'

He deliberately chose an armchair so Maggie couldn't sit beside him and cloud his judgement. She sat on the couch at right angles to him nursing a glass of water. He studied her as he sipped his whiskey. She looked as though she'd lost weight, if that was even possible, and her normally pale complexion seemed to have an underlying touch of green.

'I imagine you've got some questions,' she said.

'You're absolutely sure you're pregnant?' He knew, even before he saw her expression, that it probably wasn't the best opening question but it was the thing he really needed to know. It was the reason he'd flown halfway around the world. He needed to see for himself. Now he was here, looking at her, he didn't really doubt it but he still had to ask.

She frowned and a little crease appeared between her eyebrows. 'That's a strange thing to ask. Surely you wouldn't fly nearly eight thousand miles if you didn't believe me.' She paused and the crease on her forehead disappeared. 'Oh, I get it. You want proof.'

'It's not—'

She held up one hand. 'Don't.'

She stood and left the room. Now what? Should he follow her?

She returned before he'd worked out what to do. She was holding an envelope and she withdrew a piece of paper from it and handed it to him silently.

He unfolded it. A referral letter to an obstetrician. It was real. She was pregnant. With his child.

He knew with utmost certainty that the baby was his. That part was never in doubt.

'It says here you're seven weeks.'

'Eight now.'

He frowned, trying to recall how the dates were calculated. Maggie obviously guessed he was doing sums in his head and she explained it to him.

'The first two weeks don't count. Six weeks ago we were at Gabby and Finn's art gallery.'

'Oh.' That weekend was vividly etched in his memory. His mind drifted back to the art gallery, to the picture of Maggie in her purple dress and black boots, to the taste of champagne and the orange-blossom fragrance of her hair. It was an almost perfect memory. Was that all he would have left? Memories?

'So how was Uganda?' Maggie's voice cut into his reverie. 'Did you have trouble cutting your trip short?' She was making conversation, trying to fill what she must think was an awkward silence.

'No, there're others who can hold the fort until I get back.'

'You're going back? When?'

He wondered why she sounded surprised; she knew he was supposed to be in Uganda for eight weeks. 'In a couple of days. I thought that would give us enough time to work out what we're going to do. '

Maggie frowned. 'Do?'

'Yes.' He sipped his whiskey, resisting the temptation to swallow the lot in one gulp. 'You know I don't want to be a father, and I assume you're not planning on having more children so we need to discuss our options.'

She sat back in the couch, her arms crossed in front of her, a stubborn expression on her face. 'I wasn't planning to have more children but that doesn't mean I won't.'

He finished his whiskey in one mouthful as he worked out what to say next. 'I thought you felt the same way I did about having children.'

'I wasn't planning on having more so, in theory, I suppose we did. But choosing not to have *more* children is very different to choosing not to have *any*. Unfortunately life has a way of dealing out some unexpected cards, and you don't always want the hand you get. If you're really so against being a father perhaps you'll be more careful next time.'

He'd make sure there wasn't a next time, he thought as he got up and refilled his glass from the whiskey bottle Maggie had left on the kitchen bench. This conversation was going to require more than one drink. 'I take it that means you're planning on having this baby.'

'It looks that way.'

'And what do you want from me?'

'I have no idea. I haven't thought about the logistics yet. You're not the only one who's surprised by this. What I don't understand is why you're so certain that you don't want to be a father.'

'It's a long story.'

'It may be, but I think you owe it to me to tell me.'

Did he owe her an explanation? He wasn't certain that he did. He looked at Maggie as he tried to decide what to tell her. Her expression vacillated between looking as though she was about to burst into tears and looking as though she wanted to throttle him. In the interests of everyone's safety he thought he'd better explain. 'It goes back to when I finished my residency. That was when I first planned to work in Africa. I'd decided on my specialty but I thought it would be good to get some general experience first. Africa would give me experience I couldn't get in the western world. I arranged to spend six months in Uganda after travelling for a bit.' He swirled his whiskey around, watching the way the alcohol clung to the sides of the glass. 'I was in the Greek islands when I got a message from my girlfriend telling me she was eight weeks pregnant.'

'Oh.'

He looked away from his glass and looked at Maggie, waiting to hear if she was going to elaborate on her reaction.

'My phone call was a bit like history repeating itself, wasn't it?' she said. 'What did you do?'

'I cancelled my plans for Africa and came home. I thought it was the right thing to do.'

'So, you already have a child.' Her tone was harsh, accusing. 'Have you told me the truth about anything?'

'There is no child. We lost the baby at nineteen weeks. Our relationship didn't survive.'

'Oh, Ben.'

He shrugged. He didn't want her sympathy; all he wanted was for her to understand why he wasn't going to sacrifice his dreams a second time. It was all in the past but he'd sworn never to put himself in that situation again.

'And Africa—you said last year was your first trip there?'

He nodded. 'By the time all this happened it was too late to go—I was due to start my specialty training. Studying and then establishing myself as a private specialist took years, years where I couldn't leave for extended periods of time. So I wasn't able to get away until last year. I know it sounds selfish but I've chosen to concentrate on my career and I want to be able to continue to work in Africa. I can't do that and have a family too.'

'So you sacrificed your dreams ten years ago, and now you're worried that I'm going to make you do it again?'

'I don't think you can make me but it would be the noble thing for me to do. I feel like a complete heel but the truth is, I don't want to be a father and I think I'll resent feeling like I have to do this. Like I have no choice.'

'You have a choice. We all do. Can you honestly tell me, now there's a chance you could be a father, that you don't want children at all?'

'Yes, I can. You know how many things can go wrong. Especially...' Ben bit his tongue, knowing his next words would be like a red rag to a bull.

'Especially what? Especially at my age? Is that what you were about to say?'

It seemed he'd stopped himself a fraction too late. 'You know the risks are greater with older mothers.'

'Yes, I do know that. And I've thought of that too.' She sighed. 'Look, I understand you need to know what I expect from you but I don't think I can make those decisions right now. But are you positive you don't want to be a father?'

'I don't have time for children.'

'That is ridiculous. Look at the time you spend with Rory and look at how much you enjoy that.'

'But that's on my terms.'

'And you don't think you'd enjoy your own children just as much?'

'I made a decision a long time ago to focus on my career. I can't do both.'

'Of course you can, if you want to. I know your job is important to you and I know you love Rory but all of that would pale into insignificance against your own children.'

'I've made a commitment to my career,' he said again.

'So you can commit to a job but not to a relationship?'

'We talked about our future. I was prepared to commit to seeing you when I got back from Africa. I wanted that.'

'I'm not talking about a relationship with me!' Maggie raised her voice. 'I'm talking about a relationship with your own child. I don't need you to be involved with your child for *my* sake but for their sake, and for yours. I think you should consider it.'

'I don't want to make promises I can't keep. I never thought I'd be in this position.'

'Neither did I,' she said with an exasperated sigh. 'But we *are* in this position. And you played a part.'

'Yes, I'm aware of that and I take responsibility for that too but *you* are the one choosing to have the baby. I don't want children.'

'Fine.' Her voice was tight. 'It's obvious we're not going to resolve this tonight. Why don't we sleep on it and talk again in the morning?'

He could see the conversation going around and around in circles and he knew his fuzzy brain wouldn't cope with more discussion after the long flight. He had another sip of his whiskey and was surprised to find he'd finished the second glass, but the alcohol hadn't made him feel any better. If anything, he felt queasy. 'You're right.' He put his glass down and stood. 'I'll see you in the morning.'

'Where are you going to stay?' Maggie stood too, a frown creasing her forehead.

'I'll go to a hotel. I've been up for about twenty-four hours and I can't think straight. I probably shouldn't have come directly here. I need a shower and a sleep.'

'You're welcome to stay here.'

He should have known she'd offer. He should have

thought of this earlier. He should have checked in to a hotel first and then he wouldn't look quite so awful when he walked out.

'Thanks but I think we could both use some space.' He had to get some distance. Some perspective. Some control. He wasn't stupid. He knew he had to take some of the blame for this predicament. He hadn't been careful enough. From now on he'd show more restraint.

Maggie tossed and turned most of the night. She'd desperately wanted Ben to stay with her; she hadn't realised how badly she'd missed him. But staying with her, spending time with her, obviously wasn't on his agenda and that realisation cut her deeply.

When she'd seen him standing on her doorstep her heart had grown wings; all the worries she'd had lifted the minute she opened the door. He was back. He'd come back for her.

Or so she thought. She couldn't have misjudged the situation any more incorrectly. He hadn't even asked how she was.

She knew he'd been hit for a six with the unexpected news. She knew exactly how he felt and she knew she could easily make excuses for his behaviour, could easily justify his reaction. But she knew she shouldn't.

She'd pinned her hopes on him wanting this baby. On him wanting to be a father, but he wasn't here for her and he wasn't here for their baby. He was here to make his point. For him, nothing had changed. But everything had changed for her—she was pregnant with a baby she wanted from a man she loved.

No! She couldn't possibly love him. What a ridiculous thought. She couldn't be in love with a man who didn't want to be a father to his own child.

She turned onto her side, hugging a pillow to her chest. She was just hormonal and emotional and not thinking clearly, she told herself. She wasn't in love. She couldn't be.

Just as the birds began their morning chorus, just as she finally fell asleep, she made her decision.

She wanted this baby. With or without Ben.

When she rolled out of bed around eight, she felt awful and knew she probably looked worse. The first trimester of pregnancy never agreed with her, and she knew she looked wrung out but, today at least, she could be prepared. She showered and took some time to apply make-up. Today she could try to hide the ravages of a bad night's sleep, out-of-control hormones and morning sickness. She checked the time; he'd be here in an hour. She'd feel a lot more confident if she looked good.

Despite her pledge to do without him her heart was its usual traitorous self, leaping in her chest at the simple sight of Ben as he walked through her front door. He looked fit and tanned; just three weeks in Africa had darkened his olive complexion, giving him a healthy colour. But he still wasn't smiling and she wished, almost more than anything, to see him smile again. She thought she knew how to make that happen.

She waited until he was sitting at her kitchen table before she started talking. She didn't have time for pleasantries this morning; there was no place for them and she knew she just had to get this conversation over and done with. 'I've made a decision.' She waited until he met her eyes; she needed to have his full attention. 'I'm having the baby.' That certainly got his attention. 'If you don't want to be involved I'll respect your choice and I'll raise the baby on my own. I've been a single mother before and I know I can do it again. I don't expect anything from you.'

'Nothing? What about money?'

She shook her head. 'No, if I'm choosing to have this baby when I know you don't want it, then I don't expect you to help support it.'

'I might not want children but I can at least pay for my mistakes. Money isn't the issue.' His voice was tense; she could hear his anger.

'I realise that. But I don't want or need your money. I work now because I want to. I don't have to—Steven's life insurance has been well invested and I can support myself and the baby.'

'I'm not going to let you use another man's money to bring up my child, not when I can easily afford to do it. What sort of man do you think I am?'

I don't know any more, she thought. Her heart was heavy in her chest.

'How will you manage?'

'The same way I did last time. My children were my priority. I had to make sacrifices but I was happy to do that and I'll do it again.' Her own words pierced her heavy heart; she could feel it breaking in two. Yes, she would manage but how could she tell him she'd prefer not to? She couldn't admit how much she longed for a happy ending.

But Ben didn't argue the point and he didn't change his mind. That had been it—end of discussion. She'd given him what she thought he'd wanted—his freedom—but he still hadn't smiled. How she wished she was the type of girl who threw vases and other assorted household items. She imagined it would have been extremely satisfying to have hurled various objects at Ben as he'd walked out her door. But she kept her cool and managed not to dissolve in tears until he'd gone. Then she channelled her energy into looking after the family she already had.

CHAPTER NINE

MAGGIE'S children had been out of the house all day but tonight she needed them home. She sent messages to both their mobile phones, making sure they'd be home for dinner. She needed to tell them her news before any more time passed. Despite her complaining stomach she got to work in the kitchen. At least that kept her hands busy even if her mind still had time to wander.

She wasn't surprised by Ben's decision but she was hurt and disappointed. At least he hadn't doubted that the baby was his. But it hurt that he could still be so removed from the baby and from her. Despite his explanation she still couldn't understand why he was being like this. It wasn't what she'd expected, and she was having difficulty associating this Ben with the one she'd known before she was pregnant.

Maggie watched as her children polished off the last mouthfuls of their roast dinner. She'd barely touched hers; she'd eaten some of the vegetables but she'd just pushed the meat around on her plate. It wasn't nausea that was ruining her appetite tonight, it was apprehension.

'That was terrific, Mum,' James said as he cleared the plates from the table. 'Did you make dessert?'

'Are you still hungry?' Maggie asked. James had eaten two servings of dinner but she supposed for a boy of nineteen there was always room for more food. 'There's an apple crumble in the oven.'

'Told you so,' Sophie said to her brother as he cleared the plates from the table.

'Told him what?' asked Maggie.

'Soph said that when you make sure we're going to both be home for dinner it means you've got something to tell us, especially if you make dessert,' James replied.

'Am I right?' Sophie asked. 'Is there something we need to know?'

'Do I really do that?' Maggie thought back; she shrugged. 'Maybe you are right, because there is something I need to tell you both.'

'Oh, my God, you have cancer too,' Sophie burst out.

'What do you mean too?'

'Like Auntie Jules.'

'No, no, it's not *bad* news. I'm perfectly healthy. I'm just pregnant.'

'Pregnant!' Sophie said. 'That's worse.'

'How can that be worse?' Maggie asked. She hadn't meant to blurt it out quite so quickly but in comparison to cancer she felt the news was relatively good.

'Aren't you too old?' said James.

Maggie smiled. 'Obviously not.'

'How did that happen?' Sophie asked. She saw her mother's expression and added, 'I know *how* but what about safe sex? You've been preaching that to us for as long as I can remember.'

Maggie shrugged. 'It's not one hundred per cent foolproof, I guess.' She wondered whether she'd be struck down for lying. The first time she slept with Ben they'd gotten so carried away they hadn't even thought about protection until it was too late, but she didn't think her children needed to hear that!

'So what are you going to do? What did Ben say?' Sophie paused. 'It is Ben's, right?

'Of course it's Ben's.' What did her children think she'd been up to? Maggie didn't want to hear the answer to that question. 'And he didn't say anything I didn't know already. He doesn't want children. He told me that almost when we first met and it seems he means it.'

'He doesn't want children?' Sophie asked. 'What does that mean exactly?'

'He doesn't want to be a father.' Maggie shrugged. 'He doesn't want to be involved.'

'What are you going to do?' James asked as he returned to the table, dessert forgotten in the oven.

'Obviously, this wasn't planned. As you so kindly pointed out I'm no spring chicken, and if you'd asked me last week, hypothetically, what I'd do I would have said it would depend a lot on the baby's father and on you two. But now it's *not* a hypothetical situation and there's only one answer—I have to have this baby. The two of you are the most important people in my life—you have been since the moment you were born—and this baby will be the same. I couldn't give it up at any stage any more than I could give either of you up.

'So, it looks like there'll be a new addition to our family. I don't expect you to be jumping for joy but I'd like to think that when you've had time to process this I can count on your support. Not with raising the baby—I don't expect that—but I think I'm going to need your support emotionally.'

Sophie stood from her chair and came around to Maggie's

seat and hugged her tightly. 'Of course you have our support. You're a fabulous mum—you can do this and of course we'll be here for you.'

'Do you think Ben will change his mind?' James asked.

'I don't know. I'd like to think so but he's always made his position pretty clear.'

'When is the baby due?'

'January.'

'So there's plenty of time for him to change his mind.'

'I guess so.'

Maggie didn't tell her children she was wishing for the same thing.

Ben had been gone again for two days but she had a plan to keep him in the loop. She had no idea if it would work but she was prepared to give it her best shot. She hoped that by keeping him informed he'd start to feel part of it all and maybe change his mind about being involved.

She waited to see if he rang her once he got back to Uganda but the phone was silent. She sent her first email a few days later.

To: Ben
From: Maggie
Subject: URGENT!
Sorry to be asking but I've been reading up on all the tests that are recommended for mothers over thirty-five and the chorionic villus sampling can be done around now. It tests for chromosomal abnormalities, things like cystic fibrosis and Down's syndrome. I'm not that keen to have the test done because of associated risks but if there's any family history on your side that I should know about could you tell me please? I'm still not sure if I would have the test,

probably depends on what you say. I've attached a
file explaining the test. I'm not sure how much obstetrics you remember from your med school days,
probably not a lot.
Thanks.
Maggie

Ben's fingers hovered over the keyboard as he thought
about his reply. He hadn't wanted to open Maggie's emails—
he didn't want to be dragged into any discussion, didn't want
to care—but he hadn't been able to ignore this one, not with
that subject.

To: Ben
From: Maggie
Subject: Test update
Thanks for your reply. I was glad to hear there's no
history on your side either 'cos it made me feel that
I've made the right decision. I'm going to wait a
couple of weeks and have the nuchal translucency
test instead. Much lower risk of anything going
wrong and I'm only considered high risk for chromosomal defects because of my age so I'll wait.
Maggie

There was a week of silence following Maggie's last
email, and Ben found himself actually wondering if anything had gone wrong. He was contemplating emailing his
sister, Gabby, to see if she'd heard anything on the grape-
vine but he restrained himself, reminding himself he didn't
want to be involved. Maggie's next email arrived later that
same day.

To: Ben
From: Maggie
Subject: Ultrasound
I had an ultrasound scan today. The obstetrician was checking the baby's size against my dates. I've attached two pictures for you in case you'd like to see the baby.
Maggie

Ben deleted the email without opening the attachments, before he could be tempted to peek. He emptied the trash folder. He didn't want to see the baby; that would make it real.

Half an hour later he was still thinking about the email, wondering if he should have been so hasty.

He grabbed a cup of coffee in between consults and pulled out his wallet as he sat at his desk. Tucked inside, behind his driver's licence, was an old picture. He pulled it from its hiding place. It was an ultrasound picture. Taken ten years earlier, it was of his first child, his daughter, Angeline.

If anyone had asked him why he'd kept it all these years he probably couldn't tell them. He couldn't remember the last time he'd looked at it, yet he'd never forgotten it was there. It was the only reminder he had.

There was no grave, no birth certificate. She hadn't made it past twenty weeks so there had been no legal requirements for burial or even to name her. But of course they had named her and now that was all he had—an old photograph and a name.

He'd sacrificed everything at the time but he'd done it without a second thought. He'd done it willingly and it was only when Angeline died that he felt it had all been for nothing. So why wasn't he prepared to do it again? A child didn't ask its parents to make sacrifices but surely a child deserved that much.

Ben ran his fingers over the picture. He was getting a second chance. Should he take it—could he afford not to?

To: Ben
From: Maggie
Subject: Twelve-week update
I heard the baby's heartbeat today; it's good and strong. It was quite fast. There's some correlation between the heart rate and the sex and I'm tempted to check. The baby is starting to develop the relevant bits depending on whether it's a boy or a girl. I might be able to find out the sex when I have my eighteen-week ultrasound. Would you like to know? I'm not sure if I want to know but I have been thinking about names. Do you want the baby to have your name? I was thinking of giving it mine so it's the same as my other children. Do you mind if it's a Petersen? Lots of questions today…sorry.
Maggie
P.S. The nuchal translucency test is scheduled for next week.

Mind? Of course I mind. Ben's immediate reaction was one of outrage. There's no way my child won't have my name. This child is a McMahon, he thought, a split second before he caught himself. He frowned and wondered when he'd started thinking of this baby as his child.

But that was the reality, wasn't it? His reality. Maggie was twelve weeks pregnant and in twenty-eight weeks she'd be having a baby, his baby. He was going to be a father, whether he liked it or not.

He leant back in his chair and rubbed his eyes. He was

thirty-nine years old; he was going to father a child—a child who wouldn't know him, who wouldn't even have his name.

But he couldn't have it both ways, could he? He couldn't refuse to be involved in the child's life yet still expect Maggie to give it his name. Why would a child want its father's name in place of a father?

This child, his child, deserved better. Ben knew he was capable of being a father, a good one. He was penalising his child for something that wasn't its fault—penalising it for his mistake.

Was it too late to make amends?

His plane touched down on the international runway at Kingsford Smith Airport on a bright winter's day. His first impulse was to head straight to Maggie's but he'd learnt his lesson last time. He wasn't going to have another conversation while suffering the effects of jet lag.

He'd booked a room at the Park Hyatt in The Rocks, close to Maggie's house, and he planned to sleep off the plane flight and see Maggie tomorrow. He hoped and prayed another day wouldn't matter.

He checked in and went to bed, waking at six the next morning. It was still too early for an unexpected visit but he didn't feel like eating breakfast yet so he took a towel and swam laps in the rooftop pool as the sun rose over the harbour. He finished his laps and towelled himself dry as he watched the early-morning commuter ferries heading in to Circular Quay. It was a glorious morning, the gods were smiling, and he hoped this boded well for his day. He'd arranged for an early delivery of flowers to Maggie and had asked the florist to call him to confirm the delivery. Once he knew Maggie was home he was ready to visit.

He'd rehearsed his speech many times but his words

almost failed him when he saw her. Her dark hair was pulled back into a ponytail, emphasizing her oval-shaped face. The freckles across the bridge of her nose were conspicuous today against the pale shade of her skin and her blue eyes were piercing in their intensity. They were missing their usual sparkle. Her gaze was cold and, unlike his last unexpected visit, there was no welcoming smile this time. She folded her arms across her chest in a defensive pose when she saw him at her door.

'What are you doing here?'

'I came to apologise.'

'What for?' She frowned and the familiar little crease appeared between her eyes. He wanted to reach out and smooth it away, wanted desperately to make everything all right, but he was finding it difficult to recall his well-rehearsed words.

'For my reaction to your news, our news. I realise it wasn't what you needed to hear. Or what you wanted to hear. I'm here to try to make amends. Please can I come in?' His palms were sweaty and he was aware of a feeling of disquiet. What if she didn't let him explain? He didn't have a plan B.

She let him sweat for a moment before turning and leading him into her house. As they walked past her children's bedrooms another thought occurred to him—was he going to have this conversation in front of an audience? They were another factor he hadn't considered.

'Are Sophie and James home?' he asked.

'No, it's semester break at uni. They've gone to the ski fields for a week,' she replied as she sat on the sofa.

He took the same armchair as before, facing her. His flowers were on the mantelpiece—that was a good sign. She hadn't tossed them straight into the rubbish!

He took a deep breath and started his apology. 'There's so

much I need to tell you but now I'm here I don't know what to say first. It's all important but what I really came to say was that I'm sorry. Sorry that I was halfway around the world before I realised I have an obligation, a duty, to do what's right. I want to be a part of my child's life—if you'll let me.'

'You want to be a father?'

'Yes.' He was sitting on the edge of his chair, leaning forward, his hands clasped between his knees. 'I'm sorry for the things I said. I have no excuse except to say I wasn't thinking clearly and I'd spent so many years telling myself I wasn't going to have children that my first reaction was *how did this happen*? It wasn't part of my plan and I reacted badly.'

Badly! That was an understatement but she wasn't about to debate that point with him now. There were too many other things being said. 'I don't understand what's changed?'

'I've been doing some soul searching. I gave up all my plans ten years ago when I was expecting to be a father. No one asked me to—I did it because it was right. But when it turned out differently to what I'd expected I threw myself into my work, deciding to revive my dreams.' He stood and started pacing the floor. 'I realise now my initial reaction was purely selfish and I'm ashamed of that—it's not how I like to think of myself. Avoiding my responsibilities isn't right and it's not fair on my child. I think I could be a good father and I'd like to try.'

'What about Africa?'

'It will always be there. I might get back in a year—it might be ten, there's no way of knowing but that's OK. My priority now is the baby.'

'You're not leaving again in a couple of days?'

'No. I was thinking you might need me here. I'd like to come with you to the nuchal translucency test. It's tomorrow, isn't it?'

Maggie nodded, pleased he'd been reading her emails and paying some attention. 'Can I think about it?' she asked. She knew what her answer would be but she wasn't planning on capitulating immediately. It was his turn to wait.

Maggie was perched on the edge of the seat. She could feel the waistband of her jeans digging into her stomach and, while that was uncomfortable, she was too keyed up to sit back in the chair and relax. She'd left the waistband button undone—at thirteen weeks she couldn't fasten it any more—but perhaps she should have left the zip undone as well. She was aware she was jiggling her legs, unable to sit still.

Ben reached across from his chair and held her hand, his touch settling and unsettling her at the same time. 'Are you cold?'

'No, I need to go to the toilet!' She'd spent the morning drinking copious amounts of water, filling her bladder in preparation for the ultrasound. She did need to go to the loo but that wasn't why she was fidgeting. She'd been unexpectedly nervous today, and sitting, waiting for the diagnostic ultrasound, was giving her too much time to think. She couldn't explain her nervousness. It was easier to blame her restlessness on a full bladder.

'It should be our turn next—it'll soon be over.' Ben let go of her hand and returned to reading the newspaper.

Maggie didn't feel like talking but she was still annoyed that Ben wasn't making more of an effort. She was being unfair, she knew, because every time he'd tried to talk to her today she'd just about bitten his head off. She was nervous but she wasn't sure if she was worrying about the test or worrying about Ben. He'd talked about being a father in terms of obligation and duty—she had no doubt he'd do the right thing by her and the baby—but was that enough? She knew she wanted more; she wanted the fairy tale. Was she asking for trouble, for heartache and disappointment?

Should she settle for whatever he could give her or continue to hope that he might actually fall in love with the baby? And with her?

'Ms Petersen? You can come through now.'

The technician's voice interrupted her thoughts and as she was whisked away to get undressed her nervousness increased. She got changed as quickly as possible—she needed company; being alone wasn't helping her nerves.

Maggie had changed into a hospital gown and was lying on the examination table. She had a sheet over her legs but the gown had been lifted up to expose her abdomen. Her skin was pale, her stomach only slightly rounded.

Ben was standing beside Maggie's head, trying to stay out of the way while still making sure he could see the screen on the opposite side of the bed, the screen where the image of his child would be displayed.

The radiographer, Jade, was fiddling with equipment and getting things set up. She looked about twenty years younger than him. Surely she wasn't in charge of the test? Ben was tempted to ask to see her qualifications.

'So, Maggie, Ben, you're a nurse and a doctor, is that right?'

'Yes.'

'Are you both familiar with ultrasound pictures?'

He assumed Maggie knew more about all the various tests and procedures than he did. He was quite prepared to admit his ignorance so he answered the radiographer. 'I'm a plastic surgeon and I must admit I didn't pay a lot of attention in obstetrics. Let's pretend I'm just like all the other fathers who come in here—I know nothing!'

'Is this your first baby?'

He hesitated very slightly. 'Yes.'

'OK, then, I'll tell you what you're looking at but if you're used to reading X-rays this shouldn't be too difficult. Let's give you a look at your baby. The image will come up on that screen on your left.'

Jade applied the gel and began to move the ultrasound over Maggie's stomach. Ben saw her flinch as the cold gel made contact with her skin.

'The baby's in good position,' Jade said. 'Look—' she held the transducer steady, freezing a picture on the screen '—that's your baby's profile.' She rolled a finger over a button and a little arrow appeared on the screen. She used this to point out the baby's features. 'Forehead, nose. Oh, look, he's sucking his thumb.'

Ben was awestruck. He could see the baby's fingers curled into a little fist, pressed against his mouth as he sucked on his thumb. The picture was brilliantly clear—technology had clearly advanced in the past ten years—and he could scarcely believe he was able to watch his child moving in the womb. It was the most amazing sight he'd ever witnessed. His child. A perfect little person.

He hadn't expected to feel a connection but the bond was established now. That was his child on the screen.

Jade clicked a button and handed Ben a piece of paper that popped out of the printer. It was a copy of the image of the baby's profile. He immediately thought of the other, similar picture tucked away in his wallet. He was getting a second chance. This time he'd get it right.

The technician moved the transducer and a different image

appeared on the screen. Ben could see something pulsing, expanding and contracting. 'This is the baby's heart,' Jade explained. 'He's got a good strong heartbeat.'

That was twice she'd used the masculine pronoun. Curiosity got the better of him. 'Is it a boy?'

'No. Just a figure of speech. Do you want to know?'

Ben looked at Maggie. They hadn't discussed this. He remembered Maggie mentioning it in one of her emails but he couldn't recall whether she'd been keen to find out or the opposite. 'What do you think? Shall we find out?'

She shook her head. 'No. I'd rather have a surprise.'

Personally he'd had enough surprises but he guessed it wasn't a big deal—they'd find out sooner or later. 'OK, we'll keep some secrets.'

'All right, then.' Jade was waiting for their decision. 'I'll just take some measurements to check the baby's size against your gestational dates. I'll measure the femur first—' she moved the machine, then held it still and clicked a button before moving it again '—and then the biparietal diameter across the baby's skull. How many weeks pregnant are you?'

'Thirteen.'

'OK, I'll do the nuchal translucency measurement now. That just involves measuring the fluid at the back of the baby's neck. He's in a good position so I should be able to get that done through an abdominal ultrasound without any trouble.'

Ben watched as Jade positioned the transducer twice, clicking a button each time to record the millimetres.

'Are you thirteen weeks exactly?' she asked Maggie.

'Thirteen weeks and two days.'

'OK.'

Ben watched as Jade took more measurements—was she double-checking her calculations or taking new ones?

'You're forty-two, is that right?' Jade's questions for Maggie continued.

Maggie nodded.

Jade removed the ultrasound transducer and wiped the gel from Maggie's stomach before covering her with the gown. 'I'm just going to ask the radiologist to check these measurements. I won't be long.' She flicked the machine off and the screen went blank.

Ben's heart froze in his chest. Going to get a second opinion was almost never good.

'Something's wrong, isn't it?' Maggie sat up on the bed and turned to face him. Her expression was pleading, her eyes begging him to make everything all right. 'Did you get a look at the measurement she took before she turned the machine off?'

Ben shook his head. 'No. Maybe the baby isn't in a good position after all. Maybe she needs someone with more experience. Jade looks about fifteen—she can't have been doing this for long.' Ben made excuses, saying the first things that came into his head, hoping his words would alleviate Maggie's fears. Telling her he shared her concerns wouldn't help matters.

Jade returned, bringing with her the radiologist, a softly spoken man who Ben guessed would be in his mid-forties. Jade got Maggie repositioned on the bed and repeated the ultrasound while Dr Evans watched. He nodded his head as Jade recorded the figures.

'Maggie, Ben.' Dr Evans turned to face them. 'What we're looking at is the thickness of fluid at the back of the baby's neck. More than three millimetres of fluid is considered greater than normal and puts the baby in the increased-risk category for Down's syndrome. Your measurement is three-point-five millimetres.'

Ben heard Maggie's sharp intake of breath. 'There's something wrong with our baby?' she asked.

'No, this test just suggests an increased risk—it's not conclusive. There are other factors to consider, and these include the mother's age and estimated gestational age. All these factors combine to give us a risk factor. A blood test can give us a more accurate picture. Did you have blood taken before you came here?'

Maggie nodded but Ben wondered how much of this information she was absorbing. Her response was delayed and her expression was unfocused.

'Good. Those results may take a couple of days to come back to your obstetrician but when they do you'll have more information to examine. Combining the nuchal translucency test with the blood test is about eighty-five per cent accurate but it's important to remember that this means there's a fifteen per cent chance of false-negative or false-positive results. So the scan is showing that you're of increased risk but it's not one hundred per cent accurate.'

Ben waited for Maggie to ask more questions but she was silent. He jumped into the void. 'So what do we do?'

'My recommendation is to wait for the blood results, get that information and then consider your options.'

'What are they?'

'Further testing, like an amniocentesis, or you can choose to do nothing. The test today is not definitive, it's just an indication. You need to get more information and you should have that in a day or two. Once you have more information, then you could elect to have an amniocentesis or you could choose to do nothing. Counselling can be helpful when you're trying to make a decision but I wouldn't jump to conclusions yet. Get your results and gather your facts and go from there.'

Ben wondered again how much of this information Maggie was absorbing. She hadn't said anything for several minutes now and her expression was introspective. Jade and Dr Evans left them alone, and Maggie stood from the table and went to get changed, all without uttering a word. He suspected her silence wasn't good.

CHAPTER TEN

SHE didn't speak until he pulled out of the car park and was headed towards the city.

'Please, can we just go home? I don't feel like eating.'

'Are you sure?' He glanced over at Maggie; she looked miserable. 'It might be a good idea to keep busy.' They'd planned to go out for lunch. Maggie's appetite had returned now she was almost in the second trimester, and Ben thought they should stick to their plans.

'I'm really not in the mood to do anything and I can't see how you can be either.'

'It's only a preliminary test—it's not conclusive. You're worrying about nothing.'

'It's not nothing! There's a chance our baby could have Down's syndrome. I need to think about what that means. In my mind that takes priority over everything else. Please, just take me home.'

Maggie bent her knees and put her feet on the seat, hugging her knees to her chest. She looked defeated and Ben was worried. In his mind she was overreacting, jumping to conclusions, but he wasn't sure how to tackle the issue. He had a feeling that anything he said now would only make matters worse.

They drove home in silence.

Maggie went into the house and headed straight to her bedroom.

Ben followed her inside. She was sitting on the edge of her bed, small and vulnerable. He wasn't sure what he should do. He had a feeling she'd push him away if he tried to comfort her but he couldn't continue to stand in the middle of the room like a monolith. He felt large and cumbersome. He sat next to her, close beside her but not touching. He needed her to know he was there for her without feeling as though he was overpowering her.

'Talk to me, Maggie. I think we need to work out what's just happened. I don't think we're on the same page.'

'You were there, you heard Dr Evans. Our baby has a genetic deformity.'

'*Might* have. There's a risk, that's all.'

'But if our baby has a genetic condition, what do you want to do?'

'I'm not going to discuss hypotheticals. Let's wait until we have all the facts.'

'The blood test won't be back until tomorrow at the earliest. There's no way I can just ignore what happened until then. I'll be going through every scenario.'

'Well, make sure you include one where our baby is perfectly healthy as that is still the most likely scenario. I don't think anything will be achieved by you focusing on things that may or may not happen. If the baby has some issues we'll deal with that when we get confirmation. There's nothing we can do to change that.'

'I'm scared.'

Ben wrapped an arm around Maggie's shoulders, half-expecting her to push him away. 'All anyone wants is a healthy baby—you and I are no different to the next pregnant couple—but please don't blow today's events out of proportion. I know you're worried—that's to be expected—but don't forget the other possibilities. Whatever happens we will deal with it.' He didn't want to downplay her concerns—they were justified—but he didn't want her turning those concerns into unreasonable fear. 'Why don't you lie down and I'll bring you a cup of tea.'

'I don't want tea.'

Ben held his tongue as he tried not to take her tone personally. All he wanted was for her to be patient and wait for some more information. He supposed he should be patient in return.

She curled up on her side, her back towards him. He waited a few minutes to see if she said anything further but she continued to ignore him. Eventually he heard the change in her breathing—she'd fallen asleep, emotionally exhausted. There was a blanket lying across the foot of the bed and he draped it over her before he left the room.

He wasn't tired and he couldn't do nothing while a million thoughts ran through his mind. Maggie was hurting and he needed to find a way to fix things. He knew there was nothing he could do to change the outcome of any tests—that die had been cast—but he knew any delay in getting results was only going to compound the problem. There was nothing worse than waiting to hear bad news.

As a doctor the one thing he could do was call in favours, and he had no qualms about doing that on Maggie's behalf. He called Dr Bakewell, Maggie's obstetrician, and gave him a summary of their day before asking him to get the blood work hurried through.

He knew that an increased risk meant just that, an increased risk. It was by no means definite that there would be an abnormality. There was a much greater chance their baby would be perfectly healthy, and he hoped the blood tests would support his point of view. Seeing his child on the screen today had blown him away. He'd realised then that he didn't have to make an effort, he wanted to. His child and Maggie were more important than anything else, and there was no longer any point denying that was the way he felt. He'd made a silent promise to himself today to protect Maggie and his child but already Maggie was hurting and he was powerless. All he wanted was to give Maggie some good news.

The ringing of the telephone woke her. Her bedside clock read a quarter to five in the afternoon—she'd slept for hours! Afternoon naps always left her disoriented and Maggie lay still, putting the day's events back into order.

She remembered lying on the bed; she remembered being scared. She remembered telling Ben she was scared. He hadn't asked for more information, and she hadn't explained.

She was terrified he wouldn't want a disabled child. He'd only just come to terms with the fact he was going to be a father at all. She was scared she may end up being a single mother again and this time with a special-needs baby.

How could she have told him all that?

She was terrified he'd leave again and she couldn't bear that.

But now all she was aware of was silence. She was alone. Where was Ben?

She sat up, pushing a blanket from her shoulders. Her bedroom door opened and he appeared. He was holding the phone and he looked drained. The day had obviously taken its toll on him too.

He sat beside her and switched on her bedside light.

'Who was that?' Maggie nodded her head at the phone.

'Juliet. She was ringing to find out how the scan went.'

Maggie took a deep breath. She should have called her sister but she hadn't gotten her head around the scan yet and wasn't ready to talk about the results. 'What did you tell her?'

'I told her about the scan but also that we're waiting for the blood test. I said you were sleeping and would call her later. Is that OK?'

She nodded. She didn't want to think about today. She wished she could forget about the scan but it was impossible. The pictures were going around and around in her head.

What if the blood test confirmed a problem? She already loved this child and she'd do anything to protect it. What terrified her now was the thought that Ben might not feel the same way. What if he didn't love this baby like she did? What then?

A wave of claustrophobia swept over her. She couldn't breathe; she needed some fresh air. She pulled on her shoes and grabbed a jacket. 'I can't stay here, I need to get out. I'm going for a walk.'

'Do you want some company?'

She didn't want to leave him but she needed some time alone. She shook her head. 'I need some space to think.'

She walked out of her house with the image of Ben standing marooned in her bedroom. While not overtly feminine it was definitely a female's room, and he looked out of place. The room didn't suit him; he didn't fit and she wondered whether he fit with her life at all. The changes he was making for her were huge, and she wondered whether it was too much to expect him to achieve. Was it just change or was it sacrifice? Was he really prepared to make the necessary sacrifices? Could she afford to believe he'd had time to make a rational decision?

She needed to believe him; she knew she wasn't strong enough to do this on her own. She loved him but she also knew that, unless he loved her too, there was no hope of a future together. He could be involved in the baby's life but she couldn't have him in her life without love.

Ben checked his watch—it was getting dark and cold, and Maggie had been gone for almost an hour. He knew, or thought he knew, what was going through her mind. He had to get her to see reason—there was no need to worry until their concerns were confirmed. It was really a waste of energy to spend time imagining *what if*, but she was obviously going through various scenarios in her head and he needed to fix this.

He needed to find her but he didn't have a clue where she might have gone. Where did she go when she was worried? He had no idea.

He couldn't wait any longer; he had to try to find her. He grabbed her car keys; he'd have to drive the streets. He didn't know what else to do.

She was walking just one block from home. Her head was down, watching the footpath, and she didn't see him approaching. He pulled up alongside her and he could see it took her a moment to register her own car, to register him behind the wheel.

'Maggie, get in, please.' He got out of the car and walked around to open her door and only then did she move. 'Are you ready to go home?' he asked once she was settled in her seat.

She shook her head.

That suited him; he knew exactly where he wanted to take her.

He drove to The Rocks and pulled up in front of the Park Hyatt. He took Maggie's hand and helped her out, handing his keys to the valet.

'Where are we going?' she asked.

'You'll see.' He led her into the lobby and crossed to the bank of elevators. He was still a guest of the hotel and neutral territory was the perfect place to have this conversation. They rode in silence to the rooftop and stepped out into the dark. The Sydney Harbour Bridge arched before them, and he heard Maggie's small intake of breath as she saw its famous shape illuminated against the night sky. It didn't matter if you'd spent your entire life in Sydney, every single view of the bridge could still take your breath away.

The air was cold but still and only a faint hum of engine noise from the evening traffic heading north over the bridge carried across to them. Ben took Maggie to the rooftop wall. He faced the harbour and turned Maggie so she stood in front of him, encircled in his arms, facing the bridge. At least she wasn't pushing him away physically; perhaps she needed the contact, perhaps she needed the comfort.

She hadn't spoken as they'd moved through the hotel, and he hoped, by letting her face the ocean and not him, she'd find it easier to tell him what was troubling her.

'Are you worried about coping with a disabled child?' he asked.

'No.' She gave the smallest shake of her head. He felt it against his chest. 'I'm scared of getting these test results.'

'What do you mean?'

'I'm scared of what will happen if the test confirms a problem. You've been so adamant that the nuchal translucency test only showed an increased risk and that everything will be fine but what if it isn't? I know I'll manage but what about you? Are you prepared to raise a child with a disability?'

'Of course I am.' He'd been watching the lights of the

traffic as the cars traversed the bridge but now he looked down at Maggie. 'Why would you think otherwise?'

'You spend all your time fixing people. Making them whole and perfect. What if your child *isn't* perfect and you can't fix it?'

He'd thought she was worried about raising a child with a disability but her doubts were about him? Did she really think he would reject someone for being less than perfect?

'I don't want perfection. My job is to make a difference to people's lives. Sometimes I'm able to improve their quality of life, sometimes their self-esteem, but it's never about perfection. I'm not egotistical enough to believe I can make people perfect. I don't even know what perfect is, but I can try to make people whole. Sometimes that's physically whole and sometimes it's emotionally. Right now I'm just trying to be positive. It doesn't mean I'm going to run if the going gets tough.'

'But that's my point—you're not going to be able to change this baby physically. Are you OK with that? Are you prepared for any eventuality?'

How did you prepare for every possible outcome? How did you prove to someone you were up to a challenge that was yet to arise?

He shrugged. 'I'm prepared for the idea that our expectations may differ from our reality but it's not my way to worry about hypothetical situations. I deal with facts, but whatever the facts are, I will be around, and together we will work everything out.' All he could do was give Maggie his word, his promise to meet any challenge.

'Even if some things are out of our control?'

'Even then.' He turned her around to face him; he needed to see her, to make sure she was listening.

'I am responsible for somebody else now—totally responsible—and whether or not our baby has a disability won't change how I feel. If our child has problems we will manage. I know we will.' He picked up Maggie's hand and held it close to his chest. 'Do you have any idea how amazing today was for me? Seeing our baby on that screen, sucking his thumb, watching his heartbeat, was a life-changing moment. To me our baby is gorgeous and always will be. This baby depends on us both, and I intend to be there for the baby and for you. No matter what issues we might face I have no intention of letting anyone down.' The wind had picked up a little and was ruffling Maggie's hair; he brushed a strand from her eyes. 'I'm here for the long haul, for the good times and bad.'

He was totally committed to her and to the baby, she had to understand that. He knelt on the terracotta terrace tiles, on one knee, still holding her hand. 'I need to do this properly.'

'No.' He looked up at Maggie. She had a horrified expression on her face, almost as if she were afraid. She was tugging his hand, trying to pull him to his feet. 'Please. Get up. Don't do this now.'

Ben held his position. 'Why not?'

'I can't.' There were tears in her blue eyes, gathering on her lashes, threatening to spill over.

He took hold of both her hands, ensuring she couldn't pull away. 'Maggie, look at me. I'm on my knees, begging you to give me a chance. Let me prove that I'm as good as my word.'

'I can't do this now. Please. Can we do this later?'

'Talking about it later won't change the facts. We are going to raise this baby together—I'm here to stay. I'm prepared to discuss details later as long as we are agreed on those two things. OK?'

She nodded and only then did he get to his feet. Only then

was he prepared to postpone the conversation. 'OK.' He'd thought that what she wanted, what she needed, was confirmation of his commitment. Maybe it was, maybe it wasn't, but at least it seemed as though she'd heard him. Maybe he'd never really understood women. He certainly couldn't understand Maggie's reasoning at times. 'I'm flying to Melbourne in the morning. Can we talk about this when I get back? Or would you rather come with me?'

'No.' She shook her head. 'I want to stay here. I want to speak to Dr Bakewell, get some information.'

'What's the hurry? Why don't you wait for all the results first?'

'I need to sort out a few things.'

'Just remember, you don't get to decide whether I'm allowed to hang around or not—that's not negotiable—I am here to stay.' He hoped she understood he wasn't going anywhere. No matter what the future held he intended to share it with her.

The airport was busy; the usual hive of weekday-morning commuter activity was all around them. Maggie held tight to Ben's hand as they negotiated the crowds, her hand at odds with her mind. They'd been existing in an uneasy truce all morning, not talking and not arguing.

She felt the burden of the nuchal translucency test weighing her down and she realised she wouldn't really be able to move on or make any reasonable decisions until she knew those results. She was sure Ben had things on his mind too. Things he wasn't disclosing to her.

She could feel the weight of their unspoken words, each word like a brick, slowly piling on top of one another, making a wall, and she wondered if that wall would ever come down.

Would they be able to speak the words, take them one by one from the wall and say them out loud until the wall was gone?

She needed time to sort things through in her own mind before she'd be ready to tackle the wall.

Ben had offered to be a part of their child's life but she knew he still imagined working in Africa again one day, travelling the world. That might have been possible with an able-bodied child—would it still be possible with a disabled child? Could she expect him to give up his dreams forever? Because there was a strong possibility that's what this would mean. Would he stay or should she set him free now?

Her brain needed to get him on this flight. She couldn't think clearly when he was around and she desperately needed to think, but her hand was holding firm, her body wanting to keep him close, making the most of every minute in case she had to let him go. Each minute could be bringing them closer to the end.

She remembered his words from the night before—*you don't get to decide* whether I'm allowed to hang around or not. He was right—she couldn't make him stay and she couldn't make him leave. It was all up to him. But what he didn't understand was that she could give him permission to leave, and she still wondered if that was what he was waiting for. This was what she needed to decide today—should she give him permission to leave and how did she do that?

She walked with him to the departure lounge where they were calling his flight.

'Will you be here when I get back?' he asked.

'Of course.' Her words came easily. She didn't dare stop to think if she was speaking the truth. She hugged him tightly, wanting to savour the feel of him in case it was goodbye. She loved him; that was why this situation was impossible. If only he could love her too. 'I'm not going anywhere. I just need to get my head straight.'

He leant away from her a fraction. 'You'll be OK?'

'I'll be fine.'

'I'll see you soon.'

She stood still as he turned to board the aircraft, her arm stretching between them as he held onto her hand until it could go no further, finally letting go.

She waited as he handed the flight attendant his boarding pass and she saw the appreciative glance the attendant gave him as she processed his ticket. He turned in the doorway and she waved, staking her claim. She didn't move until he was out of sight.

She hadn't gone far when her mobile phone rang. The conversation was brief but the news had her hurrying back to the departure gate. She ran to the front of the queue, not caring that passengers were still waiting to board.

'Excuse me.' She confronted the flight attendant, the one who'd so shamelessly checked Ben out as he'd boarded. 'The man who just boarded, Dr McMahon, you have to get him off the plane.'

'Is there an emergency?'

'I need to talk to him.'

'Sorry, that's not an emergency.' The flight attendant's tone was smug and Maggie wanted to slap her.

'Please, I have to speak to him. He's right at the front, he had seat 2A. It will only take a minute.'

'I can't get him off the plane. He has checked-in luggage and he's been marked off as boarded. He doesn't come off until we get to Melbourne.'

Maggie felt her eyes narrowing and she fought to stop herself from glaring at the woman. 'Can you let me on, then?'

'Do you have a ticket?'

'You know I don't.' Maggie just managed to refrain from stamping her foot in frustration; she was ready to explode.

'I'm sorry, there's nothing I can do.'

She didn't sound sorry!

'Is there a spare seat? I'll buy a ticket.' She had to get on this plane.

'There are some seats available but the plane leaves as soon as everyone has boarded.'

One of the other flight attendants came to her aid. 'You could try the customer service desk at gate four. If you're lucky you might make it.'

'Thank you,' Maggie said as she spun on her heel and raced to the next gate lounge, dodging travellers and their bags. She bought a ticket, a horrendously expensive one, but considering seat 2B had been vacant she didn't care. Now she just prayed she wasn't too late.

She made it. She thrust her boarding pass at the smug flight attendant and ran down the air bridge and onto the plane.

Ben was already settled in his seat, reading the newspaper, and the flight attendants had begun their preflight safety talk.

She slid into her seat. 'Excuse me, is this seat taken?'

'Maggie! What are you doing here?' The look of surprise on his face was priceless. He leant across the armrest and wrapped her in a warm embrace. His reaction released her heart. The phone call had lifted a weight from her chest and now Ben's hug set her heart free. She was back where she belonged—beside him.

'I'm coming with you,' she said as she buckled her seat belt.

'To Melbourne?'

She nodded and grinned.

'What's going on?' he asked as the plane began taxiing to the runway.

'I just got a phone call from Dr Bakewell. He got the blood test results back.'

'And?'

'Everything's normal, the ultrasound was a false positive.'

'What?'

'He thinks our baby is perfectly healthy. I can have an amnio to double-check if we want to but he's confident everything is fine.'

'That's fantastic,' he said as he hugged her again. 'You got on the plane to tell me that?' She nodded. 'You know we would have managed if our child had a disability. I love our child and I love you and we would have survived.'

'You love me?' When had he decided that? And why had he waited until now to tell her? 'Why didn't you tell me?'

'It took me a while to work it out.'

'Is that why you came home?' Had he come back for her after all? Had he realised he loved her but not known how to tell her. He was shaking his head.

'I came back from Africa because I thought it was the right thing to do. I felt I owed it to our child. It deserved to have two parents. But sitting at the radiologist yesterday with you, looking at our child on the screen, I realised I wanted to be there. I want to be here for our baby and for you. I love you both—that's what I was trying to tell you last night when I was trying to propose.'

'You were?'

'Yes, but you wouldn't let me finish.'

'You never said you loved me. If you'd proposed and I'd accepted I would have always thought you'd felt trapped, forced into marrying me.'

Ben reached out for her then, taking her hands in his. She looked down, scarcely able to believe he was back, that he was holding her, that he *loved* her!

'I'm in love with the woman who is going to be the mother of my child. I think I've loved you for a long time but I've been too scared to admit it.'

'Would you try proposing again? I'll let you finish this time.'

'You're serious?'

She nodded. 'I am. You must know by now that I'm not the sort of girl who dates. I'm the sort who falls in love. And I'm in love with you. So, if you're willing to propose again, I won't interrupt.'

He laughed. 'All right, this is what *I* know.' His thumb was making tiny circles on the back of her hand, and she fought to concentrate; she didn't want to miss a word. The wall was coming down, and she was going to make sure it never came back. 'You have changed my world. You have taught me about love and commitment. Since falling in love with you I've realised some things are out of my control. There will be some things I can't fix and that's OK. It might take me a while to get my head around the idea but I will. You have shown strength and courage and altruism, and I love you more than I thought possible. Believe me when I say I'm committing to you of my own free will. I *want* to spend the rest of my life with you. Maggie Petersen, will you be my wife?'

'You're sure about this? What about your dreams—Africa, your work?'

'I thought you promised to let me finish.'

'You did finish. I'm just clarifying a few things.'

His laugh washed over her, and it was the most beautiful sound she'd ever heard. 'I was trying to hang onto my dreams instead of realising I could make new ones, with you. I have a different dream now. One where I am married to the woman I love and raising our family. One where I'm trying to be the best father I can be. And in that dream I take my family with me to Africa and to show them the world. My dream has expanded, and it's going to be better than you or I could ever imagine. So, what do you say, Maggie, will you marry me?'

He reached inside his coat and when he brought his hand out again he was holding a small box. The box was duck-egg blue. He opened the box, holding it towards her. Nestled inside was a stunning square-cut diamond set in a ring of platinum.

'You bought a ring?' It was her turn to be surprised.

'Yes, I bought a ring.'

'From Tiffany's?' Her heart was racing and her words were tripping over themselves as they tried to keep pace with her pulse.

'Yes,' he said with a grin that had his turquoise-blue eyes sparkling.

'When?'

'Yesterday afternoon, when you were sleeping.'

'You've had it all that time?'

'Yes! For pity's sake, Maggie, would you answer the question!'

She laughed. 'Yes.' She kissed him. 'I will marry you.'

He took the ring out of the box and slid it onto her finger. It fitted perfectly. She closed her eyes as he kissed her and she could taste his promises and knew he would always be there for her.

'I love you, Maggie. I love you and I love our child.'

She knew she could believe him. She lifted her sparkling eyes to his. 'Here's to new beginnings, new dreams and new life,' she said.

Ben rested his hand on her stomach, joining the three of them together, and kissed her again.

Maggie sighed as they sealed their promise to each other with that kiss. The next stage of her life was about to begin—her world was complete and it was perfect, she couldn't ask for anything more.

NEW VOICES

Do you dream of being a romance writer?

Mills & Boon are looking for fresh
writing talent in our biggest
ever search!

And this time…our readers have
a say in who wins!

For information on how to enter
or get involved go to

www.romanceisnotdead.com

MEDICAL™ 2-in-1

Coming next month

WISHING FOR A MIRACLE
by Alison Roberts

Mac MacCulloch and Julia Bennett make the perfect team. But after an illness left Julia unable to have children, she stopped wishing for a miracle. Yet Mac's wish is standing right in front of him – Julia...and whatever the future may hold.

THE MARRY-ME WISH
by Alison Roberts

Nine months pregnant with her sister's twins, paediatric surgeon Anne Bennett bumps into ex-love Dr David Earnshaw! When the babies are born, learning to live without them is harder than Anne expected – and she soon discovers that she needs David more than ever...

PRINCE CHARMING OF HARLEY STREET
by Anne Fraser

Temporary nurse Rose Taylor is amazed when her playboy boss, Dr Jonathan Cavendish, expresses an interest! Swept off her feet, shy Rose realises she's misjudged this caring man, but when her contract ends she knows she *has* to walk away...

THE HEART DOCTOR AND THE BABY
by Lynne Marshall

When Dr Jon Becker agrees to father his friend René Munro's baby, he's determined to support her...but his attraction to the radiantly pregnant René takes him by surprise! Jon's got used to the idea of becoming a father – is becoming her husband the next step?

On sale 6th August 2010

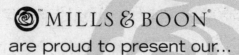

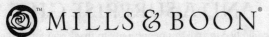

2 FREE BOOKS
AND A SURPRISE GIFT

We would like to take this opportunity to thank you for reading this Mills & Boon® book by offering you the chance to take TWO more specially selected books from the Medical™ series absolutely FREE! We're also making this offer to introduce you to the benefits of the Mills & Boon® Book Club™—

- **FREE home delivery**
- **FREE gifts and competitions**
- **FREE monthly Newsletter**
- **Exclusive Mills & Boon Book Club offers**
- **Books available before they're in the shops**

Accepting these FREE books and gift places you under no obligation to buy, you may cancel at any time, even after receiving your free books. Simply complete your details below and return the entire page to the address below. You don't even need a stamp!

YES Please send me 2 free Medical books and a surprise gift. I understand that unless you hear from me, I will receive 5 superb new stories every month including two 2-in-1 books priced at £4.99 each and a single book priced at £3.19, postage and packing free. I am under no obligation to purchase any books and may cancel my subscription at any time. The free books and gift will be mine to keep in any case.

Ms/Mrs/Miss/Mr _____ Initials _____

Surname _____

Address _____

_____

_____ Postcode _____

E-mail _____

Send this whole page to: Mills & Boon Book Club, Free Book Offer, FREEPOST NAT 10298, Richmond, TW9 1BR